Sara Barnes lives in the Lake District a ... outdoors woman: trail running, cyclii ... 2017, her life changed when she was d... arthritis and underwent extensive surgery on both legs at once. Zero rehab left her believing her physical life was over.

But then Sara realised there was one thing she could do to get back outdoors whenever she felt the need to dull the emotional and physical pain caused by the surgery: swim, dip, jump and dive, whatever the season, into the lakes, tarns and river pools of home. Gradually, the cold water released her on many levels.

Her creativity and love of storytelling, which had become trapped, burst back into life. In November 2022, her debut non-fiction book *The Cold Fix* was published by Vertebrate Publishing and sold out within four months and is now on its second reprint. A lifetime's worth of aspiring to be a published author took another exciting turn, when her emotional love letter to the power of cold water was spotted and evolved into *The Winter of Our Lives*.

Sara is often to be found wandering through the wilder parts of Cumbria, seeking quiet places near waterfalls and mountain rivers, both of which feed her soul and imagination. When not in the Lake District she travels to Scotland, Norway and France, alone or with friends and family.

www.sarabarnesauthor.co.uk

instagram.com/bumblebarnes

One More Chapter
a division of HarperCollins*Publishers*
1 London Bridge Street
London SE1 9GF
www.harpercollins.co.uk

HarperCollins*Publishers*
Macken House, 39/40 Mayor Street Upper,
Dublin 1, D01 C9W8, Ireland

This paperback edition 2023
First published in Great Britain in ebook format
by HarperCollins*Publishers* 2023

A catalogue record of this book is available from the British Library

ISBN: 978-0-00-863960-0

This novel is entirely a work of fiction. The names, characters and incidents
portrayed in it are the work of the author's imagination. Any resemblance to actual
persons, living or dead, events or localities is entirely coincidental.

Printed and bound in the UK using 100% Renewable Electricity
by CPI Group (UK) Ltd

To the Whisky Pool and those I have lured there in the name of love, friendship and cold water.

THE WINTER OF OUR LIVES

SARA BARNES

Chapter One

STEVIE

October

S tevie was the only human down at the lake. She was ageless, sexless, fearless, and weightless. After removing her layers of material comfort, she stood naked at the water's edge. Her toes crinkled into the hard, cold stones. As the early morning air explored her curves, she lifted her long hair away from her neck and shoulders, piling it on top of her head. Armpits, freshly shaved, greeted the sunlight; elbows, in need of a slather of moisturiser, pointed at the clouds; breasts, lifted to pre-children perkiness, invited almost-forgotten attention; baby belly stretched and flattened; waist defined and bottom naturally rounded from the tension of trying to keep her balance.

Experience had taught her to slow down her breathing as she started to walk barefoot into the lake. She stretched her arms out wide and discovered her natural balance. Peering down into the clear water, she was able to weave past small rocks and one or two branches. Instinctive thoughts of survival threatened to spin her back around, but instead, she walked on, the hairs on her thighs standing to attention. She wanted to squeal in shock as the water reached her groin, which automatically contracted, and just as she was in up to her waist, the pain across her ribs stopped her thinking about what might be happening down below. She pulled down her goggles and her world went blue. It was time to plunge forwards, succumbing to the bittersweet embrace of the water.

It was as if she were flying. Her fingertips reached out in front of her – long, straight fingers, unfettered with diamonds or gold bands. Arms endless, toned, and strong. Chilli prickles taunted places that you would never ever spice or season. She could feel the blood leaving every part of her body except a place deep inside her, right in her core, where there was enough warmth to keep her vital organs working. But she knew she was playing a finely balanced game.

Thanks to the blue lenses that protected her eyes, she was no longer stimulated by the natural tones of a Lakeland landscape. Instead, there was a green-blue world of shivelight, which had no edge, no end, no landmarks or definition. Bubbles of air streamed out in time to her stroke and she only briefly caught a faint scent of the external world each time she rocked to one side: damp moss, cold stone, silty earth and, if she was unlucky, goosy feathers.

Swimming in the wild would leave many people vulnerable. But she was at her most powerful. This was the place – the only place – where her true Self came out to play.

She took home a tiny piece of that Self every time. She wondered whether her friend Emma down in Oxfordshire did it, too. She made a mental note to bring it up the next time they saw each other. For her, it felt almost like a game of swop: in exchange for receiving people's grumpiness, the water gave unconditional love. She could feel it in every cell as she walked out of the lake. This early morning act of self-love had become a daily routine for Stevie.

Chapter Two

CHRIS

October

C hris's calf muscles were on fire, but he kept pushing down on the pedals and then pulled up as hard as he could without his lungs exploding out of his chest. He was standing up on the pedals for the first time in months and it hurt everything, even his teeth from clenching his jaw as he went up the sharp twisty road out of Buttermere village.

Sweat ran into his eyes, but the pain it caused made him push and pull with an emotion he didn't fully understand: it burnt like anger, but hurt like his heart was splitting down the middle.

As he approached the top of the hill, his stomach was right at the back of his throat and his whole body was starting to shake. Sitting back onto the blade-like saddle when he passed over the summit, he sank his shoulders forwards and allowed his legs to relax a little. As he moved back up through the gears, his heart rate went back down to somewhere closer to normal. The ugly emotion that had kept him going had sizzled out for now. He felt drained, but better than he had for months. Moving everything to the extreme had been physically painful, but cathartic. Pure muscle memory and grim determination had got him up the hill.

The morning light was soft; he noticed it now and breathed the fresh air deep into his lungs, his eyes half closing in long forgotten pleasure. He glanced at his outstretched arms, coated lightly with sweat, and noticed the hairs were standing up in an effort to escape the dampness and cool down. He wore fingerless cycling gloves, the backs of which were criss-cross cream cotton like old-fashioned driving gloves and had soft suede pads. Only his thumbs and index fingers were visible as he gripped the hoods of the handlebars, ready to tweak the brakes as he descended the long sweep of road out of the village and towards the end of Crummock Water. He had always kept his nails closely clipped, but over the last few months, he had taken to nibbling them without even realising it was becoming a habit.

After the shady and sometimes slippery with leaves and sheep poo bends by the posh B&B that never had vacancies, the road dropped down more sharply and he had to pull hard on the brakes. His left foot twisted slightly, ready to unclip if he wobbled. But he caught himself just in time and glided down to the large lay-by under the stand of Scots pines by the lake end. He often stopped here on his way back from Honister; it reconnected him to his life before everything had gone wrong. This morning was no exception.

As he stood astride his bike, quenching his thirst from his water bottle, he allowed his eyes to feast on everything that was laid out in front of him. The tall, dignified trees that provided a natural windbreak in the winter and cool shade in the summer; the blue of the deep water, so calm that it reflected the greens, russets and coppers of early autumn fells; a tiny island, where oystercatchers made their nests in spring and which noisy teenagers invaded by paddleboard and rubber canoes during the first hot spell of summer; and right down in the distance, the giant lump of shattered rock, airy ledges and sheep-nibbled grass that was Melbreak.

Something pale caught his eye down on the beach below the road. It was a person – a solitary figure of a woman. She was naked. He was so deeply lost in memories that he hardly reacted; she just seemed to be part of the landscape that he knew so well. But as she lifted up her long, dark hair and held it on top of her head, he found himself examining the shape of her body. He wanted to be closer, even though it felt slightly voyeuristic. He felt guilty for intruding on her obvious pleasure in soaking up the early morning beauty, believing herself to be alone and unwatched.

But he was mesmerised. From the road, he couldn't tell who she was, how old she was, or whether she'd just been or was about to go for a swim. It was her nakedness that caught him by surprise – or rather, his body's reaction to watching her bare body, even though he knew it was not an invitation for anyone or anything. Feeling uncomfortable in many ways, Chris hurried to get back on his bike and cycle on down the road before she turned round and saw him watching. He put his reaction down to having raised his blood pressure cycling up the hill, but for the first time in months, possibly years, he felt a vague connection to his body and another, more intriguing, part of his being: desire.

Chapter Three

ANGELA

October

There was one silver lining tucked away in the folds of Angela's everyday loneliness: the lake and the web of footpaths that wove around its shoreline. She often thought about how she had first met Stevie, down there on the shoreline at the end of September, while she had been searching for a lost ewe. Angela had vaguely recognised the woman from town, older and taller than her, and with blue eyes that lit up as she described how she'd just had a swim in the dark waters of the lake. It sounded scary, but weirdly wonderful: the risk of hypothermia and being out of your depth balanced by feeling alive and strong enough to battle your fears. Stevie had given Angela her mobile number and invited her to try it out as soon as she felt ready.

Angela wanted to so much, but she was scared: not of the lake, but of what her husband and his mother would say if they found out she was swimming there.

The thought had played in her mind for ages, and as the

daylight hours started to grow shorter and her time outdoors, which was her only escape, was pinched by darkness, she'd texted Stevie. They arranged to meet at the same place on the lakeshore early one morning before anyone else was around.

The water was still pretty warm, but no longer at its warmest as night-time temperatures began to drop. Every time it rained, a degree was knocked off the thermometer. They met by the stile that marked the beginning of the footpath along the western lakeshore. Angela had climbed over this stile many times during the five years that she'd been married to Ed, but, even then, when she was very much in the giddy early days of love, her heart hadn't thumped so loudly in her chest as it did now. She felt excited and guilty all at the same time. But Stevie exuded such calm and reassurance that it was hard to remain agitated. Very soon, the absolute beauty of the scenery spreading out before them worked its way into her being. She could tell by the way that Stevie had quickened her pace along the path that she too was being drawn down to the crescent-shaped bay that lay in the shadow of Melbreak.

'Beautiful, isn't it?' Stevie turned to smile and put out a hand to help as Angela slipped on the damp grass. The cows had been gathering to drink from the water trough down here at the gateway, so there was a mixture of grass, mud, and deep hoof-shaped pools of water. Neither of the women cared about getting their boots messed up. Once home, these same boots would be hosed down and stood to dry somewhere near a radiator – or in Angela's case, would join a collection of wrecked boots and footwear that cluttered up the farmhouse porch.

This beach was formed of small pebbles and stones in no particular size or colour: there were flat ones, coveted by stone skimmers, and surprise quartz ones that glittered like a vein of diamond but had no value other than to tease and tantalise. Angela thought the lake seemed particularly dark here. It always did. Whether that was just the way Melbreak's bulk loomed so close to shore here or because more underwater plant life grew here, she didn't know. But she was unlikely to find out because she didn't intend to open her eyes. It would be achievement enough to lift her feet off the lakebed and push her nervous body forward into the depths.

Stevie stopped by a broken iron fence that followed the slope of the beach right down into the water, dropped her rucksack onto the pebbles, and reached into her jacket pocket for her phone. Angela hardly ever took photographs, but used her eyes to absorb the magnificent view of this wilder side of Crummock Water, with the distinctive shape of Rannerdale Knotts jutting out into the lake and the layers of mountains down at the southern end. Every time she was here, on Dead Sheep Beach, there was something different in the light, the clouds, the colours on the fellside, or the reflections on the water's surface.

They both stripped down to their swimsuits very quickly, eager to do what they had come to do. The air was still but held a slight frisson of expectation. It was enough to make Angela hug her arms around her slight body. Her plain navy swimsuit hung loosely on her slight, almost fragile figure, disguising her forty-two years and giving her the appearance of a woman wanting to hide from public gaze. She noticed Stevie wore a fairly low cut and high-legged red one-piece and looked amazing. How old was she? Angela couldn't quite guess. It was always hard to tell someone's age once they were over forty, but judging by the lines on her face, the patches of age spots on her chest and arms, and just by the way she held herself like she knew her place in the world, perhaps she was mid-fifties?

Angela's feet hurt as she trod carefully across the stones. She noticed Stevie was wearing red-and-white-stripy slipper-type shoes, which clearly protected her feet from the stones because she did not hesitate in her graceful walk into the clear shallows lapping onto the beach.

The water felt cold as soon as Angela walked in and she couldn't help but wince, instinctively wanting to walk straight back out. She'd felt worse pain, but didn't want to think about that time, or how the horror of it had changed her. If the passing of the years could numb the memory of something so terrible, then surely physical numbness from the cold could ease this supposedly positive pain. It was only her brain warning her body to get out of the water and she knew she was able to curate her brain if she needed to. It was called survival.

She looked over at Stevie, who was standing thigh deep in the water with her arms bent, holding her elbows and hands out of the water for as long as possible: two areas that were often the most sensitive, especially the elbows. Angela's intuition told her that this physically strong and capable person had also had to find a way to cope with difficult thoughts and feelings. There was something about her serenity and composure, the straight set of her shoulders, and the way her chin tilted upwards to expose her still-slender neck to the gentle breeze drifting down from the steep sides of Melbreak.

Stevie explained in a quiet voice that in those first moments of cold-water immersion, you needed to project your thoughts inwards, right down to your soul, while the physical body righted itself. This channelling of inner strength and poise helped to calm Angela's own chaotic thoughts about whether she would be safe or would need to retreat.

Stevie conveyed calm and understanding. It would be safe to lower her guard, concluded Angela, smiling inwardly with relief. No need for the litany of self-reproach and self-checking that haunted her every waking hour on the farm. If being down here, with this woman, doing this wild swimming thing was going to work for her, it had to be her sanctuary. It had to restore her rather than drain her increasingly depleted resources.

'One, two, three…' Stevie's firm voice penetrated Angela's fog of uncertainty, her brain frantically trying to work out what to tell her body as she fought against her instincts. Simple words, but ones that acted as a call to action.

Without allowing any further thought, Angela launched herself forwards, kicking gently off from the lakebed with her bare feet and bracing her whole body for how awful it would feel. *Don't scream*, she repeated silently, but screamed anyway as her chest hit the water and the waves splashed over her head.

She hadn't meant to go under the water, but as she emerged, gasping and spluttering from having swallowed what seemed like a gallon of cold water, she felt glorious – like she had jumped off a cliff, hoping she could fly.

'Angela, stop swimming for a minute. Now, breathe. Wait until you've got yourself under control and this time take a breath in *before* you submerge!' Stevie's voice held her away from panic, which was seething in her stomach and the back of her neck, threatening to burst out.

As she took a deep breath in and then out Angela felt her panic subsiding. Gradually, her heart rate slowed and the tension in her shoulders released, allowing her to sink a bit deeper into the lake and then she assumed a more natural swimming position – more like a human doing breaststroke than a wind-up froglet trying to escape the bathtub.

However empowering and good it felt to be swimming in the lake, Angela knew that it was a world she would have to keep secret from Ed and his mother. She desperately wanted to do this again, but knew that they just wouldn't understand how it made her feel or how safe she felt with Stevie there beside her.

To them, it would simply be an act of outrageous disrespect

towards Ed's late father, who had died in tragic circumstances in a beck high up on the fells that surrounded the family farm.

It would have to become just one more secret in her lonely life. If Angela came again, she would have to pretend she was doing lanes in the leisure-centre pool instead.

Chapter Four

HOLLY

October

T he first time Holly met Stevie had been at the beauty therapist. They'd started chatting after the therapist asked if they wouldn't mind waiting while she made a few phone calls to sort out a personal crisis at home.

Holly's frankness about why she was there seemed to take Stevie aback, as if they were in the doctor's waiting room and she'd told her she had haemorrhoids.

'Too much alcohol,' Holly groaned, pointing at a small patch of spidery red veins on her face. 'I get them lasered every now and again, which seems to do the trick. What are you here for?'

'Eyebrows. They're fading fast, but getting fluffier, too... if you know what I mean?'

Holly nodded and rolled her eyes. Stevie continued.

'It's my only bit of pampering and the thought of waxing them myself has always terrified me after hearing stories of women who apply too much wax and end up with no eyebrows at all.' They both laughed.

'Besides,' Stevie added, 'I don't wear much make-up, so it helps to have them defined a bit. I don't look so grim when I'm swimming then either.'

'You swim?'

'Yeh, I go to the lake first thing every day.'

Holly uncrossed her legs and leant forward, her interest piqued. 'Ooh, isn't that very cold? I couldn't do that. Not with my veins.'

'It's been a lifesaver, to be honest. I've always swum, with the kids in the summer and the occasional New Year's Eve crazy dip, but one year something happened that changed my life and I needed to find a way to keep myself sane. So, I started to go for a dip every morning in the lake and I just kept going right through the winter. It makes me feel great. I love it.'

'In a wetsuit?'

'I did to start with, but now I just go in my cossie or nothing at all. So much easier.' Holly's jaw dropped and she was intrigued by Stevie's smile. It wasn't smug exactly, but seemed to convey a sense of feeling special, somehow empowered by the reaction her response elicited. Holly wanted to experience some of that feeling.

'Can I come with you sometime?' she asked. 'Seriously, I need to do some kind of exercise and I've read that this outdoor swimming lark is good for you.'

'But what about your veins?' Stevie teased lightly.

'Bugger the veins! What's your number?'

The following Sunday, as Holly patted herself dry with a tumbled-soft bath sheet in her luxury en-suite, she thought about what she had agreed to do: swim in the lake with the woman she'd met at the beauty clinic. As she hung the bath sheet on the hook on the back of the bathroom door, she took another look and chucked it in the wash basket. Fake tan had ruined the pristine white cotton towelling. It had been so long since she'd bothered to apply it that she'd forgotten about the mess it made. She wondered what swimsuit to wear and whether it would still fit. Nervous anticipation, the kind she hadn't felt for years, bubbled up in her belly.

Later that day, as she drove slowly along the eastern shore of Crummock Water, her wobbly belly was the last thing on her mind. The dark surface of the lake looked terrifying. Was it really as deep as they said? How many bodies lay hidden in it? Was it true that the giant pike had been swimming around since the Ice Age? She'd hastily removed all traces of nail polish from her toes just minutes before setting off because she remembered someone once telling her that pike go for blue toenails – not that hers were painted blue, God forbid! But better safe than sorry.

What the hell had she been thinking when she had agreed to meet up with a complete stranger, let alone swim in what was surely going to be extremely cold water?

Fortunately, the sun was shining, though that wasn't unusual for October. Almost as soon as the schools broke up in late July, the skies darkened and a cloud of rain and low temperatures normally sat right over Cumbria. Then, typically, on the first day of the autumn term, the sun and blue skies would reappear and sometimes last right through until the end of October. She had grown to hate Cumbrian weather and dreamt of southern France or Italy where it would be hot and sunny.

When they had lived in London, she and Simon had shared a dream of escaping the rat race and living somewhere beautiful. They had talked of going to Scotland or somewhere in Europe, but in the end they had found this huge place in the Lake District. He could go mountain-biking, she could use her creative eye to refurbish luxury holiday cottages out of the various outbuildings. At first, it was exciting and although the two new cottages on the property now looked fabulous and were often fully booked, Holly was gradually finding her enthusiasm for small windows, stone walls and slate floors waned on a regular basis. It was hard to get jobs finished as all the tradesmen were up to their necks in work. The task of transforming the main house seemed overwhelming at times, but every time Simon came home, he always complimented her on how good it was beginning to look. She just wanted him to be there with her for longer periods so that they could get on with jobs together and not have to rely on vanishing joiners and decorators. He kept reminding her that it was only for a few more years and then he would be up there with her full-time and everything would be so much more fun.

Feeling completely inside out with frustration and regret at having agreed to leave a successful career as a recruitment consultant and move up here, she pulled up and parked next to the stand of tall, dark trees. *Some sort of pine,* she thought as she glared at their Mediterranean-type outlines. That association didn't help one bit with her mood. *Get a grip,* she told herself. *The decision has been made. You agreed to move here and now you just have to find a way to live happily or you will go mad!*

Her thoughts turned to what she was about to do and whether she could get out of doing it. But that seemed churlish and cowardly. Besides, she couldn't turn on the TV or pick up a magazine these days without some celebrity extolling the benefits of wild swimming. Was it possible it wasn't all just media hype? Had she awkwardly stumbled upon something that could actually be a positive to living in this godforsaken arse end of nowhere?

She shrugged her shoulders and pulled down the sun visor with its small mirror so that she could stare herself into a different frame of mind. Those blue eyes Simon had once said he loved, but did he really? This morning they looked on the piggy side because she'd left off mascara and just relied on eyelash tint. *Come on, Holls, leave all this back at home and deal with it later. You've got this. It's just a swim. In and out in a jiffy, what's the big deal?* She glanced back down at the lake and swore she could see white horses beyond the shore. The wind did seem to have picked up, but it had been reasonably mild when she left the house.

She wriggled on her leather seat; her swimsuit was feeling a bit 'tuggy' around the crotch area. It took a bit of groping around down the front of her joggers to sort herself out. For a moment, she had an image of someone looking in the car window in shock at a middle-aged woman with her hand down the front of her trousers. With a quick glance back in the mirror, she saw a hint of a twinkle in her eyes now.

And then she jumped as something banged against the side of the stationary car. She looked in her wing mirror and saw the back ends of two large Herdwick sheep rubbing up against the bodywork. Their complete disregard of her taking up space on their road was evident and made her smile. Who gives a hoot? They certainly didn't.

This was it then. The time had come. Her baptism into outdoor swimming was unfolding and there was nothing she could do to stop it. In fact, she had this funny, excited feeling in her stomach, almost as if she was looking forward to it. She firmly believed that things happened for a reason. Like the night she met Simon for the first time; like the beauty therapist having to leave her and Stevie waiting while she dealt with her domestic issues. If that was the case, then Holly had learnt from experience not to fight it.

'You never forget your first time.' That's what Stevie had said to her during a series of text messages to arrange this first plunge into the lake. It could have been a threat or a promise. Right now, it felt more like the former.

There were no other cars parked under the conifers, so when

she saw one coming up the narrow road that snaked alongside the lake, she suspected it was Stevie. Sure enough, two minutes later, the white Suzuki had parked up and out jumped the same smiley woman, dressed in loose fitting trousers and an oversized hoodie. Her head was covered with a blue bobble hat and Holly could see that she wore Crocs with socks. *Heavens!* She sighed. *Is this my future?*

Planting a fake smile on her face, she climbed out of her Audi TT, pushed her sunglasses up onto the top of her head and called out a cheerful hello. Her eyes automatically went to the other woman's eyebrows because that's how they had met a week ago. *Yes, definitely a good idea to have them done,* Holly thought. *It's probably the only thing that's well kempt about you.* Harsh! Why was she being so harsh about this woman who was giving up some of her day to introduce her to a new activity? It was a nasty habit that she knew she'd got into since moving up here and stemmed from being so dissatisfied.

'Hi! How're you?' asked Stevie, reaching out to give Holly a hug. Holly accepted it rather reluctantly because although in London she'd moved in circles where air kissing and showy hugs were the norm, since moving up to Cumbria, she hadn't had the opportunity.

'Good! Looking forward to this… I think.' She laughed off her awkwardness and hoped Stevie hadn't noticed any reticence to hug back, because in the end, it had felt really good. She grabbed her big shopper bag from the tiny boot, locked the car, and smiled once again in Stevie's general direction.

Off they set at a slow amble back along the road a little way before dropping down to the lakeshore via a steep, stony path worn into the short, sheep-nibbled grassy bank. The bracken on either side of the path was starting to dry and crinkle up, making it catch on their legs rather than just allowing them to brush through.

'I've got my cossie on already,' Holly said. 'And I brought a towel to change under like you said.' It was a vast designer bath sheet, brand new and ready to attract some sheep poo, no doubt, and never be the same again. But she was in a Herdwick's 'who gives a hoot' kind of mood now for some reason. *Hey*, she thought, *go with it!*

Stevie caught two corners of the voluminous rectangle of soft towelling that Holly wafted across at her and the breeze caught it like a sail. Holly could tell from the other woman's face that she was amused by its size and newness and made a mental note to bring an older, grottier one next time – if there was a next time!

'Ready?' Stevie had already stripped down to her black swimsuit, cut for swimming rather than the beach, but it suited her still athletic figure and her seemingly practical nature. It was almost as if she didn't want to be noticed, thought Holly. She, on the other hand, emerged from her baggy jogging bottoms and hoodie wearing a piece of orange Lycra, which was a perfect fit in all the right places and definitely wasn't designed to keep her hidden. Holly wasn't sure how old Stevie was, but suspected there wasn't much difference in age between them, though they were light years away in body confidence.

'Wow! You look stunning,' she heard Stevie say. But the compliment felt slightly out of place now that she was here about to swim, thought Holly. Could she do this? Could she handle the lake's temperature, which Stevie had told her was in the low teens?

She heard Stevie's calming voice. 'I want you to love it Holly, so that you want to come and do it again, to really experience the benefits in this beautiful place. Take it slowly, remember to breathe, and give it at least two minutes. That'll allow your heart rate to readjust back down to normal and get your breathing nice and strong and slow.'

'I'll just see what it feels like,' Holly said as she picked her way down the beach into the gently lapping water. At first, she felt nothing as her feet were fairly insensitive. As she walked in though, one step at a time, the cold began to seep into her nervous system like a slow wave of pain. She mustn't think of it as pain. Stevie had told her cold-water swimming was eighty per cent a mind thing, a question of training your brain to switch off the cold receptors, or at least not catapult the body into full flight or fight mode.

Was it like childbirth? Holly wondered. But she'd had no experience of that either, so had no benchmark of pain management unless she counted period pain or body waxing. As the water reached her mid-thighs, her eyebrows went into a funny puzzled shape and her mouth became a small O. Now she could feel it. The weird prickliness was creeping up towards the place she knew would sense it most and— She let out a sudden shriek and clamped her hand over her mouth, giggling.

She turned to Stevie, who was slightly taller than her so hadn't quite reached the 'oooh' moment. The woman was smiling with an annoying knowing smile and waffling her hands about in the water on either side of her thighs as if to warm it up. Or was she actually having a wee in the water? Holly stifled another giggle and then, as she tried to compose herself, she saw Stevie sink down while exhaling loudly.

The lake drew her body down, leaving only the tops of her shoulders, neck, and head exposed to the sunshine and breeze. The rest of her was now settling into the magic of below the surface.

So tranquil, so brave, so impossible, thought Holly. *But I can try.* She stepped forward once, twice – oooh – three and… she was in. It was as if the water grabbed at her torso, hungry for warm flesh to suck on. The pain was so intense and there was a clamping feeling on everything below her narrow shoulders. She closed her eyes and tried desperately not to jump up and run out. *Two minutes. How long is two minutes? One, two,* three… but her brain was in panic mode and numbers came and went with no meaning. All she wanted to do was escape this horrible, horrible feeling. But still she crouched, her eyes open now and staring straight ahead of her towards a little island with a couple of trees: Bird Poo Island, Stevie had called it. *Bloody birds,* thought Holly. *I could do with some of your frigging feathers now in a bloody duvet!*

'Remember to breathe,' she heard Stevie say softly from where she was now swimming in gentle circles close to Holly.

Of course! It's all about breathing after all, remembered a now slightly more comfortable Holly. She moved her arms suspiciously around her, almost afraid to swish the water in case the cold bit into her nipples again. But, surprisingly, it felt no colder. In fact, she now felt okay actually moving a little. The next second, she was swimming in a breaststroke towards Stevie.

'You're smiling,' called the other woman cheerfully. 'That's it. Relax, enjoy moving your body, and keep breathing.'

Afterwards, while they were getting dressed and enjoying a hot drink, Stevie asked Holly if she'd like to swim again.

'I think I would actually, yes! I didn't think it'd be something I'd do, but I can honestly say I haven't felt this good for years.'

Stevie laughed. 'It has that effect.'

Silence fell on them then, a warm, companionable silence. Neither of them wanted to go, but eventually Stevie stretched and stood up.

'Time to leave, I'm afraid. Things to do back at home. Work for the next three days, but then I've got two days off, plus the weekend. Are you busy?'

'Nothing that can't be got round, although Simon's back on Thursday evening, so I maybe should be around on Friday. But he goes mountain-biking on Saturdays, so I could do then, if you're free?'

'Well, yes, I could be. I was wondering whether you'd like to meet Angela, who I met for her first swim a week or so ago. It might be nice for us all to get together.'

'Sounds good to me.' Holly hiked her large bag onto her shoulder before starting to walk back up the path towards the road above and their cars.

'Brilliant. I'll message you both and make a plan. Are you on WhatsApp?' asked Stevie. 'It's about the only phone thing I'm any good at! Shall we make a group swim chat thing?'

Chapter Five

STEVIE

October

As the first frosts of October snapped up September's last glow and the nights grew longer, Stevie felt the usual dread of winter seeping into her bones: the threat of damp days that never seemed to get light and the emptiness of a stone-built house that was hard to keep warm.

She became even more grateful for her part-time job in the admin office at the Theatre by the Lake in Keswick: a multifaceted role in which no day was the same. She knew she had made the right decision to stand down as a partner in a law firm when her marriage exploded and had focused on picking herself up and protecting what was left from further stress. It suited her need to be distracted from her own thoughts and meant she got to meet an eclectic mix of actors, musicians, theatregoers, artists, writers, and tradesmen. And, once she'd done this next lot of three days, it would be time to meet up with Holly and Angela. She'd kept her promise to Holly and set up a WhatsApp group so they could message each other to make arrangements. But, for various reasons, it had taken a few weeks to finally get all three of them together on the same day.

She wasn't sure what the quieter Angela would make of Holly, but time would tell. She was looking forward to the company of both women again and was pleased to learn that they were sometimes available during the week because of the nature of their work. All she knew about them so far was that Angela was married to a farmer and worked alongside him, but she said she could probably escape a couple of times a week to meet at the lake. As far as Stevie could make out, Holly didn't work, or at least didn't have a traditional full-time job. Instead, she ran the two holiday cottages that she and her husband owned on their property.

They'd arranged to meet in the same place she'd met Holly: under the stand of conifers opposite Bird Poo Island. She was amused to see that, as she drove down the side of Crummock, two vehicles were following her closely. Holly and Angela, she assumed. She recognised Holly's car, but she and Angela had met on foot. Still, the large red 4x4 didn't surprise her, as it was typical of farmers round here to own a smart vehicle alongside numerous tractors, quad bikes and maybe a Land Rover.

'Hello,' she called as she walked towards the other two women, who were shaking hands and introducing themselves already. Lots of smiles and laughing, some of it obviously nervous, especially from Angela.

'Good to see you again, both of you. How come our paths have never crossed before?' She hugged the smaller, auburn-haired woman first, and then turned to Holly, who came forward to reciprocate the hug. Already a warm, strong connection between virtual strangers. Stevie felt a wave of affection for these women who she sensed were going to become important to her. It wasn't the warmest or sunniest of days and yet here they were, ready to strip down to swimsuits and brave the cold water.

She did indeed wonder how they had never come across each other before in town, at one of the supermarkets or even at one of the performances at the theatre where she worked.

'Good question,' said Holly as she was arranging the contents of her huge bag on the grassy bank by the little beach. 'Simon and I don't go out at weekends. He's usually too tired from the week in London or exhausted from mountain-biking – it's a shame, though. We used to go to the theatre a lot in London. And I get Sainsbury's to deliver.'

'I'll let you know what's coming up over the next few months, then, and see if there's something on you'd enjoy?' offered Stevie.

'I'd love to go to the theatre, too,' piped up Angela, 'but Ed wouldn't go, I'm sure. It's not his kind of thing.'

'Well, why don't the three of *us* go sometime?' Stevie laughed and made a mental note to take a look at the upcoming winter programme.

'It's just odd that I've never seen either of you in town.' Stevie was now undressing and her voice was a bit muffled as she pulled her hoodie over her head.

'Actually, I'm sure I have seen you in Sainsbury's,' admitted Angela. 'Several times. I'll say hello next time!'

'Talking of random sightings, we did accidentally meet at the beautician's that time,' Holly broke into Stevie's thoughts. 'Not quite the same as the tinned fruit aisle in Sainsbury's, but pretty random.'

'Yeh, you're right.' Stevie laughed. She admitted that she didn't even know all her daughters' friends even though she'd ferried them to and from parties over the years.

Angela piped up, 'And I hardly ever leave the farm. I go to the leisure centre to swim twice a week and the supermarket maybe twice, too, but, otherwise, life is extremely limited up on the farm.'

Stevie caught a slight sad tone to Angela's voice, but didn't follow it up. As they got to know each other better, maybe the reasons would be explained. Or perhaps Angela wouldn't be the sharing type.

The three women stood at the edge of the lake, shivering slightly in the cool breeze coming across the water from Bird Poo Island. Stevie wore a plain black racerback swimsuit and had tied her hair up in a high ball on top of her head. Holly stood next to her, jiggling up and down as if she was very nervous, but she said it was because she needed to pee. Her swimsuit today was slightly more conservative than it had been the first time she'd met Stevie, but, even so, it couldn't hide her curves. Stevie scrunched her toes in the tiny stones at the edge of the water and noticed that the pairs of feet on either side of her did the same. Angela, who was standing on the other side of Stevie, started to walk into the water, slowly but steadily, as if she had done it hundreds of times before.

This was the cue for the other two. Squeals and swears replaced conversation as the water reached their sensitive parts and then they all stopped and looked at each other.

It was Stevie who broke the silence, 'One, two, *three*!' and plunged forwards, swimming breaststroke with quick but strong strokes as she controlled her breath. Either side of her, Holly and Angela were going through their own baptism.

Within a couple of minutes, Stevie smiled and almost whispered, 'I can feel the change.' It was that moment when everything in her body was regulated and in balance, no longer in fight or flight mode, but relaxed and in control.

'Me, too!' called Holly with a huge grin. She'd turned over onto her back and was treading water while looking all around her: confident and sure.

'I think I might be too,' laughed Angela, sinking a little and spluttering.

And then they swam around each other in circles until Stevie looked at her watch and suggested it was time to get out.

'Oh, but I'm feeling quite relaxed, isn't that a good thing?'

asked Holly. She turned and swam back towards the beach with the other two, listening to Stevie as she explained how important it was to get out of the water before you got warm and relaxed as that was one of the earliest signs of hypothermia.

'I don't want to sound preachy, but it's really important to get to know your body and how it reacts to the cold water. It should feel good, but not too good. There's always a moment when you can sense what I called the change, but then you should still be able to notice the coldness of the water.'

'Do you always time yourself, Stevie?' asked Angela, waggling her hands around to shake off water before picking up her towel from the grassy bank.

'No, hardly ever. I did today because I thought I might get distracted by you two!' She laughed. 'But it was just about the right length of time as neither of you are used to it. Next time, we can stay in a bit longer, but it doesn't really have more benefits, just so you know.'

'It doesn't?' asked Holly, sounding a bit surprised. 'So, what is the optimum length of time to be in the water?'

'There isn't one. It varies from person to person, day to day, swim spot to swim spot, and it depends on the weather, how much sleep you've had, and on and on.'

'Interesting.' Holly's voice was muffled from under her thermal top, which she was pulling down over her head.

'Mmm, it is,' mumbled Stevie and then looked up from packing her bag. 'So, shall we swim again in a few days?'

Twice a week, they met down at the lake come rain or shine. Usually, it was all three of them, but occasionally one of them couldn't make it, leaving two of them to swim together. Each swim was different, but the common thread was a growing intimacy and shared knowledge of each other's lives as the water brought down the filters and more sensitive information became topics of conversation.

The person who kept her private life most concealed was Angela, but Stevie sensed there was a lot more going on behind the scenes. From the few things she did say, it was clear that all was not rosy up at the farm. Most of that appeared to be down to one woman in particular – her mother-in-law, who was unimpressed with her son's choice of wife.

'Oh, by the way,' Stevie said one morning while they were sitting drinking their hot coffee and teas, 'I won't be around next weekend. I'm off to Norway. It's somewhere I'd never really thought of going, but my friend, Emma, has been going on about how beautiful it is there for so long and… well, I reckon it's time I went.'

'Yeh, good for you!' said Holly. 'I've never been, but it should be nice and cold there. Will you be able to try one of their ice holes? You know, the ones with the ladders going down into them?'

'It's part of the plan, yes. And skiing. But I never learnt to ski, so not sure I'll be doing that. Apparently, the Norwegians never turn down an opportunity to ski if the snow's good. But we'll see. I'm sure I can snuggle up in their cabin instead with a good book and some Gløgg!' Stevie laughed happily, excited now at the prospect of doing something a bit different. *Who knows*, she thought, *maybe this trip will be the start of new things.*

'Just don't go falling in love with an ice hole while you're out there, will you?' Holly giggled, well aware of her double entendre. 'Some bearded Viking who wants to act out his ancestors' savage fantasies.'

'I think that was the Danish, Holly,' interrupted Angela. 'And the Swedish. The Norwegians were farmers mostly.'

'Don't worry, I've had my fill of ice holes – not going to

happen again!' Stevie chucked her swim bucket into the boot of her car and slammed it shut as if to emphasise her point.

Later that day, she reflected on how talking about going to Norway had triggered all sorts of ugly emotions she thought she had long since slung out of her life. Of course, she knew what it was, she just hadn't explained it in detail to Holly and Angela: John, her ex-husband, used to take her with him on his work trips to Oslo before the kids. It really irritated her that she still connected him with the place – not that it hadn't been pretty cool to spend time wandering around the city while he was working and then eating out every evening in some excellent, but astronomically expensive restaurants. They'd never explored beyond the city though, which now seemed a shame, and she couldn't remember why they hadn't. What a wasted opportunity! *Go away,* she said to the memories. She made herself promise to create new ones to replace them.

Chapter Six

STEVIE

November, Norway

'Saunas, ice water, Vikings and Gløgg,' Emma promised her as they each unwrapped a boiled sweet and started sucking on them to unblock their ears as the plane descended through clouds over southern Norway. Stevie remembered Angela's correction but didn't try to explain where Vikings primarily came from to Emma.

She and Emma had met up at Gate B35 in Schiphol Airport, Amsterdam because Stevie had driven up from Cumbria to Glasgow to catch the KLM flight and Emma, who lived near Oxford, had flown from Heathrow. This way, they were able to travel together on the short flight to Kristiansand, where they were going to be met by Emma's friends Eva and Harald, a Norwegian couple who had spent some time working in the same firm as Emma in Oxford before returning to their homeland.

Stevie and Emma had first met each other down in Oxfordshire when Stevie's mother had still been alive. She had spent a lot of time with her mother, but even more so while she was poorly. On one such occasion, in need of a break, she had looked up where she could swim. Queenford Lake was within easy reach, so one Sunday morning she'd gone along and found it a friendly, low-key place, albeit with changing rooms, toilets and showers and even a coffee shop/restaurant on site. Completely different to Crummock Water. These regular swims lightened the stress and heartache she felt during the last few weeks of her mother's life and she'd got to know a few of the women there quite well, especially Emma.

It was Emma's loud laugh that had drawn Stevie to her initially and then, as she got to know her better, it was obvious that they shared many life experiences, including marriages that had ended badly. A friendship emerged and the swims extended into post-swim coffee and cake on many occasions. The atmosphere of the club was eclectic and stimulated Stevie in a way that, now that she wasn't busy with her career, children, or husband, she realised she craved. She felt comfortable in the company of these businesspeople, scientists and academics, and started to form a plan: supposing she sold up her large house in Cumbria and bought a small place down here? It might give her a fresh start; she'd just need the right place to live and a job of some sort that brought her into contact with people, although her existing swim friends would no doubt also be a way into some sort of community.

As the plane dropped lower, Stevie's excitement increased. It had been years since she'd travelled outside of the UK – ironically, the last time probably had been going to Oslo with John. Craning her neck to get a good look at the terrain, she could see frozen lakes and dark green conifers: miles upon miles of emptiness, dotted now and again with a cluster of mostly red-roofed buildings, which helped them stand out against the landscape. Although it was the middle of the day, already the sun was sinking quite low in the sky. She could see twinkles of house lights and fairy lights as the plane flew lower and lower, bringing them ever closer to their destination.

Harald was waiting for them on the other side of the mirrored No Return doors and his English was impeccable – unlike his driving.

Strapped into the back seat while Emma sat up front conversing in Norwegian, Stevie began to feel increasingly claustrophobic as the electric car slid at speed along the highway and then, when they turned off to climb up into the mountains, the roads became more twisty. In the glow from the headlights, she could see snow-clad forests and snow pole after snow pole. The road had been ploughed and there was a bank of dirty snow piled up on each side of the gravelly tarmac. The three-hour journey couldn't end quickly enough for Stevie, who was already dreading the return journey to the airport in four days' time.

Darkness had fallen like a dropped cloak, intense and smothering, which was not helped by their forest location. She had no idea what lay beyond the trees, but was informed that it was stunning and all would be revealed in the morning. Tired after a 4 a.m. start in Glasgow, Stevie relished the hearty meat and potato supper that was served, but could feel herself nodding off as they sat around the huge log burner afterwards sipping wine and chatting.

She pushed herself up from the 1950s style wooden sofa with red-patterned cushions, made her apologies and said she just needed to lie down and sleep. When Emma offered to come with her over to the guests' cabin, Stevie reassured her that she would be fine. It was only a short walk across and Eva had left a lantern on the decking to guide her. Up here in the forest, there were no streetlights or ambient lights of any sort. Everything in the cabins was solar powered, with a generator as a backup. Candles and lanterns festooned every room, and if you stepped outside, it took more than a minute to gain any night vision.

Standing on the decking of this smaller, but equally cosy-looking cabin, Stevie stared out into the dark forest and breathed in and out deeply for a few minutes to catch up with herself and steady her racing mind. Specifically, the memories of John: here in Norway on work trips, but, more disturbingly, four years ago, on the morning her world had imploded. She could still hear that woman's voice screeching down the phone, thinking she was speaking to John and accusing him of cheating. So many times since, Stevie had wasted energy wishing she'd screeched back – so loud that John would've heard her from the bathroom and the woman would've realised what a double-cheating shit he was. Wasted energy because there was no turning the clock back. What was done was done.

The heaviness of missing an opportunity to release her anger and hurt had undoubtedly tainted her life since. Something needed to happen to draw a line under those memories so that she could really step forwards with confidence. This quiet reflection time on the deck allowed her to put a lid on those dark memories for the time being and bring herself back into the present: a lovely weekend with no responsibilities in a beautiful part of Norway, with no expectations of her except to relax and enjoy her time.

It was time for much-needed sleep but, first, a visit to the bathroom, which Stevie suddenly remembered was not like her bathroom at home. It was an outhouse, separate from either of the two cabins and a short walk along a solar-lit path. When they'd arrived at the cabins, she'd been shown how it worked, but was now dreading going back in. She'd avoided it all evening as the main cabin had its own indoor 'bathroom' by the porch.

Here goes, she thought as she pushed open the outer wooden door with its large wooden latch. She stepped into what looked like a shed with the left-hand end dedicated to rows of tools and a workbench. The smell was what you would expect: years of DIY projects using various oils, paints, and coatings had taken shape in here and the scent of their creation lingered not unpleasantly. She pushed the outer door closed behind her and was plunged into the dark of the night, except for a glimmer coming from under the second door. She reached out to feel for a doorknob, but only found a tiny cotton reel-shaped object, which she knew she wasn't supposed to pull on. It was matched on the other side by another small reel to pull the door closed once you'd used the facilities. Push, that's what Eva had said. If it feels a bit stiff, just push harder – the wood tended to swell in the winter.

Tiny jars of lit candles sat in rows on the small shelving at shoulder height around the room. She shivered slightly. It was well-ventilated, that was for sure. There was a distinct, but not foul, smell: wood shavings mixed with pine needles and eucalyptus and tinged with what she knew was in a heap in the pit that she was about to sit over.

A traditional long-drop toilet and bucket of cedar bark, with the luxury of a china bowl and a jug of cold water on a wooden washstand. But it was the toilet seat that made her laugh out loud. It was a factory-formed polystyrene seat made up of a 'lid' and then a 'seat', which had been glued down firmly onto the wooden platform built over the pit. She put her hand out to hold the lid by its raised handle, took a deep breath, and lifted it off the seat. In the gentle glow of the candles, she could just glimpse white scrunches – toilet paper – amid what looked like a fairly high peak of wood shavings and... she dropped the lid.

'*Eeek!*' She grabbed it again, terrified it might tumble and fall down the hole. Thankfully, it was attached to the seat by a string leash. *Oh, my God,* Stevie thought. *I am so not sure about this.*

Shortly afterwards, as she snuggled down under a weighted blanket on the bottom bunk in the cabin, sleep came more easily than she thought it would. She felt cosy and safe, cocooned in a world of hygge hints and accessories: throws and scatter cushions, lights and candles – all intended to light up the dark months and celebrate not just winter, but the cold.

For Stevie, this was a revelation. An unexpected bonus of having come to Norway might just be finding a way of coping with her ingrained dread of October sliding into grey November and then into the long, dark days of December, January, and most of February. She noted how easy it would be to transform her own home into something far more relaxing and healthier.

Stunning was an understatement for what she saw the next morning when she crawled out of her snug nest of a bed and pulled back the woollen curtain from over the window. She had to wipe away thick condensation from the small panes, but then the reason for everything became clear. Even the car trip was erased from her memory. Sharp light – the sort only rarely seen in the Lake District on a cold winter's day – flaunted the curves, edges, and depths of a frozen-mountain scene. Below the cabins, there was not just a lake, but a long wooden jetty protruding rudely into the water.

A summer haunt, silenced now for months as nature reclaimed what was hers. Human tampering was tolerated, but not treated kindly. The freezing water soaked into the wooden structure every autumn, and from then on, it started its deadly destruction once again: expanding and splitting the posts and boardwalk until the tension burst. When this was repeated over years, the damage eventually killed anything it touched.

But death was not on the agenda for their first day. A gentle stroll down through the forest to the lake was planned, which sounded exactly like what they needed to wake up, followed by a picnic on the shore complete with log fire.

'Great you've come here this weekend, Stevie,' announced Eva. 'The temperatures have really dropped over the last few weeks and the lake is frozen over, so we are going to try to cut you an ice hole. Last night it was minus ten.'

Stevie stared at her in surprise, feeling a mixture of excitement and trepidation.

'Harald is going to check to see if the ice is the right thickness at the end of the jetty so that he can make us a dipping hole at the foot of the ladder.' Emma poured some red-brown liquid into an enamel mug and passed it to Stevie. 'Drink this Gløgg. It will give you fire in your belly!'

Eva and Harald both chuckled as they swigged back the hot drink and wiped their mouths with a satisfied sigh afterwards.

'To work,' announced Harald as he strolled down the frosty jetty, his chainsaw held in one hand and an axe in the other.

Stevie watched as he crouched down by the ladder and started to chop at the ice. Satisfied with its thickness, he climbed down the wooden rungs and stepped out. Then he started up the chainsaw. The noise was deafening and stopped all conversation, but Stevie was happy to watch as the big man worked away like a professional, sliding the long blade of the chainsaw up and down. As the ice was cut, a steady arc of watery ice streamed into the air, lit by the sun like an ethereal rainbow of crystals.

'Normally, he'd cut a hole out on the ice away from the ladder, but it's not reliably thick yet, so it's safer to do this one for you right at the foot,' explained Eva. And off she marched down the jetty, brandishing a huge pair of tongs, heading to where her husband was working away. She climbed down the ladder and onto the frozen lake and started to help him pull out blocks of ice from the hole with the huge tongs.

Stevie hardly dared to breathe. She had grown up with the very clear message that you did not walk on a frozen lake, no matter how thick you thought the ice was. Yet, here were two fully grown adults working away to create a beautiful ice hole in a frozen lake.

Clearly it was heavy work hauling out the blocks of six-inch thick ice, but Eva was used to manual work and focused tirelessly while Harald stacked the blocks around the hole with some artistry.

The sun was, unbelievably, starting to sink down towards the treeline on the other side of the lake although it was only lunchtime. Stevie smiled quietly, grateful for the work that was being done to ensure she and Emma got the ice hole experience most wild swimmers only dream about.

Then it was time to take off their clothes and lower themselves, one at a time, into the dark water. Eva and Harald stayed on the ice, ready to help their guests get in and out safely, guiding them gently on the best way to get in, how to hang from the corners of the triangle rather than the sides, and telling them when it was time to get out.

Fear squatted like a toad in the pit of Stevie's stomach as she watched Emma lower herself slowly – first, just the bottom half of her legs, while she sorted out her balance on her arms. and then, the rest of her body with her elbows digging into the ice either side of her. The squeal that came from her friend as the cold water hit her armpits made everyone laugh and briefly gave Stevie the confidence she needed to step forward for her turn. Emma had moved herself down to the other end, away from the ladder, and sat with her arms flat on either side of the widest part of the hole, It wasn't what Harald would normally advise doing, but since there were going to be two of them in the hole, it was necessary.

Emma had some previous experience with ice holes and relaxed into this one as if it were a hot bubble bath. Stevie could hear her own breath, fast and troubled, and her brow was creased in concentration as she put her feet either side of the pointy end. Eva had put a carpet tile on the ice to protect their bottoms and give them something to grip onto when they pulled themselves back out. Its prickly surface tickled her bare skin, but she was grateful for it being there, something tangible in this terrifying moment of dare or go home.

'You can do it, Stevie!' called Emma. 'It's delicious in here, you'll love it!'

And so, with a bit of grunting and huffing, Stevie worked her way inelegantly into the dark triangle, trying to blot out any thoughts of lake monsters seeing her white legs dangling. Her breath was snapped away as the cold clenched around her hips and groin, but she had known this would happen and mentally prepared herself to relax and let everything settle before lowering herself and trusting elbow support.

She looked straight ahead at Emma, who was silhouetted against the now orange sky and moved herself into a state of suspended astonishment. Beauty, not only aesthetic, but emotional and intellectual, held them both in the moment and Stevie knew what she was doing was life changing.

If she was brave enough to do this, what else could she do? She was trying to overcome her deep-seated fear of not knowing what was in the depths below her, something that haunted her in the lakes at home.

But that wasn't all. This deliberate exposure to potential danger, albeit carefully managed by Eva and Harald, was like a giant dose of adrenalin, kicking her out into the rest of her life from a place in which she'd wallowed for too long. The underlying sadness and low-level stress she'd lived with since her marriage fell apart needed to be shaken off and ripped away from her shoulders. Her daily solo dips in the lake soothed and comforted, but barely scratched at the scab that had formed over her pain.

This ice hole and this different experience were two of the main reasons she had wanted to come with Emma to Norway. She saw it as a way out of her comfort zone by exposing herself, not only to travelling, but also to meeting new people by staying with Emma's friends. If it gave her the strength she thought it might, then she knew she could use that strength back home in other areas of her life. That included feeling more positive about the prospect of growing old alone and answering the question her daughters always asked about whether she was ready to invite another man into her life. That always led to the question of how the heck would she ever meet another man out in the sticks, and whether it was a good idea to move south to Oxford and start a completely fresh chapter of her life.

'Time, ladies,' called Harald, firmly.

First out was Stevie. It was easier than she'd feared to push herself back up onto her elbows then hands and, finally, scratch and scrape her frozen bottom back onto the point so she could wriggle and squirm her way onto the furry tile, where she was helped up to her feet by the strong hands of Harald. Then up the ladder. Eva held out her swim cloak and told her to remove her wet costume immediately and then hurry back to the shore and the fire. Meanwhile, Emma repeated the pushing and squirming movements until she too was safely out of the water and being looked after by Harald.

Eva had put a couple of lanterns on the beach and their warm glow flickered gently, a healing and soothing focal point to stare at while sipping more Gløgg and swaying from side to side to pump warm blood back into their legs.

The Lake District seemed light years away out here on the frozen mountain lake. Stevie could hardly believe they'd only been there for twenty-four hours. She felt invincible and her brain was on fire. Crazy ideas about being in icy water more often raced around and although she was shivering, she thought she'd never felt a more intense burning in her belly.

Halfway through the evening, which had been a lively one with some of Eva and Harald's friends round for dinner, Stevie knew she was falling asleep. She was being lulled once again into a warm cocoon by the heat from the wood stove, hearty food, wine, and not being able to understand a word of the conversation rattling around her. Emma was still alert and joining in, but Stevie knew it was time to retreat to the annexe. As she stood up to leave, Eva put a hand up to silence the group.

'Tomorrow night, we are going into the forest on our skis.' She nodded encouragingly at Stevie. 'You will come with us, yes? We take food and drink, light a fire, and then ski back.'

Emma clapped her hands with excitement like a small child. Stevie smiled to herself. It was exactly what Emma had said would happen. She just wished now that she did ski, because Eva and Harald were such sweet people and it would be a beautiful evening.

'I know you don't ski, but we could perhaps take the pulk,' said Eva. 'If you're wrapped up warm enough, we can pull you along. No one goes fast anyway. It's cross-country skiing and we never go far.'

'That sounds fun, but I'm honestly happy to stay here, snuggled up by the stove and reading my book – I'd hate for you to have to lug me along behind you!' A bit of quiet time in this cosy cabin was far more appealing. She looked at Eva and Harald. 'If that's alright?'

Harald nodded, but then turned to say something to the woman sitting next to him whose name Stevie couldn't remember. After a few minutes, Harald said, 'You are welcome to, but we have an idea.'

Harald and Eva exchanged a look, but neither of them

explained what the idea was and Stevie felt too tired to press them.

It would all be revealed tomorrow, they said. 'We just need to send some texts to make arrangements. Goodnight, Stevie, we hope you sleep well.'

'Arvid will arrive in his truck at seven p.m. He will take you to the forest for a real Norwegian experience.' Eva sounded satisfied with the arrangement that had been finalised after another text message the following morning.

Stevie wasn't quite sure how to react. It all felt a bit as if she didn't have a choice. Who was Arvid? And what was he going to show her in the forest that was such an amazing Norwegian experience? Why couldn't they just let her be in the cabin for a couple of hours on her own?

Emma had taken Stevie's hands and squeezed them encouragingly and said, 'It'll be fine. I've met Arvid. He's a great guy and I know he'll make it a really memorable evening.'

Eva and Harald both nodded enthusiastically. 'Ah, yes, Arvid. He is a good guy. You are in good hands. He knows the forest well and will keep you safe.'

Safe? She wasn't sure that was the most encouraging thing to hear, but she forced herself to ask questions.

'What do I need? Where are we going?' Her voice sounded stronger than she felt, but, as she'd always told her daughters, there are some things in life you don't really want to do, but you do them anyway and then wonder what you've been worried about. *Maybe this is a leap of faith I need to take,* she thought to herself. *Trust these lovely people. When in Norway, do as the Norwegians do and all that.*

Stevie looked across at Emma, who shrugged her shoulders as if to say, 'What? What's there to be worried about?'

'You just need to keep an open mind,' Emma warned Stevie when Eva and Harald were out of the room sorting out soup for lunch. 'Arvid is a kind man and he knows these forests really well because he's a hunter. But he's not bothered about the skiing – he finds us all too noisy and it offends him. I think you'll like him,' she added. 'Oh, not in that way! He's completely reliable, a confirmed bachelor – a bit of a recluse, really, but nothing to worry about. You told me you wanted to change your life, bury the past, look to the future, all that stuff… Well, I think this experience will be exactly what you need to set yourself free of everything that's holding you back. You're an amazing woman, Stevie. I love you to bits, but you need to let go. It's time.' Emma hugged Stevie hard and whispered one last time, 'Just keep an open mind and you'll love it.'

It was a phrase that echoed in the darkness that now crept in from all sides as Arvid dimmed then switched off the headlights on his truck. Silence. There was only her own heartbeat. Stevie turned to look at the man who had driven her out to the forest. He was a complete stranger to her, but the brother of the woman they had dinner with the previous night.

What the heck am I doing? Stevie felt her whole body tensing up. She only knew that the reason she was here had something to do with swimming, in the forest, in the dark, with a man she had never met before. Simple really! No need to be suspicious, afraid, or anything other than 'open-minded'.

Actually, Arvid seemed fine.

'Okay, it's time. Let's go.' The tall Norwegian turned to look at her and she could just make out in the dark of the cab that he was smiling. It didn't make her feel any less uncertain.

'So, I just need my bag? We don't need an axe or chainsaw?' Her voice was clear and steady even though she just wanted to run away. At this point, she had only a couple of options, neither of which appealed: get back in the truck and refuse to move until he drove her back to the house or follow him into the forest to wherever they were going. Swimming was the promise, the carrot, but her rational self thought, *Why would anyone want to swim at night in a frozen forest miles from anywhere with someone they had only just met half an hour ago?* It was utter madness. Her wild self, the one that she knew would help free her from the past, urged her to think out of the box. Was it really so perverse to think that something that didn't make rational sense could actually be good for her?

Stevie wanted to follow through. At the back of her mind was the obvious comfort blanket of knowing that Emma's friends had set this up to ensure she too had a special Norwegian experience while they were off having theirs. There was no way that they would have set her up with a psychopath (not knowingly, anyway!) who was going to do anything bad to her and then leave her body buried under mossy rocks. How would he explain not returning her to the house? Or was he planning on disappearing, too?

It made no rational sense, but to Stevie, it almost felt right – as if this was why she had been offered this trip to Norway. She felt a tingle of excitement in her belly and looked across at Arvid, who wore a look of slight irritation on his face.

'Open your coat.' He moved slightly towards her. She took a step back and pulled her heavy coat more tightly around her. Panic rushed through her body as that tingle turned to something less pleasant.

'Here.' He held out his hand and she could see something glinting in it. 'Open your coat, please.'

She did as he asked, seeing her life flash before her eyes and wishing she could remember that self-defence move where you disable your attacker with one swift leg and arm movement. But he was suddenly too close and had pulled open her coat and reached in to unzip the little breast pocket. He dropped what he held into the pocket and then zipped it back up.

'There, you have the truck keys, so you know you will be safe.' Then he turned and headed off down the track.

'Close your mouth, Stevie,' she said to herself and pushed her chin up with the back of her gloved hand. 'And don't lose that man!'

The snow on the forest floor was ankle deep and in places she sank even further, but so far, her feet had stayed dry in her strong boots. Arvid seemed to be following a path between trees and she could hear running water, a sound that got louder and louder and the snow deeper and deeper.

Arvid stopped and she very nearly collided with him because she had been scanning the gaps in the trees for signs of a river or a waterfall rather than looking where she was going. He turned and held out his hand. Then he waggled it impatiently when she seemed reluctant to take it.

As he helped her over a fallen tree and through some spiky branches, she felt her heart flip over several times: not from his strong grip, but from where he had brought her. The two of them stood in silence staring at a beautiful, but small pool, which had a tiny waterfall dropping into it and then another one, equally tiny, falling out of it. Arvid shone his head torch into the pool and Stevie could see the stones on the bottom – it seemed to only be about knee deep, but clear of branches and very dippable. The current wasn't too strong and the access was going to be a bit of a stony, mossy slide, but nothing crazy. She smiled at Arvid for the first time since she'd met him and his response was to pat her on the shoulder with an excited grin.

'Okay, I'm going to light a fire for warmth after and then we can swim. You find a place to sit,' he said, shining his head torch on the ground behind them, seeming to look for a good spot for her to place her sit mat.

'This looks flat.' She pointed at a mossy rock with only a thin sprinkling of snow. Confidence had replaced fear; they were indeed going to have a swim, or at least a dip, and she felt within her comfort zone again. Back home in the Lake District, she'd done a few night swims – never in a forest, but at least there was now something vaguely familiar about what they were doing. Lighting a fire was a bit different, but she was looking forward to the warmth it would provide after.

She sat on her boiled wool and Neoprene sit mat, which Eva had said she could keep, and started to take off her outer layers. Arvid had got the fire going and had disappeared, probably to his own rock to get changed. She'd already put her swimsuit on and was actually desperate for a wee all of a sudden – more than likely brought on by the sound of running water! But she wanted to put on her Neoprene swim socks and gloves first, so she was rooting about in her daysack to find them when she glanced up and saw a bare bottom lowering itself into the pool: Arvid was naked. Completely. Not even shoes or gloves.

He had left his head torch dangling from a tree branch so that their way into the pool could be lit from that as well as the glow of the fire, but it seemed to shine directly onto his muscular body. Stevie couldn't stop staring. How come some men just look so much better out of their clothes? Arvid was taller than her, but had given the impression of being fairly scrawny and unspectacular in the dark with clothes on. *Perhaps that was it*, she thought, *the light's playing tricks and creating shadows*. No, he was in one hell of a shape for someone his age, she admitted with a slightly naughty chuckle to herself. He had a greying head of hair and beard, which indicated he was about her age, unless he had aged prematurely.

'Hey! Stevie! Come on!' He turned to face her and that was it. Nothing hidden and nothing aged about his front view either. Stevie stood up and in a moment of bravado and un-Britishness, she pulled her swimsuit off her shoulders and down over her hips. In her haste to be rid of its encumbrance, she momentarily overbalanced on the snowy ground, but at the last moment righted herself. When she looked up to see if Arvid had been watching, she was slightly disappointed to see that he was sitting down near the top waterfall with his head bent over his hands, as if in prayer. Maybe it was only her who had felt the sexual tension?

Embarrassed now by her nakedness, she covered herself as best she could while holding onto the branch that made getting into the pool so much easier. Boobs, belly, or crotch? Which to cover? She knew she was now the one spotlighted, but if she was quick, she'd be in the water and submerged before the Norwegian had finished his prayers. It was unfortunate that she rushed the final few steps because, instead of slinking down like a wood nymph into the very cold water, she stumbled and had to reach out with both hands to catch hold of Arvid's knees, which were protruding out of the pool because he had made room for her to sit down. Suddenly, she found herself pressed up against him and squeaked as her left boob squished between her forearm and his thigh and now her chin was on his knee.

She imagined trying to describe this to anyone else and realised how it would look. Petrified of this stranger two minutes ago and now she was draping her naked body across his in the middle of a deep, dark forest miles away from anywhere.

'Oops! Sorry.' She pushed herself away and tried to squat elegantly far enough away from him, but deep enough in the pool to cover at least her belly, which she didn't need to look down at to know was like a few rolls of uncooked pastry.

'It's okay, it's normal.' Did he mean her belly or her grabbing at his body?

He held his hand out to help her settle in the water. Now he was clearly looking at her body. She knew he was, but there was nothing in his look that said 'yuck' or 'mmmm'. She felt human rather than woman. Two humans, old enough to know better some would say, strangers, crouched naked in a freezing cold puddle with their extremities wincing and screaming for help. It was an incredible feeling of liberation and Stevie was so glad she had taken off her swimsuit. It would have seemed odd to have worn it in the circumstances, she realised with a laugh. And then she relaxed completely and gave herself up to the moment.

Arvid moved over and let her share the waterfall. Their bare shoulders touched more than lightly and she put her arm under his so that they could sit comfortably. When she felt his hand on her thigh, it seemed completely natural and not at all suggestive. She looked at their knees sticking out of the water, four brave body parts, his higher than hers and with a few dark hairs quivering in the cold air. The water down the back of her neck and cascading over her shoulders and down her chest soothed and stimulated at the same time. She looked down at her breasts and saw that her nipples were like ripe loganberries, standing to attention. Arvid glanced down at them and then smiled at Stevie. She was surprised to feel a faint stirring in her groin, which she was sure must be pretty much frozen. Would he kiss her? She knew she would have let him and very likely reciprocated. There was no reason not to. It would have seemed natural and unencumbered. But, instead, he pointed at his groin and took his hand off her thigh to use his thumb and index finger to show her how men's bodies react differently to women's when immersed in cold water.

Then his hand rested once more on her thigh and they both relaxed into the moment. This was not what she had imagined she'd be doing in Norway this weekend, but it felt incredibly liberating, and she knew that deep down it would have a big impact on her.

Being discarded by her husband after twenty-five years of marriage had completely undermined her self-confidence and belief in love. The moment she realised she wasn't enough for him, she had lost all connection to physical desire and passion. It no longer existed in her world because it was now tainted with lies and deceit. She didn't believe a man would ever find her attractive again, because she didn't feel she was attractive. And her internal flame had almost been extinguished. But, tonight, here in a dark forest, with a man who she had only just met, it had felt completely natural to be naked.

Naked immersion with an attractive man who had recognised her bravery for getting out of her comfort zone, absorbed her female essence, and treated her as an equal. In this moment, she knew she deserved nothing less, but whether that confidence would carry over to her real life back in Cumbria was debatable. That was up to her. For now, she just wanted to enjoy the moment and not overthink the whys and wherefores.

Chapter Seven

CHRIS

November

C hris, aching like an arthritic old man, swung his leg over his bike and clipped into the pedals. He cursed having checked the text message earlier that morning from his cycling friend, Andy, because it had guilted him into action first thing and, reluctantly, he'd made a large bowl of porridge and prepared a bottle of energy drink.

'Remember, Chubbs, if it's not on Strava, it didn't happen,' Andy had texted.

Chris was grateful really, because without these nudges and reminders to keep going and keep busy, he still wasn't sure whether or not he'd retreat back into apathy.

It had been Andy who had dragged him out on his bike earlier that year. He'd turned up one afternoon, uninvited, let himself in the back door, and taken one look at Chris. He was slumped on the sofa, as had become the norm after his wife Gail had died, surrounded by the detritus of a man who'd given up on himself. Andy had set about getting this broken human back on track the only way he knew – cycling. He'd rifled through his friend's kit in the under-stairs cupboard to find cycling shorts, jersey, shoes, helmet, and gloves, then searched for the track pump to put some air in the tyres of the carbon machine that lived on the wall in the study.

After months and months of relative inactivity, that first ride with Andy had hurt: his backside, lower back, shoulders, hands, forearms, and legs all ached as if he had been wrestling. Slowly, the aches and pains had diminished and he noticed his muscles becoming slightly more defined again. The sharp burning sensation as he pushed down on the pedals reminded him of the days when he thought nothing of cycling fifty miles in a morning, but he still hated it.

Today, months down the line, once he was out, he felt content to be in his element again, heading down the Lorton Valley towards Buttermere and made a mental note to send his thanks to Andy for the reminders to keep going. As it was a beautiful November day, he planned to grab one of the benches outside the cafe down there. He enjoyed the feel of early winter sunshine on his face and had always been a people watcher. In spite of his reluctantly eaten bowl of porridge earlier, he now craved one of those crumbly scones washed down with an Americano. Hunger now motivated him more often and he ate a more varied diet, but he still hadn't got round to cooking himself a meal from scratch. Somehow it didn't seem important at the moment. He just needed to stop the rumbling in his stomach.

As he headed out onto the main road down to the lake, he swore at a red 4x4 that passed him just a bit too close; the driver was too busy yacking with her friends to bother to give him enough leeway. He shook his head and, not for the first time, questioned why so many drivers didn't seem to know the width of their vehicle. Irritated now, he stood up on the pedals and pumped his legs hard, feeling the burn in his tired muscles until he could see the view open out in front of him. Skiddaw, one of the highest mountains in England, then Sale Fell, Ling Fell, Whinlatter Pass, and, just visible from this angle, the tops of the fells that ringed Crummock Water. The sight never failed to move him, even though he'd known them most of his life.

As he turned right at the junction, once again his heart beat slightly faster with an emotion he'd never quite been able to understand. What was it about this landscape, the light playing through the clouds and the incredible mix of colours: green, tinged with orange bracken; black rock and grey scree. No one had ever called Chris creative, but as a young boy he'd been uninhibited in his art classes, producing work that astonished the teaching staff with its maturity. The system had stomped down on that, though, until he'd just not bothered with arty stuff anymore.

This road was freewheeling heaven as it swooped down the valley towards the mountains and lakes, but Chris knew to slow down through the narrows as the edges of the tarmac had broken away, leaving treacherous, wheel-buckling holes for unwary cyclists. Strained muscles and tired limbs brought a wince to his face when the road kicked up through the woods, which in spring wore a carpet of bluebells. He felt his stomach rumble again, but it wouldn't take him long to reach the cafe where Tom, his youngest, was working post A levels while he decided whether to take up his place at university.

A moment's lack of concentration and Chris swore when he had to brake hard and whip his left foot out from the cleats to stop from falling off. It was that damn monster of a car again – stopped in the middle of the road. Its three occupants had piled out and were pointing their phones at the sky and the mountains.

'Morning,' he snapped at them as he squeezed past, making a point of putting his hand on the side of the pristine vehicle. *Someone is very proud of this hunk of metal*, he thought, *and I don't reckon it's you, love.* He stared hard at one of the women, rather mousy-looking, in her early forties, who almost dropped her car keys and jumped out of her baggy jogging bottoms and fleecy top. Miles away. He shook his head, but held back a stream of verbal abuse.

Once far enough past the women so as not to be seen by them, he stole a glance across towards the lake. Actually, those women had a point. He unclipped his left foot in a more controlled way this time, applied the brakes, and skidded elegantly to a stop in the loose gravel at the side of the road.

Three shafts of light fell out of the chaotic clouds and struck down deep into the metallic sheen of the lake. It was like God was throwing huge amounts of energy and power into the water, not caring who he distracted. Beautiful. There was no denying it.

A loud toot made him jump as the red 4x4 rolled past him – its engine ghostly and quiet in an expensive sort of way. Nothing tasteful about its passengers though: waving and calling out 'Helloooooooo!' and 'It's us again!' Why were they so damn cheerful? Now he was stuck behind them. This section of road that ran close to the lakeshore oozed danger, not just from oncoming vehicles, potholes and rocks dislodged from the dry stone walls, but often from the nonchalant sheep that wandered aimlessly across the road, or worse still, skittered out in front of you for no logical reason whatsoever. Herdwicks, bred to survive harsh winters out on the fells, guardians of Lakeland, and, as such, to be respected and chivvied along out of the way, not sworn at and driven into.

Resigned, he hung back about 100 metres from the car, far enough to avoid being gassed by the exhaust, but close enough to see, by the way in which the three women were moving their heads and gesticulating, that the conversation was free ranging and hilarious.

He had grown used to quiet. His son, Tom, shared staff

accommodation at the hotel near the cafe and his daughter, Clare, lived with her boyfriend near Lancaster.

Needing to shrug off the sudden flood of memories that hit him when he remembered what a noisy family they had once been, he reminded himself how annoyed he'd be if those women were heading for coffee and cakes in the same cafe and took either of his favourite tables. Thankfully, under the stand of Scots pines, the red car pulled over and parked. He raised his left hand to say thanks and pushed down with some force on the pedals as he sailed past. Glad to be on the open road again, he embraced the power in his legs and dropped a gear or two. It felt good. He felt invincible.

∼

Angela, Holly and Stevie

'Did you see how cross that cyclist looked?' Angela picked up her small, neatly packed rucksack from the boot and then reached up to pull it closed. 'I thought he was going to scratch the car.' She winced, remembering how he and his bike had been within millimetres of Ed's precious vehicle. How would she explain a scratch on the door? Somebody's shopping trolley in the car park? She really didn't want to tell him the truth because she knew how he would be against her swimming in the lake because of the way his father had drowned, but it upset her to have to lie to him. Or, more to the point, she was keeping the secret safe from his mother, who she suspected would be far more vocal about the subject.

Therein lay the problem: his mother and how much Ed was under her thumb, to the point that he sided with her over so many things to do with life on the farm. It seemed an impossible situation and she just didn't know how to deal with it. Put up with it until it became intolerable, she guessed.

'Hang on, I just need my—' Her blonde expensively perfumed swim buddy nudged her out of the way and grabbed a bright pink, already inflated, tow float from the boot.

'Sorry, Holly.' Angela smiled, stepping out of the way.

'Are you okay, Angela?' Hearing her own name was enough to bring her back from wherever she had drifted. She saw that Holly was peering at her anxiously. It would have been a good opportunity to offload some of the questions that were constantly chasing around in her head, but she didn't want to spoil the day. It was such a stunning morning; no one needed to hear her moaning about stuff.

'I'm fine, thanks. Mmmm, you smell nice.' Some exaggerated sniffing of Holly made all three women laugh and that nearly triggered the tears she was holding back. 'Is that a new perfume?' she asked as she slammed the boot shut, triggered the central locking, and joined the other two.

It was a short stroll back down the single-track road towards the place where they usually swam.

'Yep, it's had rave reviews in *Elle* so I thought I'd treat myself seeing as it's nearly my birthday.'

Holly heard Stevie snort suddenly and say, 'No, it's not! 'That's not until February!' She felt herself blushing. Was she so transparent? She admitted to herself that her obsession with designer brands was definitely a protective layer of body armour. She suspected that Stevie was astute enough to see that underneath she was a warm, genuine woman who was just scared of growing old.

The water had brought them together only a few weeks ago, and now here they were, middle-aged ladies faffing at the side of the road, with Holly being the main culprit.

'*Ha!* I know my birthday's in February, but—' She swore and dropped her voluminous bag onto the ground and started to rummage through its contents impatiently.

'What've you forgotten?' she heard Stevie moan in mock despair. Holly knew herself well and admitted that for someone so outwardly glamorous and confident, she was the least organised person she had ever met. Her swimming bag contained enough kit for several people: spare costumes, swim caps, warm tops, a hairbrush, sunglasses, book, towel plus microfibre changing robe, spare socks, and Sweaty Betty joggers.

It was completely the opposite of Angela's, which was neat and inconspicuous, trimmed down to the essentials. Stevie used one of those plastic gorilla buckets sold at garden centres and DIY stores. You could easily see what was in it, and, unless you were walking a long distance from the car to a swim spot, it was practical and sturdy.

'*Aha!*' cried Holly, whipping out something pale and flimsy from her bag. 'I thought I'd forgotten my knickers.'

Stevie rolled her eyes and said, 'I never bring knickers, especially not posh ones like yours!'

They'd reached the steep, stony path that dropped off the side of the road and led down to a small pebbly beach.

'They're tiny, so they must be posh,' Angela said. 'Mine are practical black or white ones.' Her voice sounded almost apologetic, but the other two women stopped what they were doing and waited for her to continue, as if they knew she was needing to talk and not just about the colour of her knickers. 'I get housekeeping money every week. I know, I'm sure it's old fashioned, but Ed prefers to do it that way. Anyway, if there's any left over I put it straight into a grey sock that I keep hidden under the spare bedding in the airing cupboard – my "exit fund".'

'God!' said Holly, but Stevie just nodded gently in an encouraging and understanding sort of way.

'I really don't know what I would say to him if he discovered it.' Her voice broke slightly and the lake itself seemed to be waiting for her to explain what she was wanting to exit from. But, with a slightly sad shrug of her shoulders, she turned away from the others and gave herself a shake from head to toes. 'I'll explain another day.'

'No rush,' said Stevie. 'Ready everyone?'

Down on the shingly beach, each woman headed for her favourite spot on the sloping ground, each grassy dip the perfect size for their bottoms. Angela lifted her pale face to the sun, which, although it was November, still held enough warmth to make a difference.

Each of them breathed in deeply. For Angela, a clean, mossy scent, quite different to the soulless smells back at the farm, wafted across the surface of the dark-looking water. For Holly, a confusing mix of good and vaguely unpleasant made her shudder slightly. Stevie just loved it and took more than one deep breath.

'How was Norway?' Holly's voice was muffled under her thermal layer, which she was busy pulling off over her head.

'The most exciting thing about the trip was the ice hole, which I'll tell you about another time, but I was also talking with Emma about something she's doing that I think would be really cool. How do you fancy making up a mixed relay team?' She paused to pull off one functional black boot and wool sock, then the other.

Neither of her swim buddies spoke.

'To swim in a winter swimming championship.'

No response.

She tried again. 'It's not until February, so we've plenty of time to train.'

She stood up, ready to swim apart from buckling her tow float round her waist.

'In Norway?' Angela asked, adjusting her gloves and swim socks.

Whatever Holly said was just an incoherent mumble. She had one glove between her teeth, desperately trying not to transfer any of her pillar box red lip gloss onto the Neoprene, while she was pulling on the other glove. Her two swim buddies were waiting for her and getting chilly.

Finally, Holly joined them both down at the water's edge. 'I'm up for that. Sounds exciting.'

'No, Angela, it's *not* in Norway, it's in Loch Tay. The only thing is— Ooh, that's chilly!' Stevie squeaked as she walked slowly and carefully into the water. 'The only thing is, we need to find a man.'

'Crumbs!' Angela tried hard not to squeal as she crept in up to the top of her thin white thighs. 'Is that Scotland?'

'A man?' yelped Holly as she plunged forwards. Arms outstretched for balance, blue eyes closed as if in denial, she slipped and slid across the loose stones and then sploshed into the lake like a wobbly starfish.

'Oh Holly!' her swim buddies shrieked crossly. Getting splashed with cold water unexpectedly is a shock, even when you are acclimatised. It's not the cold, but the lack of warning.

Finally, they were in. Back in the lake, bringing with them a rainbow of emotions, certain that here, in this magical water, they could breathe deep, absorb the smells, tastes and sounds of nature, and re-emerge a short while later, not as three middle-aged women, but as three swim-tanned water warriors.

While she was getting dressed after their swim Stevie wondered why she hadn't told Holly and Angela about her night dip in the forest with Arvid. She'd just said she'd had a great time and then launched into telling them about the winter swimming competition idea Emma had put in her head. But it had been more than a great time; it had woken up the fire in her belly, the fire that her ex-husband had very nearly put out by abandoning her for someone else.

It had also confirmed something she'd been feeling for many years of married life to him: he was a controlling man, who, to the outside world, gave the impression of adoring her and their two girls, but in reality spent very little quality time with them. When he did, he made sure it was doing something he thought was a good idea rather than just agreeing to something together as a family. His priority seemed to be work, but he'd never go into detail, even when it took him away from home. It was almost as if he was leading a double life, but if Stevie tried to ask him how his latest trip had gone, or whether he had met any important people, he would just shut her down. It became easier not to ask.

Occasionally, he flew to Oslo for a couple of days, and she longed to ask which restaurants he'd visited and perhaps remind him of the time when he used to take her, but again, he wouldn't be drawn out in conversation about it. And yet, in hindsight, she realised she'd never once wondered whether there was more to it than work.

But, there in the Norwegian forest, in that delicious pool of very cold water, she had found her sense of self. It had been inside her all along, just buried under everything else.

Chapter Eight

CHRIS

November

Washing his bike after every ride had always been part of Chris's cycling routine, especially in winter, but now it was a necessity on a more emotional level. Every time he went out on his bike, he felt himself moving one step forward, away from sadness towards something else. He wasn't sure what that might be yet, but he was relieved that the darkest months following his wife's death were behind him. Sleep now came more easily, and if he woke in a panic in the early hours, he had a trick ready to help him drop off again: he imagined pedalling up one of the Pyrenean cols, his shaved but muscular legs slowly grinding in a low gear up the beautifully graded tarmac. The monotony was therapeutic and far more soporific than counting sheep.

So the bike, the only one of five that he kept hung up by its front wheel on his living room wall rather than in his garage, became a symbol of his strengthening spirit of independence from grief. The chrome spokes shone, the black rims reflected light, and the chain set glistened from freshly applied oil.

Ever since his wife's cancer diagnosis, Chris had realised that the clock had started ticking for the family to readjust, to reconfigure their lives without their mum and his wife. She'd be pretty irreplaceable and her absence would take some getting used to, but he also remembered finding himself cursing her under his breath when she had one of her demanding days where nothing any of them did was good enough for her.

It was only while out on his bike that he found the quiet space in his mind to remind himself of their early days together when they spent Friday nights planning a weekend of cycling and Sunday nights dozing on the sofa wrapped in each other's arms. Those were the good memories – memories of a love that, years later, had stopped him from walking out of the marriage when it all became too difficult to tolerate. Those memories were also what he held close to get him from the day her cancer had been diagnosed to her death exactly 363 days later.

Chris sighed and squeezed out the rag that he was using to wash the frame. His broad hands gripped it hard as if he wanted to throttle the life out of this inanimate object. He felt so frustrated that he'd never stood up to her and told her how she made him feel. He had avoided confrontation instead of communicating his needs and now that she was gone, he regretted the opportunities to reclaim their relationship and marriage. He hoped that one day this same frustration would become a positive force in his life: he wanted to love again, but more than anything, he wanted to know what it felt like to be loved back, to be on an equal footing with his partner.

Until then, he was relieved to be emerging from the perpetual dark grey of sadness. Andy told him feeling angry was a good sign. 'It's a journey, mate, give it time. Pedal out the emotions.'

Out here on the patio he'd laid all those years ago when the children were little, he noticed the terracotta plant pots were crumbling from the few hard frosts they'd had over the last couple of winters. The dandelions were as tall as the lavender and the birdbath still lay upside down where he'd knocked it off a few weeks ago. Would it ever matter again?

It wasn't him who had weeded the garden. He'd just cut the lawn, which he still thankfully managed to do. If he could just stop it from becoming a field fit only for sheep, then that would be something. What was it Gail had done with the lavender heads at the end of summer? He ran his fingers across one almost completely dried out purple tip after another and breathed in, hoping any scent that remained would trigger something in his memory. That's it, the large wooden bowl in the hallway – she'd always topped it up in the late summer with that year's flower heads, creating a warm, inviting aroma as you walked in the front door. It was November. Was it far too late to create his own potpourri?

He went into the kitchen and scrabbled about in the utensil drawer, searching for the scissors.

'*Ouch!*' The skin on the back of his fingers scraped across the serrated edge of the bread knife, which Gail had always reminded him not to put here, but to tuck it down the side of the cutlery tray out of harm's way. He sucked on his wounded fingers, and with the other hand, grabbed the black-handled scissors, pushed the drawer shut with his hip, and walked back out into the garden.

Unless he was mistaken, you could also cut rosemary in the same way, take rose petals and dry them, add a few bay leaves, and create your own potpourri. He wasn't sure why he was fiddling with Gail's tried-and-tested concoction, but, for over an hour, he snipped away at any plants that still had any flowers or leaves, filling a terracotta flowerpot with bits and pieces from the front and back gardens.

He went back into the hallway, tipped the pot out into the wooden bowl, mixed the new in with the old, bent over to sniff the result, and was about to pick out some of the added rose leaves when his mobile vibrated in his jeans pocket. It was Andy. There was a problem.

Andy ran his own business – window cleaning – a one-man operation with a loyal customer base covering a five-mile radius of Cockermouth. His father, who lived in Spain, had been taken into hospital and Andy had booked him and his wife onto the next flight over to Malaga. Could Chris cover for him while he was away? It might be a week, two weeks, he wasn't sure, but he was concerned that if he left a gap in the normal cleaning schedule, even at this time of year, one of his competitors would trespass on his patch.

'No problem,' Chris responded, pleased to be asked and glad to be needed. Not only did the thought of working physically hard appeal, but it was a simple, yet important way to repay Andy and his wife for how they had supported him and Gail through those last few difficult months before her death, as well as continuing to keep an eye on Chris, thereafter.

Chapter Nine

WATER WARRIORS

November

On the beach after their swim, the three silent water warriors began the process of stripping off wet costumes, gloves, and booties, drying and redressing in warm layers. It was a peculiar ritual, which Stevie did differently from the more fastidious Angela and Holly just did differently every time.

Today, with the sun's November warmth, the race against the after drop felt slightly less threatening, but nevertheless Stevie was glad she had explained the basics of how the body worked after being in cold water. During their earlier swims, she'd made sure Holly and Angela understood how the blood flows back to the extremities, which were cold, and then back through the heart. This chilled blood could cause the body's core temperature to drop by a degree or two further, which, in the worst case, could lead to dizziness, confusion, clumsiness, and an inability to rewarm without additional help. The after drop was the beginning of a slippery slope to hypothermia, she had warned the others, so it was not something she ever wanted to see them experience.

'So what do you both think about this relay team idea then?' she asked once they were all sipping hot drinks.

'Let's do it,' said Holly, hopping about to try to get some feeling back in her size four feet. 'Mind you, my feet are like blocks of ice now, so God knows how I'll manage as the water gets colder.'

'We'll be acclimatised by then. It's still a few months away,' reassured Stevie. 'Don't forget that you've only been doing this for a few weeks.'

'Hmm, when did I first come down?'

Stevie could almost see Holly's brain working its way back through her diary.

'Eyebrows! That was it. We met at the salon and you were about to have your eyebrows done.'

Angela stared at Stevie's darkish brown eyebrows but said nothing.

'My God! Stop staring!' Stevie laughed, covering the upper half of her slightly freckled face with her free hand. 'Do they need doing again?'

Holly ignored the question.

'Thank God we've sorted that one out then.' Stevie's surprisingly throaty laugh was infectious and as she stared out across the lake, she remembered what she had thought when she met Holly down by Bird Poo Island for her first outdoor swim. The woman who would look more at home in the city couldn't have brought more stuff with her if she had tried and then she stripped down to the smallest, flimsiest fluorescent orange swimsuit Stevie had ever seen.

'I thought this would be the easiest to get on and off,' Holly had chirped, grinning at Stevie. Stevie remembered wondering if she was going to actually do some swimming. From their first encounter at the beauty clinic, she had suspected that what Holly looked like mattered more than whether something was practical or not. No one was that tanned in the Lake District, either. But she had to admit that Holly had an amazing figure and not just because it was sculpted by that high-cut plunge-neck second skin.

'And I only started a week or so before you, Holly.' Angela interrupted Stevie's thoughts, and looked at her cheap pink child's watch anxiously. 'I've got to go in a minute I'm afraid. Things to do.'

From some of the things that had come out in their swimming conversations when their filters disappeared, the other two women knew this was Angela's code for 'I'll be in trouble if I don't get back on time.' There was nothing concrete, but enough to indicate that this hesitant self-conscious woman had a less than ideal home life.

But on this stunning Lakeland day, such thoughts had no place. In Stevie's heart, she knew the water was gradually opening up energy within the other two women. For herself, it was a relief to be able to let more people into her dark, internal emotional confusion about love, rejection, and her place in the world as an older woman. In return, she listened, didn't judge, held, and then let go. The water took it all and asked for nothing. Flaky as it sounded, it was what Stevie had come to believe the more she swam.

She tipped the remains of the now cold tea from her enamel mug. 'Of course. Next swim? I know we'd mentioned Thursday, but, actually, Friday's looking dry and sunny.'

'I'm free,' said Holly.

Angela nodded, her still damp hair falling loose from the topknot she'd hastily created while getting dry. Stevie noticed how feather light it appeared, not thick and heavy like hers.

'Brilliant. My turn to drive,' she said, pulling her merino wool hat down more cosily around her ears.

As they walked slowly back up the narrow bracken-edged path to the road, silence fell upon them once again. Lost in their private worlds of breathing and relaxed smiles, they were headed back to a reality that was far more complicated than wild swimming in this stunning landscape.

Chapter Ten

STEVIE

November

Stevie stood naked in front of the long mirror in her bedroom. She wasn't sure who she was looking at. Last night she had dreamt of Arvid and things had become far more intimate than they had in reality. It was such a beautiful dream, and even as she knew she was waking up, she tried to resist opening her eyes. She didn't want to lose the moment, lose the woman who she saw indulging in some pretty heavy petting on a blanket by the tiny fire Arvid had built next to the waterfall.

But looking at her reflection now, she felt those irritating internal voices battling. 'You look terrible,' said one, and, 'You are a goddess,' said the other.

'What is happening to me?' She'd grown used to seeing a tall, still reasonably slim, but less athletic, middle-aged and rather sad-looking woman. But now the mirror reflected back someone who looked different somehow; more like her younger self. 'I remember you,' she whispered.

She turned sideways. 'This angle isn't so good,' she groaned, her critical voice now butting in. She squashed in her belly and tucked in her bum, but it just made her knees stick out. She shook her head. Divorced for over four years now, it had taken forever to climb out of the dark hole into which she'd jumped when she'd answered a call on John's phone from a woman telling him she was leaving him because he'd been unfaithful to her. Unfaithful to his mistress! He had denied knowing anything about Sharon to start with and then held his hands up as if to say, 'Okay, guilty', but his body language seemed to say, 'Not bothered.'

Was it her? Something she'd done or not done? The questions surged around in her head as she watched him pack a holdall she'd never seen before and walk out of the front door. She could have tried to stop him and get him to explain everything, but something in her brain had switched off in the same way she had learnt to detach herself from some of the worst cases in the juvenile court during her career as a barrister.

The grandfather clock struck midday, which brought Stevie back into the present.

She unpacked her swim bucket: Thermos flask, goggles, enamel mug, GoPro, several swim caps, two bobble hats, swim shoes and gloves, changing robe – all of it needed to be sorted out.

She'd had a shower as soon as she got back from the lake. She didn't usually shower straight after a swim because she'd once nearly fainted in the hot water after rewarming too quickly, but, today, she just wanted to indulge herself a little. She had turned the temperature down and only gradually increased it as she felt herself warming through.

Back downstairs in the kitchen, she put the kettle on and rubbed her hands briskly together to generate some heat. It would take a while to warm up completely, but a hot drink would help. She automatically reached for the blue-and-white mug from the cupboard, then put it back; it was the one she always drank midmorning coffee from. It fitted perfectly into cupped hands and was neither too thick nor too thin. She never drank tea from it, though, and tea was what her body needed now – it was hotter than coffee. Sometimes, she felt half asleep, as if her brain was firing slower than it used to. She knew it was one of the symptoms of the menopause and rechecked to make sure the tiny transparent patch was still on her belly. It was. No need to worry then, but she made a mental note to call the doctor to discuss her dose of HRT.

Her mind drifted off to the conversations she'd had with Emma on their journey back to Amsterdam and while they waited for their connections in a bar in Schiphol Airport. One of them in particular sprang to mind and she tried to remember some details about the relay team for the winter swimming competition so she could pass them on to Holly and Angela since they'd both seemed keen.

The rules made it clear: the team had to be mixed, with either two women and two men, three women and one man, or less likely but still allowable, three men and one woman, which gave Stevie a slight problem. The only men she came across these days were the postman (nothing wrong with him, but he was Gareth, and everyone knew Gareth, he was the postman); the DPD driver (not as chatty as Gareth, but looked fairly athletic); the pizza-making man in Sainsbury's (now he was a possibility and looked as if he needed something to cure his grumpiness – did he ever smile?); and, occasionally, when she needed to renegotiate her HRT treatment, the male GP (she knew he was into running, but swimming? Outdoors?).

Obviously, she knew there were men who swam outdoors in the Lake District, mostly triathletes, but in general they were only there between April and October. After that, the lake temperature got too cold for them and they returned to the leisure centre pool.

According to International Ice Swimming Association rules, a strict 'no Neoprene' policy was enforced. That was the other problem she'd have to somehow overcome if she was to get their team a man. Triathletes nearly all swam in wetsuits, even in the summer. She knew part of the logic behind this was that the triathlons for which they were training usually stipulated wetsuits had to be worn once the water temperature went below sixteen.

She sighed. Distracted from what she had been doing, she lifted up the toaster with one hand and carefully brushed the crispy crumbs that hid underneath and then put down the toaster and swished the crumbs towards her cupped right hand, ready to drop them into the sink. Housework rarely got much tougher than this unless her daughters were home for the weekend.

She remembered the kettle had boiled, but she'd not done anything with it, so she flicked it back on again, spotted the red squirrel china mug already on the worktop complete with teabag, and finally got round to making herself the first hot drink of many. A couple of drips landed on the grey carpet as she walked up the stairs and through to her study.

When she was not working in the box office at the theatre, she created 3D artwork in box frames. First, she painted the background canvas in sky colours. Then, she built up the picture by weaving in bits and pieces she found outdoors while walking or going down to the lake to swim. Usually, the pictures had a miniature dry stone wall somewhere, with a tiny wooden footpath sign and a stile. Pieces of moss, sheep's wool, fragile twigs, and grasses all got meshed together, along with threads of the coloured twine that farmers often snipped from a bale of hay when feeding the sheep and then discarded on the ground. Her self-imposed rule was that she'd only use things she'd scavenged and never pick a flower or bud or take moss off a wall. There were more than enough remnants from both nature and humans littering the footpaths and fells to fill several plastic 'toolboxes' and keep her supplied with material for her pictures. The gallery at the theatre took them from her and sold them for a reasonably high price, yet it wasn't the money that Stevie enjoyed the most, but the tranquillity and creativity that surrounded her hobby. Books, paintings, and stacks of files made the already small room a bit of a squeeze, but she loved being in there surrounded by treasures. Nothing could take any of this away from her unless she chose to get rid of it. It was a duck-egg-blue nest of security and calm – her sanctuary.

Not today. There was a curious rattle and knocking just below the window and then a man's head appeared, quickly followed by a wet rag. She gasped, spilt her tea all over the carpet, and went to pull the little window shut so that he could wash it properly. Then she noticed that it wasn't the usual window cleaner. Andy, he was called. This man had brown eyes and was slightly older, possibly too old to be up that high on a ladder – but who was she to call him old? She laughed at herself. And he was smiling at her as if to apologise for having startled her. It was a smile that transformed his rather stern unshaven face. She couldn't help but smile back and shrug her shoulders as if to say, 'Don't worry.' She must've not heard the doorbell announcing his arrival, but then remembered that Andy always just turned up once every couple of months and worked his way round the house, popping a scribbled invoice through the letterbox when he was done.

At the back of her mind, she was wondering nervously how long he had been at the property and which windows he'd already washed while she'd been standing observing her body in front of the mirror.

His face seemed familiar, too, but she couldn't work out why.

Chapter Eleven

CHRIS

November

His first afternoon cleaning windows had put a big grin back on Chris's face. He had taken early retirement from one of the satellite companies near Sellafield to look after his wife shortly after she had been diagnosed with terminal pancreatic cancer. His twenty-four-hour availability served them both well during that time, but he'd missed the routine work brought. He'd suggested to Gail that he should use his consultancy skills on a freelance basis, which would give him some intellectual stimulation, but also give him the flexibility he needed to be on hand for her.

His suggestion was met with a disappointed look from Gail, which made him feel bad about wanting some escape from the sickroom. He'd shelved his ideas, thinking maybe one day he might resurrect them. That day hadn't materialised yet, but he was pretty sure that sooner or later, he'd feel inspired to come back from retirement and enjoy chasing down contracts and working with clients. One step at a time, though, he told himself. If finances proved difficult, then he would have to, but otherwise, for the first time since meeting Gail, he realised he could do exactly what he wanted when he wanted.

Although he was physically tired from an afternoon of climbing up and down ladders and he'd bruised his shins more than once on the rungs, even the mess he'd left in the kitchen that greeted him as he opened the back door failed to bring his mood down. He chucked the keys to Andy's van on the small kitchen table, along with his phone, and went straight upstairs to have a shower.

While standing under the stream of hot water, he closed his eyes and let his mind drift wherever it wanted. To the face of a woman. Not Gail, though. He felt a touch of guilt that lately he'd had to think really hard to see her face, along with all the details he used to remember like the back of his own hand.

This woman had an open, trusting face and eyes that seemed to pull you towards her. He'd noticed them as she came closer to the window he was about to clean and then stared at her hand as she firmly closed the same window. He couldn't tell what colour her eyes were, possibly blue, but he noticed that they were framed in dark lashes and set wide apart. And then there was her smile. The instant it replaced her startled expression, he found himself smiling back. How could he describe to anyone who hadn't been there the effect seeing her had had on him? Surprise for sure. After all, he was only cleaning windows and not really expecting to be that close to anyone inside the house. But underlying everything was a sexual tension. It was as acute for him as it had been the morning he'd first seen her: bathing naked in the lake.

In his long marriage, sex had been something he thought about more often than he experienced, even in the early years. Gail just wasn't a sexually motivated woman; she didn't like the messiness of it. It was something she tolerated to get pregnant, but as the years passed and they still shared a bed, mutual physical pleasure had long vanished.

He sighed and opened his eyes and began to wash away the day. Two weeks of climbing ladders, combined with a daily ride down the valley to Buttermere, and those love handles that he was wobbling up and down might just disappear! And right at this moment, it seemed to matter to him how he looked. At fifty, he was fit and reasonably athletic, but used to be fitter and more toned. He knew he could get it back, though, and with it, a much healthier state of mind and emotions. For him, working his body had always been very much connected to working his mind: if one was out of order, so was the other. Andy had been right. 'Get back on the bike, mate,' he'd urged. 'Pedal out the pain!'

Chapter Twelve

HOLLY

November

'Oooh, budgie smugglers!' Holly shrieked with laughter as her husband strutted around their massive bedroom modelling a piece of colourful Lycra that had arrived by Amazon Prime earlier in the day. 'How about a mankini?' She hoiked up what looked like cycling shorts, giving him a painful wedgie.

'Jesus!' he yelped and danced about on his toes until she let go. 'They're not budgie smugglers, dear, they're jammers. All the cool kids wear them. Parliament Hill Lido is a pretty cool place to swim, literally and aesthetically,' he added. 'Can't let the side down.' Simon was now naked and headed for the en-suite without answering her question about who went swimming with him at the lido during the working week.

Holly had already lost interest in her husband's new hobby by the time he turned the water on. Every Sunday was the same, or had been for the last few years. Both of them slopped about all morning doing nothing in particular, ate together in the kitchen, then went upstairs: him to shower and pack his bag with a set of fresh shirts and underpants for the week, her to keep him company and then, once he'd gone, she would shower and look respectable to greet holiday cottage guests as they came back from their day out.

Sex would have been nice. Once it had been the glue that held their marriage together. Over the last year or so, actual penetration had become painful because no matter how aroused she felt emotionally and physically, she remained dry inside. 'Bring on the K-Y Jelly', she had groaned. The very name took her back to the job she'd had at Boots between A levels and university: on the pharmacy counter selling Tunes, Settlers, and Sudafed all day long. *I'm now that woman,* she thought, *the one who came in and asked for K-Y Jelly and I sent her off to the jam making and home brew aisle. Oh God! No wonder she looked so huffy and embarrassed having to explain to a cocky teenager that it wasn't something you spread on your toast!*

The irritation and dryness she suffered from if they had sex was unbearable. It was as if someone had rubbed a mixture of itching powder and broken glass deep inside her. It was different from the times when she and Simon had used lubricant if she was a bit sore from overenthusiastic sex – that was something they resolved together and had little impact on her sex drive or need to be intimate. This discomfort and pain took about a week to recover from sufficiently to have penetrative sex again and during that time, nothing could soothe her apart from cool water or aqueous cream applied internally.

She sometimes wondered if the cause was lack of sex because Simon was away all week, but there was no way of telling until his first week's holiday came up. The first time had been really good and everything felt back to normal, so Holly actually initiated sex the next day. She felt turned on watching her husband as he tinkered with his mountain bike on the patio. She was sunbathing on a lounger and imagined what it would feel like if he came over and gave her an oily massage in the same way that he was caressing his bike. It had felt like they were the only people in the world, out there on the lounger, enjoying each other's bodies, when the pain started inside her. Simon sensed something was wrong because she'd frozen under him. As he wilted, she kissed him and stroked his back and held him close, but actually just wanted to cry.

'What's wrong, love?' he'd asked, releasing himself from her arms and moving across to sit on the other lounger. He reached out and stroked her hip and thigh tenderly.

'It hurts inside. I don't know why.' She sat up and clutched her cotton robe up to her chest, burying her face in it like a scared child and breathing in the soft scent of fabric conditioner.

'You weren't very wet, but well, you aren't always. But it's never stopped us before.' Simon seemed a little confused and Holly had a feeling he was being diplomatic.

'It's not you, it's me,' she said and then stopped because it sounded trite and as if it really did have something to do with feelings and emotions, not just a physical quirk of her body.

Simon frowned, shook his head, put his clothes back on, and returned to playing with his bike. But the seed of doubt had been sown in their relationship and there was no more sex that week. Both of them avoided intimacy and the silence around the subject grew heavy and threatening.

He went back to work and things went more or less back to normal with no further mention of what had or had not happened. Occasionally, emotion got the better of them and, as if for old time's sake, a Sunday-morning fumble gave her a slight tingle and him a silly grin, but even that became too much for her to cope with.

She went over to the tall windows that looked out over acres of green fells and slowly decaying bracken. Her yawn made Jasper, the spaniel, jump. He hated Sundays because Simon disappeared and so did unconditional dog biscuits and cuddles. Holly reached up with both arms in a massive stretch and as she did, her Missoni robe fell open. When she dropped her arms back to her sides, she stared down at her boobs with dismay. Where did they think they were going? It seemed that no matter how hard she worked at maintaining the body shape she had only come to love when she met Simon, curvy but with everything where she wanted it to be, the more out of her control it seemed to get. All those years of half starving herself in her early twenties to shed the kilos she'd hated so much as a teenager. Old habits die hard and she still weighed herself every morning and silently counted the calories at every meal. Living here in rural Cumbria, though, her resolve and self-discipline had started to slip. There was no longer any point in buying designer clothes because there was nowhere to wear them. She lived in stretchy, black tops that covered everything and leggings, just in bigger and bigger sizes. In her head she was still the curvy blonde who attracted attention, but when she had folded up yet another pair of too-small jeans and put them in the drawer of 'one day, maybes,' the disappointing truth hit her. Middle-aged spread was real and every day she told herself to do something about it and every day went by and she hadn't worked out yet whether to join the gym, get a personal trainer, or do the Couch to 5k. The least painful option, of course, was to just start walking. She stared out of the bedroom window again, taking in the natural beauty beyond the triple-glazed glass: a view which, instead of inspiring her to be active, bored her. Mud, spiky grass, boggy moss, slippery stones, and sheep shit – why would anyone actually *want* to get out into that?

'Right, I'm off,' Simon called from the landing at the top of the metal and glass staircase.

'See you Thursday.' Her voice held a measure of despondency, but she moved from the window and went to give her husband a goodbye kiss. It was a pattern they repeated week in and week out: he left on a Sunday afternoon to go back down to London, she stayed up here in the farmhouse they had taken on a few years ago, when it had been in a badly neglected state and Holly had thrown her hands up in horror at the thought of living there. But Simon had reassured her that they had the money to renovate it to a high standard, along with creating two separate guest cottages, which she could manage, but she would need to give up her job as a recruitment consultant.

At first, the prospect of being able to restore the beautiful Cumbrian building and create a really special home fulfilled Holly, but when the realities of finding and retaining tradesmen alongside integrating into a closely knit farming community just became too difficult, she admitted she had taken on far more than she had the experience to deal with. Her career up until that point had always been fairly exciting, or so she thought, either working in sales or recruitment. Apart from consuming every single home interiors magazine ever published she had no training as an interior designer. Running her own business was her dream, but she'd never had the courage to go it alone down in London.

Now here she was, waiting all week for Simon to come back up on a Thursday evening and grace her with his pale face. She felt she was just going through the motions of listening to him go on about how he was itching to get out on his mountain bike the following morning with his group of fellow MTB-ers, kitted out in hideous body armour. At first, she used to drive up to the cafe at Whinlatter Visitor Centre and meet them for a coffee mid-afternoon and cart a mud-caked Simon and his even muddier rock-hopping machine back home, but the novelty had worn thin, the cafe owners objected to filthy bodies inside the building, and it was never quite nice enough weather to sit outside.

Standing under the massive showerhead, she pondered over how odd it was that Simon had taken up swimming after so many years of refusing to swim, even when on holiday somewhere hot.

He'd been one of those kids whose parents had sent him off to swim practice before school several times a week, pushing him to compete when all he wanted to do was ride his bike and hang out with his friends. But, to Holly, it seemed a bit churlish of him to have been rebelling against that. Perhaps he'd finally exhausted his resentment and felt inspired to give it another go and get healthy by swimming at lunchtimes in Parliament Hill Lido near his office in Belsize Park?

She shivered in the steaming heat cascading onto her shoulders. Something didn't feel quite right. Was Simon having an affair? Was he so frustrated by their own less than dynamic sex life? She had to tell herself that it was highly unlikely given the way they'd first met: she'd scooped him up in a Covent Garden wine bar because she felt sorry for him. He'd accidentally knocked over the drinks she had just bought and then, after replacing them, he had plonked himself down next to her and her friend and poured his heart out. It was all around the office, he said. His wife had been caught with her knickers down, bent over the boss's capacious black Ikea desk. The regular Friday after-work drinks had then gone badly wrong for him, and there he was, a self-confessed mess. Her friend had met up with her boyfriend, so Holly sat for a while with Simon, trying to persuade him to get himself home. Finally, he agreed it was time to go, so she helped him outside and as she hailed him a taxi, he'd nearly passed out. It had taken all her gym-fit strength to shove his six-foot-three-inch frame onto the back seat before reluctantly squeezing in next to him. Even now, ten years later, if he forgot to leave his muddy MTB gear in the porch and traipsed half a trail in with him and expected any sort of sympathy, she reminded him of the gutter he would have spent that Friday night in if it hadn't been for her.

As she massaged moisturiser into her entire body, she remembered how passionate their relationship had always been.

In the beginning, they hadn't been able to keep their hands off each other. A perfect match physically and intellectually.

Until that dreadful week when they'd tried to have sex while they were on holiday.

Now, nearly every Sunday before setting off back down to London, he nagged her to go to the doctor. It was starting to make her feel like a failure, and every time they tried and it was too painful, she saw the look of rejection on his face. For a couple who had always talked about anything and everything, it was sad to now be incapable of talking this through in a reasonable and rational way. It had got tangled up with emotions and past hurts. What a mess! He was right. Once she'd made the appointment she felt a sense of relief and was cross she'd been too scared to do it sooner.

Chapter Thirteen

ANGELA

November

On the farm halfway up the mountainside, the back end of the year was all about completing plans for next year's lambs. If finances had allowed, they might have even stretched to joining a syndicate. Then their ewes would have been tupped by a £100,000 Swaledale ram. But as usual, this job fell to one of their three ordinary rams who had been resting over the summer.

Angela found this part of the farming year more interesting than most of it because it was about business planning and one day she hoped she might be invited to offer her opinion about the future of the farm. There was a lot of rather graphic detail about the mating credentials of sheep, but she could ignore that and focus on the facts and figures, which spoke more to her own experience when she was running the pub in the village.

She hated lambing because everyone got extremely short-tempered from lack of sleep. With her small hands, her presence was often in demand, so everything else to do with running the farmhouse, the chickens, and the mother-in-law's list of jobs fell by the wayside. Human interactions were limited to head nodding or shaking, shoulder shrugging, and sofa snatching. It was a hard few weeks and the rest of the year seemed to build up towards it – without a successful lambing, the farm wouldn't prosper.

The only month of respite was June, but that depended on the weather. Grass cutting had to be completed, once, if not twice, between about May and July or August. Lakeland weather played nasty tricks on those who showed any sign of complacency; some years it rained every single day in June and whole fields of grass could be ruined. Grass became silage, which is what supplemented the bought-in animal feeds, so the more that was cut and the higher the quality, the healthier the animals and the smaller the financial outlay.

She longed to talk about something other than silage, muck spreading, and dipping. Ed, her big silent bear of a husband, lived for the animals in his care while his mother lived in her own world of memories and sadness. Quiet evenings hung heavy in the stuffy sitting room. There was no conversation or loving teasing between her and Ed like in the old days when they were dating and used to stay up long after his parents had retired for the night. Instead, there were just stares from Ed's eighty-one-year-old mother as she sat on the tartan sofa under the window, lost and vacant, occasionally turning to look at the open door as if expecting to see the big frame of her husband filling the space, a mug of steaming tea in each hand. But he would never stand there again. He was dead.

Angela would never forget the night it happened. It had been nearly five years ago and only a few weeks after she had gone from being just a visitor to moving into the farmhouse as Ed's wife. He drowned in the beck up in a remote corner of the farm's rough fells while trying to rescue a stranded ewe and her lamb, which had finally been swept away by the torrent. He'd been left trapped between two rocks, but no one knew he was there. They just thought he was out on his quad bike fetching ewes down into the sheep shed for their protection from the sudden perishing weather. When he didn't return by the early hours, Ed had called the police who called Mountain Rescue, although he was sure he kept hearing the sound of the quad bike's engine coming into the farmyard.

The body was retrieved by the Mountain Rescue team and brought down on a stretcher, an awkward carry because he was frozen with his arms up around his head to protect it from the debris being carried downstream and his legs broken from being wedged between the rocks. It was a grim task for these volunteers and a terrible shock that tore open the close relationship between mother and son, leaving them both locked within themselves.

How on earth was Angela going to survive the solitary and silent world she now occupied? It baffled her and kept her awake at night as she lay overheating next to the bulk of her husband. Ed wasn't a snorer, but his mother was. Every pig-like grunt from down the hallway prompted Angela to clench her teeth and her fists so tightly that in the morning, her jaw ached and there were indentations like fresh cuts and markings deep in her palms. Even with the window wide open and her side of the duvet thrown back, her whole body often took her by surprise with the intensity of feeling like she was burning up. It embarrassed her to find she had soaked the bed sheets. She daren't wash them too often for fear of getting the 'look' from her mother-in-law for wasting water and electricity, so, instead, she pulled back the duvet each morning, left the window open, and prayed her mother-in-law wouldn't come into their room.

Angela's suffering was silent until she couldn't hold it in any longer. Then the sheep shed was her crying place, the vast empty space in the summer months still scented with eau de dried-up sheep urine and lanolin oil. She could crouch down inside a pen, pull some straw over herself, and let out all the pain until she was done. She wasn't sure what was happening to her or why she felt so emotionally unstable. She didn't know what she wanted or needed, but knew it was more, more than this existence was giving her.

When she'd met Ed for the first time in her life she felt loved by someone who wanted nothing from her that she wasn't prepared to give. His love was helping her to move away from her past and that terrible day when, as a fifteen-year-old, she had been raped by a neighbour while her mother was out at work.

She was reluctant to let this terrible secret out now. She should have told him when they first met, but she had been scared he would think less of her. It seemed too late now and she really didn't know how to start such a conversation. Ed had asked very few questions about her past, so she hadn't given much away, and they rarely discussed their emotions.

The fogginess in her head was growing worse and worse, and the knowledge that her struggle to feel happy at any point in the day was also getting worse. The only time she felt any clarity of mind was when she was in the lake with Holly and Stevie. It was this clarity that was gradually making her feel strong enough to talk with him and explain how she was feeling.

Maybe now was also the time to tell him about the rape. Did she have PTSD? Would that explain how she was feeling? She was scared. The risk that he might be upset that she had never told him about it before was a difficult one to take.

Chapter Fourteen

CHRIS

November

'Good to see you, Dad.' Chris's son placed two Americanos down on the wooden table and slung his long legs over the bench to sit opposite. 'On the house.' He smiled. It was his morning break and no one minded if he grabbed a couple of coffees, or even a slice of cake, especially midweek when it was quiet.

'Cheers, son,' said Chris, sliding one of the coffees towards him. 'How's life?'

'Oh, you know, quiet.' Tom laughed. 'How about you? Thought any more about buying that van?'

'*Hah!* Not really the right time of year is it, back end?' Chris picked his cup up and had a sip. Hot. He blew and sipped again. 'Made your mind up yet?'

'Pretty much, yeh.'

Chris raised an eyebrow and put his cup down. 'And?'

'Well…' Tom's hesitation was followed by a deep drawing in

of breath. 'I'm not going to uni.' He looked at his dad. 'I'm going to Spain. With Con.'

Chris's eyebrow lifted again. Then a slight frown. 'Who's Con?'

'Dad? I told you about her ages ago. You know, she's been working here for the last year or so, Spanish. We're—' He sighed. 'We're friends, just friends.'

'Good friends?'

'Very.'

'She must be special.'

'She is. Besides, Dad, I never wanted to go to uni.' Tom hesitated, before adding, 'It was you, Dad. You wanted me to go.'

Chris heard the worry in his son's voice and said gently, 'It's okay, Tom. You're right. *Hah!* Your mother was right, too. She told me to stop pushing you to go. She always knew.'

He felt himself withdrawing and knew he was on the edge of crying. He prayed he could control himself. He felt one tear escape and run down his cheek and knew that Tom saw it because he asked, abruptly, 'So— Are you okay with me not going to uni?'

'Yes, of course I'm okay with it. Come here.' Chris stood up and held his arms open, grateful that Tom had brought him back into the moment and saved him public humility.

The two men hugged each other tightly, holding on for much longer than usual. Chris felt a shift in their relationship from father and son to two adult men and knew that his son must've felt it, too, from the way he was holding on. Chris tried to ignore the wave of darkness that washed over his soul.

'Have you told your sister?' Chris eventually managed to ask, sitting back down on the slightly cold wooden bench and wincing. Not even the padded cycling shorts stopped this all-pervading Lakeland damp. He'd spent his whole fifty years in this climate, but it didn't mean he particularly liked it.

'Yeh, she's known for ages.'

Chris reacted by reaching over to cuff his son's blond head. Tom responded with, '*Ouch!* We talk, you know. She's my big sis.'

'That's good.' Silence. Comfortable, but with an edge of there still being more they needed to talk about.

Over the 363 days in his role as a carer, Chris could see for himself that he had started to carry himself differently: no longer upright and straight shouldered; his comforting, strong voice had become monotone; the smile lines round his eyes had faded from lack of use; his dinner plate-sized hands had nothing to keep them occupied now except the handlebars of his beloved bike and now seemed smaller, more feminine. Tom and his sister, Clare, were both suffering from the loss of their mother; she had been the hub around which they revolved on a daily basis. But Chris knew they hadn't shut themselves away from the world like he had. It was wonderful to see how his children's lives were embroidered with so many opportunities and possibilities, but all the more heartbreaking to know that his own life had been left frayed and ragged.

Tom was waiting. Chris knew his son really should be finishing his break and getting back to work. It touched him to know that the young man was holding back for him, to make sure his old dad was okay.

Chris hugged his son again and reassured him that he was fine. But he felt empty. If Tom really did commit to a life in Spain, what was there left for him here in Cumbria? Ghosts? Steep, winding roads to cycle up? Perhaps he should give up the house, buy that van, and become a digital nomad – which is what Tom and Clare fondly teased him he needed to do. 'Go and find yourself, Dad,' they had both said an irritating number of times.

The thought scared him because of how true it was. He might have a bricks and mortar house, but love had left home. Slowly, he had acknowledged that he had a choice: continue to wallow or take a few risks. Gail had never really encouraged him to take risks and she hadn't taken any herself. Was that it? This emptiness that stopped him moving on, was it actually a fear of change or a lack of self-confidence now that he no longer had anyone to tell him what to do? Whatever it was, he moved between states of hating it and giving in to it. He didn't want to feel like this anymore.

All it had taken to wrench open the door on his feelings was for his son to tell him he was going to live in Spain. His son could stand on his own two feet – the realisation felt brutal, but also like a relief. He had done his job as a father and he had held together a marriage that he now admitted was not perfect like it appeared to be, but most of all, after years of holding back his feelings and his needs in order to preserve that marriage, he was at last in touch with his emotions again as evidenced by his reaction to watching the woman bathing naked in the lake.

Tom's news left him feeling excited and sad all at once. Clare was still around, albeit an hour away, but she, too, was living her own life successfully. This moment of true empty nesting was something he had expected to share with Gail, not do on his own. He'd been lonely in his marriage, but to be growing old and alone was a different prospect altogether. Didn't someone once say: life was painful, but you could choose whether to suffer? A tingly feeling lay in the bottom of his stomach, like butterflies. It was a fragile sense of liberation.

Chapter Fifteen

WATER WARRIORS

November

'So,' announced Holly, 'I've got an idea. I think I might know a man who could swim with us.' She did a little dance on her changing mat. Dressed in just a bright blue, plunge-neckline swimsuit, she laughed and slapped her hands across her bouncing boobs.

'Go on…' said Stevie, strapping her tow float round her waist and cupped her own boobs as if wondering how unruly they would get if she jumped up and down like Holly.

'The postman?' grunted a squirming Angela as she struggled to pull her swim booties on.

'Simon.' The way Holly said it with such confidence left little opportunity for the others to express a different view.

It made total sense to Holly, but obviously not to the other two she suddenly realised, judging from the looks on their faces and their silence. She let the idea sit with them for a bit and was just about to justify her reasoning when Stevie broke the awkward silence.

'What a great idea… but I didn't know he was a swimmer.'

'He's not, well, he used to be a reluctant one as a child, but for some reason he's taken it up again.' Holly shrugged her shoulders in a more casual way than she was feeling.

'But surely he wouldn't do it in the lake in the winter?' Stevie's voice was almost a laugh and she clapped her hand over her mouth almost immediately as if desperate to stifle it.

It was too late. Cobalt blue swimsuit aside, there was nothing bright about Holly now: crestfallen. Stevie had unintentionally hit a raw nerve. But, given that she could hardly understand why herself, Holly wasn't in the mood to explain how she was feeling to the others. She knew she often talked about herself and how much she hated living in Cumbria, but said very little about Simon unless it was to complain about the mud he left on the new white-tiled kitchen floor after a mountain-bike ride. From the way Stevie was looking at her, Holly knew she must be thinking *What's going on?* Maybe once they had been in the water for a few minutes and it had worked its magic, she would feel able to open up.

Sunshine isn't always available on a wild swim in the Lake District, even if it has been forecast. This didn't seem to bother Stevie and Angela, but Holly wished she wasn't there at all. Her feet were slipping around on the tiny, sharp stones even though she had invested in a pair of slipper-like swim shoes, her skin was a mass of goose bumps, and her mind was racing as if on a high-speed train to nowhere. She felt doubly exasperated: not just in the way that she always did when she thought of Simon down in sunny London, possibly at the lido posing in his 'jammers', but also with Stevie and Angela.

They were not her usual type of women, but they were her

only friends up here in this backwater town she'd agreed to live in. It wasn't their fault, she knew that, but that didn't stop her feeling trapped and resentful. This time of year was always difficult with the nights drawing in and a feeling of decay pervading everything: the leaves needed raking up, the drains unblocking around the holiday cottages, the heating bills crept up, and lights were left on from dawn to dusk just to feel as if she was actually living in the twenty-first century. It was depressing and drained her energy.

Walking the dog resulted in muddy boots and a stinking dog – nothing delightful or romantic about that. The only thing that didn't seem to give in to the weather was this swimming thing she'd got roped into: if the sun was out, it was a bonus, and if it was raining, Stevie would remind them that they'd get wet anyway. Holly had to admit it sometimes felt better in the lake when it was raining than when they were back on the beach trying to get dressed again.

'Come on, let's swim.' Holly tore herself out of her thoughts and back into the reality of this uncomfortable but strangely addictive thing she'd got into since meeting Stevie.

Today, they had decided to swim from the northern end of the lake, which was marked on the Ordnance Survey map as Lanthwaite Woods. If the sun did decide to come out, they would be right in it from midmorning onwards. And if it didn't, well, at least they'd warm up on the walk back to the car park through the woods.

The view down to Rannerdale Knotts and Hause Point was unrivalled from this beach. Unless there was a strong southerly, it was also relatively sheltered, open, and light. To the right, the sound of water gushing down the fish ladders was mesmerising. Most visitors paused here for a while on the shingly beach, then walked across the two bouncy narrow wooden bridges built over where Crummock Water had been damned by the ladders. United

Utilities planned to remove this structure in a few years' time and the level of the lake would drop by at least a metre. Areas of the lakeshore not seen for decades would be exposed and the lake would go back to flowing out into the River Cocker as nature intended.

For now, though, it was safer to avoid swimming or kayaking too close to the weir, as it was known locally, in case you got sucked down into its spin cycle. Even the triathletes angled their diagonal swim back from the oak tree with caution.

The walk into the water was as difficult as always, not just from the sudden feel of cold on their skin, but because the stones moved as they walked on them and it was more of a slip and slide before giving up any hope of being elegant and serene.

'One, two and three,' called Stevie, and the other two automatically followed, squealing, swearing, and embracing the water.

After a minute or two of fast heads-up breaststroke while trying to control their gasps and breathing, all three got a grip and could talk again.

'Mountain-biking is more Simon's thing, isn't it?' Stevie asked, as she swam slowly towards the boathouse about 500 metres along the wooded lakeshore.

Holly forgot her earlier frustration and opened up a little; who else did she have to talk to? 'Well, that's what I thought. But he's started to swim at the lido in London near where he works. Funny time to start, I thought, the end of summer, but he's dead keen. He even bought himself some fancy swim trunks!' Holly laughed.

'My God! He *must* be keen. I thought only Frenchmen wore those?' Stevie spluttered suddenly because an unexpected wave had slapped her in the face.

'Jammers, they're called,' Holly said, laughing. 'I think you're imagining something else completely.'

Angela swam along quietly, dipping her face down into the water now and again to feel its soothing wash. She loved to peer down and watch the stones and branches that littered the lakebed a few feet below her. The women swam fairly close to the shore, but still Angela's imagination ran away with her sometimes while she was sculling along on the surface, goggled eyes alert to anything that looked like a fish with large pointy teeth. To her right, she could catch a glimpse of darkness where the water suddenly became deeper. The other two swam close to that part – it didn't bother either of them, but they knew she preferred to be on their left-hand side where the clarity of the water was more reassuring.

She wasn't thinking about Simon in swim trunks, but about her mother-in-law's teeth, or lack of them. It was disgusting at mealtimes. The noises and the way the crow-like woman chopped each piece of food so slowly and carefully before squashing a piece of meat, a small piece of carrot and potato onto the back of her fork, then smearing gravy with her knife onto the mushed mess before bending her small head with its white-streaked short black hair down towards the plate. *Why on earth didn't she lift her fork to her mouth?* thought Angela angrily. *No manners. Uncouth. God!* How she was growing to hate her.

She dipped her face down once more into the softness, allowing the bad thoughts to be gently wiped away as if she were a baby whose mother was stroking her face with softened cotton wool. Clean again. It always worked, this beautiful lake with its slate bed and algae-free water.

Voices travelled across the few feet separating her from the other two women. She was ready now to join in the banter. Something about swim trunks, she recalled. Stevie called across to her and asked her if she was alright? Was she ready to turn back or did she want to swim on a bit further?

They always kept an eye on each other, especially now the water temperature was falling. That had been one of the first things Stevie had made them agree to when they started to swim together as a group in October. Everyone swam at their own risk. They were responsible for themselves, but obviously as swim buddies they were sharing the water, so they all shared the good and the bad times too. If one of them needed a bit of help to get dressed afterwards because they felt a bit shaky, it was natural to help them into their layers or pour them a hot drink.

'It's weird, though. He used to swim as a kid, but he's never really shown any interest, even in a heated pool on holiday. Maybe he's having an affair? But I suspect it's more likely got something to do with his new boss. She's some whizz kid from the States, got the whole office wrapped round her immaculately manicured fingers. Maybe jammers are the new office uniform.' Holly giggled at the thought of men conducting serious business meetings wearing a shirt and tie to fool Zoom, but semi-naked from the waist down.

'Is wearing swim trunks a sign of a man who is having an affair?' Stevie asked. 'I'm trying to imagine my ex-husband bounding downstairs wearing a pair, as if to announce, "Darling, I don't love you anymore. I'm taking this hot package to another woman who'll appreciate it."'

'What colour are they?' Angela blurted out, anxious to break the slightly shocked silence that had fallen after Stevie's heartfelt joke, which clearly wasn't a joke. 'I imagine navy ones are more a sign of wanting to swim faster or something, whereas black or red, well—'

'*Angela!* You're not helping!' Holly laughed. 'Actually, I can't remember. I was too busy looking at what was in them.' *My God,* she thought to herself, *that wasn't meant to be said out loud in public.*

This water did funny things to your sense of decorum and modesty, that's for sure.

'Well,' interrupted Stevie, 'I think we should turn back and do a bit of action planning while we have a drink and a piece of cake.'

'Agreed,' said Holly. But she then turned onto her back and, just for a moment or two, floated with her arms wrapped round her bright orange tow float, which she liked to strap round her waist for just this purpose: to float around like an otter more than to be visible to other water users. Indeed, there were no boats on Crummock Water. Ottering got the back of her head wet and it felt good to be wet all over. The image of Simon had left her feeling sad, almost as if she was in mourning for feelings she had once definitely made clear to him on a daily basis.

If he were starting something with another woman because he wasn't having good sex with her, then they needed to have a proper grown-up conversation about where their marriage was heading. She needed him to stop teasing her about what she was experiencing 'down there'. She felt like reminding him that she was about to see the doctor for some advice on what was causing the discomfort and maybe also explain why she was so disinterested in sex. She loved Simon and hated him being away. Holly knew it wasn't going to be just her up there forever – just until they'd paid off the massive mortgage on their property. Then she was sure things would come right again. At least she really hoped they would because it would be unbearable to live here alone permanently and she did absolutely adore her lanky, actually very sexy, husband when he wasn't being secretive.

A couple was standing on the beach, watching the women. Their dog was running in and out of the water barking until they threw a stick in for him to fetch. This always happened. Just when they were about to walk out, with wet swimming costumes stretched across every lump and bump, what had been an empty beach would suddenly become populated with dog walkers, families, or more disturbingly, men pointing their iPhones at them. Holly had worked out that the latter were easily thrown off balance by a request to see the photos they'd just taken or even better, she'd casually say to them, 'Here's my husband's email address. Why don't you send them to him?'

Today, the dripping, sliding walk out was accomplished quickly, with no one slipping and falling back in: water warriors returning successfully to dry land for some rest and sustenance.

'So going back to this swimming event you were talking about.' Holly wanted to shift her thoughts away from her body and how it was failing her. 'Is it in a lake?'

'Yes, a loch – it's a lake. They may have to cut a hole in the ice,' Stevie added.

'What? You're joking?'

'Only if it's very cold, but it's Scotland, so it may not be much colder than here. However, in Russia and Slovenia, well… I've seen the videos on YouTube.'

'God, we'll freeze our bits off!' squealed Holly from under her second thermal layer. She'd already pulled on baggy jogging bottoms and was manoeuvring a sleeveless vest up her body with the straps over her shoulders, all while keeping herself covered. On this beach, with members of the public popping out from behind the trees, they all felt more comfortable with the slower, but more modest, method of getting dressed. However, if the weather was particularly horrible, decorum went out the window and nudity became an essential tool for survival. Then it was simply off with the wet and on with the layers. No argument.

'Well, look, you have a chat with Simon, but we should maybe have a backup plan. What do you think?' suggested Stevie.

The three of them were now dressed and pouring various varieties of herbal tea into enamel mugs. Stevie pulled out a plastic box from her bucket and handed round slices of homemade lemon drizzle cake.

'Yum,' said Holly, taking a piece and biting into it with relish. 'Okay, oooh, sorry, shouldn't talk with my mouth full, but hmmm, this is delicious.' She rolled her eyes and took another bite. 'I'll have a chat with Simon this weekend, see if I can sound him out a bit.'

'Right-o.' Stevie nodded. 'Um, I'm not meaning to pry, but you said you were worried Simon might be having an affair – has he done anything else other than go swimming at lunchtimes that makes you wonder?'

'I can't put my finger on it, or even really believe he would, but it just seems so odd for him to be going swimming.'

'Trust your gut, Holly. If it doesn't feel right, then it probably isn't.'

'My Ed is so predictable I'd know instantly if something had changed,' said Angela, rolling her eyes.

'Yeh, but sometimes predictable is good,' said Stevie. 'So, Holly, is everything alright at home? I mean, nothing's changed there, has it?'

Holly braced herself to tell them how bad things had got between her and Simon – and that she had booked an appointment to talk to someone and hopefully be reassured that everything was normal, just part of growing older. But it was so personal! *Go on*, she urged herself, *just say it.*

'It's hurts to have sex,' she blurted out. *Oh, God*, she thought, *no one wants to know, too much information!*

'What do you mean, it hurts?' asked Stevie, concern deepening the blue of her eyes. 'During?'

'Well, yes, I suppose it is during. I can't really remember, it's been so long since there was any regular "during", but it's not like it used to be, if you know what I mean.' Holly cringed and just wanted the lake to mass up in a huge wave and wash her back out with it.

'Have you been to the doctor?' asked Angela.

'Nope, but I've got an appointment tomorrow and I am going to ask whether he thinks it might be the menopause. I haven't had a period for ages, either, so I was going to check that with him. Do you think that's what it is then?'

'How old are you again?' asked Stevie.

'Fifty in February.'

'Oh, yes! How could I forget?' Stevie laughed. 'Well, yes, then. In fact, you've probably been perimenopausal for a few years now, which can make you feel very peculiar sometimes. But the doctor will explain everything I'm sure.'

'Good. I can't wait to get it sorted out!'

'Have you ever thought about HRT? I'm on it.' Stevie pointed at the tiny oblong piece of plastic right at the top of her thigh. 'Patches – what a lifesaver!'

'Doesn't that give you breast cancer?' Angela looked horrified. 'I've read articles about it and Ed's mum says it's natural for women to go through the change. She doesn't understand why everyone's making such a fuss about it. Just keep quiet and get on with it. Fact of life, like periods and having babies.'

'Great help she is. Thanks, Ed's mum, wish there were more women like you around to spread a bit of cheer!' Stevie's astonishment was tangible. 'I'm so sorry, Angela, that you haven't got more support at home.'

'But she's got a point, hasn't she? I mean, there's nothing we can do about it, and it goes away, eventually, doesn't it?' Angela looked worried and also slightly embarrassed to be talking about it.

'Well, it seems I know more than you two put together.' Stevie laughed, before adding, 'Oh, I'm sorry, that sounds very pompous! I just mean I did a lot of reading up on it because I felt so awful and wanted some sort of explanation for why I felt I had lost myself. Oh, and Holly, just so you know, I went to the doctor, but just got handed antidepressants. It took a while to find the right doctor and funnily enough it was a male doctor too.'

Holly raised her eyebrows. 'I wonder if it's the same guy?'

'This one recommended taking a daily cold shower.' Stevie grimaced. 'I told him, "No way! I'd rather be in the lake." And then he ran through a list of the benefits, physical and mental, of cold-water swimming. Things like better skin tone for sagging skin, reduction of blemishes, soothing hot flushes, increased libido due to a combination of being more relaxed and having regular rushes of endorphins.' She could have gone on, but Angela suddenly jumped up.

'*Crikey!* Is that the time?' She sounded in a panic and was looking at her phone.

'You got to go?' asked Stevie, packing away her mug and Thermos and taking a quick scan around the beach for anything they'd forgotten.

'Be with you in a minute, ladies,' said Holly, her red-painted nails hastily tapping out a message on her phone. There wasn't much signal down here at the end of the woods, but she wanted to get in touch with Simon as soon as possible about swimming with them.

'What's our plan B, then?' After pressing send, she caught up with the other two as they walked back quickly through the woods to the car. 'In case Simon isn't up for it?'

'Well, I did wonder whether we might try the Internet, like Facebook or something?' suggested Stevie.

'How about Internet dating?' Holly piped up. 'Yes, that's it. Stevie?'

'What?'

'You're the only one of us who's single, are you up for a bit of online dating?'

'You're joking?' Her answer was clear. Then she explained that she had actually meant one of those outdoor swimming Facebook groups.

'It's a good idea actually, Stevie,' said Angela as she stood by the car, waiting for Stevie to unlock it and open the boot.

'You do it then,' quipped Stevie, chucking her bucket in the capacious boot. 'I can't think of anything I'd rather do less, except possibly hang around in local pubs until I get talking to a man who looks vaguely like he can swim. How would I test him out anyway? Get him to pull his trousers down and dip his testicles in a pint of freezing water at the bar?' The look on Holly and Angela's faces was priceless.

'The men round here would probably form an orderly queue to do something like that,' she added, 'but it doesn't mean they'll agree to get in the lake for a swim.'

'We can create a profile for you. It doesn't need to say anything that's not true. Just say, "Looking for a man who will swim with me in cold water."' Holly's blue eyes twinkled as she glanced at Angela as if hoping for back up.

'We'll take some photos of you,' offered Angela, nodding her auburn head.

Stevie rolled her eyes in despair. But how could she say no? After all, it had been her suggestion in the first place to swim in this bloody championship. It was the least she could do to help find a man. 'Okay, I'll do it.'

The other two cheered.

'But on one condition.'

They stopped cheering and looked worried.

'Yes?' they both asked at the same time.

'The photos should be of all of us walking into the water. Not just me.' *Hah!* she thought. *That will shut them up. Get their backsides on the Internet, too, not just mine!*

Holly was the first to agree, but Angela hesitated, 'I'm okay with it, but... I'm just trying to work out if Ed would ever come across my photo. Unlikely, but he does know lonely farmers looking for a bit of under-the-duvet action on a cold winter's night.' She shuddered at the thought.

But, as they drove back towards town where Angela had left her car, they began to formulate a plan. Stevie would check the forecast and on the next fine day, they'd go down to the lake early in the morning and, by using her old tripod and Nikon SLR, take some group shots. Meanwhile, Stevie promised to join the biggest online dating site and they agreed to share the cost of a month's membership. This would mean they could send and receive messages from all those brave, but lonely, men out there who would leap at the chance to freeze their bits off in the name of love.

Chapter Sixteen

ANGELA

November

Angela stopped the car at the bottom of the track that led up to the farm. She closed her eyes and let out a long, weary breath. She sighed a lot these days, mostly when she was trying to calm herself, and especially when she was returning to the farm. There was nothing rude about her sighs, unlike her mother-in-law, who since the death of Ed's father had mastered the art of speaking without words. *Clever,* she thought, *all the woman had to do was put her scrawny hands either side of her plate, close her eyes briefly, and let out the foul air for a deliberate length of time.* It was just enough to give her son the impression she was tired and full after the meal; almost like a reminder to him to devote his time to her rather than his wife or himself. To Angela's ears, it was scalding criticism, directed at her and most likely at her cooking, or something she'd said, or not done in the 'right' way. Oversensitive and exhausted from holding back, she knew it was only a matter of time before the tiniest thing would trigger a flood of emotion that quite possibly might drown them all.

Later, as she cleared away the evening meal, she could hear the TV blaring from the front room, where they typically spent their evenings. Usually the sound irritated her further, but tonight her mind was still down at the lake with Holly and Stevie. Those women only sighed in mock anger when she said something silly or naive. She remembered her attempt at a joke about the colour of swim trunks. Poor Holly. Imagine feeling suspicious about your husband; you wouldn't be able to believe anything he said after a while. Ed couldn't hide his emotions, so she doubted he'd be able to keep an affair a secret for very long – certainly not from his mother!

They still didn't have a dishwasher, even though she'd once ordered one from the Internet. When it was delivered, Ed had refused to sign for it, so the delivery guys had taken it away. He said they didn't need one. Angela suspected it was more likely that his mother, who was too mean to spend any money, had been behind it.

Angela's mouth set grimly. She couldn't remember the last time she and Ed had had a laugh together. She knew farming wasn't the easiest of professions, or lifestyles, but there were fun moments to be had if you shared the work, dealt with the ups and downs together, and took everything in your stride. The paperwork got her down, but now that she dealt with most of that, it offered her an escape from her mother-in-law's post-tea grunts in the permanently fetid atmosphere of the front room. Ed's father's gruff but gentle presence was sorely missed. It would have cut through the wall of silence that had fallen on the family; the trauma of his violent death had changed everyone.

She heard someone come into the kitchen, but didn't turn away from the drying rack where she was sorting out Ed's socks, rolling them into matching pairs. She felt strong hands grip either side of her waist and pull her gently back until she met the large warm body of her husband. He wrapped his arms around her and held her, nuzzling gently into her neck. It felt safe and good. And made her want to cry.

'Ed—' she started to speak, but his nuzzling had got more persistent, less loving, and his hold around her felt restrictive. One of his hands had moved down to her crotch and he was pulling her hips back and bending her slightly over. She could feel he was hard and pressing himself into her. And then he let her go. This was as far as it went these days, what their love had become. He was frustrated because he wanted her and didn't understand why she pulled away all the time. She needed him and loved him, but just didn't feel any sexual urge whatsoever. And they didn't talk about it, but left the subject to grow like a barrier between them. She saw him readjust his trousers and look up at her sheepishly, almost apologetically.

'Ed?' she tried again. 'Shall I put the kettle on?' *Come on, be strong,* she told herself. *Look at him, he's suffering. You both are. He loves you. He'll listen.*

'Angie, love,' he said, 'what's wrong?' His hugs were always comforting, but this time it was not enough. She knew that if they continued to ignore their lack of physical intimacy because it felt reassuring just to hug each other and too scary to open the can of worms that was festering within, nothing would change.

She virtually forced herself to start trying to explain, to open up a conversation about how she was feeling, how she'd been feeling for months now. Each day, her inability to think clearly and focus on tasks grew worse and her anxiety levels shot higher. She found herself reflecting more and more on her darkest moments, which she thought she had buried forever. She really was beginning to feel overwhelmed by it all.

'Here, sit down, I'll make a pot of tea and we can talk.'

'Right-o, let's do that. Mother's got her telly, so you and me can have a chat.' He pulled out a chair and sat down, arms folded across his chest, legs stretched out into the kitchen.

Angela sorted out the big brown teapot, two mugs, and sugar bowl. Then she sat down herself, bolt upright, legs tucked under her chair, and busied herself with pouring the tea.

'Go on, then, what've I done? Get it off your chest. You've obviously got things on your mind.'

'Well, you know I've been having trouble sleeping – too hot, not wanting to be, you know, physically close, well, I think it's the start of the menopause.' There. She'd said the word. The one that was forbidden in this house even though there was another woman present.

'Women's troubles, Mother calls it,' responded Ed. He helped himself to sugar and stirred it into his tea vigorously. He picked up his mug. 'Ahh, that's good. The first sip is always the best.'

Angela's temper flared and she banged her hand down on the table. 'Never mind what your mother thinks, Ed, this is me. I want to talk with you about it, how it makes me feel, why everything feels so difficult all the time. And there's something else I need to tell you, something really serious—' Her words trailed off as she saw Ed's mother standing in the doorway. She must have heard everything. Angela winced.

'Go on, tell me, love,' encouraged Ed.

'Son!'

Ed jumped and spilt his tea over his lap. *Ouch, that must have hurt!* thought Angela as she watched this grown man turn into a guilty boy, caught by his mother doing something naughty and forbidden.

'Mother.' He used a tea towel to wipe down the worst of the tea. 'Angela and I were having a chat. I'll be through in a minute.'

'I heard. Load of nonsense. Forty-two is far too young! And, anyway, if it were true, you'd just have to get on with it, Angela. I never had any problem. It's a fact of life; no one wants to know about it. Ed, I need you to fix the telly, it's gone again.' She turned and walked slowly back down the hallway towards the front room, but Ed didn't follow immediately.

He turned back to his wife, who still sat at the table, her face white, her eyes staring right through him to the woman who did everything she could to control their lives.

'Don't be hard on her, love.' He patted her shoulder. 'She's not been the same since Father passed.' He paused and closed his eyes as if trying to compose his own thoughts. Pushing his dinner plate-sized hands down on the kitchen table and pushing himself up from his chair signalled the end of that conversation, Angela realised. As always, something, or someone, got in the way of them having a real conversation these days.

'I'm sure she's right, though. Everything will sort itself out, you'll see.' He kissed her gently on top of her head and followed his mother down the hallway.

Angela could hardly breathe. Her chest was tight, her neck taut, her fists clenched. The back of her neck ached and she was grinding her teeth. But the tears wouldn't come. It was true that grief changed people. She'd changed when her mother died a few years ago; she'd allowed herself to be swallowed up by Ed, his family, and the farm, and now it was all she had left. The outside world meant nothing to her with the last of her own family gone.

Stunned by the woman's words and total lack of empathy, Angela sat on that hard wooden chair until her bones felt cold and her knuckles had lost all colour. The inside of her cheek was bleeding from where she had been vigorously gnawing it. Her head pounded and her throat was dry.

What was there left to say? What was there left to stay here for? Would Holly or Stevie let her move in with them? They were the only flash of colour in her monotone world, like a lakebed jewel glinting in the shivelight. She dived down to reach for it in the silt, feeling her body pulsing strongly through the water. A mermaid's long auburn hair and bubbles of human breath trailing behind her in the green-blue depths.

She felt herself stand up, push back the chair, walk from the kitchen and down the long, cold, stone-floored passageway towards the front room. She stopped at the dark stained doorframe to the sitting room and forced her fingernails into the palms of her hands as she scrunched them up into angry fists. She opened her mouth, but instead of the pent-up words she'd been trying to suppress, out came a simple, honest fact. 'I go swimming in the lake.' And then, just in case they hadn't heard it, she repeated it. 'I swim in the lake with my friends.'

Two shocked faces turned to stare at her.

'Yes, that's right. With friends. Several times a week. It makes me feel good,' she continued.

Nothing could have stopped her, but almost as soon as she'd said it, she regretted it. Her beautiful sanctuary of friendship and nature was now lying exposed and vulnerable on the grim-patterned carpet of this fart-filled over-lit chamber of grief.

If she could have morphed into a tiny spider and scuttled away into a dusty corner, Angela would've gladly done so, but her feet were rooted to the hideous swirls and lines of fake Persia and her trembling hands were the only things that held her upright in the slightly sticky and grimy architrave between escape and death by stony silence.

'It's okay, Mother,' said Ed, gently patting his mother's knees as he stood up. Angela noticed that the old woman tried and failed to grab at his huge hand with her own frail, claw-like one before crumpling down into her own body like a paper bag that was no longer needed. Then Angela's eyes flickered to Ed, who appeared to loom over both women. She'd never seen him look so massive and angry before. Silence held them all, like three stone statues.

Who would speak first? Ed or Angela? The wounded or the

knife-bearer? Angela wasn't sure who was who anymore. She frowned, and from somewhere deep within her body, she felt a bizarre rush of energy over which she had no control. It released her from her state of uncertainty and she heard her own slow but steady words stride into the room.

'When I am in the water, nothing else matters. For those brief moments, I am ageless and fearless, capable of being the best I can be.' Her voice grew stronger, which seemed to be having an effect on her mother-in-law, who withdrew even further from them both as if she was scared or maybe had even finally realised that this was a conversation between her son and his wife. Angela took one, two, three steps towards her husband and then she spoke again, this time in a quieter, more intimate tone.

'Ed, my love.'

He tensed up again, so she took another step towards him.

'I need you to hear me out. The two women I swim with are my friends. We look after each other and help each other. I need to do this thing with them because it will make me more able to help you and your mother here on the farm. But I would like your blessing, so that I don't have to hide it anymore.'

This time, Ed's stance seemed a little less defensive and Angela dared to walk near enough to be able to reach out and take both his hands in hers. Without casting a glance anywhere else in the room, Angela placed his hands on her hips and encouraged him to pull her body towards him. It was an awkward moment, but something within her spirit needed physical contact to melt the cold distance between them.

He didn't respond, so she put both her hands up on his shoulders and pushed her hips towards his at the same time as sliding one hand up to the back of his head. A yearning to be enfolded within his arms compelled her to act as if they were the only two people in the room, naked and ready to gorge on each other. Her rational self shook its head and shouted, *What on earth do you think you are doing?* And the woman who bathed like a selkie in the cold waters of the lake felt her husband's body beginning to respond to the connection she was creating. Love wasn't dead, but it had been crushed beneath grief and jealousy. She felt it stir and for the time being that was all she needed to know.

As Ed clamped her in his arms, she felt his body shake as painful groans rose up and out of his belly and chest. He'd kept it all locked in so that he could focus on his mother and the farm, but instead of giving him the strength to step into his father's boots, it had been a barrier to love and healing.

'You can't swim, Angela. I won't permit it.' His words felt like needles jabbing into the back of her neck. She pulled away from him as if she'd received an electric shock. Words crashed through her head, but even as she tried to form them in her mouth, he'd already pushed her away and was walking back towards his mother, who wore a flicker of a smile across her tight lips.

Chapter Seventeen

STEVIE

November

Whisky Pool takes your tears and turns them into bubbles. That was why it was Stevie's pool, her tiny piece of heaven where no one could see her, judge her, misunderstand her, lie to her, or desire her. She had found it many years ago when her children were small, up-river from the troll bridge, and far more exciting than paddling about at the edge of Crummock Water.

They used to pack a bag of food and goodies, dry clothes, and sitting mats and drive down to the telephone box in the lay-by and not return until the sun was setting over the trees above Maggie's Bridge. It had always just been her and the children; she now kicked herself for not having realised this was a red flag. She'd made it so easy for her husband to say he needed to work. But those times with her daughters had been all that mattered at the time. Giggles and squeals echoed around the little river gorge as they scrambled up along the tiny sheep track, stopping every now and again to straddle a gap between two rocks or slide on their bums down a mossy rock face rather than walk through the cold water in the beck.

She knew every stone that rocked, every boggy bit that swallowed your boot; the dripping algae after a snowmelt, the crunchy bracken that grazed bare legs. There was that singular stake, hammered down into the bank until just the top two foot remained, pale wood with a flash of red paint, marking it out for some mysterious purpose.

From here, her ears searched out the waterfall, her nose twitched, and she felt the anticipation in her belly rise into her throat. Today, the clarity of the water – nature in a playful, joyous mood – was what she needed to shake off the solitary hours of creating an online dating profile that would be detailed enough to reel in an ice man, but anonymous enough to protect her dignity and real identity. She longed to immerse herself with no agenda, silence unwelcome memories that had come to the surface, and chill old fears that threatened to knock her off balance. Neither Holly nor Angela would ever know the Herculean task that they had set her, but if it meant they got the all-important final member of the winter swimming team she had set up, then she believed it was her duty to take it on. She just needed to be brave, which is how the cold water made her feel. Brave enough to form a relay team and compete against other teams in front of hundreds of spectators in a cold Scottish loch in winter.

She could see the tiny tree on the left-hand bank, its roots gripping to whatever thin soil it could find among the rocks. Below that was an almost perfect circle of turquoise water with a short three-foot waterfall feeding into it from the rushing beck above.

There hadn't been too much rain, so she knew the flow would be safe, because the pool had a natural lip and she could still get in when the water was no longer turquoise but a boiling mass of white bubbles after a rainstorm.

Once there had been a dead sheep on the little beach next to the pool. The children said they felt sick, even though it was mostly fleece and bone, with everything else having been eaten away by foxes and other scavengers and its rib cage washed out by the rain and water.

They'd moved on upstream after finding that and soon the carcass was forgotten as an even bigger, even better pool was discovered where they could slide in under an overhanging rock and pretend they were freshwater octopuses lurking in wait for tasty little wiggly sprats.

Nothing like that today, thank goodness, Stevie thought, as she set out her swim kit carefully and deliberately before removing any layers. Just her body and a bit of nerve was really all that was needed up here, but she always found herself bringing basic kit, plus a few extras: a Thermos filled with a hot drink, swim shoes or booties, goggles, GoPro, bobble hat, changing robe, warm clothes. And a mat to sit on because the rocks were cold.

The OS footpath, which ran up from the road, over the bridge, and up across the fell to the ridge high above, was well used at weekends by runners and walkers. They all headed for the horseshoe walk above, but during the week it was less likely anything or anyone would disturb her. The path she took was just a sheep trod, sketchy and tricky in places.

Her mind was a jumble of pictures and words after staring at the blank boxes on an Internet dating site. Photographs she'd tried and failed to take of herself looking relaxed and friendly, but not overtly flirtatious; answers to inane questions she'd never ask anyone, such as: What's your ideal first date? What sort of films do you enjoy watching? How would you describe your body type? And it got worse. Questions designed to categorise people into easy to digest one-dimensional shadows. She hadn't been on a date for over twenty years – not since marrying her ex-husband. Now, she had to admit, any date would be acceptable, so long as it didn't last too long and was in a public place with an easy exit. Films? Romantic ones made her cry and feel even lonelier. Action films reminded her of her husband; they had been his favourite. Horror? Not when you lived alone. Feel-good British films were fairly safe territory, but once you'd watched them several times over, it was more exciting to get an early night with a book.

Body type is an interesting question, Stevie thought, as she rolled out a bathmat onto the slightly wet ground. It would keep her feet dry and clean while she got changed and was far nicer than sludging about in grassy mud. How would she describe her body type? The last time she'd looked in the mirror after swimming with Holly and Angela she knew she'd been confused by what she saw, but how could she describe herself in a sentence? *Saying your boobs are no longer perky, but not too bad either wasn't going to sell many tickets to the show. There they are,* she said to herself as she pulled the last layer of clothing up and over her head. Holding her hands under her breasts and supporting their weight like a good fitting bra, she jiggled around for a few seconds, noticing that her nipples had instantly reacted to the cold air. It made her laugh out loud. *Good grief!* she thought. *I really hope there's no one on the footpath watching me!*

She unfastened the button and zip of her walking trousers and had to sit down on the rock to get them off over her feet. Knickers followed, carefully placed on the pile of dry clothes ready for after her dunk in the pool. Sitting down like this, she knew her belly slumped and her backside splayed out, thighs pressed together.

She jumped up and jiggled about again, shaking off the feeling of self-loathing she felt creeping out from the shadows in her being. *Who cares? My body type is perfect for what I love doing. Just enough body fat to keep me warm for long enough.* She always remembered her mother's favourite saying: if elephants didn't have folds and creases, they wouldn't be able to move, stretch, or breathe.

Into the pool she tiptoed. The only thing she wore was a pair of pink swim shoes with a little toggle on the front. Her dark brown, grey-streaked hair was loose and hanging over her shoulders. A girl-woman, Stevie May, freed from time, thoughts, and the chains of other peoples' criteria. Knee deep, she stopped to calm her breath and relax once more. Then she walked in further, wincing slightly as the moving water swirled around the tops of her thighs. She did a few pelvic floor exercises just before the water reached the point of no return, locking up the hatches and then dunked down.

She said to herself, 'Going down, going down.'

It was a private ritual, not one she'd shared yet with Holly or Angela, but she did wonder whether all female swimmers automatically did the same or whether it was just something you had to do as you got older and your intimate body tissues lost elasticity and tightness. Not exactly a routine topic of conversation, but maybe she could introduce it as an exercise at the beginning of each of their swims from now on. A kind of shoulders back, boobs out, tummy in, bum up, flaps up type of discipline on the walk of no return into the cold water.

Embraced by oxygenated very cold water made her feel like a goddess bathing in her very own elixir of life. A cocktail of sound, touch, smell, and taste, poured into a glass vessel of blues, purples, greens, rusty-reds, blacks, greys, and frosted round the edges with white and pale pink sugar crystals.

Stripped back of meeting society's expectations, completing tick boxes, grieving a lost love, or even her fading youth, this was Stevie May. A beautiful, strong, intelligent, surprising, creative, warm, caring, and funny woman, perfect in Nature's eyes, a survivor, a giver, and a water warrior. Here, the sky was her mirror and the reflection was sparkling.

Chapter Eighteen

CHRIS

November

D own at the lake there was no breeze at all. It was one of those early winter days when time stood still. A shroud of mist hung over the water, rolling down lazily from the damp fells and kissing the black surface of Crummock Water.

Chris loved mornings like this when nature chose to be nothing but stunning. His first night in his newly acquired campervan had gone well and waking up to this amazing view confirmed he'd been right to take the plunge and buy it. All he had to do was slide the door open and he could stay lying in the bed, mug of tea in his hands, and listen to the geese gathering in a raft on the cool water.

Since his conversation with Tom, Chris had talked himself into going on a campervan hunt, at first through the Internet and some local contacts, and then to a man in the Borders who had been converting them for over a decade. Always thinking of himself as risk-averse, this deliberate act of pushing himself out of his comfort zone felt strangely liberating. No one, not even Andy, had known what he was thinking while he sat slumped on the sofa surrounded by empty beer cans and takeaway containers after Gail's death. If he'd had too many beers, his thoughts were extremely jumbled and blurred, leaving him paralysed and in a catatonic state. On sober days, he'd been tortured with bolts of anger and disappointment in himself for allowing Gail to belittle him on an almost daily basis, but in such a subtle way that he was pretty convinced no one else noticed. It seemed to be a control game she played of criticising him for nearly everything he did and then saying she loved him. It was strange now to just get on with everything exactly how he wanted to. So strange that sometimes he felt giddy with excitement and rebellion. He was relearning who he was and how he wanted to live.

Day by day, he grew stronger. It was simple, he realised: life went on and time only stopped when you were dead. Without Gail, he now needed to make his own decisions, find his own way through the rest of his life, and not allow the loss of the woman who had cushioned him in the palm of her hand to suck him down into a dangerous spiral of a half-life even after her death. He had finally admitted to himself that love with Gail had been a complex game of giving up much of his own identity over the years to fit her expectations, upbringing, personal issues, and taboos. Alone now, with no one to create his boundaries on his behalf, or ensnare him in theirs, he had felt his heart beat: a single beat, desperate to be heard in the silence.

But he had heard it. It had been a visceral awakening of something forgotten and abandoned. His shoulders may have slouched under the weight of wanting to live up to someone else's song, but his heart was still beating. He'd heard it, felt it, and wanted it to beat harder and faster. He wanted to feel it burst out of his chest or just be strong and steady when he rested, but he never wanted it to be a robotic murmur in the background again, something he merely took for granted. It was up to him to grab whatever life threw at him with both hands. Someone had given him a second chance – a choice about how he lived his life.

This morning as he rubbed his bleary, sleepy eyes, he noticed there was a red 4x4 parked in the lay-by under the stand of conifer trees; the one which had irritated him so much the other morning. Automatically, he groaned and pulled up his duvet, tempted to slide the van door closed again. But his gut was telling him to take another look. Now that he was awake and he'd finished his tea, he may as well get up. He had always been an early riser, unlike Gail, so he'd often gone out on his bike first thing or walked up a fell with breakfast neatly packed into his rucksack. It was something he'd stopped doing when they had children; it seemed unfair to leave Gail to do all the work. During the teenage years, they'd lounged around later in the mornings, so it was a habit he had grown into again.

As he was pulling on his clothes from the previous day, he put the kettle back on the little two-ring burner resting so neatly on top of the small kitchen unit. Sitting back on the raised bed, he pulled on his boots, but didn't bother to lace them up.

With a mug of freshly brewed tea in his hand, he stepped out of the van, crossed the road, and stood under the conifer trees sipping the hot tea. Wiping his mouth with the back of his hand, he watched the figures below. Two of them were actually in the water and a third was crouched over by what looked like a tripod set up on the beach.

He scrunched up his brown eyes and tried to focus more clearly on the figures. It was hard to tell from this distance, but he swore they weren't wearing anything. He blinked and stared again in disbelief. Good grief, they were stark-bollock-naked! It was the same three women and they were standing in the lake with no clothes on.

He chuckled to himself, but also felt a bit awkward and

voyeuristic. He was pretty sure that they didn't know that they were being watched.

Right, I'm off, he decided, tipping out his undrunk tea and not wanting to be caught staring at them. Just as he was about to climb back into his van, he heard a shout. He was being yelled at. Were they telling him to bugger off and stop being a pervert? No. They were waving at him, trying to get his attention, and signalling for him to come down to the beach. What the heck? No way was he going down there. Put some clothes on, he wanted to shout back. *Then I might consider it,* he thought.

The last thing he wanted was to see his picture on the front of the local rag with the headline: CRUMMOCK CRUMPETS CAVORT WITH CYCLIST. Jesus. No way. He knew the local press was desperate for sales, but no. Cumbria was a small world where everyone knew everyone else's business, or at least thought they did. It wouldn't take long before a story like that would do the rounds and next time he went out for a ride with the local club, questions would be fired at him more rapidly than he could pedal. All in good humour, admittedly, but something he'd just as soon not lay himself open to. Being the centre of attention in any shape or form never sat comfortably with him.

The women were still waving at him and trying to get him to come down. He'd better go and see what they wanted. Crazy women. He walked carefully down the steps, remembered his boots were unlaced, stooped to do them up, and then pushed through the kissing gate.

As he approached the women, he sighed with relief. Thank God, they'd put some clothes on: swimming costumes and those voluminous swim cloaks.

A tall and very attractive woman greeted him. 'Hi, I'm Stevie and this is Holly and Angela.'

It was the woman he'd seen through the window when he'd been cleaning for Andy.

'Chris,' he said, shaking her hand firmly and wondering if she'd recognise him. Those eyes, an extraordinary dark blue framed with heavy lashes. Sad eyes. But her wide smile lit up her face in recognition: she was one of those naturally beautiful women who don't know it. He felt as if he was grinning like an idiot; it had been so long since he had smiled sincerely.

Holly, who was not quite as tall as Stevie, certainly had some very attractive curves and, from how she held herself, seemed pretty self-confident, but he didn't feel drawn to her. She reminded him of Gail's younger sister, who had tried her best to comfort him during those difficult days after the cancer diagnosis. All a bit overpowering, even if well-intended. Then there was the quiet one, Angela, who he'd very nearly been rude to the other week. She was auburn-haired and slightly built.

'Angela, hi,' he said, shaking her hand more gently. 'Sorry about the finger marks on the car. I hope your husband didn't notice?'

There, how difficult was that? He was pleased with himself, but it had not been easy. He felt as if he'd completely got out of the habit of being sociable. Not surprising really. He'd shut himself away and spent over a year of caring, worrying, and then losing and coming to terms with everything. Chris didn't matter anymore. Who was Chris?

'Thanks, Chris. Sorry to drag you out of bed, but can we borrow you for a few minutes?' asked Holly, pointing towards the tripod. 'We're trying to get a photo of the three of us walking into the water.'

'With our clothes on this time,' added Stevie. She was blushing and Chris thought how beautifully it enhanced her natural colouring.

Holly laughed, but didn't blush in the slightest. 'Well, we did think no one else would be around this early in the morning. Otherwise—' She laughed again. 'So, is that alright?'

'Yep, sure, no reason why not. Shouldn't take long.' Chris coughed a little and recomposed himself. 'Is it all set up? Shall I take it off the tripod?' He went over to the camera. 'I can walk around then and get the best angle.'

'You must have strong hands from cleaning windows,' said Stevie, an innocent comment twisted by the look Holly gave her. She hastily unscrewed the Nikon camera from the tripod, while Angela held the tripod steady for her. 'We used this.' She pulled a wireless remote from her cloak pocket. 'Trouble is, it only works up to a certain distance, so you can't be sure you've taken a photograph.'

'Ah, right.' He nodded. Then he asked nonchalantly, 'Is that why you were running in and out of the lake?' He felt pleased that Stevie had recognised him, but decided not to bother with an explanation of how he'd only been filling in for Andy.

The women looked at each other and Holly burst out giggling. He could see Stevie and Angela almost shrinking away from him and wanting to disappear into the ground. Holly, on the other hand, obviously had fewer issues with body image. Her lack of modesty made him relax just a little bit more.

'There you go then. Well, we're ready when you are. Let's do it!' Holly laughed, pulled off her coat, checked her swimming costume was pulled down in the right places, and hoisted it up under her boobs.

Stevie explained to him that the main photo they wanted was of them walking into the water, but once he'd got that, it'd be good if he could take some front shots of them as a group as well.

Chris wondered what they were going to do with the photos, but guessed they'd tell him if it mattered. For now, he'd just do as he was told and then grab his bike from the van and pedal down to the cafe to see Tom.

The mist had started to lift from the surface of the lake and gradually drew out into thinner and thinner streaks. Blue sky was beginning to appear between them and the light was growing stronger by the minute. The water reflected the sky and the island appeared vivid green. The women wore black swimsuits and that was about it. Aside from that, they just had Neoprene swim socks to help them walk in across the stones. How they did it amazed him. He'd briefly dipped his hand in the edge of the water and he was shocked by how cold it felt. He shuddered as he thought how much colder it must be further out in deeper water.

And this was November when the water temperature was probably only just starting to drop as the nights grew colder and longer. It was at its warmest around late summer. *Bah!* Summer? He used that word carefully – it was summer, but not as most people know it. Rain, low temperatures, and too much wind. This year, they hadn't even had the typical early two weeks of settled weather in May.

Oh, well, he thought, *it keeps the lakes full*. How he hated it when other people used that well-worn phrase. Personally, he'd prefer the lakes to be less full and get a bit more vitamin D for a few months. And be able to ride his bike every single day without having to check the forecast on an hourly basis. It had that weird habit of doing something completely different to what he expected, especially if he'd planned a long cycle ride.

He was quite happy to take the photos. As a teenager, he had made a hobby of it to the point of processing his own film in a makeshift dark room in his parent's cellar. Another of his interests that he had given up when he met Gail. He sighed. What better way to spend an hour or so than staring through a camera lens at three attractive ladies in their swimming costumes while they walked slowly into the lake? The camera never lies, apparently, and from what he could see, women around his age hadn't lost it. Okay, so their bodies might not be quite as pert or toned as they used to be, but then neither was his. *My God*, he thought, *they've only asked me to take their bloody photograph. Concentrate.*

He knew how to get the best out of a camera, even a digital SLR on automatic. It was all in the composition and lighting. Nothing he could do about the lighting, but he moved around on the beach and took various shots from different angles. He stood up on the natural sandy bank over on the left so he could get a shot looking down on them, then stretched out on the pebbly beach to see how that looked. He liked that one. It elongated their legs; very flattering. The water patterns around their legs as they strode slowly into the lake looked good, too.

It was just as he was adjusting the focus so that their legs really stood out that another memory popped into his head. He took his eye away from the camera lens and stared at the women: actually, one woman in particular. The one called Stevie. Then he remembered that not only had he seen her through the window he had been cleaning, but before that, just like this, walking into the lake. There was no mistaking her figure and ease of walking into the water. The natural sway and stride, which her swimsuit couldn't disguise, seemed too young for the age he guessed she actually was now he'd talked to her face to face. Did he need to feel awkward? He was convinced that on that first occasion, she hadn't been aware of anyone watching her, let alone him. He felt a bit more relaxed and put the camera to his eye again. Something to share with her one day maybe? The thought was strangely exciting.

Holly turned round and called back to him. 'Are you done?' It was almost as if his temporary lack of attention had transmitted across the water.

Coughing to disguise his embarrassment at being caught off-guard, he called back, 'Just one minute. I was about to focus in on your legs.' How weird did that sound!

Shame, he thought, *I was just getting into it.* Some deeply buried creative kernel inside his brain had come back to life. Behind the camera, he'd forgotten where he was, who he was, and why he was there. He'd just been. Just was.

A few minutes later, the women were busy getting dried and dressed. To give them some privacy, he walked along the lakeshore and took more photographs of the landscape. He liked the way the mist had completely disappeared apart from the odd wisp here and there. Shadows lurked on the bulk of Melbreak in the distance as a cloud or two drifted over the sun. He was enjoying this and wracked his brain to think where he had put his own camera. He wasn't quite sure how he'd carry it on his bike though. Maybe he'd need to invest in a handlebar bag or panniers? He laughed. *Watch it, Christopher,* he said to himself, *you'll be buying a touring bike next to strap to the back of your hippy love shack on wheels!* But he did fancy giving it a go. His phone took good photos, yes, but getting back into serious photography – now that would add another dimension to his solo wanderings.

'Here, would you like a hot drink?' Stevie approached him carrying two enamel mugs of steaming liquid. He met her halfway and took one of them, murmuring his thanks. He'd not noticed feeling cold, but now he thought about it, he was. Not surprising really as he was just wearing what he'd crawled out of the van in. There was nothing in her body language that suggested she recognised him from anywhere other than up a ladder though, so he breathed a sigh of relief.

'Thanks, Chris.' All three women stood round him, sipping tea and now and again pacing around to keep warm. Their smiles and sparkly eyes were infectious. What the heck do they put in the water? They seemed to be high as kites now.

'My pleasure. Are they for anything special?'

The women looked at each other as if wondering whether to tell him or not. He was intrigued.

'It's complicated,' piped up Angela.

'Yes, it is, rather,' added Stevie.

'We need a man,' Holly said with a laugh. 'Well, Stevie does.'

Everyone looked at Stevie, who backed away in embarrassment, one hand up in the air as if trying to stop the conversation from going any further.

Chris frowned, completely lost. Where was this conversation going? He breathed a sigh of relief when Stevie spoke above the giggles and he moved closer to her so that he could hear properly.

'We're entering a winter swimming competition and we need a man to make up the team. So, funnily enough, these two—', she nodded her head towards Holly and Angela, '—volunteered muggins here to go looking online… so, I'm doing my profile photo.'

Silence.

Even the other two had stopped messing around now. Chris didn't know what to say. 'Ah, I see. Well, don't you need some photos of just you then?' It sounded obvious to him if it was her profile. 'I can take a couple now if you like?'

He started to get his phone out of the back pocket of his jeans.

'No, it's okay.' Stevie put her hand on his arm and smiled. 'I've got a couple of more dressy ones, but we wanted to be very specific in who we attract, hence the swimming shots.'

'But she didn't want to be posing on her own,' said Holly, 'so we promised we'd be in them with her, but only rear-view shots.'

Well that all sounds overcomplicated, thought Chris, checking the time on his Garmin. 'Ladies, I need to go. Um, well, thanks for the tea and—' He looked at Stevie, who was still standing next to him. 'Good luck with finding a man.'

He shivered. He was definitely cold now. He needed to get moving. 'See you, then.' He started to walk away. How on earth did those women manage to stand around in their swimming costumes, let alone swim in the lake?

Angela, who was definitely the quiet one, touched his arm as he walked past her and said, 'Chris, just a thought, but are you a swimmer?'

He was just about to say, yes, he did swim, when he heard Holly pipe up, 'Hey, what a good idea! Well?'

Just before he answered, he saw Stevie staring at him intently, her dark blue eyes looking right into him from under her grey bobble hat. Those eyes didn't deserve to be lied to. In that split second between having that thought and opening his mouth, he knew someone had lied to her before and it still hurt her. 'No, not really. I'm more of a cyclist. I'm sorry.'

He looked at Stevie, but she was now bent over what looked like a gardening bucket, sorting out her things. He wanted to kick himself. What an idiot he was. It wasn't as if he'd never swum in the lake. In fact, as a child, he'd learnt to swim here rather than the pool. What was he so afraid of? Spending time with strangers? Not being able to do something that pushed him out of his comfort zone and made him look weak in front of someone who mattered? Did Stevie matter? Or was it just that, for some reason he didn't understand yet, she touched something inside him that he'd been forced to bury increasingly deeper over the last couple of decades? All he knew for certain was that it wasn't just a case of being afraid of a bit of cold water.

Angela broke the uneasy silence. 'Okay, no problem.' He hardly heard her soft voice because he was feeling so uncomfortable at having lied.

'Anyway, thanks for the photos,' said Holly.

Thank God neither of them seemed to have noticed the look that had passed between him and Stevie.

She stopped what she was doing and said, 'Yes, thanks for doing that, Chris.'

'Not at all. I enjoyed it, Stevie. Well, ladies, good to meet you all. And good luck!'

Chapter Nineteen

ANGELA

November

'So how will we know which photo to choose?' asked Angela on the drive back from the lake.

'If it's okay with you both, I'll download them and see what we've got, then why don't you both come round one evening?' Stevie seemed distracted. 'Actually, I'll choose. I've already made a bit of progress on the profile, so I can activate the account, see what happens, and then you come round. Does that sound better?'

'Aren't we going to help you write the blurb though? Could be fun,' Holly added with a suggestive grin.

Stevie shook her head. 'All I'm going to write is, "Winter swimming team looking for male swimmer to join their team – message if interested." Does that sound okay?'

Holly rolled her eyes. 'Bit boring, but I guess it will do. Hang on, what about your details? You know, personal details.'

'I'd rather keep it very *im*personal, thank you.' Stevie laughed. 'I'm not even sure why we're doing this to be honest. It's not as if I'm actually looking for a man man, as in partner man!'

'I agree,' said Angela. But she didn't elaborate. The other two looked at her, expecting her to give some reasons, but they could tell that her mind was somewhere else completely.

Her altercation with her mother-in-law first thing in the morning had stressed her out completely and she was scared of what she'd find when she got home. God knows what the woman might have said to Ed. Maybe now was the time to count how much was in her exit fund.

It had still been dark when Angela snuck out of the kitchen door, desperately trying not to let the latch drop back down as she shut it behind her. She prayed the farm dogs would know it was her and not start barking. Ed was already out in the field, checking a couple of ewes, but she'd laid out his breakfast on the table as always and left the coffee brewing in the pot on the Rayburn.

His mother normally didn't get up until a bit later, which gave Ed and Angela a peaceful hour or so at the beginning of the day – a special time when Angela actually felt brief happiness. They worked really well as a team on the farm. That was what it was all about: supporting each other through the bad times. There were two people in this team, but three people in the marriage.

No time to dwell on that, thought Angela as she crept across the yard to where the 4x4 was parked. Once again, Angela breathed a sigh of relief that the close encounter with Chris the cyclist hadn't left any lasting damage, so she'd never mentioned it to Ed.

The air was chill and smelt of sweet silage from the barns, damp grass and vegetation, and wood smoke from the Rayburn that had to be kept going twenty-four hours a day for hot water, heating, and cooking. It was a good smell this morning and felt like home. Her spirits were high and excitement brought colour to her normally pale face. Maybe life wasn't so bad after all?

In her rucksack, she had her swimsuit and all the kit she needed for a normal swim, neatly packed into the small space. In one of the side pockets, she'd included a comb and a lipstick because today was special. It was their photo shoot for Stevie's online dating profile.

'Where are you going?'

Angela spun round in surprise. She hadn't heard the kitchen door closing or footsteps across the yard. Ed's mother stood a few feet away from her with her grey dressing gown tightly wrapped across her scrawny body and slippers on her small feet. She was peering at Angela, taking in the bag and the car keys.

'Does Ed know where you're going?' *Of course he doesn't,* thought Angela. *I promised him I'd stop swimming in the lake because it upset you too much.* But she couldn't say any of that out loud. She had to try to keep the peace somehow even though inside it was killing her to lie and break her promise to Ed.

Angela thought quickly and decided to go for damage limitation rather than the truth. 'Of course he does. The pool has an early session and by the time I've swum my lengths, the shops will be open.' She pulled open the car door, chucked her bag onto the passenger seat, and was about to climb in when she felt a bony hand on her arm.

'His face. I'll never forget the fear on his face when they brought him back to the house, Angela. God help him, how he must've fought to stay alive, but the water, it was too cold, it sucked the life out of him.' The shadow of emotional pain cast over her mother-in-law's face intensified the guilt Angela was already feeling, but there was nothing she could do. Her own sanity depended on the lake and the two women she swam in it with. The woman's grief was not her grief, and she knew she was just not strong enough to take it on as if it were.

She shook her arm firmly until Ed's mother let go. The pent-up frustration and irritation that seemed to engulf her body more frequently over the last few months made her actually feel like pushing the old woman over onto the cobbled yard. The image of her spindly legs poking out from under her nylon nightie almost brought a giggle up from her tense and knotted gut.

'Let go of me, Margaret.' It wasn't often that she used the woman's name, but she had to do something to calm the situation down. 'I'm so sorry you lost your husband. It must be awful. I can't imagine how you must be feeling.' She hesitated, pulled herself up to her full height, and spoke words she should have spoken years ago. 'You make me feel so guilty all the time, as if I am not good enough for your son. Is it because I couldn't give him children? Huh? Is that it? Well, I'm sorry. I'm sorry I am not the woman you wanted your son to marry. But we were happy and we could be happy again, but not like this. Not with you punishing me constantly for something that's not my fault. I love Ed. He's a good man. I'm a good person, but you just can't see that, can you? You shut me out and I am so lonely. So lonely.'

It was enough. She'd said enough. She couldn't get any more words out without crying and she was sick of crying. Today was meant to be a good day. It was time to leave and when she got back, who knew what she'd find, but nothing was going to stop her from enjoying this day with the two women she loved most in the world.

That made her smile as she started up the engine and reversed out of the yard. Taking a glance in the rear-view mirror just before driving away down the track, she could see a golden rectangle, which was the open kitchen door, and a small figure standing, alone, in the shaft of light that penetrated the shadows of the yard. The security lights had gone off because there was no movement. Ed's mother stood, still as a statue, her dressing gown hanging open and wafting in the slight breeze.

'Angela!' A screech from Stevie in the passenger seat brought Angela back into the present moment as she narrowly avoided the farmer's truck speeding down the narrow green tunnel.

All three women stared at each other in shock. That was close.

Then another sudden gasp – a great intake of breath as if she was in excruciating pain – from Holly on the back seat made them both jump.

Stevie turned to look at her. '*Holly?*' Stevie looked concerned and Angela tried hard to keep her eyes on the road. Fortunately, they were back at the lay-by where the others had left their cars so that they could travel down the Crummock road in one car.

'That's it! Arctic flaps!' Holly clapped her hands and did a little jig on the back seat, her eyes glinting dangerously.

'Pardon?' Stevie frowned then added, 'Oh! You mean what we were talking about this morning about the importance of pelvic floor exercises!'

Angela, on the other hand, hadn't a clue what either of them were talking about.

'Well, if you're not keen on the Internet-dating idea, how about setting up an Instagram account—'

Holly was interrupted by Stevie, who swung round in the front seat, her hands holding onto the headrest. 'Called Arctic Flaps?' She laughed. '*No way!* God knows who will follow us!'

'Block them.' That was Holly's answer to everything to do with Stevie's resistance to social media and her fear of unwanted comments.

'What are arctic flaps?' Angela's small voice sounded embarrassed to be asking.

'Oh, Angela, come on – what were we talking about just now in the water?' teased Holly, giving the younger woman a gentle shove on the shoulder.

Clearly Angela's mind did not work in the same way as the other two, or she hadn't been listening to the 'tense your pelvic floor before you go in the water' conversation.

Stevie's questions about Instagram and how it might help them find a man for their team changed the direction of the conversation. 'Apart from the name, Holly, it's not a bad idea – are there lots of outdoor swimmers who post on there?'

The car windows were beginning to fog up as they were all a bit damp from swimming, so Angela pressed the button to lower the two front windows just a crack. She was relieved that the conversation was now on less intimate topics. She knew that although she was ultra-sensitive about anything to do with her body or its functioning it did her good to listen to the other two talking quite openly about anything and everything. Just not in an overheated, slightly claustrophobic vehicle that she was driving.

Chapter Twenty

CHRIS

November

H is son was at the counter piling pieces of gingerbread onto a flowery plate when Chris pushed open the glass cafe door. For a split second, he thought he was looking at Gail. It was something in the way that Tom moved and how carefully he was stacking the cake in a perfect swirl of gingerbread loveliness. He remembered Gail always saying that you eat food with your eyes. Chris, however, had thought it was all about the taste.

'Morning, son.'

Tom jumped and a few slices of gingerbread wobbled, but because he'd placed them at just the right angle, nothing fell off.

'Hey, Dad! You're late. I've just had my break. You okay?' Tom started to sort out Chris's usual coffee and then waved the tongs about while he waited for his usual dithering over which cake to have, or whether to just go for a scone. 'Here, try this for a change.' He made his dad's choice for him, handing him an extra large slice of gingerbread that didn't quite fit on his spiral.

'I've been taking photos,' said Chris, coming back to the counter after having put his helmet and gloves down at a table in the corner. It was his favourite table inside, because from here he could watch people as they walked in. It was easier to sit alone in a cafe if he knew who was around him, he'd found. It gave him a chance to look busy if he didn't want someone to talk to him, to look as if he were saving a seat for a friend, or just sprawl about and generally look so uninviting and grumpy that no one would want to sit next to him anyway. Stupid, he knew, but it worked for him.

'Good work, Dad. On your old camera?'

'No, no. I wish I knew where that was though. I quite fancy taking photography up again. No, I've been helping out some ladies down at the lake.'

Chris picked up the tray laden with coffee and cake and started to walk over to the table. His son followed him and cleared away the single cup, saucer, and plate that were on it. He came back and sat down, half an eye on the door. Chris was the only customer in the cafe, but given that it was getting closer to lunchtime, it was more likely people would begin to appear, either before heading off round the lake or on their way back.

'What ladies?'

'Doing some kind of swimming thing and they needed some photos.' Chris bit into the gingerbread and rolled his eyes with pleasure. Now that was good cake.

'Right, well that sounds interesting. Were they hot?'

'Tom, please. Give your old man a break. Actually, I didn't notice,' he lied and took a big mouthful of coffee to avoid having to say anything more.

'You're blushing, Dad. Go on, tell.' Tom jabbed him in the ribs.

'Nothing to tell.' Chris kept his cool, praying his face would calm down in a minute. *For goodness sake, man,* he told himself, *get a grip*. It wasn't as if they were *that* gorgeous, just attractive, and it had been a bit of a surprise. Especially *before* they'd put their swimsuits back on. 'They're entering some winter swimming competition and apparently it has to be mixed, so they're looking for a man to swim with them.'

'I hope you offered?'

'You must be joking! They're swimming in February in Scotland. No bloody chance!'

'You've got a wetsuit, Dad.'

'Something tells me no wetsuits are allowed, son. Have you seen those YouTube videos from frozen lakes in Russia and Sweden? I may be carrying a little extra round the middle, but I'm not built like those guys!' He took a slurp from his cup and then demolished more cake. Tom was tapping something into his phone and then waiting impatiently for the rural Internet connection to respond.

'What're you doing?' asked Chris, wiping some crumbs from the corner of his mouth.

'There!' Tom turned his phone round to show Chris the screen.

'Uh? It's no good, you'll have to read it.' Chris pointed at his eyes and shrugged his shoulders. 'No glasses.'

'International Ice Swimming Association rules state no Neoprene, just an ordinary swimsuit and swim cap to be worn—'

'There you go,' said Chris, almost triumphantly. But Tom wasn't going to give up that easily.

'I think you should do it, Dad.' He put his phone face down on the table and leant forward while reaching both hands out across the varnished wood. Palms face up, he motioned to his dad to place his own larger ones on top. Chris did so, puzzled, but welcomed the physical contact. And that was the trigger he needed.

The two men gripped each other's hands for longer than

they'd ever done before: 'I know something like that could be fun as well as a challenge, but I need to have a think about it.' The simple words made Tom flinch, but he held on tighter to the older man's hands. White flesh interlaced with pink, with every tiny muscle, ligament, and blood vessel tensed up.

'Don't think too long, Dad.'

They let go of each other's hands and Chris cuffed his son round the head playfully. '*Hah!* Seriously, they must be bonkers if those are the rules. Anyway, I'll consider it.'

'It'd give you something to focus on.' Tom cleared away his dad's coffee things and went back to the counter. He turned to an elderly couple who were kitted out in brand new waterproofs and were eyeing up the scones. 'How can I help you?'

He was in work mode again and Chris waved at him as he went past.

'See you, Tom,' he called and grabbed the door handle just as another customer pushed it open. He held it open for the man and then went out to his bike.

Cycling back along the lake until he reached his van, which was now surrounded by cars and a couple of other vans, he looked down to where he had been taking the photographs. The women had long gone. *Mad,* he thought. *They must be mad. It was cold enough now, but, in February, in Scotland? There could even be snow.* The lie he'd told Stevie about not being a swimmer played on his mind though. Yes, he was primarily far more interested in cycling than swimming, but he did swim, pretty well actually, but mostly in the indoor pool. As a kid he'd swum in the lakes and when his kids were little, he'd taken them into the lake and done a bit of ghyll scrambling, hence the wetsuit.

Those dark blue eyes had been so soulful; he just couldn't get them out of his mind. There was something about her – or was it just that he found her attractive and intriguing? He half wished he had agreed then and there to be 'her man', but the thought of freezing his balls off in ice water for her? He laughed out loud. Even his laugh sounded fake for some reason.

Maybe Tom was right. Perhaps he did need something other than cycling to focus on; perhaps it was time to take the first steps towards whatever now awaited him.

Chapter Twenty-One

HOLLY

November

Holly drew the curtains across the dark night, checking to see if the outside lights were on over the porch and in the yard. There were people staying in the smaller holiday cottage, a young couple, and she wanted to make sure it looked inviting for them when they got back in from their day out. Their way back to the cluster of buildings at the end of the track would only be lit by stars. There were no streetlights this far out of the village, but each gatepost was adorned with a string of bright fairy lights set to come on as dusk fell and she'd carefully wound more twinkles around the evergreen shrubs that divided each holiday cottage from the main farmhouse and cobbled yard. The cost of electricity to create a welcoming and enticing ambiance was meagre in comparison to the lifting of spirits she always felt as she drove in, so she could only imagine how appreciative her guests would feel. She'd enjoyed chatting briefly to this particular couple that morning when they were on their way out into the Central Lakes.

She looked at her watch; the others would be here soon. Stevie and Angela were coming round to talk about creating their Arctic Flaps account using some of the photographs that Chris had taken. Holly had invited them to hers because it was closer to Angela's farm and she had said she couldn't be out very long. The poor woman – from the little she'd said about her mother-in-law, it sounded awful. How could she put up with such negativity and downright bullying? She needed to stand up for herself. Or maybe her husband, Ed, needed to be more of the man around the place and not let his mother tell him what to do. Even as Holly thought it, she knew that would never happen, not from what she'd observed and overheard since she'd been living here. There was just something about mothers and sons who had been left alone to run a farm. Any other woman involved in that particular relationship was like a threat to the mother, it seemed. If Ed wouldn't retire his mother to a bungalow in town, her place was with them in the farmhouse in which she'd grown up. She was the boss.

She and Stevie had tried to gain Angela's confidence and get her to open up more, share her stuff with them during those unfiltered moments when the cold water made them swear or afterwards while they sat huddled up in layers of warm clothes sipping hot drinks and consuming cakes none of them would normally eat. Somehow, it was all part of being a swimmer.

Holly knew that she was the only one who didn't hold back. Sometimes the other two women squirmed at the details she gave about Simon and her sex, or lack of, sex life. "Do you think it'd be less painful if he were smaller?" she'd asked them, which had made Angela giggle so much that she nearly wet herself, which was when it dawned on her what the other two had been saying about arctic flaps and vowed to do pelvic floor exercises every time they swam from now on. The notion of thinking 'squeeze and up, up and up' triggered more laughing.

Often, the howls of laughter, even from Angela, echoed round the Crummock valley. The loudest definitely came from Holly. Never, in all the time that she had been living up in the Lakes, had she imagined there would come a time when she forgot where she was and who she was with, but those moments were more frequent now as she got to know the other two women better. During the long hours she spent in the overly neat house that was supposed to be a luxurious escape from the city, those moments were fast becoming a string of emotional fairy lights to add to her artificial ones that danced in the shadows and made her smile.

What was even more surprising to Holly was that she thought about Stevie and Angela every day, not just in terms of swim buddies, but as real friends: who shared her sense of humour, who were slowly changing her opinion about the landscape, and who had become mentally and emotionally resilient themselves.

Holly opened the door of the wood burner with the heatproof glove, chucked another couple of logs on, closed the door up again with a twist of the handle, and watched while the flames licked up the dry wood. Fire: bewitching but dangerous. *Not too dissimilar to love between two people,* she thought with a wry smile.

Half an hour later, armed with glasses of wine and Stevie's laptop, the women settled down on the floor at the low coffee table. Six slippered feet scrumpled up on the expensive designer rug and Jasper the dog was watching them with half an eye open. He'd already sniffed Stevie and Angela when they arrived and had latched on to Angela, probably because she'd stroked his head and tickled his ears in such a confident way that they were now friends. He was still checking Stevie out from time to time, but gradually, the warmth of the stove and the sound of the women's voices seemed to lull him into a state of complete serenity.

'So, here we are,' said Stevie after various clicks and scrolls, tuts and mutters.

'*Whoa!* Don't we look the part,' said Holly, peering more

closely at the photo of the three of them walking into the lake. 'He's good.'

'He had great subjects.' Stevie laughed, but agreed it was a good photo, well composed, and Chris had shot them from a flattering angle so their legs looked endless and the lake absolutely stunning.

'So, what do we do with them now?' Stevie looked at Holly, who was already tapping on her phone and was in the process of setting up the account.

'Arctic Flappers is better, I think, don't you?' Holly typed it into her phone before the other two could answer.

Stevie didn't think it would make a huge amount of difference. It still embarrassed her.

Holly continued, 'I need you to send me some of the photos. One for the profile photo and then we'll do a couple of posts now while we're together.'

'How do I do that?' Stevie's brain panicked, looking from her laptop to Holly's phone as if she literally hoped she would see a handful of glossy photographs floating in the space between them.

Angela snorted and the others both looked at her. 'Sorry,' she muttered. 'Your face, Stevie. No! I can't help! I'm no better than you!'

'Here, give it to me.' Holly tried not to sound frustrated at the IT ignorance of her friends. 'Let me. It's quite straightforward... when you know how.'

Stevie passed her the laptop and flopped back on the sofa, but not before she had grabbed her glass of wine and taken a big swig out of it. 'I'm just worried my bottom won't look as perky as either of yours,' she said with a moan. 'Note to self, start doing squats tomorrow!'

'You have to turn your Airdrop on,' Holly muttered, looking up from the screen with her finger poised on her phone. 'Stevie! Are you with us or fantasising about Chris?' She shook her head in mock despair, but then resumed flicking up and down and tapping on the screen for a few more seconds. 'Done!' she declared with a sigh of relief.

Her glass was empty, so she stood up, grabbed the bottle, and topped up Stevie's glass then her own. Angela refused any more since she was driving and would be leaving fairly shortly, she said, looking at the wall clock.

Stevie was staying over at Holly's, so wasn't too bothered about how much she drank. Besides, she was in the mood to let go a bit.

There was a series of pings from Holly's phone to indicate the transfer had been successful. Stevie shook her head and laughed. How easy if you knew how. The other two immediately started to speak excitedly about what they should put in their – the Arctic Flappers' – first post.

'Who are we, first of all?' Holly's fingers were poised on her phone, but before either of the other two could speak, she'd already started typing. 'We are unflappable: even when our bits are immersed in cold water,' she said out loud and then added a frozen face emoji at the end.

Stevie frowned. 'Maybe take out the "our bits"?'

'Or maybe something more like "bracing ourselves for our first winter swimming",' Angela said.

The others' pretend yawns woke the dog and he snuffled and groaned as if in agreement.

'I think what I suggested will do to start with anyway,' said Holly as she finished typing their bio. 'Right. First post. I think we need to just have a photo of all three of us walking into the lake – um, this one's good. And some text.' She typed a few words. 'And some hashtags.'

'Hashtags?' Stevie was lost but intrigued.

'Yes, people search based on hashtags, so if we want to be found by the right people, we need the right hashtags.' Holly sounded so confident that the other two just sat back and watched the master at work.

'Sorry, but I'm going to have to go.' Angela said as she started to get up off the floor. 'I told Ed that I was just popping out for an hour. Stevie, how about your friends down in Oxford?' Then she frowned. 'Sorry, I can't remember whether or not I've already asked you that? I think my brain fog is getting worse – maybe it's because I'm awake most nights sweating and trying not to wriggle around too much in case I wake Ed!'

Stevie grimaced in sympathy and then added, 'It's alright, I've already told Emma I'm getting a relay team together, but forgot to say that finding a man up here is a bit tricky! Do you fancy a trip down there? We could do a bit of recruiting down south. Maybe the men are more suitable?'

'Do you reckon?' Holly raised her eyebrows. 'I'm up for that. Can you get away, Angela? Shall we talk to Ed?'

'No! Don't do that. Um, I'm not sure, but you two could always go without me.'

'It'd be nicer if we could all go. Let me message Emma and see what she reckons,' said Stevie. 'I'm sure she could put us up if we go. She's got a sort of annexe attached to her house; we could just squeeze in there for two nights.' She hugged Angela, who looked as if she needed a grizzly bear hug, kissed her on the cheek, and moved aside to let Holly do the same.

As the rear lights of Angela's car disappeared from the yard in a red blur, Holly closed the front door, checked that the dog hadn't escaped with his new friend, and then suggested to Stevie that they move to the comfy chairs, refill their glasses, and put their thinking caps on.

'So, how're things with you and Simon?' Stevie spoke the

words before realising she had even had the thought. Maybe Holly didn't want to talk about deep stuff? She almost immediately attempted to lighten the conversation. 'And his swim trunks! Did you ask him if he was interested in being our man?'

'Yeh, I did.' Holly laughed. 'As expected, he shrieked in horror and asked me if I wanted to join their mountain-biking team. "Same thing", he said. "I'm not trained up to swim seriously. I'd die, or my bits would drop off!"'

'Ha-ha, he's probably right!' There was a slightly uncomfortable silence. Both women knew what the real question had been. It was Holly who saved the awkwardness from deepening.

'But I've talked to him about my worries, if that's what you mean.'

'Go on…' Stevie wasn't quite sure how far the conversation was going, but sensed that Holly would be open and just needed a bit of gentle encouragement.

'I couldn't think how to put it at first, you know, which is strange, because I've always been able to talk to him about anything. But in my head, the painful sex and an affair are linked. Maybe it's my fault?' She looked at Stevie with such confusion.

'No, no, Holly, don't ever think anything like that is your fault!' Stevie grabbed the younger woman and hugged her so hard they both winced.

'*Ouch!*' Holly laughed. 'I know, I know, it's crazy, but sex has always been such a big part of our relationship. It's just,' she said with a sigh, 'if that goes, I'm not sure what we've got left.'

Stevie felt a shudder go across her shoulders as if Holly's words had stirred up her own pain, which she'd been trying so hard to bury. 'I understand, honestly I do. But, from what you've told me about Simon, how you met, and your plans for the future, there's tons of stuff going on between you.'

'Yeh, you're probably right. I still asked him, though. I said,

"Do you still love me, Simon?" And he looked at me as if I'd gone mad. Actually, he looked quite angry! Of course, then I felt defensive, which never helps, and we had a massive argument.'

'Oh dear!' Stevie shook her head and empathised completely with how the conversation had gone for her friend. Talking about emotions had always been difficult with John, too. In fact, she'd stopped trying because he just shut her down by walking away.

'But in the end, that was a good thing,' Holly explained, 'because after the storm comes the calm, if you know what I mean?'

Stevie didn't really, but guessed Holly meant they had make-up sex. *Ah,* she thought, *I know what's coming.* Still, she let the younger woman finish her story and get everything off her chest. This was a safe space here between the two of them. Knowing this made Stevie feel quite emotional to the point of having to catch her tears with her finger and take a few deep breaths until she felt okay again.

'It's okay, I've got it.' She waved Holly's hands away as her friend reached out to hand her one of the napkins on the coffee table.

'We tried to have sex, it hurt, we stopped, but this time I explained to Simon exactly how it felt physically and how bad it made me feel emotionally. I asked him if he was worried about it, about not having good sex anymore... which led to me saying that I wouldn't blame him if he went off and had an affair!' Holly was crying now, but still managed to speak through the hiccups and croaky voice. 'That started another argument and Simon walked out.' Then she looked at Stevie, who was making funny noises.

'Oh, Stevie! Are you okay?' Stevie's face looked so, so sad. Absolutely devastated, in fact.

Holly knelt in front of the sofa, put her hands on Stevie's knees, and spoke gently to her. 'What's wrong, love? Hey, it's okay. You're here. You can talk to me. All this talk of arguments and affairs, it's my fault. I'm sorry.'

In between hiccups, Stevie managed to calm down a little and Holly could see that her friend was trying to work out whether to just let it all go, let the dam collapse and release a load of swirling, polluted water all over a sociable evening.

'Talk to me if you want to. Or we can just sit and cry. Both of us. It doesn't matter.' Holly's tone was warm and reassuring.

It took a few more minutes and much nose blowing before Stevie composed herself. Her eyes were once more focusing on where she was and, more importantly, thought Holly, how safe she was here. Even the sceptical dog had come to comfort her. He'd jumped up on the sofa and nuzzled his big head onto Stevie's lap. She was stroking him without seeming to realise it.

'I think it's all this talk about affairs, dating, trust. It's thrown me. I thought I'd got over it, but obviously not!' Stevie said with a sigh, holding out her glass for Holly to refill.

Then Stevie continued while Holly listened in dismay. 'You know my husband cheated on me? I've told you, I'm sure, but I've never told you anything else, like how we met or what we were like as a couple.' She shook her head and stared into the flames of the wood burner.

'I met John in our final year at university. I guess you could say he swept me off my feet, but the relationship didn't last because he took a job with an American firm who sent him to Chicago to work in their head office. He asked me to go with him, but I wanted to continue my law training and see if I could make it to the Bar. I remember how surprised he was that I would put my career before being with him. Oh, God! The argument that ensued afterwards was horrendous. But it was all I'd ever wanted to be. Anyway, I suggested we could take turns to visit each other until either his secondment came to an end or I qualified. I should have seen the red flag then! He just refused to listen.

'Years later, we bumped into each other in a city wine bar one Friday at lunchtime. He bought champagne and insisted we celebrate each other's success. And then, for the second time in my life, he swept me off my feet and back to his apartment. He said he liked strong women and how it turned him on to hear me describe how much I wanted him. At first, it was exciting to be with him again and I ignored all those red flags, such as his increasing need to control me, not just physically, but emotionally. Within months of reconnecting, we'd conceived our first daughter, then got married shortly afterwards.'

Stevie knew Holly was staring at her intently. She felt her cheeks glowing and knew it wasn't just the heat from the log burner. It had been so romantic to be blooming with child as she walked down the aisle with this successful and attentive man by her side. But then she fell silent because there was the other side to her marriage, the one where that same man she'd fallen in love with had gradually drained her self-belief and hope. She looked across at Holly and debated how much detail she could bear to share with the other woman. But it felt so good to be talking about it, such a relief to not hold it within her heart where it sat like a leaden weight.

'I warn you, Holly, it's not pretty from this point on. Are you sure you want to listen?'

Holly nodded.

'It got to the point where I sometimes felt intimidated, not just by his coldness and lack of empathy, but also by his strange sexual tastes: persuading me to have sex even if I felt too tired, suggesting we watch porn films together, buying me 'sexy' outfits to wear and then giving me the silent treatment and withholding sex for a week or more if I refused to wear them.' This revelation clearly shocked Holly, Stevie could see it on her face, so she was really grateful to be allowed to just continue. Now, she knew she needed to get this off her chest.

'You know, sometimes, I thought about leaving John and taking the girls with me, but he adored them so much I just felt too guilty to make any real plans.

'After a short career break while the girls were very little, I returned to work, but instead of lifting me up and reminding me of what I had achieved professionally, it became a battleground: between work, motherhood, and John. The other partners in the firm suggested I reduce my hours so that I could spend more time with the girls. I was really grateful for their understanding, and it did help. And, you know what, for a while John's behaviour became more loving and supportive. I remember wondering whether the problem had been my pursuit of professional accolades all along. Maybe John felt jealous or like less of a man the more successful I became?

'He used to look at me sometimes with a mixture of sexual greed and arrogant pride.' Holly raised her eyebrows, but Stevie shook her head vigorously. 'No, not good, it was just weird! I felt completely stripped naked, but in an exposed, not loving, way.'

'Your hands are shaking, Stevie,' said Holly, immediately taking hold of them and forcing her own strength into them.

Stevie stared down at her own ring-less hands in the loving grasp of her friend's carefully manicured ones. Every time she divulged another snippet of her previous life it felt as if this woman was ready to catch her. But it was taking a huge effort to open up, even though she so desperately wanted to.

She held on tight to Holly's hands and squeezed them hard. 'Thank you for being here,' she said quietly.

'It was a Sunday morning and I'd been looking forward to a bit of a lie-in after we'd had dinner guests round the night before for rather a late and alcohol-infused evening. It ended up with me and my husband having the sort of sex I'd given up on – the kind where I actually got a choice in what happened. Maybe he'd let his guard down because he was drunk? Either way, it just felt so good to lie there in bed enjoying the feeling of sleeping naked and waking up next to the man who'd had such a hold over my emotions for so many years, but who I still didn't really understand.

'He was lying on his side, facing away from me, still asleep. Hugging himself. I remember watching for a few seconds, examining his long fingers and carefully clipped nails and thinking, Why oh why did he not just love me in an ordinary sort of way? It's all I ever wanted.'

She looked at Holly, who didn't smile. Stevie took a deep breath and began again.

'I don't know why he had an affair. I know we had our issues, some of them quite serious, but in our own funny way we got on. Or at least brushed the issues far enough under the carpet to stay together for the children. Anyway, the weird thing is, as we were getting ready the evening before, he had started a conversation about how friends of ours all seemed to be having affairs and weren't we lucky to still love each other so much. I remember thinking how out of character it was for him to be talking about our marriage at all – we just never did. He never wanted to talk about emotions or love.

'Then our friends arrived and I didn't give it much more thought, really.' She took a big mouthful of wine and sank back into the sofa again.

'I don't think he did it because he didn't love me anymore. On the contrary, according to him, I'd stopped loving him and he felt rejected by me.' Stevie's face showed her misery.

'I didn't understand what he meant. I'd always given him everything he asked for and done everything how he wanted it, including sex.'

Holly raised her eyebrows and asked, 'How did he tell you?'

This was the part that had hurt Stevie the most. As she slowly described what had happened that morning, she felt herself slipping back into all the emotions she'd gone through.

While her husband had been in the shower that morning after the party, she'd been sitting up in bed, sipping the mug of tea he'd brought her. His mobile had pinged – not just once, but several times. She'd never touched his phone before, so it was really out of character for her to reach over to his side of the bed. There were a couple of message notifications, which she could read the first line of without even trying to unlock the screen. It was enough. And then she nearly jumped and spilt her tea.

His phone had started to ring, a woman's name appearing on the screen: SHARON. Perhaps because of what she'd read in the messages, or her female intuition, she pressed the green symbol and waited, holding her breath.

'John! Answer my messages, you bastard! Who is she? John? I know you're there. Say something.'

And then the shrill voice stopped and was replaced with the sound of panicky, quick breathing, which made Stevie's stomach churn. Her throat was tight with horror and disbelief. It felt so odd to just stay quiet and not respond. But shock had paralysed her. In hindsight, what she had wanted to do was find out who the heck this woman was, and who else her husband, with whom she'd had such amazing sex only the night before, had been sharing his body with. But even as the full truth of her husband's double deception hit her like a cold wave of water, the woman, Sharon, said, in a tone devoid of emotion, 'Don't bother calling, John. It's over. I'm done!'

In spite of how her relatively peaceful world had just exploded, Stevie remembered feeling a wave of protectiveness for her husband. Then the penny dropped. Protect that bastard? The man who had cheated on her? Her husband had been screwing another woman... two other women. How many more?

Anger and panic made her dump the phone back on the mattress and pull the duvet over it. The sound of the shower and the singing had stopped. She didn't know what to do. Confront him? Lie back and continue sipping her tea and pretend nothing had happened? Or grab her fleece dressing gown from the back of the bedroom door and avoid John by going downstairs? But he'd see that there had been a call from a Sharon and that it had been answered. She had no choice. Perhaps if she just closed her eyes it would all go away and her life would not get sucked down some dark, suffocating plastic pipe like the ghost spiders she so often hoovered up from the corners of the house. She had thought about how next time she would leave them be. Even fragile, seemingly irrelevant creatures have a right to exist. She squeezed her eyes hard like lemons, trying to stop the hot tears. But it was pointless.

'Alright?' Her husband's voice brought her back into the now, but she just couldn't pluck up the courage to do what she knew she had to do. Not yet. She needed a moment or two. Once he had seen his phone. Then there would be no alternative.

In the end, she made her escape by taking a shower. Never had hot water gushing over her head felt so welcome. Her shoulders were strong and had supported many troubles in the past, but her instinct told her that this was about to be one of the messiest shitshows yet.

'Anyway,' Stevie dragged herself back into Holly's beautiful, cosy and safe sitting room, complete with gently snoring dog. 'I couldn't forgive him. I just couldn't. It hit me hard. I told him to leave and said I never wanted to see him again. It was the first time I'd ever stood up to him. Then I walked into a lake.'

Holly's jaw dropped as she gripped Stevie's hands. 'What? You walked in—'

'Yes, and I wasn't going to walk out again. I just wanted to go, leave him, the children, everything. It felt as if he'd stripped me of all dignity, self-esteem, love, imagination, dreams, respect—'

'And where? Where did you go? Was it Crummock?'

'Yes, where else?' Stevie instantly regretted snapping at Holly because of course her friend knew that it was the *only* lake as far as she was concerned. None of the other lakes or bodies of water in the Lake District had her heart or soul. 'Down at Bird Poo Island. Where we swim.'

Holly's eyes gave away her concern. Stevie could see that she had almost reached the limit of the information she could handle in one go, but she needed to say just one more thing.

'I think if it had been anywhere else, I might not be here today. I can honestly say that for some reason, as soon as I was waist deep, I knew it wasn't the right thing to do. So, I just swam until I was thinking more clearly. I know it sounds completely barmy, but that water is unique. There's something about it that accepts fears, tears, and worries, and takes them away from you. It washes you clean and releases you.'

She stopped and looked at Holly. 'It released me from everything that day. I walked back out feeling calm and knowing that I was going to be okay. What had happened hadn't been my fault, but it's taken me a long, long time to truly believe that.' She ignored Holly's look of disbelief. 'And I've been walking into that lake first thing in the morning ever since.'

Holly sank down on the floor next to the sofa and leant back against it. She stared into the flames of the stove. 'Sorry, Stevie, but I've just got to say it: what an absolute First Class bastard. Not only did he have an affair, but why the hell would anyone do that to a woman as beautiful, inside and out, as you?'

Both women sat for a little while deep in thought. It had been a huge deal for Stevie to talk to someone about what she had done that day. She'd never told anyone before, but it had felt right to trust the truth with someone she now shared the water with, someone who would appreciate seeing her for who she really was.

Both of them sighed in unison, then laughed at the ridiculous way life tossed you around like flotsam. A log popped, the tension burst, and the dog jumped, then put his head back down on Stevie's lap. Holly pulled herself up and looked at her watch as she did so. 'It's getting late. Would you like another drink, a cup of tea, talk some more?'

'I'd love a cup of tea, if that's okay? Not sure I can go to sleep quite yet. I think I need to have a bit of ordinary, if you know what I mean?' Stevie gently nudged the dog off her lap and stood up, stretching a bit. 'Shall I put another log on for you?'

Chapter Twenty-Two

ANGELA

November

As she drove back up the dark farm track with her headlights on full beam, Angela felt increasingly sick, even though nothing at all had been said about what had happened in the yard earlier that week and her mother-in-law had given nothing away – no funny looks, no pointed comments. It was all very odd and the very lack of repercussions had made Angela feel uncomfortable. Was it because she'd stood up for herself? Had what she said sunk in? Perhaps from now on things would be different around the farm. If that was the case, she wished she'd done it sooner!

She could see a light on in the kitchen, its warm glow shining out through the seventeenth century window into the yard. She could just make out Ed at the sink, probably washing the dishes. Tea had been eaten and tidied away before she went out, but Ed had offered to wash up so that she could get off out to Holly's. His mother had made no comment at the time, but just gone as usual into the sitting room to watch TV. Something as domestic and calm as washing up being done should have reassured Angela.

Instead, it raised alarm bells and her throat felt as dry as sandpaper.

She parked up, turned off the engine, and sat for a couple of minutes trying to control her increasing sense of unease. It just wasn't what she had expected after the last week or so. It didn't make sense.

As the kitchen door opened and more light spilt out into the yard, she looked across to see Ed standing there, his arms folded across his chest and his legs planted firmly shoulders' width apart. His body acted like a barricade into the house. He wasn't smiling. Angela knew her gut instinct had been correct. The temptation to start the car up again and drive away was intense, but she had nowhere to go. Slowly, she pushed open the heavy car door and stepped down into the concrete yard.

'Angela.'

He *never* called her by her full name. She made herself approach the kitchen door, praying he would step aside or come towards her with his arms open in a hug. But he didn't move. This was serious. What had happened?

'Mother's gone to stay with her sister.' His voice was monotone and quiet.

'What?' Angela's heart was beating so fast she thought it was going to shatter into pieces. This was not what she had expected or feared. 'What happened? I've only been gone a couple of hours. She was fine at teatime.' Angela tried to push past Ed and get into the kitchen to look at the clock on the wall. But he was like a solid piece of granite that would weather time and centuries. Immovable.

Then he relented and let her past. It was a little after eight. Yes, she'd been gone about two and a bit hours. The silence was unbearable. Why didn't Ed tell her what was wrong with Margaret? Why was he just standing there staring at her? Choosing the right words was proving difficult and she had no idea why, except she felt guilty. Did Ed know about what had gone on the other morning?

In the end, her love for her husband, in spite of how he consistently failed to stand up for her or their marriage, proved too strong. Instead of fear of how he might react, she found tenderness for him.

'Ed, what's going on? Are you okay?' She put her hand on his arms, but they were locked tight. His face was tense and his eyes red – he'd definitely been crying. 'Ed, my love, please tell me she'll be okay?'

He nodded, but still didn't say anything.

'It's me, isn't it? She's gone because of what I said about going swimming.' The instant she said it, she regretted it.

Ed moved away from her and back to the sink. He pulled the plug out and swished around in the water to get it to go down the plughole, along with any bits of food that had come off the crockery and cutlery. He was seething and upset, but said nothing, leaving her to assume that she was right. She hated the fact that it was her who had caused him such pain. Was the lake more important to her than him? It was a question she didn't know the answer to.

'Angela, I think you knew how Mother would react. How could you believe otherwise?' He shook his head in exasperation. 'How could you be so selfish?'

'Selfish?' The word was terrible to hear and Angela's whole body was consumed with the same rage she'd felt rise up from her belly the night she'd walked into the sitting room to tell them about the lake. She took a step towards Ed and then made herself stop. Perhaps she had been selfish to do something so inextricably and tragically bound up with this family she'd married into, but it was the only thing she had here that she could call her own and it was precious. Couldn't her husband see that? Was he so under his mother's influence that he had no dreams or secrets of his own?

His face was impassive and he wouldn't look her in the eyes. *So that's it*, thought Angela. Emotional blackmail. Whatever had happened to his mother was Angela's fault. Ed's face showed her that's how he felt; he didn't need to say anything else.

She felt physically sick. When Ed's mother returned from her sister's, where did that leave Angela? Without farming blood in her veins, maybe she would never be good enough. Old school, that's what Ed's mother was, and she was never going to change, even though Angela knew plenty of farming families where non-farming people had been welcomed in, along with new ideas, fresh energy, and an enthusiasm for much-needed diversification in order to protect the future of the farm.

She'd told Ed when they first met that she didn't want children and it didn't seem to bother him at the time. Had his mother been pressuring him about children? Had he told her that he would never produce an heir so long as he was married to Angela? He never spoke about wanting a family or needing the next generation to take over the farm – it was almost as if the only reason he put his life's energy and focus into acres of upland and flocks of tick-ridden sheep was to keep the memory of his father alive and to make his mother's last years more bearable.

Angela had lied to him, though. It wasn't that she didn't want children, it was that doctors had her told after her miscarriage at fifteen that she was unlikely to be able to have them. Not telling Ed about that time sat heavily with her, but she just didn't know how to broach the subject after all these years. She'd been raped. The pregnancy was the result of forced sex, not love. She'd been worried he would change his mind about being with her and now she was sure he'd hate her for having lied to him. It was a no-win situation. There had just never seemed to be a good moment to tell him.

What kept her going now, though – and she hated herself for even thinking this – was that if Margaret stayed at her sister's, then Angela could see a light, or at least a glimmer, at the end of the dark tunnel. She and Ed would be left to run the farm themselves and they were good at that, or maybe they could sell up the farm and start a new life somewhere else, just the two of them – what a relief that would be!

'Ed, listen to me. Your mother and I had words, yes, but we can work this out. I'm so sorry she felt she had to do this. Please tell me what happened. How long will she be there? Please talk to me.' Her voice sounded shriller than she wanted it to, but that nauseous feeling had turned to panic. Angela shook her head and plonked herself down on one of the kitchen chairs.

'She's staying indefinitely.'

Those words were like a huge full stop at the end of the conversation, but she needed to hear them. The next few days would be significant and might even give her the opportunity to have a real conversation with him, get everything off her chest and out in the open. But she could tell that nothing else was going to happen tonight. Ed had reached his limit and needed time to work out how he was going to deal with the situation.

He left her sitting in the harsh fluorescent-lit kitchen. The space he had left was almost instantly filled with the greasy smell of recent cooking and the slightly antiseptic own brand washing up liquid drifted up and worsened the nausea she already felt. She tried to hold it back, but she only just made the sink in time before everything she'd consumed over the last few hours poured out of her small body. And again. Until there was just a rusty taste in the back of her throat from the effort of retching. The taste instantly whisked her back twenty-seven years to when she had just wanted to die because of shame and the damage that she had suffered, both emotionally and physically.

She'd been sick like this every day for a few weeks, which was how she'd known the seed of violation and abuse had germinated. When the vomiting had stopped on the seventh week, instead of feeling relief, she had felt fear. What now? Did this mean the baby was no longer living? Or would she now start to grow a belly and have to hide away even more from her parents and friends? She was only fifteen – not a child, but not an adult either. The father of what was growing inside her lived in her street and she hated him.

Towards the end of that seventh week, all feeling of being pregnant had vanished and the bloody mess that passed from her one morning into the toilet bowl looked nothing like a tiny human being. But she cried. She cried for her innocence, which had been flushed down into the sewer, along with the evidence of a heinous crime. But most of all, she cried for the knowledge that even if she ever could bring herself to be intimate with a man again, she wouldn't be able to enjoy any pleasure –not with the images of the toothless, dribbling old man who had raped her digging his puny but still functioning penis into that most private, sacred part of her, back and forth so fast that his eyes rolled like the devil back into his head and she prayed he would have a heart attack.

On the ninth week, she'd been rushed to hospital bleeding: the miscarriage had not been complete, so they'd had to perform some emergency surgery, which caused some damage to her uterus.

Still, she kept the identity of the man who raped her a secret and made up a boyfriend to keep her parents from further questioning.

But the perpetrator had watched her, and she had never dared tell her mother what their 'friendly' neighbour had done during the holidays while she'd been out at work. He was an old man who sat in his front garden in the summer watching the children play on the communal grass area. He walked his scrawny dog round the same patch of green twice a day, both of them slow and grey. Physically impossible, they'd say. They'd laugh at her. So she had kept silent.

Chapter Twenty-Three

CHRIS

November

The white horses charging down the middle of Crummock Water resembled the pain in his head that morning: fearsome and unrelenting. It was impossible to make any headway at all on his bike so he turned around at the National Trust car park just before dropping down into Buttermere village. It was pointless to go on any further as it was too early for the cafe to be open. He didn't feel like going in anyway because he knew Tom wasn't working there today.

It would be far easier cycling back as the wind would be behind him. He just wanted to get home, take some painkillers and crawl into bed for the rest of the day. It had been madness to head out so early on such a stormy day, but he had taken a chance that it wouldn't be so windy down the valley. As he approached the tall conifer trees, he glanced down to the lake, half hoping to see the naked woman, who he now knew was Stevie. He reckoned she could be called as daft as him if she was out here in this weather, but still he looked.

And there she was. Not naked, but standing in a huge coat on the beach staring out at the angry water. *Good,* he thought, *she's not going to chance it.* A sudden gust whipped across the lake and half blew Stevie off her feet. As she lost her balance, her coat blew open and Chris could see that she had nothing on underneath. So she was planning to swim! He had to admit that he was concerned about her going in on her own in such conditions. His fear translated into spontaneous action and he dismounted from his bike, wheeled it over to the stone wall leading down to the lake, unbuckled his helmet, and started to make his way down to the lakeshore. As he did so, Stevie took off her coat, folded it firmly into a sort of square, and wedged it down behind a rock near the water so that it didn't blow away. She didn't look up or she would have seen Chris on the footpath.

As she stepped into the frisky waves that lapped the tiny stones on the shore, her hands went up to her hair, pulling it into a pile on top of her head and looking where she was placing her feet. Her neck was exposed and, more to the point, so was her body apart from knees down where she was being washed by the water. She must've had a sixth sense, because in one fluid movement, she turned round and looked straight at Chris.

He paused on the path, frozen, with one hand up as if in a greeting and the other on top of his head as if he was checking to see if he was still wearing his cycling helmet. Embarrassment made him turn a shade of beetroot, or at least that's how hot he felt in spite of the biting wind. To be caught as if sneaking up on her when she was having a private moment seemed weird and voyeuristic. He wanted to sink deep down into the beach and through the stone wall and then grab his bike and pedal away.

'Morning,' Stevie said, saluting him with her free hand and smiling lightly. She made no attempt to cover her body, or to move further into the water to hide, or back out to grab her swim cloak. It was almost as if she believed she owned that hour of the day – it was hers to do what she liked with and if Chris had chosen the same hour to be down here, he'd have to muck in with her rules.

Unapologetic and completely at ease in her nakedness, Stevie turned back to face the onshore waves. This time, she lifted her arms up above the spray and allowed the water to smother her in coldness and tiny twigs and leaves.

Chris stood where he was on the footpath and watched. He felt no compulsion to leave. In fact, he almost wanted to strip off and join her. It looked fun and clearly she had no ulterior motive other than to immerse, reset, and start the day. But he didn't dare. Instead, he felt slightly intrusive in spite of her calm acceptance. And he just wasn't ready to expose his naked body to a woman, not even in this non-sexual non-threatening way.

He stayed long enough to make sure she'd walked out again safely and then with another wave of his hand, a few words of congratulations, and a 'that must feel good, what a way to start the day,' he headed back up the footpath to collect his bike and start the ride back home.

All day long, his mind was filled with Stevie's naked body and how strong it had looked as she stood half in and half out of the lake, defying the waves to unbalance her. He'd noticed the curve of her hips, the slight narrowing of her waist, the heaviness of her breasts, how her nipples stood to attention in the cold wind and how his body had responded to what he saw. Her eyes had dared him to join her, but her mouth hadn't spoken an invite. It was a challenge from deep within her, not from her conscious self. If she'd asked him, it would have been almost impossible to have refused, but for those few moments, it had hovered like a cloud of mutual curiosity between them. The intensity was tangible.

Chapter Twenty-Four

HOLLY

November

I t felt odd to be walking around the kitchen wearing just a corset, G-string, hold-ups, and high heels – and rather on the chilly side. Down at the lake that morning with Stevie and Angela, it was what she had agreed to do to test out the oestrogen tablets she had been prescribed by her doctor.

'Get sexy,' Stevie had said, twirling her wet swimsuit around her head and shaking her bum.

'Make sure you've got some lubricant handy,' Angela suggested with a giggle. 'It'd really ruin the moment to have to dash to the bathroom cabinet to find it.'

When Holly had shared the gory details of her visit to the doctor, it had become the only topic of conversation before, during, and after their swim. Angela said she had the same problem 'down there' and wanted to know what sort of lubricant the doctor had prescribed. Stevie wasn't sure if she needed lubricant, but had been told that the HRT patches she had been using for a couple of years to treat mood swings and hot flushes were supposed to help with that too.

'I just need an opportunity to try it out!' The cackles had echoed round the valley and Stevie hadn't minded one bit because they were laughing with her, not at her.

The Prosecco was already in the fridge and Holly had spent the afternoon preparing a delicious but light supper for that evening. Nothing too garlicky, spicy, or fishy – easy to eat off their laps in front of the wood burner, which she'd been stoking all afternoon so that the sitting room was cosy enough to not wear too many clothes. She'd bought a couple of huge glass jars from a homeware shop on the edge of town and filled them with unscented night lights.

She peeked out of the kitchen door and smiled: the gentle reflective glow created just the right ambiance of warmth and hygge she had seen in the magazines she'd been reading recently. Bringing light into the darkness of winter was a Scandinavian tradition she'd known about for years, but never really felt the need to practice in her city home. The darkness was different in this remote corner of Cumbria where there were no street lights and people kept their curtains drawn tight across tiny windows and barely a soul ventured out on the road after seven p.m.

Now, the glass jars of light just outside the porch would add their friendly presence to the existing holiday cottage fairy lights. The only problem was if it rained, the candles would be extinguished. Tonight, though, it was a clear sky, the stars were starting to come out, and the night lights would burn for hours. Holly would deal with the practicalities of outdoor hygge another time.

All this effort was directed at having sex with her husband when he came back from mountain biking. She didn't even care right at that moment whether he was caked in mud or walked into the kitchen wearing his muddy boots. Dressing up was a game they used to play when they were first together, a bit of role play, but nothing kinky. Just enough to tease each other, but it had been many years since she'd put this particular corset on and it was so damn tight that she hoped Simon would get home soon and rip it off her or she'd pass out. The heels were excruciating. How on earth had she managed a full day at work in them when she was younger?

Then she heard a car pulling into the yard and click clacked over to the window to peer out. The yard was so well lit up with fairy lights and night lights that she had no trouble seeing that it wasn't Simon's car, but one that she didn't recognise. *Help!* she thought. *Who the hell is that?* There weren't any guests expected today, or had she got the bookings mixed up?

Hopping about in her heels, not quite sure what to do, but hoping the couple would go away, she grabbed her phone from her handbag and tried to log into the holiday cottage owner's page. Too late! There was a loud knock at the door and Holly stood completely still. Then a face peered in at the window. *Oh, God!* She squealed and tried to cover herself up with her hands. Then she heard another car coming into the yard and she knew instinctively it was Simon. A car door slammed, voices were now at the door, and in walked Simon, followed closely by a man and a woman. All three stopped, a stunned look on their faces at the sight of Holly standing in the middle of the kitchen dressed like a porn star.

If anyone had told her what had just happened and how she and her husband would react, she would not have believed them. Right at that moment, she just wanted the ground to swallow her up. *My marriage is over,* she thought.

'Darling, I'm home,' Simon said in a perfectly normal, calm voice. His eyes told another story.

'Oh, good, the Prosecco is in the fridge,' replied Holly. Her heart was going like the clappers, but she stood, paralysed, as if the music had stopped in a game of musical statues.

'*Fuck*,' Simon mouthed at her as he fumbled for the key to the cottage on the back of the larder door, took one more glance at his wife, and beckoned the staring couple to follow him back out and across the yard.

Those poor people. They'd driven all the way from London for a romantic week in a Lakeland cottage just to be confronted with that! Holly could breathe again, but she knew she had to do something pretty quick before Simon came back in. An idiotic thought flashed through her head. If she changed into jeans and a T-shirt, perhaps he'd think he'd imagined it all?

'You're in trouble, girl,' Holly said to herself.

She hobbled upstairs in her stupid shoes and reached for her Missoni robe off the back of the bedroom door and yanked it around her shoulders. Not wanting to break her neck falling down the stairs, she fiddled with the flimsy straps round each ankle, trying to undo them, but her hands were shaking. By the time she'd got them undone and flung the shoes into the corner of the bedroom, she heard the kitchen door bang and then there were noises downstairs as Simon pulled off his muddy shoes. As she tiptoed down the stairs, she heard the kitchen tap start to run as he washed his hands.

'Hello,' she said quietly from the doorway.

Simon was drying his hands on the kitchen towel, but turned round to look at her. 'What the hell's going on?' He chucked the towel down in a heap on the draining board and went over to the fridge, probably looking for a beer. She felt desperately in need of the *whole* bottle of Prosecco.

'So?' His voice came from inside the fridge. 'And what's this Prosecco doing in here? Have I forgotten our anniversary?' She hoped it was her cue to go up behind him and try to placate him, reassure him that it had been a surprise, a romantic surprise.

'Let's have some now, shall we?' she suggested, trying to remain calm. 'Here, I've got two glasses.' She grabbed a couple of vintage crystal wine glasses from the shelf and put them on the table. Her dressing gown fell open. She saw Simon looking at her.

'Why are you wearing that anyway?' Not the reaction she'd been hoping for.

'More to the point, why didn't you remember that we had guests arriving today? That was rather embarrassing.' Simon popped open the bottle and poured two glasses. 'To say the least,' he added as he handed one to her.

Without another word, he walked out of the kitchen and into the sitting room.

Never in the whole time she'd known him had Simon turned down sex with her. Her outfit had clearly been intended to be provocative, not promote rejection. Holly was dismayed and embarrassed. She felt smutty and ridiculous. She thought he'd be pleased she was actually initiating sex after all the times she'd complained about it being painful. What was wrong with him? Had something happened at work? Perhaps he really had been having an affair and now found her repulsive?

The sitting room was roasting; the dog was virtually passed out on the rug in front of the stove. He was so out of it that he hadn't even appeared in the kitchen when Simon came back. Perhaps he had sensed trouble and had stayed out of the way.

Holly curled her feet up under her bottom and squeezed herself into the corner of the huge sofa. The corset was digging into her and she could hardly breathe. She didn't want to fiddle about with it now and further irritate her husband, but she longed to unlace the damn thing and chuck it on the stove. He sat on the sofa opposite in silence.

'Cheers!' she said raising her glass, but he just drank his down and poured another one. She tried to open the conversation. 'I was dressed like this, and still am, because I had planned for us to have a cosy evening in together, darling.'

Simon snorted. 'Ridiculous.'

'What? I'm ridiculous? Or the idea of spending some time together is ridiculous?' snapped Holly. That was the last straw. Why should she even try to explain something that had been planned so carefully and only with the best of intentions? It wasn't her fault it had gone tits up, was it? Possibly if she'd remembered the guests then it might still have worked out alright, she thought with a squirm. Her head had been on other matters instead, such as lubricants and swimming in ice championships.

She looked across at Simon slumped in his muddy mountain biking clothes nursing his glass. He was staring towards the dog, though the dog might as well have been in space because there was absolutely no connection between Simon's brain and anything else in the room. Where was he? What else had she done wrong? Everything had seemed fine yesterday. He'd been chatting about his week at work, checking his bike over, all the normal Friday stuff. She sighed and it was a proper sad, fed-up sort of sigh, which made both Simon and the dog shake themselves and look at her. The dog pulled himself up, stretched and walked over to Simon for an ear scratch.

'Sorry, darling,' said Simon, smiling weakly at his wife. 'I'm sorry I snapped at you. Stuff going on at work: people getting fired. I may not have a job there for much longer, but I'm doing my best to make myself indispensable.' He chuckled and scratched a bit more vigorously on the dog's ears until the animal shook his head in irritation and walked off into the kitchen to sniff at his bowl.

Holly felt an enormous sense of relief and patted the sofa next to her. 'Come here, love. I'm sorry about your work and I'm sorry about tonight too. I don't know where my head's been at, but I shouldn't have forgotten those people. Good grief! What on earth must they have thought when they saw me dressed like this?'

'You look very nice.' Simon's voice was sad, which was also not the reaction she'd been hoping for.

There was no point feeling disappointed.

'It's killing me,' she said with a laugh, wriggling about until her robe fell off her shoulders and she had her back to Simon. 'Loosen off the lacing before I pass out.'

He put his glass on the floor and reached for the black ribbon that laced the corset all the way down the back. The irony of it wasn't lost on Holly: compassion rather than passion. Were they getting old?

At least she could breathe. She stood up and let the corset drop down around her waist and then wiggled it off over her hips. She heard Simon chuckling at her and she wanted to whack him round the head with the torturous garment, hoping the hooks and eyes on the front would scratch his face. *Don't take it personally,* she reminded herself. *Next time, check the cottage diary first before sex.*

'I love you just the way you are, Holly.' Simon pulled her down next to him and held her very close. 'You don't need all that stuff. You're a beautiful, gorgeous, sexy, and...' he said, hesitating, 'very funny woman.' He nuzzled into her neck and it felt so good.

Her brain was shouting so many questions at her: what about the swim trunks, what were they all about? Would the oestrogen tablets the doctor had prescribed really have kicked in by now? Where did I put the lubricant in case they haven't? Would the cottage guests give them a shit review on TripAdvisor? Her mind was chattering away while her body was beginning to respond to Simon's touch. *Oh, well,* she thought, *I'll just have to pray the doctor knew what he was talking about.*

She braced herself for the usual pain after the initial moment of penetration, but, so far so good. In fact, very good. And she started to remember what it felt like to make love, to lift her hips up and encourage her husband to go deeper and harder.

Chapter Twenty-Five

CHRIS

December

How did Stevie and the other two women walk in so calmly? Chris winced as he stepped across the tiny stones on the beach he had always called Dead Sheep Beach because someone once found a very dead one there and called the National Trust ranger, who had removed it.

This was perhaps the most private and most dramatic place to give this wild swimming thing a go. He didn't want to do it anywhere in public in case someone he knew saw him and word got round the cycle club. It was going to be a one-off experience, just to see what all the fuss was about. Seeing how brave Stevie had been in the wild weather the other morning had inspired him to put his big boy pants on and stop fannying about on the sidelines.

Chris wanted to challenge his own personality, which automatically winced at this sudden desire of his to experience something his brain judged to be 'sketchy and flaky'. The image of Stevie, walking naked into Crummock Water on that windy morning, had never left his head. There was something about the way she had accepted the stormy conditions, lingered, dipped her hands in the water, looked up at the sky while she let her long hair be blown around her naked back and shoulders... true beauty and connection. He wanted to experience a similar connection. He wanted to be naked and feel the water with nothing in the way.

But the stones hurt his feet, the breeze made him shiver, and it was as if the lake was holding its breath, poised to wrap itself around his body if he asked it to. He was almost ready to give himself to whatever the water could do to help him step into his new life. He wanted something to guide him as he moved away from sadness and submission. He sought something to fill his soul to the brim in a way that he had never experienced before.

His nakedness somewhere other than the privacy of his own shower was a new feeling, a combination of curiosity and shame. Once both children had left home – Clare to move in with her boyfriend, Tom to live down in Buttermere with other staff from the cafe – Gail had left their marital bed. She set up her own space in the spare room and that was how it had stayed for the rest of their time together. From time to time, Chris was invited between her sheets, but he knew the no mess rules she insisted on were non-negotiable, so once she had orgasmed, she patted him on the shoulder and pushed him off so that she could roll over onto her side and go to sleep. He'd been left with no option but to stop mid-stroke, push himself off her, and go into his own room or the bathroom to finish himself off. The mechanical act had become so habitual to him after a while that he didn't even think of it as odd. There was physical contact of a sort and he enjoyed giving her pleasure – it made him feel wanted, if not actually loved. Or was it love? Even though she always said 'Love you' afterwards, he really didn't remember how love was supposed to feel. It just felt easier to accept that this was what their marriage looked like. And then it didn't matter anymore because she got sick.

As Chris stepped into the lake, he was careful where he placed his feet, avoiding larger rocks and trying to keep to the patches of smaller pebbles or shingle. By staring down at his feet, he also saw his body from the waist down: body hair thinning and fading to grey as it tapered towards his penis and scrotum. Why doesn't the hair on the legs go grey too? Should he pluck the grey ones from his pubic area? Did it matter? Why was he even thinking about his pubic area?

He put his hand under his scrotum and squeezed just slightly, noticing that his penis became slightly erect even in the chill air. But then he let go. It may have been early in the morning and this beach was known as the quiet side of Crummock, but even so, this was not the place to be doing that sort of thing!

The further out he walked, the more peculiar he felt – not physically, but emotionally. A part of him was drawn to just keep walking until the water swallowed him up. Was that how Stevie felt every time she walked in? What was it like to let yourself just go like that? He shivered. *Come on, man, focus on this thing you're doing, nothing else. Plunge in, get it done.* He winced as the water bit into his testicles. It felt as if they were retracting back inside his pelvis. And it was only going to get colder as winter set in and by February… definitely at its coldest. Swimming with those ladies in February? Not a chance!

Taking a massive breath, he flung himself forwards, head down and as he sank down into the swell, he let out that same breath through his nose, watching the stream of bubbles under the water and feeling the cold on his teeth even though his lips were closed tight against them. Rising up through the surface, he let his feet sink until he touched the bottom on tippy toes and the roar that came from his throat rang out loud. The sound echoed around the lakeshore and was testimony to the conversations he'd never dared to have with Gail, the sexual frustration he'd always felt when she made him stop, the virile man who lived inside his body, but was never allowed to come out to play. He hated and despised himself, not her. The emotion he had allowed to be trapped for so long had rotted into pent-up violence and self-disgust. Astonishingly, he craved this new feeling, this shock of cold immersion as it ripped at his body and his mind, desperate to get at the warmth of his heart. He wanted it to suck him dry, make him reel from agony and ecstasy, and leave him drained but deeply cleansed of all that had become so negative over the last twenty or so years.

Now he understood the woman whose face he saw reflected on the water's surface close to his own. Hers was calm and tender, his in agony. Knowing her more intimately was something he knew he needed, but how that might happen, Lord only knew! A glimmer of a thought came into his head, probably put there by the water he'd just submerged in: perhaps if he offered to join their team? Did that mean he now felt ready to become 'her man' and strip down to Speedos several times a week with her and the other two women?

He knew that even if he did, she was highly unlikely to look at him in any other way than as the missing piece to their damn winter swimming team. It certainly would not give him permission to fantasise about holding anything other than her hand to steady them both across this uneven and slippery lakeshore.

Chapter Twenty-Six

ANGELA

December

After she'd wiped her hands on the towel by the sink, Angela took a deep breath. It had been a week since Margaret had moved out to stay with her sister and almost the same amount of time since she and Ed had spoken more than ten words to each other. At night, the gap in their bed seemed to grow wider and Ed's bulk more solid and defensive. If something didn't thaw out the tension pretty soon, Angela knew she would feel compelled to move out herself – she bet it would then only be a matter of hours before Ed's mother came home. But that's not what she wanted, not at all.

Ed mattered to her, and her life on the farm was exactly that: her life. Where else would she go? It wasn't as if her old life, which now seemed so carefree and simple, even existed anymore. It had just been her and her mother most of her life, which had felt more like two friends sharing a house together. When Angela was only twelve, her father had left them for another woman, who it turned out he'd been having an affair with for many years. Angela had taken care of her mother for months, making sure she ate well and actually went to bed rather than fall asleep on the sofa with an empty bottle of wine in her hand. It hadn't been easy to witness the devastation, but deep down, she knew her mother would survive and have a happier life for it.

And so she had for quite a few years. Then she was diagnosed with advanced breast cancer and needed care of a different sort. It had drained Angela of any energy she had left after working full time in the local pub. After her mother's death, she had sold their few belongings, given up the tenancy of their small house, and moved into the accommodation that came with the job at the pub.

A few more years passed where she lived a simple, but peaceful life. The landlords, Bruce and Ann, trusted her implicitly with running the pub on her own if they wanted to take some holiday. She managed everything, including staff, kitchens, menus, and rooms. It was her life and left her no time to dwell on the future or the past. One night a big, smiling man had walked in and turned her world upside down. It was Ed, out for the night with some other young farmers, and from the moment he spoke to the slim, auburn-haired woman behind the bar, he was smitten. A romance that looked perfect from the outside, but it wasn't without some complications. Not only did Angela not really want to give up the pub, but she sensed already that Ed's mother didn't approve of her.

Still, she loved the big man and felt confident enough in what they felt for each other to be able to surmount any problems they faced then or in the future. He put a ring on her finger the day before the owners announced they were selling the pub. The two events couldn't have occurred more serendipitously.

Wind forward five years and now the other secret she was keeping from him was being a member of Stevie's winter swimming team and going to the championships in February. It was time she told him.

She could hear the television was on in the living room and she could visualise Ed slouched on the sofa, his long legs akimbo and his chin down on his barrel-like chest, probably snoring, but maybe with his eyes half open vaguely watching the screen. During the week, while driving to meet Holly and Stevie at the lake, she had been rehearsing how she was going to tell Ed, but had never practised it in front of them. Now she regretted that. Their support was sincere, but it felt disloyal to Ed to go into too much detail about her marriage or life at the farm.

After a few phone calls to her friend, Emma, Stevie had organised what sounded like a really fun weekend down in Oxford and needed to know for sure whether Angela was able to go. Going with the other two felt like a massive deal to Angela, but she knew that in the current circumstances, she would have to explain to Ed very clearly why she wanted to go. Having his blessing would make it all possible and give them both some space to reflect on recent events.

Turning off the kitchen light was a signal to herself that the moment had come. There was nothing like darkness to remind you of the innate human need for warmth and love. That need could be met if she and Ed talked – she had every confidence, even though her hands were shaking and all she wanted to do was waste some more time doing chores.

Now she was marching down the stone-flagged corridor towards the sounds of a familiar soundtrack: *The One Show*. Not a programme Ed would mind missing, so the timing was perfect. The conversation opener she'd been practising was at the front of her mind, so she had no idea why, when she opened her mouth to speak, something completely random came out instead.

'Ed, love, the engine light on the car has come on. Shall I book it in to the garage or will you look at it tomorrow?'

It did the trick. Ed moved his head slightly, reached for the remote, and turned the sound down on the television. 'What?'

'I said the engine light—'

'Nah, I'll take a look.' He turned the sound up again and shuffled about a bit on the sofa making himself more comfortable.

No, no, no, thought Angela. *I'm not going to give up so easily.* 'Ed, I thought I'd tell you what my plans are for next weekend, I'm excited about it and I'd love to share it with you.'

She winced. It sounded so like therapy jargon, not her way of talking at all, but desperate measures were needed and it was all she had.

'I'm listening,' said Ed, but didn't move or take his eyes away from the screen.

'If you're listening, then why not look at me too? How do you know I haven't grown horns or dyed my hair black?'

The television went off and Ed sat up and turned to face Angela, who was perched on the edge of the chair by the stove – his mother's chair.

Angela one, Ed zero. She felt a tiny lurch of her stomach. Here goes!

'I've been invited down to Oxford to stay with some friends, well, friends of one of the women I swim with.' She decided to go the whole hog and tell him then and there about the winter swimming championships, but wanted to take it slowly and get Ed on board with the idea of going down to Oxford first.

Ed shook his head and he reached for the remote again, but Angela was quicker. 'No. Let's just take a few moments to talk about how and when I'm going, what it means for you here on the farm on your own – the practical things, you know.'

To Angela's relief, his face relaxed a little and she felt able to continue, but instead of sitting in Margaret's chair, she moved to perch on the edge of the wooden chest they used for a table in front of the sofa. It was close enough to Ed, but not squashed in next to him on the soft cushions – maybe they'd get there at some point if all went well, but she kept a lid on such a hopeful thought.

'So, when are you going?' asked Ed, actually looking into Angela's eyes for the first time in a week. 'Mother's wanting to come home. I don't know what to say to her.' He shook his head sadly and sighed. 'I can't live like this, Ang, it's ridiculous. I feel caught between a rock and a hard place.'

His words hit her like a ton of cold, powdery soft snow, leaving her buried under emotion and struggling for breath. While she metaphorically spat out snowflakes, reaching for the right words, Ed had time to continue to talk and it seemed there was no stopping him.

'I love you both, but I can't live with you both if this nonsense continues. It's Mother's farm still, but you're my wife. Can you see how impossible it is? If I take Mother's side, I'm hurting you and if I protect you from her crazy behaviour, it'll only get worse and we'll get more of this.' He waved his arm across to the now empty chair by the fire. 'Mother is a good woman, you know.'

Angela wanted to say otherwise, but having recomposed herself, she knew now was not the moment to disagree.

Ed continued, 'Losing Dad near killed her. It's certainly warped her sense of normal and tolerance. You won't remember much of how she was when Dad was alive, though. We'd only just met really.'

Angela shook her head and smiled and Ed smiled back. Something in him had softened slightly and she felt her shoulders ease down from round her ears.

'He was her world, her everything. It was a Great Love. Did I ever tell you more about him?'

Angela shook her head; Ed had hardly ever talked about his mother and father even when they first met.

'He didn't come from a farming background, you know, but they met when he was here one summer vacation from his university, working his way round farms to learn more about animal husbandry. He was training to be a vet.'

Angela was astonished. She knew the farm had been handed down to his mother from her family, but had assumed his father came from another farming family. No wonder Ed had never been bothered about her own lack of farming genes, but surely his mother should have been more understanding given she'd married a man from 'outside', so to speak.

'That's quite a sacrifice he made for love! I'm so sorry about your dad. Your mother's grief is completely understandable and I've never doubted it.' She hesitated, then found the courage to add, 'All I've found unfair is why she's never taken the time to get to know me and I've done nothing but be kind and patient with her. Well, until recently! But I was pushed too far, she pushed me too far, and I had to react. I'm sorry.'

'You did. And I get it, Ang. I've watched how you've been with her and I've prayed every day that gradually her thorny exterior would soften, she'd let her barriers down, and allow you to come into the family.'

'Were we getting close?' asked Angela with a tiny chunk of hope and even greater sense of fear that if she'd just waited a bit longer...

'No, I don't think so. Your announcement about swimming in the lake knocked it back a few months, but to be honest, I think her grief is so engrained in her psyche now, there's little you could've done to change things.'

'Could've? That sounds so final! As if I'm not going to see her again – what do you mean, Ed?'

'Slip of the tongue, Ang.' He reached out his huge hand and patted her knee, but didn't leave his hand there. 'So, change of subject, when, why, how?' Ed leant back into the sofa and looked at Angela, waiting for the detail.

'Oh! Right, yes, going to Oxford.' Angela paused and with an enormous leap of faith, said, 'Ed, can I tell you the truth, I mean the whole truth? About why we're really going, I mean?'

Ed frowned, not in an angry way, but more as if he was confused. 'Why wouldn't you want to tell me anything but the truth? I can take it, Ang, I was brought up having to make life and death decisions, given jobs that were maybe too tough for my age, but out on the fells in a blizzard there was either a ewe missing or there wasn't. Think of the time and effort to search by quad bike and if I'd counted wrong, or not bothered to count the ewes at all, there'd be consequences. Mother will tell you that I just did as I was told'. His voice trailed off and for a moment or two he was elsewhere, lost in memories. And then he shook his head slowly before sighing deeply.

'For God's sake, Ang, I'm exhausted from all this. All these emotions. I can't handle it. Just tell me and we can deal with it. It can't be that bad! Or is there something you're not telling me about, like another man?' His laugh was half-hearted, but gave Angela the confidence to realise that the corner had been turned. Now it was down to her to share everything, just as Ed had spoken out about how he felt so trapped by the situation too. She took a deep breath and started to tell him about the winter swimming championships and how much it meant to them all.

Chapter Twenty-Seven

THE ARCTIC FLAPPERS

December, Oxford

As Stevie reached the suppository-shaped orange buoy anchored in the far-right hand corner of the lake, she trod water briefly to check where Holly and Angela were. There they were – not that far behind, swimming breaststroke and chatting away as if out for coffee and not doing the 450-metre course in an old gravel pit outside Oxford. The water temperature was a chilly six degrees and rather blue from the chemicals the owners put in it to stop algae and weed proliferating. Heads down front crawl meant Stevie saw more blue water than sky, but even so, she didn't really take in anything under the surface aside from the one or two wafting weeds now and again, which made her twitch slightly when one of them trailed through her fingers. It was strange swimming here because it was probably only about ten feet deep maximum, but she couldn't actually see the bottom except around the edges.

Sometimes a few rocks and weeds loomed up in front of her because it suddenly got shallower, but on the whole, it was just like swimming in a tank of Radox, just without the bubbles. It was quite relaxing and gave her the chance to really stretch out and concentrate on her technique. It was getting too cold in Crummock Water to do heads down front crawl.

They'd driven down from Cumbria yesterday and stayed at Emma's house just outside Abingdon. Today, they were swimming in this lake at the morning session, then they'd go into Oxford for some culture and lunch, then there was a Full Moon Mermaid Swim in the river that evening.

The main reason for the spur of the moment flying visit was to try to find that elusive man to swim at the championships with them. Their Arctic Flappers Instagram account was attracting a lot of followers, but all women. She didn't count the random men with zero posts and zero followers who sent dubious private messages, which she immediately deleted. More than likely they weren't men at all but bots.

There were loads of swimmers, like them, making their way around the course. They'd chosen the middle distance course, which took them round the edge of the lake, past a few fishermen to an orange buoy, then across the lake to another buoy before cutting back diagonally to where they'd started. Emma had to be on safety duty for an hour and Stevie waved at her as she sat in a deck chair on the jetty, peering through binoculars at all the swimmers. There were also a couple of safety kayaks floating about, checking everyone was okay.

And there were men here too! Quite a few of them. All ages, sizes, and abilities. Surely this was the perfect place to scoop one up and invite him to join their team?

Stevie had got out, pulled on her swim cloak, and was having a chat with her friend when Holly and Angela finished their loop. Used to changing out in the open on the lakeshore, it was weird to see picnic tables, wooden shelves, and even a few hooks there for swimmers to use. But even more of a luxury was a communal outdoor changing room right in front of the clubhouse, which was in fact a converted shipping container. If people preferred, they could use another container, which provided the luxury of toilets and showers.

Stevie cringed at the thought of this in the Lake District, but the activity and buzz here was exciting: young kids from the local swim club like a pod of dolphins whizzing round the circuit with a coach tucked into a safety kayak in fairly close proximity, offering encouragement to them to keep going or instructions to lift their arms a bit higher, reach out further.

'This is Stevie from the Lake District,' said Emma when she joined them after completing her safety duty. 'She's looking for a man!' Everyone snorted with laughter or looked shocked.

Stevie found herself explaining over and over again that it wasn't that sort of man she wanted, but a specific man who would swim with them. She found it hard to get a word in edgeways because everyone knew each other and her conversations with people were constantly getting interrupted as their own friends joined them.

Holly and Angela, who were both now dressed, also squeezed into the clubhouse and were ready for a mug of coffee. They regrouped around the kettle and shared their views on how they were getting on, how much they'd loved swimming there, how friendly everyone was, and had Stevie found a man yet.

'I saw you chatting to a group of men,' said Holly with a wink-wink nudge-nudge expression. 'Any luck?'

'Nah! None of them swim skins through the winter. They all wear wetsuits. There are a few who don't, apparently, but they're not here today. Maybe tomorrow.'

Then Holly stepped backwards onto someone's foot as she was getting out of someone else's way. 'Oops, sorry!' she said.

It was getting very busy inside the building, partly because there were three huge sofas and not enough standing room. It was a man, and, to the embarrassment of Stevie and Angela, she went straight in for the kill.

'Um, I was just wondering, do you swim just in trunks right through the winter?' The man nodded and smiled at Holly. Encouraged, she continued, doing a sort of wiggle and a sway as she spoke to him. She was flirting! Stevie and Angela exchanged glances and laughed. Go, girl!

The rest of the conversation was swallowed up by the general buzz. *Time to escape,* thought Stevie. She gesticulated towards the door and she and Angela squeezed carefully in between people and out into the fresh air where they both took a long, deep breath and smiled.

'What a morning,' said Stevie. Angela nodded but seemed distracted.

'Are you okay, Angela?' asked Stevie now that she could hear herself think.

'Hmm, so-so.' Angela seemed to be caught off-guard and blurted out, 'Things really aren't so good with Ed. His mother has gone to stay with her sister because of me.'

'Oh, my God! Really?' Stevie wasn't sure whether to feel pleased or concerned. If anything, she'd half expected Angela to say that she had decided to move out, not the mother-in-law. 'Sorry,' she said, giving her friend a hug. 'But why do you say because of you?'

'This swimming thing.'

'My God! Surely not? It's just going swimming with friends, it's—'

Angela interrupted, 'You know that her husband, Ed's dad, he drowned? I told you about that, didn't I? Okay. Well, I think Margaret is still paranoid about anyone going in the water.' She shrugged her shoulders. 'That's what I think anyway. But the good thing is we've talked about it all, Ed and I.'

'That's good,' said Stevie, thinking, *What a weird situation.* 'So, he knows you're down here with us. How did he feel about that?'

'Oh, he wasn't worried about me going away, but was not happy about the swimming championships.'

'Hey! I've got a possible.' Holly's voice interrupted what Stevie had been about to suggest to Angela. 'He's called Mike, he's an experienced winter swimmer, and he's going to check his diary to see if he's available for the championships!'

'Well done, you,' said Angela quietly.

Emma reminded them that there was a group of ladies going down to the river that evening for a moonlit skinny dip. Stevie knew her friend had in the back of her mind how much of an impact the naked forest swim in Norway had had on her. They both agreed that perhaps Holly and Angela would benefit from letting go of worries and basking in the moonlight naked. 'There's something mysterious and slightly illicit about night swimming,' said Emma, 'as if you were stealing something from the dark and turning it into your own special bit of warmth and light.'

One by one, as jeans, hoodies, T-shirts, bras, and knickers were pulled off and neatly folded or carelessly chucked down onto the grass, the figures became women: breasts, buttocks, hips, and bellies. Emma pulled something long and glittery from her bag and flapped it about in the frosty air – a mermaid's tail, complete with fin. She pulled it on over her legs and posed for a photograph, stretching her arms across herself in feigned modesty.

The air filled with the sound of giggles, whispers, and squeals as hands grasped hands to help each other down the steep, muddy bank onto the little beach by the river. Only the mermaid was left and she hopped across the grass until she was right at the edge of the slope. Nothing for it but to sit down and slide onto the sandy beach four feet below. There she sat, giggling until tears ran down her face; mascara and sequins mixed together in a sparkly mess down her cheeks.

Someone had to go in first or they'd be standing there all night for the early morning dog walkers to point and stare at. So two women braved it. The first waded out up to her waist clasping her phone protectively, wanting to photograph the moon, which cast its white glow as it hung huge and low above the river. She beckoned to the others to join her for a selfie – a teetering, beautiful tangle of arms, curves, beaming faces, and hair.

The water on this winter night was bitingly cold and a bit rivery as the women swam against the gentle flow towards Little Wittenham and Dorchester. Heads-up breaststroke allowed disjointed conversations about currents, cow poo, who could wee while they were actually swimming, whether your boobs caused drag, and what would they do if a boat came along and had anyone ever seen a boat on the river at night in November? Squeals erupted now and again as the mermaid tail swished against someone's leg.

The riverbanks loomed high above them, mostly inaccessible because of the brambles and bushes, even in their winter state, and the water was too deep to stand.

'Did someone leave a light on the beach?'

A moment's panic, until one of them piped up that she had brought battery-powered fairy lights and left them in a huge glass jar on the bank above the beach to mark their point of access.

The swimmers had abandoned their clothes, along with their human trappings, to become part of the river and the life that belonged in the water. Long hair wafting around their shoulders joined the weeds that brushed against their bellies like a dead man's fingers. Ring-less hands spread like frog's webbed feet pulling through the water. Nostrils twitched close to the surface;

every breath a palette of decaying greens, woody browns, goosey greys, and sulphurous yellows.

All was silent now on the riverbank near the piles of clothes as a tiny water vole scuttled out of its home, ran along a precarious twig, paused to sniff the air, and then plopped into the water, scaring the lone swimmer who'd turned before the others to float gently back downstream to the fairy lights. Once safely in the gently illuminated sandy shallows, she wallowed, relishing the feeling of complete liberation here in this secret world of water.

It was Stevie, listening to her own body as it spoke to her of connection to its wilder self, a self that had never been allowed to truly flourish, but which had come out to play in the icy river pool in the Norwegian forest.

A woman of logic and stoicism, it had always gone against her nature to be flowery and spiritual, but slipping naked into the watery artery of London with other women of all different shapes, sizes, abilities, and backgrounds had felt so completely natural. It was as if with a flick of the mermaid's tail, society's units of measurement and quantification had vanished, replaced by emotion, sensory overload, and a desire to be at one with the world.

'I am slowly changing,' she told Holly and Angela on the walk back across the water meadows to the car. 'I am starting to see my body in a completely different way and I feel good about it.'

Back in Cumbria the next evening, it was hard to leave Stevie's car and the warmth of friendship to step out onto the muddy, stony track and begin the walk back up to a life Angela wasn't sure existed anymore. She'd asked Stevie to drop her here because she didn't want her friends to get involved in any awkward situation; it seemed unfair after such a long drive. Ed hadn't objected to or supported her trip down to Oxford, but he had not been happy about the winter swimming championships. He thought it sounded frivolous and potentially dangerous. This was her problem, though, and she had to deal with it. She had absolutely no idea whether Ed would be on his own in the house, or whether his mother might have used the opportunity of Angela being away to come home.

The kitchen light and the yard light were on. Angela felt her heart pounding under her hoodie and was feeling far too hot. Stress had increased the frequency of her hot flushes over the last week or so to the point where it could happen at any time, anywhere. This was not a good moment to be having one. It made her feel lightheaded and not in the mood at all for facing whatever was behind that kitchen door.

She pushed down the handle, half expecting it to be locked. Inside, Ed was sitting at the kitchen table eating his tea. No sign of his mother – still at her sister's, hopefully. He looked up as Angela walked in out of the dark. She noticed that his knife and fork were shaking slightly as he held them in midair above his plate. She instinctively wanted to reach out, take the cutlery from him, and hold his hands to stop the shaking. But she didn't dare to speak, let alone touch him. Her throat was so dry. How many steps was it to that glass she noticed sitting on the draining board? Why was she even counting steps across her own slate floor? She walked in across the mat, closed the heavy door quietly behind her, put her bag down and said, 'Hello.'

Ed dropped his cutlery on his plate with a clatter and stood up. Angela wished he'd stayed sitting down because then he seemed less large. 'Hello,' she said again, more quietly, trying not to convey her nervousness. She went over to the sink and poured the glass of water she needed so badly. Her tired imagination flipped into scary film mode and she spun round, half expecting to see Ed standing right behind her with a knife. *For God's sake,* she told herself, *get a grip!*

'Are you okay?' His question took her by complete surprise. She walked slowly towards him, put the glass down on the table, and stood right up close to him. She was desperate to be hugged and told everything was alright. But he just stood, his arms hanging down by his sides. She realised that all the fluster and anger had drained out of him, if there had ever been any. Maybe it had all been in her imagination?

She took a risk and put her arms around his waist and pulled herself closer to him. He didn't respond and that's when she realised that actually, she'd been right. All was not well. Something had indeed happened.

'What's wrong, Ed?' She held onto his arms and stood back a little so she could look into his broad, wind-chapped face. Those brown eyes that crinkled around the edges when he smiled – but it really had been a long, long time since she'd seen him smile, a proper big smile.

'Mother's in hospital. They had to do emergency surgery last night.' He pushed her away from him gently, stepped back towards the table, and slumped down in his chair, unable to continue.

'Oh, Ed! Why didn't you ring me?' She felt awful that she hadn't been there to be with him. Whatever she thought of Ed's mother, as Ed's wife, she should have been with him. This was all going horribly wrong. Now, instead of resentment and fear, she felt guilt and anxiety. 'Is she okay?'

'She's comfortable, but her heart is very weak. I need to go back into the hospital shortly to sit with her.'

'I'll drive you. Give me two minutes to use the bathroom and I'll be back down. You can't go alone.'

Ed said nothing. He just sat. Angela thought he was probably in shock and had been coping with the situation because he was alone and had to. Now she was here, it was all coming crashing down. It certainly was for her, but she also knew that all she wanted to do was be with him. There was no place she'd rather sit than at his side until this went one way or the other. Nothing else mattered. Nothing.

Chapter Twenty-Eight

ANGELA'S LAST SWIM

December

Early-December sunlight no longer contained much warmth, but it highlighted the last threads of the year's colours, strewn like discarded rags across the fells and hedgerows. It intensified the russets, browns, burgundies, and yellows of the dying bracken, bare branches, and stripped back tree trunks. Evergreen leaves and tempting red berries shone and quivered in the slight breeze. The greyness of stone walls and scattered rocks echoed the mood of the three women who stood on the lakeshore slowly undressing.

This morning there was no excited chatter, rants, or giggles, just silent, thoughtful companionship.

Angela's last swim was not a time of celebration or even sorrow, but just a quiet acceptance that, for now at least, priorities beyond her control had swept her away from the lake and into something bigger than any of them.

Ed's mother had not recovered well from her heart surgery and was unlikely to leave the hospital. Angela had to take over the work on the farm herself so that Ed could sit by his mother's bedside for as long as he wanted or needed. He was struggling to deal with the situation – not sleeping, not eating, and hardly talking. As soon as he had told her the news, she had gone with him to the hospital.

In her head, Angela had said goodbye to the woman who had either ignored or criticised her since the day she'd married Ed. Anyone dying was sad, but it was far sadder to see someone she loved hurting so badly and being unable to soften his grief.

Every day since returning from Oxford, she had pulled on the foul weather gear and taken over responsibility for ensuring the livestock had enough to eat, that none of them were stuck on their backs and needed heaving back over, fences and walls were in good repair, the books were updated, and records maintained.

But, after a few days, she knew she needed a last moment of serenity and friendship in the lake to give her the strength to sustain this new regime. Would Ed crumble completely at the inevitable loss of his mother? How long would he need to recover? The winter was a tough time as a sheep farmer, but on top of that, she was scared about how well she'd cope on her own and whether the physical and emotional stress would trigger anxiety and an inability to function. Would the relentless cycle of each day be enough to stop her struggling with the loneliness she already experienced? Wild swimming with Holly and Stevie had started to give her some self-confidence, purpose, and happiness, but with that gone, how was she going to hang on to those shoots of hope?

She tried to imprint this last swim onto her soul, mentally noting down exactly how she felt. *If I don't say a word as I walk into the water, every tiny change in sound, touch, and sight is intensified until the heat of the chilli prickles becomes unbearable and my breath escapes in a shriek of joy. As the splash of the lake hits my face, smell and taste rush into the mix – it becomes a full orchestra of sensations as my mind fights with my body and my soul comes out of hiding, holds itself strong and invincible, the true warrior comes out to play.*

'Oh God, how am I going to survive without this?' Angela spoke at last as she pulled through the water in the space between her swim buddies.

'Don't,' groaned Holly. 'Don't think, just swim.'

Angela wanted this last swim to go on and on, possibly forever. They wanted to swim right down the length of Crummock and back, but the water was now hovering around five degrees, too cold to stay in for more than a few minutes. Even if Angela had not turned round, she was sure they would have grabbed her tow float and made her swim back to the beach. It felt good to know that because this swim might be their final one for however long it took for her to join them again, neither of them wanted her to feel too down. She hadn't needed to explain how much she would miss spending a couple of hours away from the responsibilities of the farm with nothing to worry about except not staying in too long, being able to pull her socks onto blue-cold feet, and finding the strength to twist open the lid on her Thermos. They had been disappointed too about giving up her place in the championships, but they understood how worried she was about Ed. If anything could give her the proof that it was all worth battling for then it would be the memory of a really good, happy, safe swim here, where neither of them had ever made judgements, or asked anything of her except to walk in with them, dunk down with them and swim back out again with them.

Sitting on the beach wrapped up in their layers, half hidden under thick bobble hats, the women shared hot drinks and cake. Stevie told them that she'd had a message from the Oxford ladies: the man Holly had spoken to had strained his shoulder so wasn't swimming at the moment, but a man who used to swim at the club and now lived in Scotland was keen to meet them and join the team. He was an experienced ice swimmer, had just finished working on the rigs, and it would fill in his time before he went travelling. It was the news they wanted to hear, but it was received with mixed emotions. If he was suitable, then how ironic that they'd now be looking for a woman to replace Angela. Of course, there was a slim chance they'd find two men. After all, there was nothing in the rules about male/female balance, just that the team had to be a mixed four.

'Yes, but that'll be so much easier,' said Angela. 'You could even go up to the championships and find someone there if necessary.'

'It'd be mad to leave it so late, though. We'll have to try and find someone before then,' said Stevie.

'What about your Oxford friends? One of them still might do it.'

'I know they're all already sorted, but I'll ask just in case things have changed. Ohhh, isn't life shitty?' said Stevie, giving Angela a one-armed hug.

'You can say that again.' Angela's smile was sad. She hugged Stevie back, but then jumped up and turned to face them both. 'Right, you two... You two strong, beautiful women. You go get your man! Do this for me okay? I'll be fine. Keep in touch with me. Come and visit? I can give you jobs!' Angela laughed. 'But seriously, do not give up on this just because of me.'

Chapter Twenty-Nine

CHRIS

December

The more he considered offering to be 'Stevie's man,' the more often Chris thought of her until he knew he would do it, if for no other reason than to just see those blue eyes light up with pleasure.

But the moment to offer never seemed to come along. He didn't know how to contact her and every time he cycled along the lake, even early in the morning hoping to catch her, he was the only person there, not even another swimmer unclipping their tow float from around their waist as he unclipped his feet from his pedals to stop and look for her on the lakeshore or out in the water.

It felt important to Chris to tell her himself, face to face. He chuckled because it reminded him of when he'd had to pluck up the courage to ask Gail out on their first date. He'd hung around where she worked on the off chance he'd catch her escaping the office to get a bite to eat at lunchtime, or later in the day happen to bump into her as she left at five p.m. In the end, it was her who asked him out and he'd been grateful. It saved him further awkwardness and made him feel wanted.

There he went, using that word: grateful. He shook his head in disappointment at himself for being such a spineless idiot for too long. He had been drawn by her quietness, her constant state of calm, and had chosen to ignore the flashes of irritation and unkind words that punctuated each month, then each week, until he came to expect at least one outburst each day.

It became easier to submit than to keep fighting to stay afloat in the sadness and hurt their marriage had become for him. The two bright sparks of hope in his life had always been his children: Tom and Clare.

But everything felt different now. In the same way that his late wife's moods had deteriorated from rare to frequent, his self-confidence was increasing from zero to tangible. The emotional bruises were fading and he took pleasure from something new each day: the fit of his jeans, the bulge of his calf muscles as he stood up on his pedals, the taste of a homemade pasta sauce, and the teetering pile of books on the bedside table. Everything he did felt like the first time because he could choose exactly how he did it. Adding six garlic cloves to the pasta sauce was starting to feel normal now, not rebellious. The first time he got carried away while he was touching himself one afternoon and orgasmed messily onto the duvet cover, he felt like a warrior. Afterwards, he realised the window had been open and his elderly neighbours were sitting on their patio having forty winks after lunch. Flooded with embarrassment, he had to stop himself from stripping the cover off and racing to the washing machine before he got found out and told off.

On other days, he missed Gail – not the difficult and unforgiving woman she had become before her diagnosis, but the one who had grown more gentle and loving as she surrendered to the terrible disease and asked for his help. He had seen the fear in her eyes, the fear that he would refuse to care for her after all the unkind things she had said to him over the last few years. Short of asking for his forgiveness, she had allowed him some autonomy, even if it was just because she had no one else to turn to. It was a weird kind of love, but it made Chris feel far closer to her and more valued. He had, once more, been grateful.

Chapter Thirty

STEVIE

December

'You two strong, beautiful women.' As Stevie pulled up outside her house, Angela's words echoed in her ears. She turned off the engine and sat staring into space. Were they? Or were they just two middle-aged ladies trying to hold back the years, trying to prove something to themselves?

An image of her ex-husband flashed before her; he was laughing with her about something the children had done when they'd spent a family weekend in a holiday cottage in the Yorkshire Dales. She remembered how much fun it had been there, the walk to Malham Cove and then on up the steep path to the side, right onto the limestone pavement: clints and grykes. Strange words, which the girls had giggled about at the time. Then, on a balmy evening, they'd walked all the way to Janet's Foss from the village. The air had been scented with wild garlic, a smell that now brought back memories. There had been a certain warmth between John and her. Why had it been so fragile and transitory throughout their relationship? What had she been doing wrong?

She buried her face in her hands; they were still cold from being in the lake, slightly paler on the tips of her fingers than her palms. Cold seemed to seep from those ten tips right down into her core again and she just didn't know whether she'd ever be able to warm through completely. Ever. Some days she didn't feel strong or beautiful. She felt as old as her years and ten times as lonely. That burning fire in her belly that she usually felt after swimming hadn't lasted this morning.

She questioned why she had suggested doing the winter swimming championships in the first place. Wasn't it enough just to swim regularly with a couple of friends and then resume her quiet age-appropriate life? She frowned. What was age appropriate though? Just because she was in her fifties, did that mean she had to stick to certain rules and not live beyond society's expectations? There was nothing wrong with putting on the kettle, slouching on the sofa, going to the book club, or having an early night with a book, but what if she wanted something different? What if she didn't want to be single for the rest of her life? What if she wanted the full-blooded passion she had felt in her youth? What if she did want to be loved and adored by someone who wanted to rip her clothes off rather than watch Netflix? What if she really wanted to know what it felt like to be loved on a daily basis and to give such love in return?

It would certainly be far easier if she told herself she was happy to be on her own and truly believe that singledom was liberating, because it was sometimes just so damn painful to feel the energy – often sexual energy – flow from her core, especially after being in cold water. The world seemed to assume that when women went through the menopause, the desire for intimacy and sex disappeared along with your hormones. The tide seemed to be turning as more and more women spoke out about how they really felt, but Stevie preferred to observe from a distance and just navigate her own thoughts and feelings. What she wanted above all else was a relationship. She now felt ready, switched back on emotionally as well as physically. Arvid had been the trigger and her vivid dream about him afterwards clear proof that everything was well and truly functioning!

She couldn't imagine herself going back to the Internet-dating profile she'd started to create to find a man for their swimming team or hanging around the pubs in town, though. That wasn't the sort of experience she yearned for.

What does that have to do with pulling together a team for a swimming championship in the middle of winter? Come on, Stevie. Get a grip! She switched off the engine, grabbed her phone from the glove compartment and stepped out of the car. Easing back her shoulders, she looked up at the sky: *please, someone, something, show me what I need to do. Show me where I can find someone to love.*

Chapter Thirty-One

THE ARCTIC FLAPPERS

December, Outer Hebrides

W here to swim first? Which turquoise water lapping gently onto white sand should Stevie and Holly tiptoe into? In spite of the Bahamian hues, the sea around Lewis and Harris squeezes hold of your delicate anatomy within seconds, stopping breath, thought, and movement while you stare in disbelief. How can it look like this but be so cold?

The trip had been weather dependent, given that it was mid-December and snow would have made the long journey up to the north of Scotland challenging if not impossible. Fortunately, they were blessed with clear winter skies and unseasonably warm temperatures. The plan was to drive from Stornoway to Tarbert, Harris, where they were going to meet Tors, the ice swimmer. He'd got an itinerary in mind for them, which included some of the most famous beauty spots such as Luskentyre and Horgabost. He really wanted to show them a special place that visitors didn't get to so much, Hushinish, on North Harris and if they were really feeling adventurous and fancied a walk and a skinny dip, he offered to take them over the hill to swim from a stunning beach opposite the island of Scarp. The wink he gave them made their stomachs churn, not flip.

Their man was not what they expected. They looked at each other as they walked towards someone who was shorter than either of them, much hairier, and considerably un-Viking-looking. The Viking persona had developed on the long drive up as excitement bubbled up every time they turned another corner, saw the stunning distant mountains, wooded valleys, sweeping roads, tumbling rivers, and finally the ferry that was drawing them ever closer to Tors, the answer to their prayers.

'Why do you fancy Vikings, Holly?' Stevie had said when she was at the steering wheel for the second time on their long journey. 'They did nothing but murder, rape and pillage – not exactly romantic souls!'

Holly carefully handed Stevie a roll, which she'd filled with pastrami and a few lettuce shreds, and didn't let go of it until it was safe in Stevie's hand.

'Dunno, I guess it's to do with their height, manliness... a sort of mystique, you know.' Holly had taken a huge bite out of her own roll and sat chewing thoughtfully. Then with her mouth still full, she continued, 'I reckon you can tell a lot from a man's height, but only if you look at his feet and hands too.' She tried to keep pastrami and chewed-up bread from falling out of her mouth as she laughed.

Now that they had met Tors in real life, both recalled the fantasy man they'd been creating, but it was Stevie who whispered to Holly: 'So, Tors isn't a real Viking then, given his lack of height? Not that you're going to get the chance to find out, I hope?'

'It's tempting, I must admit, the way I feel about Simon at the moment.'

'No, that's never the right thing to do, even if you're not happy,' Stevie said.

'No, I know. But I feel cross and that makes me do stupid things,' warned Holly.

'I won't let you,' said Stevie and both women smiled.

Was he even a swimmer? There was absolutely nothing attractive about him, not even his smile. If his teeth had been clean, it might have helped, but whenever he grinned, mostly at Holly, the first things she noticed were the nicotine stains and one or two bits of gunk firmly wedged between his teeth.

Stevie sensed Holly was like a coiled snake in the back seat of Tors's tatty 4x4, on the verge of gagging because he kept turning round to leer at her. Stevie prayed that Holly wouldn't feel her usual travel sickness. They'd both taken some tablets earlier because they knew the roads would be twisty. Whatever had been spilt on the matting beneath their feet was still going through the decomposition process. All they could do was leave the windows open a crack to let the stink out and not too much cold air in.

Stevie nearly jumped out of Tors's car when she felt his hand land heavily on her thigh and squeeze it suggestively. She hardly dare look across at him or give him any encouragement. When she didn't respond, he moved his hand back onto the gearstick and started to rub the top of it with his thumb. What should have been an amazing trip to swimming heaven was turning into a queasy war of attrition.

She caught Tors's twinkly blue eyes and quickly looked away, but not before he had winked at her again.

First, he drove them to Luskentyre, where they parked up above the beach in a sandy car park, empty except for his vehicle. From there it was a short and easy stroll along a pretty river, sheltered from the slight breeze that had appeared as soon as they left the car park. The sun was warmer than it had been for a while down on the beach at Crummock. It was a different climate, further north but exposed to both warming and cooling winds and currents. Tors explained how he was originally from Oxfordshire, but had bought a croft down on Harris and now that he was retired from his job on the rigs, he planned to travel for a few months then would settle into life as a crofter, hopefully with a girlfriend at his side. He needed to find one first, he laughed. Holly nudged Stevie, but received a hard look in return. Surely no woman in her right mind would have been tempted to have sex with this awful man, let alone shack up in a lonely croft with him!

The view that greeted them as they arrived on the beach could not have been conjured up in the dreams of an artist, photographer, or poet: it was the perfect sea and beachscape, composed of long lines of light and colour, texture and tone. Blues, whites, creams, blacks, greys, and yet more blues as far as the haunting island of Taransay. That island seemed to beckon them towards it, urging them to run into the delicious-looking sea and swim, swim like bionic creatures to explore its tempting beaches, mounds, coves, and rocks.

Tors led them down to one end of the beach, not far from some rocks. They could hear a waterfall. There it was, tucked away – so bizarre. A freshwater shower dripping from moss and lichen onto pure white sand and then running into the river and out to sea.

'We swim from here,' he said and started to strip off.

Holly stared at his torso. Like a bear. She looked across at Stevie, who was also staring. It appeared they had underestimated him and his obvious swimming attributes: his massive chest and shoulders, built to cut through waves and currents. His legs were strong too; he was a climber, a scrambler, used to forging his way across this craggy island stuck out in the middle of the Atlantic Ocean or working his way up and down ladders, harnessed for safety but needing strength of mind and body to power through the bite of cold metal, the rasp of sea winds, and the loneliness of rigging life.

The women removed all their outer layers down to their swimsuits and couldn't wait to run into the clear water. Stevie dipped one foot in gently and squealed loud enough to be heard on Taransay. Holly bent over laughing and Tors shook his head in amusement.

Stevie reached out to grab Holly's hand. 'We're doing this together.'

Tors, on the other hand, had marched in and was now submerged up to his chin, laughing at them. He'd gone in without a murmur as if it was tropical. He swam a few strokes of front crawl away from the shore and then came back towards them doing fly, one of the hardest swim strokes and so easy to get completely wrong. When performed well, it could be extremely powerful and incredibly beautiful to watch. He almost looked desirable from a seal's eye view. Holly and Stevie counted to three, let go of hands, dunked down, and jumped up again almost immediately in absolute shock at the bite of the water.

Then they swam, quick short strokes to get their blood flowing and leave their fears behind. The man they'd come to meet was now swimming next to them, telling them about some of the area's history. Once they'd swum through the cold, they floated and took in the view from the water, looking back towards the beach and then doggy paddled round to stare at the mass of the island. Not even Tors, who was now doing porpoise impressions, could take away from the sheer raw beauty of this wild landscape carved out of the rock and ocean.

It was time to move on to Hushinish, Tors told them as they were walking back to the car park. He'd prepared a rough picnic for them, although they'd also brought their usual hot drinks and cake, plus a few extra snacks just in case it wasn't easy to buy things.

In the car, he asked them for more details on the championships and what he needed to do to be part of the team.

At the mention of fifty metres, he roared with laughter. Now, having seen him killer whale-like in his comfort zone, they understood why. They definitely, if not a bit reluctantly, had the right man for the job. They didn't have to like him, did they?

The road from Aird Asaig to Hushinish left nothing to the imagination – it was pure adrenalin as a passenger, driver, or cyclist. This perfectly smooth, incredible thin line of black tarmac snaked its way into every nook and cranny for about fourteen miles. At some points, it clung to the rocks above a steep drop to certain death on the rocks below, where their bodies and vehicle would be thrashed to pieces by the waves and power of the sea.

'Look at that! It's a tennis court!' cried Holly, pointing out of the window. Tors nodded and pulled over so they could get out and take photographs.

'It was built about twenty years ago. They were trying to bring more recreational facilities to the island. The kids used to play tennis in the road.'

'Fabulous,' said Holly, crouching down to capture the light on the sea beyond this tiny piece of flat land where the all-weather court had been built. 'Fancy a game, Stevie?'

'Oh, you can hire rackets and balls, it's not a private court,' said Tors. 'Maybe another time?'

'Yes, let's go on, I'm looking forward to seeing Hushinish. Such a great name,' said Stevie, climbing into the back seat of Tors's car to give Holly a turn sitting in the passenger seat and be subjected to Tors's arousal technique as he rubbed his thumb round and round the top of the gearstick. She looked up and saw Tors looking back at her in the rear-view mirror. She groaned. Outside, it had just started to spit with rain and was also getting chilly.

About halfway along, the sea came right up to the road.

'But,' said Tors, 'unfortunately, you are not allowed to stop your car on this section as you are driving through private land. Permission is only given to drive through the grounds of

Amhuinnsuidhe Castle, not stop to take photographs, walk, swim, or launch a boat into Loch Leosavay, beautiful though it may be.'

The swooping road down to the beach at Hushinish revealed a strip of white sand that stood out in stark contrast to the black clouds that were gathering over the island. Out to sea it was brighter, but Tors warned them that bad weather was coming in. If they wanted to swim here, it was best to do it now. How wrong a weather forecast can be!

After their first swim, they had changed straight into dry swimsuits before adding their layers so that they were ready to swim again. It was a shock to the body to pull those warm layers off, so they wrapped their swim cloaks around their shoulders to prevent any more heat loss. No need for shoes on this beautiful fine sand. Tors set off down some shallow wooden steps leading from the car park to the huge crescent-shaped bay. There were a few white horses on the sea and the women felt a familiar childlike excitement propel them down to some black rocks, where they folded their cloaks fleecy sides inwards in case the rain came. Then they ran squealing into the breaking waves.

Light rain or sea spray? It was hard to tell. Or a bit of everything mixed in with a sprinkling of madness? Not silent water warriors, but brave nymphs marching forwards into the sea to receive its salty healing. Positive ions joined the rush of endorphins. Holding hands and raising their arms high above the waves, they shared a thought for Angela and silently thanked her for encouraging them to continue with their adventure to find a man worthy of their challenge.

~

Later that day, in their B&B, Stevie admitted to Holly that although he was genuinely disgusting, Tors would be better than nothing to keep you warm on a winter's night snuggled up in a gale-blown bothy.

'You can't be serious?!' squealed Holly.

'He's built for it! Swimming in ice, that is. And no, he is not getting anywhere near my duvet. He could be perfect for our team, but not my life.'

Holly readjusted her face from a look of utter disbelief to a huge grin. 'Oh, my god, Stevie! Not that I wanted to imagine you in bed with Tors, but at least it means your natural urges are alive down there somewhere!'

Chapter Thirty-Two

CHRIS

December

I f birthdays and anniversaries are tough for those who've lost someone special, then Christmas is even tougher. And this year, it was a double whammy for Chris: his son was leaving before the new year with his Spanish girlfriend to start a new life over a thousand miles away in her hometown near the Picos de Europa. A beautiful part of northern Spain, but it might as well have been on Mars, as far as Chris was concerned.

The emptiness looming ahead in only a matter of days left him floating on a wave of constant anxiety and irritation. Instead of just sitting back and allowing his daughter to organise the Christmas food, he took it on. If they were all leaving him, they could damn well do his traditions for once. He knew he was being childish and ridiculous. In fact, Gail's presence behind his shoulder every time he bought more crackers, or stocking fillers, only served to make him more stubborn.

He'd come down with a bad cold shortly after his solo swim in Crummock and blamed it on wild swimming – so much for all those media reports that hyped up its miracle immune system boosting properties! So he had spent a lot of time indoors in the run up to Christmas, flitting from one chore to another, achieving absolutely nothing significant and often going to bed more exhausted than if he'd run a marathon.

But in the end, the substantial meal round the over-decorated table had been fun. There had been five of them: him and his offspring and their other halves, as well as the shadow of Gail in the empty chair at the other end of the table. Halfway through the meal, he had got up and dragged the chair out of the room and found a good place for it in the hallway. He ignored the looks his son and daughter gave him. His house. His rules. As everyone rejigged their chairs slightly to make the empty space seem less obvious, he felt a shiver run down his spine. For some reason, the image of Stevie walking into the lake that first time flashed across his eyes. His legs prickled as if he was walking into the water alongside her; his feet stung as if the stones were jabbing into his own soles. Phantom cold-water immersion: now there was something some clever journalist could write about.

Just fleeting thoughts, nothing he could catch and explain to anyone, but he allowed them to slide away, knowing they'd be back.

Christmas had been mild, with no bright sunny days or night frosts, but even so the lake temperature had dropped down to about four degrees, which was excellent news for Holly and Stevie as they planned how they would increase their training for the championships. Snow tinged the fell tops one day and was gone the next, a bit like Tors, who had been such a welcoming host on Harris and perfect as their male swimmer in every way but personality, but a couple of days after the festivities, Stevie had received a long email from him. She'd read it out to Holly while they were sitting drinking hot tea after an early morning swim. His apologies were nearly as broad as his chest and shoulders. It seemed that everything that could possibly have gone wrong in his life had. He was now on his way to sunnier climes to soothe his wounds, chill his beans, and have a bit of fun. But as he planned to be abroad for quite some time, he was terribly sorry, they would need to find someone else to take his place.

'Damn his hairy arse,' swore Holly. 'I never trusted that horrible wink of his. Do you know what? I reckon he asked us up there on spec.'

'What do you mean?'

'Well, he was looking for a woman, wasn't he?'

'And we were looking for a man,' butted in Stevie, not wanting to let him off the hook, but surprised at how angry Holly was.

'Yeh, right,' Holly scoffed. 'No, I reckon he got us up there to see whether either of us would, you know, fit his purposes so to speak, before he spent a load of money going off halfway round the world to find some other mug.'

Stevie shook her head in disbelief. 'Really? But it was my friend who suggested him. I don't think she would have given us a duff so to speak.'

'Sorry, I didn't mean to question your friend, but how well did she know him?'

'Well, I don't know, but—'

'Anyway, that's it then really, isn't it?' Holly sighed. 'I'll ask Simon again. Promise him a blow job a day if he'll do it.'

Stevie nearly choked on her biscuit. Then the cold air filled with the two women cackling like wicked witches cooking up some disgusting concoction.

But Simon wasn't interested, not in the competition, not even on the terms his wife was offering him. He admitted he was still going to the lido at lunchtimes and that, yes, the water was getting colder. But, no, he didn't want to be on their team. Swimming in the pool was one thing, but the lake? In winter? He couldn't think of anything worse.

When Holly asked him for the second time if he was having an affair, he just burst into laughter. Who with? Oh, his boss. Yes, the new boss was a woman, but no, she didn't even know who he was. Yes, she did swim, too. There was a group of them who went, a sort of team building thing – very popular in the States, where she was from.

'The last thing on my mind,' he said, 'when I'm in that pool, terrified of drowning and looking a right twat, is sex.'

The Christmas holidays were busy down at Lanthwaite Woods, especially on a dry, sunny day when families were made up of visiting grandparents, noisy children, and overexcited dogs walking down to the beach for some post-lunch exercise, stone skimming, and stick retrieving. Not ideal for a quiet, soulful swim, but it was where Stevie's grown-up daughters wanted to go before they each headed back to different cities. She had brought her swim kit just in case the water drew her in.

And it did. The beach seemed to have emptied of people and the sun cut across from above Melbreak, but it was not quite ready to sink down to the horizon and cast the lake and this northern end in shadow. Stevie was happy to swim by herself, so it didn't faze her to walk in alone while her daughters had a stone-skimming competition, which degenerated into a pushing and shoving tussle with neither of them giving in. As she swam slowly, gazing down through the water, she thought once again of Angela. She'd never had a chance to swim down to the boathouse because she'd not been strong enough when she first started and then the water had got too cold for any of them to swim that far. They'd talked about doing it the following summer.

She gazed down to the boathouse. It was not achievable today, but hopefully Angela's life might soon reach a happier place so that she could join them. Stevie missed her, but in particular she missed seeing how she had embraced the wild swimming from the moment she'd taken her first tentative steps, her hands held up above the water as if by holding them high enough she could make herself warmer or get less wet. Stevie had gradually coaxed her to go in slightly further and stay in for a bit longer once she realised how wonderful it was. Every swimmer is different, though, and it had never mattered to any of them how long they were in for or how far out into the deep they swam. What overrode everything was safety and then enjoyment.

As Stevie turned back to face the beach, she noticed that there were two figures by her two girls: it looked like two men. There was now also a family with young children and two dogs creating quite a commotion nearer the weir. The dogs were running in and out of the lake, the three children were screeching, and one of them was actually crying. It was tempting to just head for the boathouse after all and sit on the quiet beach until people had gone home.

Walking out of the water when you're cold and your frozen feet are sliding about on uneven stones and rocks is never dignified, she thought, *especially if you're trying to pull your tummy in and walk like Ursula Andress.*

'Brace yourself,' she muttered under her breath, deliberately engaging her core and pelvic floor and trying to walk from her hips and nonchalantly swing her arms by her sides rather than holding them out like a butterfly in panic. She'd almost cracked it when she tripped over a rock that obviously hadn't been there when she'd walked in, of course, but must have been dropped in by the gods.

'Oh, crap!' She squealed and tumbled face first into the shallows.

Why, oh, why does it matter, anyway? she asked herself. It was much easier to get out of the lake as normal and scurry up the beach with a cheesy grin slapped on her face than it was to play a game. Who was looking anyway? Then she realised that one of the men was Chris. *Great,* she thought, as she headed towards her pile of clothing. Her eldest daughter held out her changing robe so she could get into it quickly and start disrobing.

Dropping her swimsuit to the ground, she stepped out of it and then pulled off her soaking bobble hat and discarded it on top of the swimsuit. She wouldn't be able to wear it soon, anyway, not once they were in the last few weeks of training. But she had agreed with Holly that it would be the last item of 'illegal' clothing to be dropped.

As she pulled on knickers, her hand deliberately brushed against the top of her thigh to check for the HRT patch. Sundays and Wednesdays were new patch days and she had to think for a minute whether she'd already put a new one on.

Legs, she had thought. *I'll make my left leg Wednesday leg and my right one Sunday leg from now on.*

Sometimes after a cold swim, Stevie found that her thoughts were very random and this morning was no exception. She wasn't sure whether it was the brain fog often associated with the menopause or something to do with being in the cold water. One thing she did notice, though, was that if she had got her head wet, her thinking became clearer momentarily afterwards, but she needed to put a dry bobble hat on or that clarity would turn into a headache.

Looking across from her youngest to her eldest daughter, she realised any grumpiness or sense of disorientation might have had nothing to do with her hormones or the cold water. As an empty nester, it seemed strange at first to have her daughters back in the house, but by the time they left again, she'd got used to them. She didn't want to let go again and fall back into the bad habits she'd acquired over the last few years: lack of housework, not cooking properly, sitting staring at the walls hoping this wasn't how the rest of her life was going to be – all those foolish things that they told her off for doing. They warned her that it was a slippery slope to being bitter and unhappy. God, she never thought she'd be learning about life from her children!

Dressed and feeling ready to be sociable, she went over to where her eldest was talking to the young man with Chris, probably his son. Yes, there was definitely a family resemblance in the way they held themselves: confident, but with an edge of shyness and uncertainty about their place in the world. Chris seemed slightly taller than she remembered, but his handshake was just as firm, his palm warm around her own cold one.

'Still swimming, I see,' he said, nodding towards the lake. His brown eyes held hers for a second or two longer than necessary.

'You noticed.' She laughed in a giddy kind of way that wasn't really her. 'Happy Christmas,' she said to cover up any awkwardness. 'A bit late, but better late than never and all that—'

'Mum?' said her daughter, giving her a look as if to say, *What the heck, Mum, stop acting like a teenager.* 'This is Tom. He took over my job at the cafe, but now he's about to move to Spain. I've been telling him and his dad about your swimming championships and how you're looking for a man.'

'Oh,' she answered. 'Well, thank you, but Chris already knows. He took some photos for us a couple of months ago—'

'I hear you were let down by Ice Man?' Chris butted in. 'Sorry to hear that.'

'More like The Invisible Man,' added Stevie's daughter. 'Still, Mum, you're always open to offers, aren't you?'

'I guess, but, well, Holly and I may just not do it after all. You know Angela has had to pull out, so we aren't really a team anymore. So... Chris, don't feel you need to volunteer or be pressured into anything!'

'Oh, that's a shame about Angela. Well, if you're not going to enter a team anymore...' said Chris, pulling the neck of his down jacket up around his ears and shivering slightly in the breeze that was picking up.

'Dad, come on,' urged Tom, nudging his dad on the shoulder. 'Just now you said you were going to tell Stevie you wanted to be her man!'

'That's not what I said, I was—'

But before Chris could finish, Stevie's daughter, Beth, interrupted him. 'Well, that's it then. Problem solved. Mum, meet your new Ice Man. Chris, meet one of the most wonderful, crazy, tenacious, but tough cookies you'll find in the tin.'

'Ah, but—'

'Too late, Dad. You better find your trunks and get training.'

Stevie smiled at Tom and said to Chris. 'Thank you so much! I can't wait to tell Holly. This might just mean we can go to the championships after all, even without Angela. On the day, there's a much greater chance of finding a female swimmer than a man.'

She looked at Chris and his eyes held hers. It was Stevie who glanced away, but she was blushing.

'If you're serious' – she looked at him again – 'meet Holly and I down here tomorrow ten a.m.' Then she added, 'Remember, it's no wetsuit.'

Chris cringed. 'Oh, crap! Okay, I'll do it. I'll be your man.'

'You've got plenty of time to acclimatise,' Stevie reassured him.

Chapter Thirty-Three

CHRIS

January

S hortly after agreeing to join their team, the reality of what this entailed began to sink in. His solo dip earlier in December had not been as awful as he expected, but it would only get more difficult as winter sunk its claws in and the temperature continued to drop. But then, he reminded himself that he'd learnt to swim in the lake. In his youth he'd been one of the lads who had gathered down at the Ledges at the diver's car park on long, warm summer nights. High on testosterone, they had dared each other to jump off the wall into the deepest part of Crummock Water. Nothing could have been colder and he certainly wouldn't do it now. Thank goodness, Tom had never got into that crowd. When he cycled or drove past the Ledges now, he cringed. The wall looked so high; the water so dark. The innocence of youth!

The water was already in his soul. He knew he could do this. He hadn't expected to feel so positive now that he was committed, but he even felt excited about training for something completely different and challenging himself on a new level. Hadn't Tom urged him to try something new?

Training was something he took seriously, so he wrote himself a training programme for the swimming, just as he always had for cycling events. He started to read up now and again about cold-water swimming to give himself the best chance of succeeding. The hardest bit would be the first few swims, everyone seemed to say, but the general consensus seemed to be that if he swam three or four times a week, he should start to acclimatise.

He liked the sound of gradually building up his tolerance to cold water. So, he plotted out eight weeks and decided that if he had a cold shower every morning and went to the lake twice a week, that should be enough. On the other days, he would cycle and run. Surely it was just like training for any other event, which was a methodical process of building up muscle strength, stamina, and memory with recovery days in between. As far as he could tell, the only training the team would do together was the swims. It was up to him what background work he did to get himself in the best possible condition. It would have been good to have sorted out an overall team training plan, but Chris quickly realised winter swimming wasn't as predictable as other events, so he'd have to adopt a slightly different, maybe more relaxed attitude to it.

As he browsed a few posts on Facebook, which was the only social media platform he used, he realised that, not only was he entering a winter swimming championships, but he was also being drawn into a worldwide phenomenon. There was a community of outdoor swimmers and within that huge community there was this smaller, more niche, group of swimmers who did it for the buzz, the natural high they experienced after cold-water immersion. As he dug deeper, he discovered that, even amongst the cold-water swimming aficionados, there were those who swore by Neoprene gloves and socks, those who went the whole hog and swam with zero Neoprene, known as skins, but with a bobble hat, and those who craved frozen water, the true ice swimmers.

The championships fell more or less into the strict skins section, but fancy dress and crazy hats were encouraged for the relay races. This sport, it seemed to him, was like no other he had ever been involved in.

As he'd discovered from watching yet more YouTube videos from Eastern Europe, no Neoprene in any shape or form. He was surprised to find that he now wasn't too concerned about that. His hands were pretty tough from being out on the bike in all weathers – he wore fingerless gloves unless it was absolutely freezing.

He was more worried about his feet. How cold would the loch be in February? Definitely below five degrees and that was bloody freezing! But he only had to swim fifty metres. That was two lengths of the leisure centre pool. *Get a grip,* he told himself. *What could possibly go wrong?*

Worst case scenario, he'd be in the water for about two minutes max. Hardly time to catch his breath, let alone freeze his toes off. It was all going to be fine. And anyway, by then he would be used to it. No worries.

'Christ!' he yelped as he prepared to take his first cold-water shower. People really did this every morning? It took all his will power to stay under it until he felt his body begin to relax, his teeth stop hurting, and his hands unclench. *That was bloody awful,* he thought as he turned the handle anti-clockwise and the pain stopped. Why did it feel so much worse than his dip in the lake? He gasped and reached for his towel, which was draped over the heated towel rail – oh that felt so luxurious against his burning skin, scorched from the cold water. *Note to self,* he thought, *cold showers are off the training programme.*

While he rubbed his body dry and warm with the towel, he

glanced at his reflection in the bathroom mirror. *You daft bugger, what have you let yourself in for now?* But he noticed the smile lines around his brown eyes were working again, his skin glowed, his hair stood up in perky tufts, and he hadn't thought about being lonely all morning.

In his rucksack, he packed a Thermos of hot Ribena, thermal gloves, beanie hat, cycling buff, spare thermal top, sit mat, towel, and a pair of Crocs. He knew what the stones felt like under bare feet, so he planned to attach his Crocs to an empty plastic water bottle so they'd still be there to slip back on when he was in the shallows after the swim. He was still relieved he'd gone in the lake once on his own already, albeit a few weeks ago now. At least it wouldn't be so much of a shock. He'd be able to handle himself very well. If those ladies were expecting to see a grown man cry, they'd be in for a surprise.

He was dressed in Lycra swim trunks. Nobody wore Speedos these days, thank goodness. More Daniel Craig, he liked to think. Then he put on his thick jogging bottoms that he normally pulled on after a shower when he'd got back in from a long cycle ride, one thermal long-sleeved layer, a lightweight fleece, and his super warm down jacket.

He arrived in the car park early, so he walked on down through the woods to wait for the women. He'd throw a few stones in, take some photographs, psych himself up – better than having to walk with them and be sociable. Perhaps once he knew them better it would be fine, but this morning, this first time with the group, he needed tranquillity so that he could focus. He always needed mind space before a cycling event; it was his way of dealing with any last-minute nerves and gave him time to run through his mental checklist.

The lake was glassy this morning as there wasn't a breath of air. It looked silver and blue, reflecting the sunbeams and blue sky. *Rather inviting,* he thought. *Thank goodness it isn't blowing a hoolie for my first group swim. Easy.* He was tempted to just go in now before they got there, get it over and done with. Instead, he dropped his rucksack down near a little wall at one side of the beach.

There was a wooden bench set a bit further back from the beach, which the male triathletes used as their 'changing room' during the summer months, and the women used the 'posher' bench over near the woods.

He heard the women's voices and looked back up the path that led into the woods – two tall, cloaked figures strode towards him like wizards ready to cast their spell. Hoods pulled up over their heads, arms tucked into their sleeves, their religiosity caught him off-guard and reminded him of the serious side of winter swimming.

This was going to be grim. He sighed. But he smiled at them with the best smile he could muster. More than anything he just wanted to pick up his rucksack, say 'You can stuff your championships' and scarper back through the woods. Would that be cowardly? Or just admitting he was scared? Chris had been brought up by parents who taught him that emotions were good and people weren't mind readers. But, during his marriage to Gail, he had learnt to suppress his emotions because she made it clear that she thought it was weak for a man to cry or be afraid of things. That was her upbringing showing through, but it did cause some conflict on how to bring up their children. After initially trying to discuss it with Gail, he gave up and went down the easiest route, which was her route. He looked at his hands and saw they were shaking.

'Morning!' The women greeted him as if they were about to sit down for a business meeting. They started to organise their swim kit ready to put on post-swim, before finally checking that the hot drink and enamel mug were at the ready.

No faffing? He was taken by surprise. He thought this would

all be a much more relaxed and laid-back thing. Did him being there change how they did things? Were they worried that he'd be a complete wuss, or panic, or freeze to death?

Chris noticed that Holly even had a pair of fuchsia pink bedroom slippers, the kind you pull on. How strange.

He tried to copy what they were doing, reminding himself that he had to learn how to do this, not just jump in gung-ho and expect to survive. This was serious shit. He muttered to himself as he pulled off his layers, all warmed up nicely from his body. It felt so bizarre given that the air temperature was hovering around four degrees and the water probably around five, possibly six as they hadn't had too much rain or too many cold nights.

Stevie handed him a bright orange bag with a strap. He knew it was a tow float and would make him visible. If he got tired, he could hang onto it briefly for a rest. He puffed into the non-return valve and strapped the plastic bubble round his waist, adjusting the size to fit him. Then he walked in his Crocs down to the edge of the water and stood waiting amongst the collection of debris that always lay there from autumn onwards: leaves, twigs, sticks, beech nuts, the odd bit of string or bottle top.

'You okay, Chris?' Stevie called. 'We're just about ready. Don't want you getting cold.'

He turned to look at the women as if to say, 'Cold? Me?' A huge shiver ran down his back and he had to admit he was beginning to feel slightly chilly.

He watched as they picked their way barefoot across the stony beach.

'You can't swim in your Crocs, you know, but it's okay to walk in with them on,' Holly said, taking several quick breaths and wincing as she joined him. 'It's even worse on your feet when they're cold.' She groaned.

'It's okay, I've got it covered,' he said, holding up the empty plastic water bottle and pieces of string to attach his Crocs once he was in up to his waist.

Stevie stood on his right side. He noticed she was wriggling her toes and her toenails were painted red. 'Does that keep your feet warmer?' he joked nervously.

'*Hah!* I wish,' she responded. 'Right, are you ready? The key thing is to breathe slowly and relax.'

'Okay,' he said, taking a deep breath. He wanted to tell them that he'd already been in once and had found the breathing part came quite naturally, but it felt a bit like pride before a fall, so he kept his mouth shut.

'You're allowed to swear,' said Holly as she stepped carefully into the water, 'especially when it gets to your nadgers,' she added, grinning at him.

'Thanks.' *Oh, God, sorry, boys, you're going in again.* He groaned inwardly, but walked forwards, his arms out slightly for balance. In spite of his confidence about walking into the lake, a mixture of excitement and nerves rushed about in his body, so he automatically slowed down his breath.

Jesus! The pain was creeping up his legs and when he dipped his hands in by his sides, he immediately pulled them out again. He heard Holly's and Stevie's voices, but he didn't understand what they were saying. He could hear nothing but a rushing in his head. Why was it so different this time? This was a good moment to take off his Crocs. He fiddled about a bit with the floaty device he'd created. It bought him time and helped him refocus.

'Okay, now wait a moment, Chris.' Stevie tapped him on the arm and he stopped what he was doing. 'Right, splash water on the back of your neck and your chest, your arms, your face. Look.' She scooped up the clear water and tipped it over her shoulders and then repeated it. She waited for Chris to copy her.

Holly had already sunk down up to her shoulders in the water. Her eyes were closed and she appeared to be meditating. Her serenity caught Chris off-guard. How could someone so outwardly confident and vivacious sit so still and appear so beautiful? He was amazed at the transformation.

With his eyes locked onto Stevie, who was now standing waist deep in front of him sculling her hands in the water, he slowly bent down and scooped up a double handful of the lake and dropped it onto the back of his neck. He closed his eyes and automatically breathed in deeply and then opened his eyes. Repeat, repeat, until he'd splashed every part of his body, but was still only thigh deep.

And now for the worst bit. Last time, he'd just thrown himself in headfirst, but he knew he had to do it Stevie's way. It was way harder to creep in slowly. For this, he needed complete silence and full concentration. It was going to hurt. He bent his knees and went down into the water inch after chilli-prickled inch until he felt his 'nadgers', as Holly had called them, contracting in fear and panic. The pain was intense and he knew his face was not a pretty picture, but he just didn't give a monkey's whatever. It was as if his testicles had been sucked up into his chest.

He waited until pain was replaced by discomfort and he could walk in a sort of half crouch into the deeper water. As the cold bit into his stomach, he winced again and then gave up this war of attrition and plunged forwards with arms outstretched just to get it over and done with.

Then his breathing went completely to pot and he heard both Stevie and Holly telling him to slow it down, relax, take longer, slower strokes, stay within his depth. Their voices did calm him down and he made a conscious effort to listen and obey.

In fact, their voices were the only things that kept him in the water; otherwise, he would have stood up and staggered straight back out. This was not the same as the first time, but he'd almost done it, he had his breathing almost back under control and his arms were still working.

He turned on his back and trod water. The two women did the same. It was as if they were leaving him on his own so that he could experience his surroundings and be completely in the moment.

For now, though, the women suggested that he get out, get dried and dressed, pour himself a hot drink, and jog up and down a bit. They were going to swim for a little longer and would keep an eye on him. To Chris, the swim seemed to be over in a flash. It almost felt dreamlike and surreal. A few moments of drama followed by serenity.

He didn't bother to try to wedge his Crocs onto freezing feet, but just picked his way painfully out of the lake. While he felt grateful to Stevie and Holly for showing him the right way to approach this, he really did prefer his way.

Still, he had to admit that his respect for them had just quadrupled and he felt as high as a kite. Wow! That was incredible. He laughed as he dried himself down with his towel and started to wrap it round his middle so that he could lose his trunks discretely.

Just as he was pulling on his joggers, he heard the two women scrunching back up the small stones, chattering happily to each other.

'Well done, Chris,' said Stevie. 'You did really well.'

'Yep, you didn't swear once!' laughed Holly.

'Oh, yeah, I can't even remember what I said, but it wasn't polite!' joked Chris.

'How're you feeling now?' asked Stevie, pulling her changing robe over her head, pushing her arms through the armholes, and then tucking them back in to pull the straps of her swimsuit off her shoulders.

'Good,' he responded. 'I feel great, not cold at all, really buzzing.'

'Brilliant. Best to get dressed as quickly as possible and get some hot drink down you. You may suddenly feel a bit colder, but it's all part of the learning process. If you listen to your body and learn how it responds to the cold water, you'll be better prepared next time. Acclimatisation only takes a few swims really, especially if you focus on that continued cooling down period after you get out,' Stevie warned.

'Oh, yes, the after-drop,' said Chris. 'I've been reading about that. Sounds a bit dodgy, doesn't it?'

'Absolutely, you don't want that,' warned Stevie.

'Have you ever had it?' he asked.

'The drop-off?' joked Holly who was nearly dressed. 'Ooh, you don't want the drop-off, Chris.'

Nothing would shock that woman, but he was glad really. If he was going to keep company with these two regularly over the next few weeks, then he wanted to enjoy it. So far, so good. He'd survived for a second time and apart from a chill spreading up his back, he felt bloody wonderful. He sipped his hot drink and turned to stare down the length of the lake, noticing not for the first time how the fells came down in swoops and layers to meet the lakeshore. Their shapes grew fainter the further down you looked. If he was going to paint this, he'd get out his blues and reds, mix a purple, and apply that as a pale wash in the distance first. And then darken it up a bit and gradually add in more reds as the richness of the bracken, trees, and rocks sharpened in the foreground.

He shivered slightly and appreciated the heat on his hands from the enamel mug he was holding.

Chapter Thirty-Four

ANGELA AND STEVIE

January

Handling a quad bike across rain-logged fells was exhausting, but Angela knew she had to keep looking for the two missing ewes. They were with lamb – twins, each of them – so that was a lot of money lost if she couldn't find them. Jet, the Collie, was balanced on the back of the bike, his body knocking into her now and again. How on earth he managed to keep his grip she'd never know, but having him there was reassuring and a bit of company. He lived in the yard and was not a house dog, or pet, but his loyalty was unlimited.

Angela hadn't grown up on a farm, but having worked at the local pub for years where the farming lads hung out, she knew what was expected of you if you married into a farming family, particularly sheep farming. No one had ever talked of the loneliness, the isolation or the relentless, physically draining nature of the job. It was a way of life, not a job. You couldn't leave it at five p.m. and go back to it at nine a.m. the next day. And now she was managing on her own. She just prayed Ed would be back at her side come lambing time, which would be any time from March onwards.

Ed had more or less lived at the hospital and was then a frequent visitor at the nursing home his mother had been transferred to. When he came home, Angela always made sure he had plenty to eat, or at least tried to get him to eat something. He was fading away, she was sure. He felt so much thinner when she hugged him and the bags under his eyes were like rainclouds: heavy, dark, and sad. It seemed to be enough for him to know that she was there, that the farm was safe in her hands, and although he hardly spoke to her because he was clearly so exhausted, she knew that she was doing the right thing. She had offered to go with him on a couple of occasions, but after a brief hesitation, he'd said no it was okay, maybe in a little while. She was helping by supporting him and that meant a lot. Secretly, Angela was relieved and glad he thought she was doing enough.

Thank goodness for mobile phones. Although reception wasn't brilliant up at the farm, she was able to let Stevie and Holly know any news, tell them she missed them, say she was going crazy without the water, and ask if they had found a man.

To hear that Chris had been roped in made Angela smile. She'd instinctively liked him that day he'd come down to the beach to take their photographs. There was something warm and solid about him, but sad too. She'd noticed the way he'd looked at Stevie – it was how a man looks when he thinks has found the missing piece in his jigsaw. Ed had watched her like that at the beginning.

As she brought the quad bike back down into the farmyard with the two ewes safely penned into the little trailer she'd hooked onto the back, she whistled to the dog that had been running behind and shut him away in his barn. She'd go back out shortly to feed him and his sister, who she had left there on guard. Plenty of opportunists around stealing farm equipment.

In the boot room, she kicked off her foul weather gear, slipped on another pair of boots, and went to the kitchen door. Now there was no one home all day, she'd got into the habit of locking it up if she was out and about. Not that there was anything of any value, but it made her feel more secure if she was coming back into the house on her own. She was almost tempted to keep one of the dogs in the house while Ed was away.

The kitchen door was unlocked. Ed must be back and found the key in the hiding place just to the left of the outside tap. She'd not noticed his Land Rover in the yard though.

Slightly puzzled, she crept up the stairs, praying it was Ed and not a burglar. She heard the shower in the bathroom and laughed. Burglars don't take showers – just money and jewels.

Back downstairs, she washed her hands and checked to see how much water was in the kettle on the Rayburn. She was flagging and needed a mug of sweet tea. Then she remembered the dogs. Slipping her boots back on, she walked back to the barn, took the two tin bowls from the stone floor, scooped some dried dog food into them, and just for a moment allowed herself to pause in her day.

One day soon, she thought, *things could be very different here.* She wasn't willing Ed's mother to die exactly, but this waiting game could not go on forever. It was draining. The dogs wolfed down their food, then started to wash themselves, nuzzling each other to find any crumbs of food caught up in muzzles or ear fluff. They were happy; content with their simple lives.

Back in the kitchen, Ed was stirring sugar into two mugs of tea. He smiled at her as she walked in, which was a pleasant surprise. She couldn't remember the last time he'd smiled. He'd also filled up two big bowls of stew and put them on the kitchen table. It was just what she needed: a little bit of someone looking after her. Angela stretched out her tired legs under the table, kicking Ed accidentally. Instead of moving his foot away, he stopped eating and put one hand on her shoulder.

'Thanks, Ang.'

Just that. But it was enough. Their team was still strong. It had taken a big knock and there were still a few things that Angela wanted to navigate her way through, but she was prepared to wait for the conversation about why she wasn't able to have children until Ed was in a better place. Her loneliness and physical irritations still preyed on her daily, but the trust her husband had placed in her to run the farm in his absence had helped her fight them off, squash them down, and let her do what she needed to do.

In a cottage not so far away from the farm, but far enough to be in another world, Stevie was sitting her desk, staring at the duck-egg blue walls. Another Christmas gone, another year beginning, the challenge she had set herself was only a few weeks away – but then what?

She swivelled round in her black chair, leant forwards and lifted the lid of a big pine chest. In it she kept all the photographs of the children when they were little, packets of prints, and about fifteen photo albums holding yet more prints in their plastic sleeves. She'd kept a promise she'd made to herself as they grew older – always print out a selection of photographs for each year rather than leaving them on the computer. It had once been a Christmas tradition in her family to open the lid and immerse themselves in 5x7 glossy memories for a couple of hours.

Divorce hadn't seen the collection split, but it did bring an edge of poignancy that they all felt but tried to ignore. It hurt to see her husband's handsome face smiling out at them, but not as much as it hurt to contemplate ripping all those photographs up or slicing him off them. Her daughters talked openly about 'Dad' and the four years without him that had passed since the divorce were only a tiny part of their life with him in the family. Adulthood, university, jobs, and partners had drawn the girls to different parts of the country, so these photographs were brought out less and less frequently and with more and more nostalgia rather than emotion. It was rare that the three of them got together in her house in Cumbria. When they did, there never seemed to be time to sit around looking at old photographs. She was sure it was only her who felt nostalgic anyway. The girls had moved on emotionally and geographically, as was normal. She missed them terribly, but treasured the times they visited or she went to see them in their new homes with their new lives.

What Stevie knew she missed most was having someone to share this next part of her life with. She imagined being with someone who would do the things John had never done, but which she saw other couples doing: someone to photobomb her snapshots, suggest an adventure, cook her a meal, ring her up when she least expected, forget to put the top on the toothpaste, tell her the barbeque was hot enough for the food now, kiss the top of her head in passing. The list was endless and all-consuming if she allowed it to be.

In the lake there were no lists, no pressures, no comparisons to her old life, no expectations to have all the answers, no secrets except what lay below you in the depths, no one to tell you they loved you except yourself. Total self-knowledge and self-belief for that brief moment you gave yourself to the water.

But she could not live every waking hour in the lake. Or use it as an escape from real life.

Bang! She dropped the lid down on the pine chest, stood up, and went into the kitchen. Time to shake up the next few months. Get the championships out of the way, get the estate agents round, put her house on the market, move down to Oxford. But was there really anything different down there from up here? She'd always thought there would be, but maybe by staying here in Cumbria and simply throwing the dice now and again, who knew what would come into her life or what opportunities might jump in front of her.

Take the forest swim in Norway. That had been an opportunity she couldn't have anticipated, or even contemplated before she'd started swimming in cold water every day. What's more, she hadn't had to sell her house and move hundreds of miles away to do it.

Come on, woman, stand tall and be proud of everything you're achieving. Look at the team you have around you: they wouldn't be out there freezing their bits off if it wasn't for you and your crazy, wonderful dream. She could understand why Holly was there come rain or shine, but Chris? What was he getting out of this apart from the odd glimpse of side boob or bum cheek if he was lucky?

She thought about the flashes of his flesh she'd seen as he was getting dressed – not that she was looking of course. It made her smile and feel good inside. Was this another one of those opportunities she might grab hold of? She smiled a bit more at the thought of grabbing hold of Chris.

Her mobile was ringing, but it wasn't on her desk where she normally left it if she was in her office. She cocked her head and listened carefully, surprised that she could hear it. Normally, all she could hear from her office was the rhythmic beat of the grandfather clock on the landing.

It was coming from the kitchen. If she hurried, she might just catch it before the caller gave up. But she was not quite fast enough down the stairs and there was no message, just a missed call. It wasn't a number she recognised. She tended to ignore these as they were usually a scam of some kind. This time, she took a chance and called the number back. She heard a man's voice on the other end. He sounded flustered, but pleased she'd called back.

'Stevie! You don't know me, but I'm Simon, Holly's husband.'

'Simon! Of course, I've heard a lot about you. Oh! Is Holly alright? Has something happened?' Panic washed over her like a cold wave. How did he get her number?

'Sure, sure, yes, she's fine. Um, actually, she doesn't know I'm ringing you. I do apologise, but I took your number from her phone.' He laughed nervously, which reassured Stevie that all was well. Now she was just curious.

'Thank goodness! So, are you okay? I mean, can I do anything?' She realised how daft this sounded as he must be ringing her for a reason, not just a random chat.

He laughed again then explained: 'Well, you probably know already, but it's her big birthday coming up soon.'

How could she not know! The number of times Holly had mentioned it, building up the tension for all of them. It was as if no one had ever been fifty before. Stevie realised that was not very kind of her to even think, so she had never voiced it.

'I'm planning something special, you see. It's down in London though. At the lido near where I work. I'll explain in more detail another time, but I just wanted to sound you out on a couple of things if that's okay?' He paused briefly, then continued: 'As I'm sure Holly has told you, we have a dog and holiday cottages, so I know it's a massive favour, but would you mind looking after him? Hopefully, the cottages won't be a problem, but I'm not sure yet.'

'No problem. I'd be delighted to help. I've often wondered why Holly never brings him down to the lake, though. Does he bite?'

'Bite? Nooo. He's more likely to lick you to death. But I know Holly's not keen to take him down with her because she's worried he might run off after something in the woods or a sheep while she's in the lake. I keep telling her he'd be fine, but, well, you know Holly, a bit of a drama queen! It would be far easier if he could be with you if that's alright? I know it's a big ask!' Simon laughed again and Stevie warmed to him even more. She was intrigued to know what he was planning, but also aware that she needed to be off down to the lake.

She checked the kitchen clock. Just gone two o'clock.

'Look, Simon, sorry to interrupt, but I need to go out in a minute. Can we talk again? I'm really happy to help out with this, though.'

'Of course, sorry. Didn't mean to keep you from things. And, thank you for calling back. I'll be in touch. Oh, and Stevie, mum's the word and all that.'

Stevie could imagine he was the sort of person who'd wink and tap on his nose as he said it. 'Absolutely, Simon. I won't say a thing. Bye for now.'

She pressed the red symbol to end the call and went back onto the landing where the grandfather clock stood in the corner – silent. It needed winding every nine days, but she usually did it on a Sunday morning so that the weights didn't go right down to full length at the bottom of the case. It had been her parents' treasure, something she'd known since childhood, and when her mother had moved into her tiny retirement flat Stevie had taken it on, along with strict instructions about caring for it. In some ways, those instructions had come with a pressure to do things as they always had been done, a pressure that Stevie had strived to live up to when her mother was still alive. Yet another person in her life who'd been controlling. Opening the glass door on the hood, she inserted the key onto the winder and slowly wound that side back up and then repeated it on the other side. Nothing. No emotion.

My God, that was a first, she told herself. Winding this clock up always carried her back into the past, a place she was trying to leave behind so that she could live whatever was her future, but today it just felt like what it was – a clock, not the beating heart of anyone's home. Maybe next week she'd leave it unwound? The rebellious thought made her smile. She was the hub, the brains, the imagination, the creator, the maker, and the leading actress – not her mother or her ex-husband. Excited now to get ready for her swim, she finished the job, tucked the brass key back on the little shelf, shut the glass door, and without a backwards glance ran down the stairs. Which swimsuit? She felt like looking good.

As she pulled out her swim kit from the swimming cupboard in the utility room, an image of the man who would be at the lake with them that afternoon floated into her head. His smile, his frown, the look of painful surprise that first time he'd walked into the lake with them. She could remember everything about his reactions. Today would only be the second time he'd swum with them as a group. She wondered what he thought of them both and whether the water would feel any different to him this time. The sun was out again, but it wouldn't make the water any warmer. She allowed herself a moment of butterflies in her stomach again.

Chapter Thirty-Five

CHRIS

January

Chris parked his campervan under the tall conifer trees a few minutes early. Here he was, back at the place he'd first come across these extraordinary women. Those few minutes on his own were vital for him to realign his thoughts, push down any misgivings, and check he'd got everything he needed before he froze his bits off in the lake again.

Two heavily fleeced Herdwicks wandered across the single-track tarmac that stretched down the valley back towards the northern end of the lake. He stared at them, his eyes not focusing on their bodies, but on a distant point in time when he'd realised his marriage to Gail was over: the physical side of it at least.

He shuddered, a chill creeping down his back at the memory of those difficult first few weeks after she'd moved out of their marital bed and existed in the house as separate entities, like platonic friends. Up until that point, even though she was a difficult and controlling woman to live with, he thought he loved her and respected her. She'd always had the final say in any decisions and it had just been easier to agree. Once they were in separate rooms, the conversations about important things in life had dried up completely. It occasionally entered his head that he might be happier without her, but he always thought of the children and made himself believe that it wasn't such a bad life, except when Gail was in a terrible mood and he didn't ever know if it was him who had caused the mood. But still, not having her in the same bed felt different and in a positive way loosened the hold she had over him. Perhaps she knew what was coming and was preparing them both for the end? He scoffed. That sounded way too spiritual for his wife. It was more likely she simply couldn't bear the idea of sharing a bed with him anymore! But that loosening provided glimpses of a possible life beyond their marriage, a life where he might have to tread on eggshells less often, if at all.

The bike had offered him a way back. Every time he slung his leg over the saddle and freewheeled down the road outside the house, he rediscovered just a bit of his younger self.

The sheep now stood at the other side of the road. One of them scrunched up and scratched its head with one of its back legs – a delightful contortionist and keeper of the fells. Chris sighed deeply and pushed his head back into the headrest. *Brace yourselves, boys*, he thought as he poked at his groin. Underneath his jogging bottoms, he already had his black swim trunks on. How he wished they were thermal lined.

He saw a car coming down the road towards him and suspected rightly that it contained the team: Stevie and Holly. No Angela, but they were still training and hoping for a miracle fourth team member to materialise between now and the end of February. They all agreed that there would probably be plenty of spare women up at the championships, so they were not nearly as worried as they had been about finding a man.

Time for action. He waved in acknowledgement and grabbed

his kit bag from the passenger footwell. Just a small rucksack, but it held everything he thought he needed, apart from his down jacket, which he pulled on over his layers of fleece. He checked that the Thermos was tucked down into the outside pocket and that it hadn't leaked and he was good to go.

He was looking forward to seeing if this end of the lake felt any different to swim in than the other. It felt less dramatic simply because you couldn't see the whole of the lake spreading out in front of you, even though the views were still incredible with the small island which lay about 400 metres out from the shore. It was just a bit too far at this time of year to swim to it. He remembered having asked about that when he was taking photographs all those weeks ago, when he was still a non-winter swimmer and ignorant of so many aspects of it.

He still felt slightly self-conscious standing around on the lakeshore in just a pair of swimming trunks in front of two ladies who were still relative strangers and with God knows who driving past.

Finally, they were ready and formed a line of human flesh and Lycra: two women and one man standing at the water's edge. The air temperature was about five degrees and Stevie said the water would probably be only slightly colder, so the shock of walking in wouldn't be so great, she reassured him. Except, it didn't really give him any reassurance at all.

It was a weird combination of giving in to the greater good, but at the same time retaining total personal responsibility and consent. Confidence would probably grow with every swim, so that after a while it would be easier to calm down the inner voice shrieking at him to get out, out now!

He daren't look at the women on either side of him, not until they had all submerged and swum for a bit, then he might brave a smile. This needed complete focus or he'd scream and run out. He was taller than either of them, so it naturally took a second or two more for the point of no return to be reached. That was the moment each of them found their own way into the water and dealt with the sharp pain either by swearing, squealing, or both at once and usually very loudly.

Holly had sworn like a trooper the other day, but he had suspected she would. Stevie had just walked in gently that first time and today she was no different. Not a sound other than 'Oooh', and then it was his turn. Jeepers! It was worse than either of the other times. He felt his face screw up into a tight ball of wrinkles, dimples, stubble, and tears as once again his 'boys' felt as if they were being sucked up into the cavity they thought they'd abandoned years ago.

'I am now a girl,' he announced out loud. Loud laughter replaced the swearing and silent cursing from the other two.

'This time, Chris, I'll count us in and then take really long, slow strokes, breathe slowly and swim breaststroke out for about ten strokes with us,' said Stevie calmly.

'Okay, ready!'

'One, two, three—'

As the cold water hit his stomach and then his chest, he instinctively gulped, which was exactly what he shouldn't have done. He started coughing rather than breathing. He carried on trying to swim, but after about ten strokes stopped and hung onto his tow float with one hand, trod water and coughed until he had got rid of that half of the lake and could refocus on swimming in the other half.

'You okay?' Stevie's voice called from where she had stopped swimming. She started to head back towards him.

'Yep,' he tried to speak, but started coughing again and he felt panic starting to invade his brain.

'Right. Chris, turn round and start moving back to where you can stand,' she told him. It took a moment or two for her words to sink in. He was terrified. He had this mental image of disappearing under the water, sinking down screaming silently.

'Chris!' He heard her voice that time and saw she was swimming close enough to grab him if need be, but far enough away so that he couldn't grab her in his panic. He forced himself to focus on the air above and not the cold danger below him. He willed his arms to pull through the water and slowly he felt himself kicking his legs.

Holly meanwhile had turned round too and was heading back to join them. He heard her voice calmly reassuring him how well he was doing. Keep going, keep going. It was a mantra and he found himself muttering it as he took slow stroke after slow stroke.

Utter relief flooded his body when he could see the bottom of the lake again through the clear water just in front of his face. Nearly back. Another couple of feet and he dropped his legs, praying he could touch the bottom. Just, but it was enough. He waded towards the beach, still pulling through the water with his arms, but not daring to take his feet off the lakebed again until he was in two feet of water.

'I forgot to breathe out rather than in,' he said now that he could breathe again more normally and actually talk. 'Sorry!'

'Don't be daft. It's a common mistake.' Stevie looked at him and smiled with relief when she realised he was fine, just a bit shaken. 'Best not to talk too much while you're swimming until you get used to the temperature and the breathing.'

'Okay?' asked Holly. She was treading water at a slight distance from the two of them with a look of concern on her face.

'Right,' said Stevie. 'I know it won't be the same, but let's try again. Only, this time, as I get to two, start to take a deep breath in. On three, when you sink down and take your first stroke, I want you to push that breath out – slowly – so that you don't take another breath until you've done a couple of strokes and your body has gone past the immediate shock reaction. Then just keep swimming, but no talking!'

Complete focus, Chris told himself, feeling slightly apprehensive. Fortunately, the sun had a little warmth and there was no breeze or wind chill. He wasn't feeling cold, just slightly foolish.

'One, two, three...' said Stevie in a firm, but quiet voice. He took in a deep breath at two and then, on three, released it slowly as he crouched down slightly.

Then he leant forwards with his arms out like a child and took his first stroke with his mouth still shaped in an out breath. On his third stroke, she saw him grin and knew he'd got the idea. Now he'd need to swim through the cold once again as it bit into his body, as his blood retreated fast to his core, and as his peripheries were left to cope on their own.

Once again, he was out of his depth. The water a couple of feet below the surface was probably far less than five degrees and he'd already been in for a couple of minutes.

'Turn. Turn, Chris, go back to shore,' she called and swam him back in.

Once he was back in the shallows, he regrouped himself and allowed his mind to wander, take in the landscape from his frog's eye view. He felt fantastic; alive! Not at all cold, but not warm either. He was not tempted in the slightest to swim for any longer. Stevie had gone back out to meet Holly and they were swimming and slowly chatting away.

By heck, this felt so good! He walked out slowly, wincing at the painfully pointy little stones that threatened to spoil the pleasure. He distracted himself by unclipping his tow float strap from round his waist.

A couple of cars slowed down on the road above and in one the passenger wound down the window and took a photograph of the lake and the two bright tow floats still moving towards the shore. He waved at the woman and she waved back. He was immensely pleased with himself – that was the only way he could have described the feeling rushing around his head and body at that precise moment.

Here he was, fifty years old, standing naked apart from a towel, in January at the side of a lake in the Lake District having done something that most people would call completely bonkers. But it felt so utterly, utterly beautiful. He felt beautiful, even though he was a gnarly old git with knock-knees, slightly drooping jawline, non-existent testicles, and sticky up hair.

Chuckling to himself, he towelled himself down and got redressed discretely because he heard the two women behind him chattering as they picked their way carefully back to the beach across the stones. He prayed his towel would not drop off and give them an eyeful of his hairy backside, but secretly knew that it really wouldn't matter now: he was one of them. He'd conquered his third swim in spite of a tricky start.

'How was that?' Stevie asked from her perch on the grassy bank. She was quickly drying herself off by patting the changing robe against her body. He noticed her nipples were erect against the microfibre material; the water had been cold and so was the air. Her costume was already discarded on the beach and a bobble hat was pulled down on her head. Holly was faffing over on another perch and was still trying to get her changing robe over her head, but kept putting her arms through the neck hole. He was almost dressed himself, so stepped over to her and held up the point of her hood on the robe so that she could see from inside where to put her arms and then it dropped down over her head.

'Thanks,' she said. 'I was dithering a bit there, wasn't I?'

He grinned at her and then answered Stevie's question. 'Bloody wonderful!'

He pulled on more layers over his head then sat back down, finished drying off his feet, rubbing off little stones at the same time, but then giving up. More important to get his socks and boots on, and finally, his down jacket.

He felt a chill creeping up his back and his neck ached just a little as if he'd been riding head down for too long on his bike, trying to look at the road ahead at the same time.

His feet were numb now, although they hadn't been when he got out of the water. But his hands were fine. He could feel everything he was doing. It was bliss to eventually cup his hands around his enamel mug filled with hot tea and take grateful sips.

'I wondered if you'd be a chatterer, but you don't seem to be,' said Stevie. She was now stood up and fully dressed, cupping her own hot drink and taking sips. She was also dancing about doing a little jiggle to try to bring some life back into her feet.

'Sorry if I gave you both a fright.' Chris looked at them. 'How long were we in?'

'Dunno. I tend not to bother timing it, just usually either count my strokes or get out as soon as I start to feel warm. But I'd say around three minutes. For you anyway, when you went back in. The first, well, we won't count that!'

'You were both in a lot longer, though,' he said. 'Maybe, seven minutes?'

'Yeh, about that.'

'So, fifty metres, how long do you reckon that will take?' asked Chris.

'About two minutes. Any longer and they'll be fishing you out.' Stevie laughed. 'Based on what we're doing at the moment, it'll be over in a flash.'

Chris agreed. Not so bad then. He'd managed three minutes today and this was only his third swim. They had a few weeks left, so it was totally possible to get to the point where it would become second nature to immerse his body in water possibly even colder than Crummock.

He sensed he was on the point of shivering, but if he

consciously relaxed and breathed more slowly, he felt that sensation pass. He loved the way every bit of his body had been put into action just now, a full body workout without masses of exertion – apart from swimming for his life. He remembered the feeling of the corners of his mouth turning up into a sort of insane grin when Stevie had made him try again. The relief he'd felt when he'd realised he was still breathing, not choking on lake water and was actually swimming.

Again, please, he thought. 'When's the next swim?'

Chapter Thirty-Six

HOLLY

February

I t was unusual to have guests checking in on a Friday, but on this occasion it suited Holly as it left her free to enjoy the entire weekend with her husband, who she hoped would spoil her rotten for her fiftieth birthday on Saturday. She admitted to herself that she had been talking about it to Stevie and Angela for a few months because in truth she was scared of starting a new decade.

Things always happen at once: a huge 4x4 drove into the yard; she suspected it was the guests; her mobile rang from the kitchen table and she saw it was Simon. *Guests first,* she thought, checking in the little mirror in the cloakroom that she looked presentable and wasn't wearing anything embarrassing. She knew she'd never ever forget that! But, despite her worries, they'd left a great review on TripAdvisor.

By the time she'd shown the couple from Cambridge everything they needed to know about the cottage and found out that they had friends in common through university, her phone showed her that Simon had tried to call twenty times and left five messages, each one getting slightly shorter as if he was getting in a bit of a panic.

'There you are!' he almost shouted at her when she rang him back. 'I was starting to get worried!'

'Guests arrived so I couldn't call you back! You okay? You don't sound it.' She felt slightly distracted because she was trying to put the kettle on at the same time so that she could fill her flask as she was supposed to be meeting Stevie and Chris at the lake for another training swim. It was the big fifty-metre first attempt today. She didn't want to miss that.

'Yes, of course, darling, I forgot about them. Shit!' He went quiet on the other end of the phone. Holly frowned as she poured a little hot water into the Thermos to pre-heat it before actually making her tea.

'What's wrong?' She was curious now. For her, it was a bonus that the guests had arrived early because it meant she could definitely make the swim. Then she would whizz home and get ready for Simon who was supposed to be getting the train home today rather than yesterday because he had had a meeting in London on Thursday night.

'Nothing, really.' He paused. 'Look darling, I've got a little surprise for you, for your birthday, but—'

'Oooh, that's exciting!'

'Yes, yes. Well I hope it is, but, um, well... Look, can you get yourself to the train station for the one o'clock train down to London?'

Silence both ends of the phone.

Finally, Holly spoke. 'But I thought you were coming up today? What's happened? Have you got to work or something?' She felt the disappointment rising. This didn't happen very often, but sometimes Simon was asked to work over the weekend, and it wasn't possible to refuse, given the pressure everyone was under from the new boss.

'No, no, nothing like that! Well, do you have time? That's why I was trying to get hold of you. I wasn't sure I could pull it off, so didn't mention it before, sorry, stupid of me I know, but I wanted to keep it a surprise until I knew it would happen.'

'What would happen?' She looked at the clock on the kitchen wall: 10.30. Yes, she'd have time to pack a few things. But what did she need for a trip to London? And she'd have to message Stevie to say she couldn't come swimming. And let the guests know that plans had changed. And the dog, what about the bloody dog? No. She couldn't go.

'Simon. The dog. I can't come down. I can't leave him, can I? You didn't think of that, did you?' she snapped and almost immediately regretted it. This was so unlike Simon to even remember her birthday, let alone organise a surprise trip.

'Well, I did, actually.' He sounded smug. 'Stevie's coming over to fetch him.'

'What? But when did you arrange that? How do you even have her number? Do you mean she knew all along?' Holly sat down on a kitchen chair. She was stunned: not only that her rather scatterbrained husband had obviously been plotting this for quite a while, but that her swim buddy had known all along and not uttered a word. Also, Simon must have scanned her phone for Stevie's number and – *oh, my goodness,* she thought. *Time's flying and I still don't know what I need to pack.*

She heard another car coming into the yard. It was Stevie, coming to fetch the dog. Holly pursed her lips. Where is the dog?

'Simon. Stevie's here. I don't know where the dog is! What do I need to pack? I'll have to call you back. Text me a list.' She tapped on the red phone symbol at the bottom of her screen.

She pulled open the door, called to Stevie to say she had to find the dog, checked her phone when it pinged to see if it was a message from Simon. Yes. It was, but scanning it quickly, she saw that all it said was 'LUBE. DON'T FORGET TO LOCK THE HOUSE!'

Blooming cheek, she thought. *As if it's ever me who forgets to lock the house! And what was that about LUBE?* She giggled. Where was that damn dog? She dashed out into the yard and saw that Stevie was chatting to the two guests and guess what? There he was. Jasper was rubbing himself up against Stevie's swim-cloaked legs. Holly walked over to the group, trying to smile through the mush that had once been her brain.

'Hi.' She greeted the guests for a second time and grabbed hold of the dog's collar before he could escape.

'Lovely dog.' They gave him an extra pat and rub on the head. 'That's no problem by the way, Holly, you being away for the weekend. Is there anything you'd like us to do?'

Holly was bewildered and her jaw must have dropped because everyone was staring at her. What the hell was going on? She wondered who else knew about this.

'It's okay, I've just let them know, Holly, don't worry!' said Stevie as if reading her friend's mind. 'And I'll be around. I've given them my number too and I know where the spare key is.'

So it was all sorted, then. Bloody hell! In the space of a few minutes, her world had turned upside down. She wasn't about to shriek to the thrill of icy cold water biting her nether regions, oh, no, she was under instructions to get herself off to the station, which was about a forty minute drive away, armed only with a giant tube of lubricant. Plus anything else she could grab in the next five minutes. She hadn't even bothered to have a shower that morning as she had thought she was going to be swimming in the lake. Her plan after that had included soaking in the bubble bath, preparing herself for the arrival of Simon, and a long weekend together of being indulged and indulging.

'Off you go, then, love,' said Stevie, giving Holly a gentle shove towards the house. 'You've now got one hour and forty-five minutes to get yourself together and get to the station! I've got the hound. We have the right man for our team. I'm happy to swim on my own with him. Go away and relax! All is good.' She smiled and hugged a still-astonished Holly, whose hand seemed stuck fast to the dog's collar. Stevie gently prized it off and pulled the dog less gently towards the back of the car. She opened the boot and he jumped in willingly without even a backwards glance at Holly.

Chapter Thirty-Seven

STEVIE

February

Fifty strokes don't sound like a lot if you are swimming in an indoor heated pool. One length of a twenty-five-metre pool or thereabouts, depending on how long your strokes are, how much power you can put into each stroke, whether you sustain the power and momentum as your arms grow more tired, and how much you use your legs. But add in the outdoor factors, which all impact heat retention and energy consumption: water temperature 4°C; keeping your head just above water; waves, even small lumps and bumps in the water; and a chilly breeze that strips heat from your body in a second. Suddenly, every stroke feels like fifty and you have no idea whether or not you're cold, warm, happy or sad – you just are on automatic pilot, silently counting.

As Stevie disrobed, she was mentally going through anything she needed to warn Chris about before they swam this morning. It would be his first fifty-stroke swim, which meant that although they could stay within their depth as they were swimming along the lakeshore towards the boathouse from Lanthwaite Woods, technically it was further than he'd swum before, so he would be in the water for at least five to seven minutes. That was a long time, really, considering the water temperature. However, she knew he was acclimatised now and so long as he was mentally prepared and physically relaxed, he would be fine. She hadn't failed to notice he swam really strongly and, combined with his wide and well-developed shoulders, it made her think *What utter bollocks he'd been talking that day down at the lake when he had taken their photographs. Not a swimmer? Maybe not in the lake, but she bet he put in a few lengths at a pool somewhere.* He had a cyclist's well-developed legs, from his backside to his calves, but she wondered what he did to keep his back so muscular and flexible. Not that she'd been staring at him or anything, but it was becoming increasingly hard not to notice how attractive he was.

He didn't appear to be worried about the championships now; in fact, his enthusiasm amazed her. Such was the power of the cold-water buzz, but, more importantly, the regular four times a week swims she'd insisted he commit to in order to acclimatise properly.

She looked across to where he was bent over his clothes, checking everything was ready to put on in the correct order when he came out. There was a strength to his body that matched her own, just naturally toned with enough of everything in the right place. *Good grief,* she thought, *imagine if he could hear my thoughts!*

She knew he had been glancing over at her too while they were changing. She'd caught him looking at her legs when she'd peeled off her leggings. It made her feel a bit giddy. Then she watched as he checked his tow float was secure around his waist and goggles were pulled down over his eyes. Only then did he turn and nod at her. Was that the signal? She couldn't resist a quick giggle at how seriously he was taking this, but stopped herself before he noticed. That would be grossly unfair of her.

'Ready when you are.' He gave her another quick nod.

Together, like a strange couple about to engage in a serious ceremony somewhere near the horizon, they slowly stepped across the leaf and twig-strewn beach, silently hating every second of the uncomfortable, wince-inducing crossing. It was worse once they were ankle deep in the water when the cold bit into already over-stimulated soles. Neither of them uttered a word, but just silently mouthed a few suitably vigorous expletives.

Nothing was forcing them to do this on a grey, blustery winter's morning. Apart, that is, from loyalty to each other as part of a winter swimming team. They strode forwards together, step by step moving from comfort to discomfort.

Stevie knew that he was now experienced enough to be left to do this on his own. She now wanted him to experience this part of the journey into the chilli-prickle world of cold-water swimming in a solitary, but supported, way. He had said he trusted that even if he just waivered or paused, hesitated or uttered the words, 'No, I can't do this,' she would be there: physically, emotionally, and mentally. It was as if that unspoken relationship between two winter skin swimmers bound them together until such time as 'normality' brought them release from each other once again. Then boundaries would re-emerge in the same way that armrests are pulled down between air passengers, providing accepted division and definition between two strangers.

Normally, the bubble of selfhood and self-protection would have burst as each of them swam through 'the change' and the corners of their mouths would have turned up into a smile. However, today was fifty-stroke day and you can't count at the same time as grinning.

～

'Fifty!' called Chris as he reached the limit of his outwards swim. Then treading water briefly and catching his breath, he turned and started the long, cold swim back. It did feel colder and it did feel longer. His stroke started to lose speed and strength. A moment of panic flitted across his face and instantly Stevie's voice broke into his feelings of fear.

'Ten. Keep counting. Keep going. Pull through, breathe, keep that rhythm, work those legs. And that's twenty; you're nearly there. And off you go again, don't stop, pull down through the water and kick, chin under and breathe out.'

She was right next to him, about a yard of dark, cold water separated them and he could see her out of the corner of his eye, while also keeping his sight pinned on the tall tree that stood on the beach. It was known locally as the Sighting Tree: it held power and reassurance.

'And you're there! You've done it!'

His feet touched down and he felt the tension in his neck and shoulders begin to slide away, but it wasn't over yet. Not until he had got himself out, dried, and dressed. Then would come the next stage of every winter swim: sipping hot tea, pacing up and down, and moving through the different stages of the body coming back to life, from the feelings of chill up the back to the tenseness in the arms, legs, and lower back to the warm afterglow, which made this discomfort all worthwhile.

'Ouch, ouch!' They both swore out loud this time because of the slippery stones on the lake bed. He grabbed her hand so that they could help each other balance.

Even so, it was an awkward walk with goose-bumped arms bashing together and half-numb bodies leaning against each other as gravity threatened to plonk them back in the shallows. Their hands remained in an unbreakable knot of white knuckles and pink pads and they didn't let go until they were both at their respective piles of kit.

Never before had he dried himself so quickly. He stripped off his trunks, not giving a hoot about exposing everything to the wind that had now started to really pick up. On with everything he'd brought, layer after insulating, protecting layer, until he was standing fully clothed, his hands beginning to shake slightly as he tried to pour sweet hot liquid from his flask. Splashes everywhere, but eventually, he had himself under control enough to bring the mug up to his lips, then swear as it burnt them and then, finally, take a sip or two. He could feel the hot goodness run down inside his gullet and drop into his cold stomach. Everything felt cold now, but he knew it was better to keep sipping and move around.

Stevie was now dressed and in need of a hot drink. There were no shakes as she poured out blackcurrant juice into her enamel mug. Those first few sips started the warming up process.

The shivering continued for Chris. She could tell from how his fingers were now turning pink that he could probably feel his hands and feet again, but only just. And there was no doubt that words were moving from his brain and out of his mouth.

'Wow! That was hard,' he managed.

His tin mug was jerking around, orange and raspberry tea slopping out of it as the shivers took over his whole body. He laughed and tried to hold his mug arm down with his other arm. It worked for a while, at least enough to get the mug to his mouth and take a sip. Then he had a sudden shiver and, with a jerk, his arm shot up to his nose and he got coated in hot liquid.

'You did really well,' reassured Stevie. She knew if she hadn't coaxed him back to the beach, his arms would have moved more and more slowly as hypothermia crept in. They were within their depth the whole time, but even so, with that cold wind, trying to stumble back along the rocky shore might have been equally risky. She knew he had the necessary grit to keep pulling his arms through and keep kicking his legs. After all, he did cycling events, so he knew how deep you had to dig when you felt like throwing up, getting off your bike, curling up, and crying.

'You've done it. You know what it is going to feel like now, only that was far worse as you swam double what you will on the day.'

'Plus, on the day, I guess adrenalin of the event carries you through to a certain extent,' responded Chris. It was what he'd always found when he trained for a sportive. The actual event was usually so buzzy that even if you'd trained just short of the distance, your natural high would take you over the line.

'Hmmm, not quite,' Stevie corrected him. 'Although it's not competitive, you will naturally want to do your best, so you'll push yourself to the limit. But factor in the cold water and exposure. That's why if we train to swim further, there should be no problem.'

'Phew, I'm quite glad that's over. At least I know I can do it now.' Chris smiled and realised he must have started to warm through just a bit because the shivering had slowed down and become less violent. 'Did you say Holly's gone down to London? Sorry, I was concentrating so hard earlier on getting in that water and not dying!' He laughed.

'Yeh, I could tell!'

'It's her fiftieth, isn't it?' he added.

'Finally, yes. Her husband has organised a swim thing for her at Parliament Hill Lido, a kind of pool party tomorrow. I've had to keep it quiet though as he wanted it to be a total surprise.'

'Sounds good. Although I'm guessing it's a darn sight warmer than Crummock?'

'Actually, no, probably as cold, if not colder. They keep it open all year now, but don't heat it.'

'Oooh, it's not going to be much of a party then, is it?' He laughed. 'More time out of the water than in, I reckon?'

'There's a band, dancing, buffet – all sorts, she'll love it! Plus, Simon's taken on the challenge of learning how to do butterfly stroke, but he wanted to do it just for Holly. I don't know anything else about it. He wouldn't tell me. But he did tell me about what's being built in her garden while they're away.' She saw Chris's brow furrow and she knew the irony of Simon and the lido had become apparent.

'So, he could have done this?' He waved his free hand across the view of the lake and back to where they were sitting. But then, for the first time since getting involved with this team of women, he felt protective of his role as their 'man'. He couldn't imagine giving it up now, or not having ever been a part of it. He looked at Stevie. She too was staring out at the lake, so her profile was all he could see. The strong line of her nose, those lips that made him feel like kissing her, and a chin that suggested she'd not give up easily on anything or anyone.

She turned her head to look at Chris and smiled to herself. He'd been staring at her. And he was still looking at her with a strange expression on his face. She never knew that brown eyes could twinkle as much as blue ones, or was it just the light playing tricks? No, it was because he was smiling, just a small smile, but it felt intimate, as if it was just for her to see – and feel. Serendipity had brought her 'man' and she was pretty glad it was Chris. How different he was to John; there was something very gentle in his manner with everyone, mixed in with a hint of playfulness. She wondered whether he got angry easily or just let things wash over him. He seemed fairly easy-going and keen to fit in with the swimming team, but not try to take over any training plans they had. She liked his sense of humour and commitment to what they were doing, as if now he had decided he was part of the team, he wanted to make it the best team it could be. In a way, it felt like he was championing and supporting her. The feeling was an unfamiliar one, given how John had been so domineering in every aspect of their lives, or simply just not available. He hadn't exuded warmth and compassion like Chris did. Somehow, although she really hardly knew him, Chris made her feel safe.

'How long is it now until the championships?' Chris broke the moment.

Stevie had to think for a minute or so before answering. 'Two weeks? Yes, that's right. Another eight swims, or so? But you seem to be doing really well already.'

'All we need now is another female swimmer,' said Chris, pouring himself another mug of hot tea.

'Do we?' Stevie was having to work really hard to get her brain back where it needed to be and away from those brown eyes: the team, February, Scotland. 'Yes, Angela. I'm not worried about that at all though. We'll find someone up there on the day.'

'I feel rather exclusive.' Chris laughed, preening himself like a prize cockerel, but with his eyes on Stevie. 'Perhaps you could hire me out at the championships?' It was a question directed at her and said in a tone that almost suggested he was throwing down a challenge: if you don't want me, I'm sure someone else will. Or was that just her imagination going crazy?

Stevie's face betrayed her awkward surprise and then real amusement at this man who somehow had found a place in her world. He was 'her man' and the thought of him swimming with any other team of women made her feel all funny inside. Was she growing attached to him? Was that why she'd secretly been really looking forward to this morning's fifty-metre swim, just the two of them?

Chapter Thirty-Eight

HOLLY

February, Parliament Hill Lido

The lido was quietly sparkling under a new moon and lights from the houses that surrounded it. Simon took Holly's hand and led her over to the closed cafe, but when they approached the door, she jumped out of her skin. Faces, grinning faces, pressed up against the glass door and music blared out of the speakers surrounding the pool. Simon put his arm around her protectively and laughed at her reaction.

'It's okay, no one's going to eat you!'

Holly frowned at him as if to say, 'Why not?'

Then the door was flung open and she was pulled inside by a couple of young women in swimsuits. The cafe, which she'd been to once when visiting Simon on a different occasion, was set up like a wine bar: a few small tables and chairs, the counter decked with fairy lights which reflected off the trays of wine glasses, and bottles of Prosecco.

The music, which was streamed into the cafe from the main

speakers, was a remix of Happy Birthday and suddenly Holly got it. So this was Simon's surprise: not a romantic moonlit swim in the zinc-bottomed pool, but a pool party with his work colleagues. Her heart sank just a little, but he seemed so pleased with himself that she forced herself to smile at ten total strangers, including a tall woman with a severe blunt bob and immaculate eyebrows. A shudder ran down Holly's back as images of a praying mantis flashed across her mind.

'Irene, meet my wife, Holly.' Holly felt Simon's hand on the small of her back pushing her gently towards certain death, but then she remembered her manners and went into full firm handshake, nodding head, smiling and inane conversation mode. This was Simon's American boss. Clearly, someone you didn't mess with. But what was she doing here, celebrating the birthday of her employee's wife? She smelt a rat. Was she wearing a swimsuit too? Holly found her eyes dropping to check out the woman's legs, which poked out from under a large coat and were suspiciously bare.

What distressed her more was that Simon had vanished and so had most of the people in the cafe; she realised she had been focusing so much on Irene's eyebrows that she hadn't noticed everyone sneaking out the door behind her back.

'Come, Holly, follow me,' said Irene, sweeping out the door and clicking her fingers as if expecting an obedient dog to follow. And Holly did. 'Sit there,' said the American, pointing at the lifeguard's high perch. 'You will get a better view.'

Then she, too, vanished into the darkness that now surrounded the pool. As she climbed up the metal ladder to the narrow seat, Holly couldn't help but berate herself for being so wet, but the woman just had this knack of getting what she wanted. No wonder Simon was so diligent about his lunchtime swims!

It was chilly up there and Holly snuggled down, grateful for her wool coat and sheepskin-lined boots. A slight breeze wafted across the pool from the houses at the northern end: chips. The smell was tantalising and her stomach growled. She could hear a police siren somewhere in the maze of roads that led to the park where the lido sat and then a man and a woman shouting at each other, their words not as clear as the angry tones. *Humans,* thought Holly. *We're a noisy, uncouth lot of creatures, blotting out the more gentle sounds of nature – even urbanised nature.* For a moment she longed to be down by the lake with Stevie, Angela, and Chris, focusing on nothing but their breathing as they walked gently into the cold water. She laughed at how much she had changed over the last few months and all because of the lake.

'Walk like an Egyptian,' screeched a voice from the darkness and Holly gasped as the entire pool came to life, a rectangle of metallic grey/blue shimmering from underwater lights set into the stainless steel lining. The song from The Bangles started to play loudly and figures ran out from the changing area: first Irene, dressed in a gold swim cap and glittery gold swimsuit with wide shoulder pads, then, to Holly's astonishment, Simon, wearing nothing but a gold swim cap and tiny gold Speedos and a collar-shoulder pad thing. These two stood on the edge of the pool facing Holly and, one by one, swimmers came to stand on either side of them. The line of swimmers then bowed to Holly and like a pack of cards, dived one by one into the pool – a careful shallow dive. And the dance began: legs reaching out of the water in a perfect circle, arms spinning round on the surface of the water like a bewildering pattern of wheels, and then the American rising up out of the pool with her feet on Simon's shoulders. Holly didn't know how to react to seeing her body-conscious husband writhing and posturing like a bejewelled snake as he kept up with the moves, which were loosely designed to tell the story of the lyrics. But it was a truly incredible sight and she realised she was actually close to tears. How could she have doubted his motives? This must be some weird kind of motivational activity, a team building exercise like no other, designed to break down barriers and reactivate people's creativity and energy.

She couldn't wait to get hold of Simon when he was dry and show him just how much she loved him.

Chapter Thirty-Nine

ANGELA

February: Two Weeks to Go

*W*hen someone you don't particularly like dies, thought Angela, can you ever forgive yourself for not liking them? Even though she didn't feel relieved that Ed's mother had died late last night, she knew she didn't feel sad either. She was so tired from running the farm on her own that her first thought had been, *Thank goodness, Ed will be back to help me.* And then she wondered if that was terribly selfish. If so, then she'd been selfish ever since his mother had been admitted to hospital because surely, if it was inevitable that someone is at death's door, don't you just hope that they won't suffer too much longer instead of counting the days?

All these questions had been jumbled up in her head as she drove round the fields on the quad bike just as it was getting light. Her only companion on the bike was the Collie dog, Jet, who hadn't answered, and she'd had no one else to ask. In the end, all she had been able to do was be practical and be ready to look after Ed when he actually did make a flying visit to the farm. Now that his mother was dead, though, she expected everything would get back to normal, or what was going to be the new normal. Did the slight excitement she felt when she wondered how different things would be make her a bad person? To take her mind off all these questions, she just kept busy.

No ewes to worry about today, fences all looked good, and the walls were shocking, but there was nothing she could do about that on her own except prop up the wooden gates that Ed had pushed against the gap in the wall to prevent livestock escaping. The wind or a fox must have knocked them down, so she pulled out her ball of twine from her jacket pocket and the little steel penknife and spent the next ten minutes sorting out some way of securing the gate onto the wire that stretched across the top of the wall. They couldn't afford to pay a professional dry stonewaller to do these repairs, so Ed would need to get up here and sort it out. Only organisations such as the National Trust had the money, so often a wall that had stood for hundreds of years fell into such a poor state that it wasn't worth bothering with. That's when a fence went up instead. The Lakeland landscape cost a fortune to preserve with miles and miles of these beautiful stone walls snaking up fellsides to points so high up that Angela often wondered how on earth they had been built in the first place.

Back in the yard, she saw that Ed's Land Rover was now parked up next to their red 4x4, home from sitting by his mother's side for the last time. She hurried to put the quad bike away and then shut the dog back up in his kennel with some well-earned food in a stainless steel bowl.

Ed wasn't hunched up at the kitchen table, but she found him in the front room sprawled across the sofa, with his eyes closed, his hands folded across his chest and his boots kicked off onto the rug. It was hard to tell whether or not he was asleep, so to be on the safe side, she left him, went back out to shut the farm gate, and then came back into the warm kitchen to make a pot of tea for them both.

Feeling chilly, she put another log or two on the Rayburn to bring its temperature up a bit more. Then she tiptoed back into the front room with two brimming mugs of tea.

Ed was now sitting on the sofa with his head in his hands, ruffling up his greying hair with his reddened hands, which were the size of dinner plates.

'Tea, love?' She put the mug down on the table in front of him and sat down next to him. Her arm went across his back and she rubbed his shoulder gently, waiting for him to respond.

'Ta.' His face was red from crying and his hair stuck up on end like a mad professor. Never had she loved him more than in that moment. Such a huge bear of a man with no puff left in his bones. She moved closer and kissed him tenderly on the cheek.

'Drink up.'

He sat and sipped the tea, staring into space and not saying a word.

It didn't matter to Angela. There was time, plenty of time to talk. For now, all that mattered was that it was over. The waiting was over. When Ed was ready, they could see where they were, what preparations they needed to sort out for a funeral, what paperwork needed catching up on, and so on. She knew that the farm must still be in his mother's name, but now, Angela suspected it would pass into Ed's ownership.

As she sat sipping tea, she thought of Stevie and the little swim team she'd had to withdraw from. Had it only been last night that she'd messaged Stevie to let her know Ed's mother had died? Had she secretly hoped that somehow she'd work out a way of getting to the championships?

Chapter Forty

HOLLY

February: Two Weeks to Go

'What the hell is that hole doing in the middle of our lawn?' screeched Holly as she and Simon walked round the corner of their house. They'd travelled back from London the previous evening, arriving home in the dark, both exhausted and needing sleep. As it was a sunny day, though, he insisted they take their morning coffee round to the gazebo.

'Simon?'

He looked sheepish, but undeterred from walking down to the gazebo, which overlooked the tiny beck that tumbled along the boundary of their property. Holly didn't follow him but stepped carefully to the edge of a massive irregular-shaped hole that had clearly been excavated in their absence. You could fit a car in it, or maybe even two, one behind the other. It wasn't deep, only five foot maximum, but with a small area down at one end that was maybe deeper. *Very odd*, she thought, but then it occurred to her what it could be. She turned and chased after Simon, who had disappeared through a wooden arch that led down to the area near the beck.

If the hole hadn't been enough to wake her up, what greeted her by the gazebo definitely did. Someone had been busy over the weekend. A barrel sauna complete with glass door stood with a view over the beck. It had been constructed on a new section of decking, along with a wooden tub, which she assumed was a hot tub. New pots, artistically arranged around the tub, contained evergreen plants and solar lights, but there was also a canopy of fairy lights woven between the four wooden pillars at each corner of the decking. It was as if the Scandi nisse had house sat for the weekend and left his trademark magic in her favourite corner of the property.

Simon had gone into the gazebo and was now standing on the decking with just a white towel around his middle. He beckoned her over, took her cup of coffee, and pushed her gently into what had been turned into a comfortable changing room.

'Fancy a bit of hot and cold?'

How could she refuse? Then it all made sense. The hole wasn't for the foundations of a new building, but was the start of something far more exciting, something she had never ever imagined she would need in her life: a natural swimming pool of her own.

Chapter Forty-One

CHRIS

February: Two Weeks to Go

'Egyptian?' Chris laughed, then his face contorted as the water reached the top of his thighs.

'Then the music started and he strutted out in teeny-weeny gold Speedos – he bloody well rocked them! I couldn't believe it. Those shoulders! It made me feel all horny, mmm... *Jesus!* This is cold.'

'That's amazing,' said Stevie. 'So pleased he managed to pull it off. The power of love, doing something like that to show someone how much you care about them. What a softie.' Stevie smiled at the thought.

'I feel really bad for doubting him now... Right, sorry, but I've got to get in,' squealed Holly.

'One, two, three,' called Stevie.

Chris counted as he swam – fifty out and then he turned and swam back towards the beach. His stroke was stronger than the last time and evenly paced, his head nicely positioned in the water. Neither Stevie nor Holly could keep up with him now.

When they had swum in closer to the beach, Chris swam back out again, this time doing heads down front crawl for about twenty metres. He popped up after about thirty seconds, swearing profusely at how much colder that was on his head.

'Wow! Bloody fantastic,' he enthused.

'I was almost crying,' Holly was saying as the two women hobbled across the stones back to their clothes. 'For once in his life he was in time with the music!'

'It's incredible. And the sauna and tub? In your garden,' said Stevie.

'You knew?' Holly shot her friend a look as if to ask if everyone was in on it.

'Most of it, yes. Plus, once I knew that Simon was actually really swimming, I wanted to encourage you to get him on our team, but didn't want to let his secret out of the bag! But it's worked out in the end, hasn't it?' Stevie patted Holly on the arm. 'Don't forget, at the time you were more concerned about whether or not Simon was having an affair than whether he'd agree to join our team.'

Holly and Stevie fell silent as they dried themselves down briskly and put their first layers on. Chris was just tiptoeing back up the beach, his head hung down slightly as he kept an eye out for larger stones to avoid tripping over.

'Hey, Stevie.' Holly nudged the other woman. They both stopped pulling down their thermal tops over their heads and peeked through the stretched neck holes at Chris. 'Not quite Daniel Craig, but close,' she whispered. Stevie reached out to whack her round the head, but Holly ducked.

'Sssh,' said Stevie. 'But, yes, I agree.'

They both smothered their giggles under another layer of fleece, not wanting Chris to suspect they had been talking about him.

'You look as if you enjoyed that swim, Chris,' said Holly

nonchalantly. Stevie looked as if she was trying to hide her embarrassed face in her rucksack, pretending to be searching for her bobble hat. Holly had to give it to Chris when he coolly responded with a cheeky wink and said, 'I'll take that as a compliment given how cold the water is.'

It set them all off and subtly shifted the dynamics – once again, filters were always lowered in the water for some reason and today was no exception. A companionable silence fell as they each hurried to pack away their things. It was a still, grey day, nothing special, neither one thing nor the other. Perfect conditions for a relaxed training swim followed by hot drink and chat.

The conversation turned to Angela and how she was coping with Ed's mother finally dying. How was Ed? Holly asked. Was he back at the farm? Would it help Angela to get out for a swim? Would she be able to?

'I don't know, Holly, you'll have to ask Angela, won't you,' responded Stevie, a little sharply. Holly suspected she'd been thinking about Chris and not really heard all the questions Holly had thrown at her, but Stevie immediately realised how spiky her tone had been and apologised for having snapped, asking Holly to repeat her questions. That man really was unsettling her! Only a moment ago, they'd all been cracking jokes, mostly at Chris's expense, and the mood had been great. Now there was an odd tension.

Holly stood up and hugged them both quickly and made up an excuse for dashing off. She had watched Stevie's face and knew there was something wrong, but she didn't like to pry in front of Chris. If it were to do with Angela and Ed, it would come out eventually; they had a lot to deal with at the moment. Her intuition told her that it had something to do with how Chris had looked walking out of the water, smiling at the world as if he were in Heaven. If that was the case, she got it, Stevie's brain had been bedazzled with emotions and feelings she thought she'd switched off four years ago, so she must now be struggling between wanting to enjoy them and protecting herself from being hurt. Time to give them some space together. She had a feeling this would happen, but maybe just not this soon.

'Chris? Would you mind giving Stevie a lift home? I really need to get off and I'm planning on going to Keswick, which is in the opposite direction really.'

Stevie gave her a quick look as if to say, 'What? What's going on?'

Chris nodded and said, 'Sure, no problem. You get off.'

Fireworks, giggled Holly to herself as she hurried back through the woods. Once out of sight of the beach, she slowed down and enjoyed her surroundings, her senses still heightened from the swim.

The River Cocker swooshed along in snake-like meanders down to her left, wide in some places and deep enough to jump in from the bank. There was a rope swing over one of the pools, and if you pushed off hard enough from the bank, you could swing backwards and forwards until you dared to let go and fall screaming into the moving water below, submerging quite some way, but still not touching the bottom with your feet.

Further down towards the car park, there was a sandy beach and the flow was weaker. Holly was sure water vole lived here, scuttling out when no one was on the footpath. When she brought their dog along here for a walk, he always sniffed around on the orangey-red sand, into the roots of the trees that were exposed after river levels had risen, and then dropped again, his tail wagging happily.

This wide path through the deciduous woods held good memories of walking hand in hand with Simon years ago when they had been debating whether to move up here permanently and then this would more or less be their back garden.

Holly had grown to like it up here, she had to admit, but this realisation was only recent and had a lot to do with being part of the winter swimming team. Since she'd found Stevie, and then Angela, the magic of the lake had helped to ease her previous concerns.

The mood swings, discomfort during sex, and general lack of energy for anything, which had all caused much grumpiness and dissatisfaction for both her and Simon – it was slowly becoming a distant memory. Whenever she spoke about it now, it was always in the past tense and as if it had happened to someone else.

She'd reached her car with no recollection of having walked back through the last half a mile or so of the woods. There were a few more cars parked up now with one or two people changing into walking boots. Stowing everything into the boot, she got into the car, turned on the engine, retuned the radio to some music, twisted round in her seat to check there was nothing behind her, and reversed out.

It had been a bloody great weekend down in London. She and Simon had spent a lot of hours in bed, making up for lost time and, again, the tablets and lubricant seemed to be working. She hadn't been uncomfortable in the slightest. *Bring it on,* she thought, smiling. *You've got this, girl. You may be sliding into your twilight years, but, by heck, there's going to be some fan-*bloody*-tastic shooting stars in your orbit!*

Chapter Forty-Two

CHRIS AND STEVIE

February: Two Weeks to Go

'Are you in a rush?' Chris asked when they got back to his campervan. 'I mean, do you fancy taking a drive down to Buttermere village? Perhaps have a walk down to the lake, or just grab a bite to eat?'

Stevie nodded. She had nothing to rush back for. Besides, she was dying to see inside his 'passion wagon', as Holly had dubbed it.

'It must be nearly lunchtime or will be by the time we get down there.' Chris checked his Garmin, which he wore permanently, even though he had only been recording his cycle rides, not these winter swims. 'Yep, it's 11.20. Fancy that?'

'Um, yes, that'd be nice. I'm not in a hurry – well, what I was going to do can wait,' said Stevie. It crossed her mind that spending a bit of time just the two of them doing something with clothes on might be healthy. It would allow them to get to know each other beyond the swimming.

She noticed how tidy Chris's campervan was, how it smelt of

pears, and how it didn't have a stack of car park tickets stuffed into the side pocket of the door like in her car.

As they drove down the length of Crummock Water towards Buttermere, they looked across at how the shafts of light were falling out of the clouds and diving down into the water. It was always distractingly beautiful here whatever the weather. It was wild and remote, except on fair weather Bank Holiday weekends when this single-track road on the eastern shore became jammed packed with tourists spilling over the mountain passes from Keswick and with locals who brought kayaks, SUPs, rubber dinghies, barbeques, and pop-up tents.

In the farming community of Buttermere, named after its lake, Chris parked up in the small car park reserved for cafe customers.

'It must've been good to come down here when Tom was working here,' said Stevie as they walked towards the glass door at the back of the cafe.

'Yeh, it was good to have a chat when I popped in. But he's doing okay in Spain, found himself a job out there. I do miss the lanky bugger,' Chris added.

Stevie sensed he was more upset about this than his tone suggested. She got that 'missing' feeling over her kids too.

He suggested Stevie take the corner table while he went to the counter and brought back two menus balanced on a tray with two Americanos, a tiny jug of cold milk, and one of hot milk. In his bid to continue doing things differently from when he'd been with Gail, he'd decided to take a risk, order the coffees, and pray that his hunch was correct and that Stevie drank hers strong. Judging from her smile, his boldness was appreciated and, bizarrely, the fact that she chose hot milk confirmed his attraction to her.

Sitting back down, Chris suddenly didn't know what to say, so he picked up and put down the lunchtime menu several times and then asked her if she'd like to have some soup. The conversation then turned to how they both felt the cold-water training was going. Back on safe ground: non-personal questions that didn't stray into the emotions he knew were bubbling around inside him, most likely provoked by being so close to her on dry land. It was striking how the dynamic between them appeared to be so different out of the water. How relaxed the team were now about stripping down to swimming costumes and then throwing modesty to the wind when it came to drying and dressing post-swim.

'This is odd, isn't it,' he said with a laugh, 'sitting here with our clothes on!'

'Yes, I guess it is,' she responded, glad he'd been the one to voice her own observations. 'Actually, I'm not sure that I'd recognise you if I saw you in town or at the supermarket!'

'You would if I just had swim trunks on.'

She blushed. Was that a dig at how she and Holly had so obviously stared at him earlier as he walked out of the lake? She cringed. But when she eventually dared to look at him, he had that brown-eyed twinkle again: he'd clearly enjoyed the attention. She felt prickles running up the back of her neck, not cold-water chilli prickles, but teenage butterfly flutters – the kind that she hadn't felt in years and completely different to the tingle she'd experienced in the Norwegian forest with Arvid. This was a whole body and mind tingle.

'*Ha!* Very true!' She stared at the menu, willing the hot flush currently flowing up her body to go away. *Did I change my patch? I'm not supposed to get hot flushes anymore, damn it!* She glanced down at Chris's hands holding his menu and an image of them holding her body flashed into her head. *How do I handle this?* She wished that Holly was there.

'Just nipping to the Ladies'.' She excused herself and Chris stood up too. He said he'd go and order two soups while she was gone.

Awkward. That was definitely the word that sprang to mind as she stared at her flushed face in the cloakroom mirror. Rosy cheeks and sparkly eyes betrayed her excitable state, or was it just that she'd been swimming so her circulation was now going into overdrive in an attempt to get back to normal? *Pull yourself together, woman,* she told herself.

Delicious homemade soup certainly reached right through their bodies, warming and filling. Automatically relaxing onto the thin cushion that slid about on the hard wooden bench, it now seemed far more natural to be sitting next to each other. Stevie no longer flinched if his arm brushed against hers when he reached for his second coffee cup. And he let his legs sprawl out within a hair's breadth of hers.

'This swimming, you've no idea how much I'm getting into it,' he commented. 'Never thought I would, thought you were all bonkers, I must admit.'

Their combined laughter made a couple of people on the next table stare. Chris stared back and smiled at them, which made them turn away in embarrassment at being caught out. 'Seriously. Thank you. Thanks for giving me the chance.' He was looking at Stevie again, only this time his gaze had weight.

Stevie blushed again and hated herself for it.

'No problem, you're part of the team. It's been a pleasure to see you learn and adapt.' *God, that sounded so formal,* she groaned inwardly. He'd done bloody well actually and they were so lucky he'd agreed to do it.

'My wife...' He hesitated and the two words hung like a shield between them.

Stevie automatically drew her body back into her own space and wondered if she'd imagined the earlier flirtatious signals.

He began again. 'Gail would have... Well, actually, I don't think she would have believed me if I'd told her what I was doing.'

His eyes seemed to no longer be looking at Stevie, or anything in the room, but far away. She didn't move an inch, but her body language spoke volumes as she crossed her legs, folded her arms across her chest, and sat back a bit on the bench. He continued talking as if to himself, unaware of how his words and distant staring had affected Stevie.

'It hurts, you know, to lose someone. It makes you hate everyone in the world for a long time. But the thing is…'

His hesitation made her sit forward slightly. She sensed he was telling her all this for a reason, something to do with her, not his dead wife. She relaxed a little, uncrossed her arms and legs, and put her hand gently on top of his – not holding on, just letting it lie there, a human connection.

'It's okay,' she said, surprised at herself for feeling so strong after having just felt so vulnerable and then defensive.

It was comfortable. Yet uncomfortable. This was different to supporting each other in the cold water and they both knew there had been a shifting of barriers.

'I'm happy to listen,' she spoke quietly, prompting him to continue the conversation. She couldn't help but notice that he still held her hand.

'Do you know what the hardest bit was?'

She knew he wasn't really expecting an answer, so she just sat still and waited.

'Seeing the light go out of her eyes. She just left her body, her soul slipped away. No word, no sound.'

God, how awful that moment must have been, she thought and fully expected a haunted look in his eyes as he turned to face her. But what she saw was something she just didn't understand. Although they'd had a few conversations about personal circumstances down at the lake after the swims, Chris hadn't really shared anything with them other than that he was a widower. It surprised her therefore to see what looked like relief on his face rather than desperate sadness.

'You may not understand this, or even want to listen, but I've been wondering if how I felt when she died is normal?' His voice was quiet and almost apologetic.

Stevie immediately tried to reassure him that grief can make you feel all sorts of things and he really didn't need to feel bad about any of them. 'I think it's normal to feel a sense of relief for the person if they were suffering,' she said. 'I know I felt like that when my mum died and then felt really guilty about it!'

'I did! You're right about that, it was awful not to be able to help her more, but I'm more confused about why it was like a weight off my shoulders. You know, a weird combination of knowing I'd miss her, but knowing I'd be free to be me again.' He looked at Stevie as if he was hoping she'd understand.

'I sort of know what you mean – although my husband didn't die, he just left!' She laughed and then regretted it. But Chris smiled at her. 'At first, I was just completely heartbroken and confused. I didn't want to be here, to live without him, you know, but then came anger, thank goodness!'

'Yes, I've felt that, too,' said Chris. Stevie nodded at him, encouraging him to explain if he wanted to. 'I suspect that from the outside everything looked good, but actually there were times when I felt like a prisoner.' He looked at her as if to see how she reacted to such a strong statement, but Stevie just nodded at him again, hoping he'd continue. It felt important that he was entrusting her with such painful and personal stuff.

'It sounds awful, doesn't it? She had her way of doing things and it was easier to do everything that way, if you know what I mean? She'd get pretty upset if me, or even the kids at times, messed up her routine. But it wasn't always like that. God! I'd never have married her if it had been!'

'Of course not! I wouldn't have married my ex if I'd known what he was really like, or what he'd become over the years.' Stevie shrugged her shoulders and smiled at Chris. 'I do know what you mean. It's okay.' She gripped his hand firmly as if to say he didn't need to worry about sounding harsh or weird.

'Good. I mean, it's good to talk to you, Stevie. It seems as if we've a few things in common, other than a penchant for immersing ourselves in cold water!' He laughed and then added, 'A recently acquired, under protest penchant I might add!'

It broke the intensity of the conversation and allowed them both to breathe again. The conversation flowed back to easier subjects, such as why they hadn't bumped into each other in the supermarket. And had their kids actually known each other at school?

Chapter Forty-Three

CHRIS

February: One Week to Go

With just one week to go before the championships, Holly arranged for the team to visit another team over in the Yorkshire Dales for some waterfall bagging and mutual appreciation of all things wet and cold.

There'd been a cold snap for a couple of days, so they were expecting the Yorkshire waterfalls and rivers to be below five degrees, which would help give them that final push to feeling completely confident about a Scottish loch. They were expecting a full day of dipping followed by an evening in the local pub and the possibility of a dawn dip the next day if any of them were awake early enough. The local hotel had good letting rooms with huge radiators, perfect for winter swimmers chilled to the core.

The whole area oozed myth, legend, and Gore-Tex, from the iconic multi-pitch routes on Malham Cove itself to the fascinating clints and grykes on the limestone pavement above, from the stony bridleways that led over grassy hills to yet another secluded valley with a pub serving real ale on a chicken-pecked lawn, to miles and miles of undulating green lanes leading down to Settle, a cobbled town square with Ye Olde Naked Man cafe.

After having frosted overnight and been gilded round the edges, this valley and those who swam there welcomed three more wild swimmers into its chilly embrace, warning them that Janet was 'a bit arsy today, so be careful how you go'.

Chris muttered to Stevie and Holly, 'She'll calm down when she sees us Cumbrians. Hard as nails, we are!'

Swimming in Yorkshire water was like swimming in Coca-Cola – even the palest of skins looked tanned as the swimmers dangled their legs in the shallows. After the clarity and transparency of Crummock Water, Chris was intrigued and kept staring down at his legs and arms as they floated about in the pool in front of the waterfall. He'd crept in over the large slippery rocks, keeping an eye on the plunging white waterfall to his left and the currents that ran out from the pool and roared down between black rocks on the other side. Other swimmers from the Yorkshire group were already down there when they arrived and after brief, easily forgotten introductions, the visitors were adopted and shown the ropes.

Feeling liberated from his usual surroundings, Chris found that he had a spring in his step. His time with Stevie in the cafe had opened a chink in his armour and he wanted to explore it further. His cheeks ached from smiling and it was still only midmorning. It felt wonderful to be welcomed so warmly by complete strangers.

Walking into a freezing-cold waterfall pool of fizzy goodness with hardly any clothes on – was there any better way to break down barriers and share random conversations? It came along with swear words and touching hands, and steadying each other across the slippery stones. No one had exchanged hugs yet, but Holly had warned Chris that by the end of the day, they'd all be on hugging terms. Not surprised at all, he just accepted it as part of this whole new world he'd inadvertently agreed to become a part of – he was now officially a wild swimmer.

Although most of his brain was focused on not falling over and twisting an ankle or breaking his leg, Chris did appreciate what a sight they must have been. Janet's Foss was a well-known tourist honey pot and to onlookers they must have appeared like a strange, water-worshipping sect. Every single one of them stripped nearly naked, but wearing a bobble hat – almost like a uniform. Their exaggerated but slow stagger and clamber across the slippery rocks created a sense of anticipation and danger. Did the crowd hold its breath or hope that one of them would tumble and slip, like a sacrifice to Janet? It must've taken at least three minutes for them to get from dry rocks to the water, following each other more or less in silence, with the occasional muffled blasphemy. Who had they come to worship? Who was Janet?

Indeed, when he looked up to the path that ran above the pool, he saw several people hanging over the fence taking photographs.

'Go away,' he muttered. *We're not some kind of exhibit at a zoo.* Then he thought rationally. What else do you expect if you take your clothes off right by a public footpath in the middle of winter and prance around in your swimming costume, letting out the odd squeal or two as you get into the water? One or two of the other swimmers, who had also noticed the photographers, told him that the question they got asked most was, 'Is it cold?'

Of course it was cold, it was nearly the end of February, this was natural, fast running water that had come down across near sub-zero ground and someone had forgotten to switch the boiler on. But that was okay because cold was good. The colder the better. God! He was beginning to sound like the others. Very Zen! Next he'd be signing up to train as a Wim Hof instructor, he thought and laughed to himself.

A cyclist at heart, Chris felt he was coming at this whole cold-water thing with a bit more cynicism than some of the others. His logical head told him that the optimum temperature to swim in was not below five degrees, even in a wetsuit. He wondered if there was a danger here of making 'winter swimming' a bit elitist just because they got their kicks from exposing themselves to the very real possibility of mild, if not full-on, hypothermia. But, then, like any extreme sport, the risk was something they had to accept, if they wanted the 'buzz' or the natural high. A conversation for the pub later, perhaps.

There was one woman who kept looking at him and smiling from under her hat, which had a ludicrously huge bobble stitched to the top of it. Or was it just that every time he caught a wobbly thing out of the corner of his eye, she thought he was looking at her? He kept thinking it was a bird or someone waving.

As he slid down into an eddy, she swam over to him and he could see her orange-coloured legs moving around just below the surface. She had an incredibly pretty face under the woolly monstrosity, so he began to feel less irritated by her bobble. He realised she had adopted him and was waiting for him to actually get in the water. Then, without a word, she tilted her head to one side like a little bird as if to say, 'Follow me.' She was swimming towards the boiling water under the fall and he hesitated, turning round for a minute to see where Stevie and Holly were.

He could just make out their hats over at the other side of the pool with about three other people. He waved at them, but didn't see if they waved back as he had already started to swim towards the woman who was luring him into the power of the water. Perhaps she was called Janet? He chuckled to himself.

There was something so strange about having very little control over which direction he swam in, even if he knew that with a few strong pushes off the bottom of the pool, he could extract himself from the fray. Abandoning himself to the fun, Chris laughed out loud and kept bumping into this woman with the big bobble. It was easy to lose track of time and place.

But then it was time to get out, dry off, wrap up, and move on to the next place. In the campervan, Chris asked them whether they'd enjoyed Janet and seemed blissfully unaware that the atmosphere had subtly changed or that Stevie had become unusually quiet.

Over the next few hours, Chris did start to notice that whenever he glanced at Stevie, she looked away or started to talk to someone else. It felt as if she was avoiding him and he was confused. Their couple of hours in the cafe had stayed with him; he felt something more than friendship had dropped into both their lives that afternoon. So for it to now not feel like that at all made him question whether it was something he'd done or said.

The woman with the big bobble seemed to be constantly at his side as the little convoy of swimmers plodded across a muddy field and down a steep and narrow track to a riverbank made up of flat rocks and ledges that overhung a wide stretch of Yorkshire river downstream from some rapids. The Eel Pool, their next peaty adventure. He just wanted to have a few moments with Stevie on her own to know for sure if anything was wrong.

But as the day wore on, Chris had not managed to be either on his own or near enough to Stevie to open a conversation. Finally, on their return to the hotel, he collared Holly when he met her in the corridor outside their rooms. In a half whisper, he asked if Stevie was okay and if she'd had some bad news.

'She seemed distracted,' he said.

'No, there's no problem, I don't think. Possibly just tired, not sure. It's been a pretty full-on day, hasn't it? But fun. You seemed to be enjoying yourself,' Holly added.

Something about the way she held his glance for just a second or two longer than usual and frowned slightly warned Chris not to answer straightaway. All of a sudden, he felt as if the question was loaded and not in his favour. He felt almost guilty because yes, he actually had been having a great time. The Yorkshire woman, Karen, was sweet and very keen to join their team. She didn't have anyone else to swim with at the championships and fancied the challenge.

'I was, yes. It's good to be with other swimmers I guess and somewhere new.' He didn't know what else to say. He almost mentioned that they might have a volunteer for the last female place on their team, but felt that it would be more diplomatic to speak with Stevie first.

Unfortunately, Karen got there before him and blurted out in front of everyone in the pub that Chris had asked her to defect and join the Cumbrians. Chris wanted the ground to open up and swallow him alive. The look on Stevie's face told him all he needed to know. He just wanted to walk over to Karen and gag her! Where this aggression had come from, he didn't know, but he didn't like it.

His gut was telling him that Stevie and Holly would not believe him if he told them it had not been his idea. He'd not been able to stop Karen once she got it into her head that the Cumbrian team needed her, or to be more accurate, Chris needed her.

He could see it now. See how this would look to Stevie. Just looking at her again, he felt awful. He kicked himself for misjudging the situation so badly with Karen, and for being so insensitive to the fledgling bond that had sparked between him and Stevie.

He wished he could find a way to undo what was already done or to at least somehow make a bad situation into a positive one for their team – they were, after all, now a full team. Maybe Stevie would thank him in the end for finding their last person? He didn't hold out much hope.

It was Holly who stepped in to rescue the awkward silence that followed Karen's announcement.

'Fantastic, let the challenge begin!' She darted a glance at Chris, which he took as a warning, unfair though it might be. He hadn't done anything! Then again, quite rightly, she was just being protective of her friend's feelings. He acknowledged her saving of the situation with a slight nod and clapped his hands as loudly as anyone else.

No one else needed to know what had just passed between them. He felt desperate to go over to Stevie and ask for her forgiveness, but he stopped himself. What was he asking her to forgive him for exactly? Their 'relationship' hadn't been acknowledged by either of them and he was basing everything on his own assumption, desire, and emotion – nothing tangible.

So, for now, in Chris's mind, it was just a balancing act of wanting to get to the championships as a full team and no one getting hurt in the process. Thinking back to the day that he'd first seen and photographed three water warriors breaching the barriers of society's expectation of middle age, Chris totally got Holly's fierce reaction. From the few conversations post-swim and particularly the one he and Stevie had had in the cafe, he got the impression that behind that strong, thoughtful exterior lay a hurt but stubborn woman who had found a way to start to heal.

It was his way, too, by being in the water and being brave enough to celebrate the cold and allow it to chip away at the pain. He knew in his heart that he didn't want to let this beautiful, special, and inspirational woman down either. He had instinctively known from the day he'd seen Stevie standing on her own down at the lake, naked, that he needed to get to know her more. In spite of how challenging it was to swim in cold water, he had been prepared to freeze his balls off for her.

How much simpler it would have been if Angela had still been their fourth member of the team. But life wasn't like that. It was all in the timing. If it got out of synch, or the unexpected jumped in, you just had to go with the flow and hope to be spat out the other end in one piece.

Chapter Forty-Four

STEVIE

February: One Week to Go

This place. This place of ghosts where clouds played with mountain tops and sunbeams flickered on the water's dark surface. Here, she could feel so alone and yet still be with those who had already passed through her life, as well as those who were yet to come.

She could stand on the shore and feel the wind funnel down from Fleetwith Pike. It gathered up spindrifts and water sprites along the way, ready to chill her right through. It whipped her long hair into tangles and made the goose bumps on her arms stand to attention until they were as taut as tiny balloons ready to pop.

Stevie stood here and abandoned every tiny slice of fear, sadness, hope, and pleasure to the elements and the landscape.

She wanted to shout out, 'I can no longer keep pretending that everything is fine, that I am happy to be like this. My needs are burning more than ever and I need to plunge into your cold safe waters so that the fires inside me are extinguished.'

Here on Dead Sheep Beach, in whichever direction she looked, she felt, saw, smelt, and tasted a part of her life that she knew she would never have again. Yet out of the corner of her eye, she caught a glimpse of something that she knew she needed and wanted. If she ran towards it, there was nothing to take hold of. It vanished. The more she ran, the faster her breath, the quicker her heartbeat, the less likely she was to capture whatever it was she had seen.

'Damn you, Chris!' she shouted into the wind. 'I saw inside you. I don't want to see inside someone who doesn't really see me. Why did you do that to me?'

She let her shouts and cries range free, like a stream of consciousness falling onto the tumbled stones, twigs, and pieces of tattered orange farm twine.

Here in this place, she let go of everything that was holding her back as she had done in the Norwegian forest with Arvid. Once again, she reclaimed her power as a woman, the power that her husband had stolen from her. She wasn't quite sure of herself yet, or what she wanted to do with that fire, but it felt so good to know it was within her, scorching energy and confidence into her body and soul. Lead her team to Scotland. That was all that mattered at the moment. After that…? Who knew?

The fiery, confident part of her wanted to talk with Chris and find out if he realised what effect he was having on her, but the cool and self-protective ever-present shell reminded her that these emotions were new, fragile, and uncertain. She hadn't ever thought of herself as a jealous woman, not until that phone call from her husband's mistress, but, if she was being brutally honest, her reaction to the Yorkshire woman's attention towards Chris had scared her.

'Stevie.' She said her own name out loud. 'Stop overreacting! He's free to be with who he wants. Forget him. Don't think about him. You don't need him.' Another quieter voice said, 'But what if he does like you really?'

The storm of emotion was calming down inside her. This place was drawing everything overexcited into a pile of tangled worms and then tumbling it out of her, only to replace it with what she needed if she were going to be strong, to be rational.

So, you are not going to have that heavy talk with Chris, she told herself. *He has done nothing wrong. He is an attractive man and that woman just fancies him, that's all.* And now she was swimming with them in their team and travelling up to Scotland with them in just under a week's time!

The waves whipped up again and Stevie had to run up and down the beach flinging her arms above her head. Laughing now, she wondered what on earth anyone looking at her would think. She didn't care. This was the perfect way to deal with these stupid, teenager-like emotions. *This is exactly why,* she told herself, *I haven't allowed myself to feel anything over these last few years. It is too hard to love again. I don't want to be hurt again.*

Now that she had admitted it, the storm gave way to a gentle breeze and sunshine lit up the last of the white horses.

Chapter Forty-Five

ANGELA

February: One Week to Go

It was at night that Angela noticed the difference most. Now that her mother-in-law was no longer with them, the tired-looking green sofa was theirs again all evening, and all day if they wanted.

Though that was unlikely to happen during the day, because now that Ed was back home, they once more worked as a team, taking equal part in the relentless number of jobs that needed to be done to keep livestock healthy and the equipment, tools, and land in good repair. Hours could pass without seeing each other, depending on their whereabouts: on the fells, in the home field, in the sheep pens, or in the house.

Mealtimes were often silent as each of them concentrated on filling their stomachs, quenching their thirst, and then stacking the dishes by the sink to be washed last thing at night. This routine would just get tougher as lambing time got underway from mid-March to early April, but for now it took the pressure off both of them after an exhausting day and gave Ed space while he processed his mother's death. It had been over a week now since the cremation and, although she wanted to be patient with Ed, she also wanted to talk with him about the winter swimming championships and whether or not she could now be a part of the team.

Holly had messaged her to say that Chris had found another woman while they'd been in Yorkshire, but if there was any way Angela could rejoin them, it would be far better for many reasons. Reading between the lines, Angela detected something was up. The words 'Chris had found another woman' conjured up unwanted images. She'd seen the way Stevie had looked at Chris when he'd been taking photographs of them and noted the way he had looked back at her. But, because she'd had to give up swimming with them before Chris had joined their group, the only way she'd kept abreast of how it was all going had been through private messages with Holly. Nothing very detailed, and nothing concrete appeared to have happened yet, but there was a strong expectation from Holly and Angela that it would sooner or later.

Getting back with the team as their fourth member and knocking this other woman off her perch was now Angela's goal. But time was running out, the championships were drawing ever closer, and Ed was the key to making this happen. She daren't go behind his back again, not so soon after patching things up with him.

So, the evenings slipped by in front of the television once they'd washed the pile of dishes from the day and checked all the outbuildings were locked up and keys taken out of vehicles. Sleep threatened to creep up on them at each end of the sofa, so Angela made sure she nudged Ed and suggested they go to bed before both of them failed to make it up the stairs. It was a slow walk up the wide shallow staircase with aching limbs. The bed they had shared all their married life had felt too small recently for different reasons; she knew each of them moved to the sides and there they stayed all night, not touching. Her night sweats had grown worse again and she made sure the window was open a crack.

But then it happened. She was stirred from deep early morning sleep by the feel of Ed's body moving across towards her side of the bed. Then his arm went around her waist and his warm body pressed up against her back. Without hesitating, she shuffled slightly backwards into him, craving the comfort he was now offering.

'I love you,' he said softly against her ear, his bristly beard scratching the side of her neck. The roughness caught her by surprise and she felt aware of her body responding in a way that it hadn't for a long, long time. She prayed for enough natural lubrication, but she needn't have worried. Her body responded and released pent-up emotions and needs for long enough so that sex wasn't uncomfortable.

'Harder, Ed. I need you.' Her voice had an urgency and she bucked her hips up towards him. He responded, saying her name over and over again as they moved together until the point of orgasm. She lay in Ed's arms afterwards, their legs still tangled and there was no sharp pain or irritation. Relieved for them both, she pressed herself closer to her husband and told him how much she loved him and how she would love him forever so long as he promised never to shave his beard off.

As the physical barriers dissolved, so, too, did more of the emotional blocks. Every time they passed each other in the yard or at the Rayburn, they exchanged a kiss or a hug and a smile. There were times when Angela sensed a deep sadness in his kind brown eyes, which seemed to be staring into the distance, but she knew those were the times when he was thinking of his mother. She felt strangely reassured though, because to her, it was a healthy sign that he was moving through the grieving process.

It was not getting her any closer to going to Scotland with her team, though, so reluctantly, towards the middle of the final week, she messaged Stevie to wish them luck in the championships. She added a brief PS: 'I promise to be back in the water with you before too long.'

She missed the lake not just because of the companionship she had found or the soothing effect it had on her hot flushes – it had held her when she felt her emotions were in tatters and given her time to regather her energy and inner strength.

There was a beautiful little beck running along the stone wall near the stand of trees. It was there, during their first summer together, that she and Ed had made love away from any prying eyes. They used to walk up to it after tea and on the secluded mossy edges of the bank find out what gave each other pleasure. Then they washed each other clean in the small pool and waterfall before walking back down to the farm and spending an uncomfortable evening in his mother's company while his father snored away in his big armchair by the fire or worked on the farm accounts in his office.

Her memory of those watery liaisons inspired her one day to tuck a small towel down the front of her overalls before pulling on waterproof trousers and a jacket. In spite of going into the busier time of year for the farm, she was determined to make time to go up to the beck. She could already sense the coldness of the water on her skin, which made her work harder and faster in anticipation of plunging into the pool as soon as she found the right moment.

Midmorning, instead of going back to the house for a coffee, she jumped on the quad bike and powered it up the track that led towards the stand of trees. She willed the machine to go faster until the track petered out. With the engine stopped, all she could hear was the beck tumbling over the black rocks, birds in the trees, and now and again a sheep complaining. It was a very short walk from the track to the beck, but it was rocky, and she knew she had to take care. Ed had always helped her across the wobbly boulders, but now it was all down to her to balance and find the best route. With a dry throat and slightly shaky arms and legs, she picked her way across without any mishap. Her body wanted cold-water immersion more than it ever had before. It was like a hunger she had to satisfy or she would die. *Crazy woman*, she thought. *Just keep going steady, not far to go now.* Excitement bubbled along with a tinge of apprehension. This would be the first time she'd swum or dipped completely on her own and she didn't have all the usual kit that she took to the lake with her, such as a flask of hot drink, spare bobble hat, or even a swimsuit!

Angela chuckled to herself at the thought of what she was about to do and how Ed's mother would have sucked her gums right in tight in disapproval until her mouth looked like a cat's bum. Then she fell. Her foot had caught in the heather and she came down heavily on her knees. The rock below the heather was hard and unforgiving.

'Ouch! Bugger!'

It was as if the floodgates had opened. She huddled where she had fallen and all the pent-up emotions of the last few weeks spilt out: relief that she and Ed were at last communicating again, intertwined with the mental exhaustion from worrying about him. Physical exhaustion from the enormous workload she had shouldered. She was so close to the beck now, though, well within dragging distance if she couldn't walk. But as she tried to push herself up to standing, she felt lightheaded and let herself fall back down. *In a minute*, she thought, *I'll try again in a minute.*

'Ang? Love?' A voice she knew well. He was there, crouching down next to her, his reassuring bulk. Her husband. Ed look anxious and puzzled, but not half as astonished as she was to see him here, of all places on the farm, this secluded spot, where they'd only come if they wanted solitude and the beck.

He tried to pull up the leg of her waterproof trousers, but she pushed his great hands away. 'It's nothing,' she said. 'I just tripped and banged my knees on the rocks, I'll be fine.'

He insisted on checking the damage. Gentle but strong hands, used to handling animals sensitively and with respect, he just wanted to do what came naturally to him. It was one of the reasons Angela loved him. She looked at his head as he bent over. His hair was wet, but it wasn't raining. Frown lines appeared above her auburn eyebrows, but she let him examine first one knee, then the other.

'Nothing serious, but you'll have a whopper of a bruise tomorrow!' He laughed.

There was a look about him, a faraway yet intense glow to his eyes. She knew what it meant because she had seen it in her own eyes after she'd got back from swimming in the lake.

'You've been in the beck, haven't you?' she asked him.

Ed nodded and looked down at the ground as if he wanted it to swallow him up.

It was unbelievable. She was furious with Ed. How dare he disapprove of her swimming in the lake – in the lake for goodness sake! With other people. And yet, here he was, taking time off while she slaved away, to climb down alone into a remote mountain beck...

She paused. Not just any beck, either! This was the same beck where his father had got trapped and drowned. She was so angry with him that she pushed his hands away, shouting at him, 'Go away, you absolute shit! I can't believe this. You – you stop me from doing the only thing I love and go and do it yourself!'

Now she was crying uncontrollably and scrabbling about on the slippery rocks and moss in an attempt to stand up, or at least work her way the last few metres to get to the beck. It would drive her crazy if she couldn't immerse herself, too. Her body was on fire and her head felt as if it was about to explode. *How dare he?*

She knew she was shouting and shrieking because her throat

felt raw. But it was as if her voice was part of the landscape, not connected to her at all. She had fallen apart and the million pieces of her were scattered across the fellside like the bones of an animal stripped bare by scavengers.

A pair of muddy boots stopped her crawling up any further. They were planted solidly and then she saw Ed's hands reaching down to pull her up. First by her hands and then, when he realised she was incapable of any further movement, he gripped her under her arms and lifted her, groaning as he did so. She was light, but the angle was awkward.

Within a couple of minutes, he had her held against him and he kept her there, close to his chest and enveloped in his arms. With one hand, he made sure she couldn't move and then he placed the other on top of her head and gently stroked from forehead to the back of her neck, calming her sobbing and cries as if she were a small animal in his care.

'I've been going for a while now,' he said quietly and continued to stroke her head until he felt her body let go of the last bit of anger and tension. She looked up at his face and was reminded of a naughty child who had been caught stealing apples from the neighbour's garden.

'When?' It was all she could manage. Even though her brain was firing out questions again, she didn't want to speak properly just yet. If Ed wanted to talk, that was good.

'I used to come up here on my way to visit her. It was the only place I found some sort of peace. In the hospital with all those machines, mother lying there staring at me but not saying anything. It was like she was blaming me for what happened, but she never said anything. Just stared. That's why I didn't want you to come and visit her. I'm not sure how she would have reacted and that wouldn't have done any of us any good.' He smiled at her and pulled her down next to him so they could be close, but with room to move.

'Sometimes it was dark, but I had my head torch and I know this place so well now. I know it sounds odd, but even the trees over there, they talked to me, calmed me and protected me from the worst of the pain. I was hurting so badly. I didn't ever give myself the chance to grieve losing Father, you see. Looking after Mother became a priority. And you. I wanted to make sure you were alright too.'

Angela smiled at him and held his hand firmly. 'You did, Ed. Don't worry. I knew you had to put your mother first at that time. Who wouldn't?'

Ed put his finger on her lips. 'Sssh, now, I know I made mistakes. You don't need to forgive me that easily! I let Mother boss me around too much, I can see that now. I didn't know how to change it once it became obvious. But I'm sorry. For pushing you away and making you feel so bad.'

She reached out and put her arm around his broad shoulders. His face was red from the wind and the cold water, his unruly hair now drying in the slight breeze.

How much should she say to him? He seemed to feel the same way about the water, but, in spite of what he had just told her, it still hurt that he had never attempted to share it with her, while he seemed to find it so easy to forbid her from swimming.

And what about the winter swimming championships? They had needed a man to swim with them. She shook her head in disbelief. He'd been there all along. Her husband. If she'd been able to talk with him without being earwigged all the time by his mother, if communication between them had been strong, if she had been braver and more honest sooner about what she was doing, where she was going.

'Ed... I need to tell you something, too. A secret. I've been scared to tell you, I didn't know how you'd react.' She took her arm away from him and wrapped herself up tightly in her own arms, willing herself to continue. It had to come out now or she knew it never would. She glanced up at her husband's kind, open face and hated bringing such an evil memory into this beautiful place where they had once found such happiness together. 'When I was young, much younger, I was raped. A neighbour, a horrible, dirty old man who I wish I could've killed!' Ed moved towards her, but she put up her hand to stop him. 'No. I need to get the story out. He got me pregnant and I miscarried, but there were complications. There was some damage to my womb.'

'Oh, my love', said Ed, and this time Angela allowed him to move over to comfort her. 'Why didn't you tell me this before? If I'd known . . .'

'If you'd known, Ed? What difference would that have made to us? Would you not have married me? Would your mother have forced you to find another woman, one who could have children?'

There was no point in 'what ifs' though. What was done was done. They still had a lot of talking to do and trust between them needed to be repaired and rebuilt. For now, all Angela wanted to do was get in the beck that was within arm's reach.

She looked at Ed, who was frowning and then, in the most alluring way she could manage with her bruised knees and heart, she said, 'Get your kit off. We're going to skinny dip together.'

Chapter Forty-Six

STEVIE

February: A Day to Go

This is a terrible idea, thought Stevie as Chris pulled his campervan over into a bumpy but wide lay-by next to Loch Etrigg. Already parked up at the other end of the lay-by was the car carrying the Yorkshire team, plus their new female team member, Karen.

'The A1 must have had less traffic than our route,' observed Chris.

The weather was dreich: drizzly, grey, and hardly any breeze. It looked like it was set in for the rest of the day.

Staring down at the loch, Stevie tried to find some beauty in its dark surface, but it was unknown water that just left her feeling uneasy. Why had the original plan been changed? Why were they going to travel in convoy from here to the venue? Why couldn't they have just met up at the championships and gone out for an evening meal and a drink once there? Instead, there'd been an exchange of messages between Holly and Karen just as they set off and then an enthusiastic and overwhelming vote to swim in Scottish waters to break the journey. Why?

In answer to Stevie's slightly petulant question, Holly had just shrugged her shoulders. She wasn't bothered so long as they got something to eat and got to the B&B before dark. And Chris? He had seemed happy either way, too, which didn't really help fill Stevie with confidence.

'I'm just the driver,' was what he actually said, but on the long journey, she had found herself second guessing what he was thinking.

Why am I even bothering to wonder? Why am I being so grumpy with everyone? This is supposed to be an exciting day! It's what we've been working towards for months. She was sitting next to the window and Holly was between her and Chris, which probably hadn't been the right way round as Holly got carsick, but then she had fallen asleep for most of the journey. From here, Stevie had been able to study Chris's profile now and again. His nose was longer than it looked from face on, but his chin was still toned. Why did men age so much better than women? She sighed, running her finger under her chin and pushing up her own slightly sagging jawline.

What did she see in him? To look at, he was completely different from her ex-husband, who had been shorter than her but made up for his lack of height with a loud voice and mass of ginger hair. Chris, on the other hand, was an inch or so taller than her, more athletic in build than her ex and had an altogether calmer more stable feel to him. He came across as someone she could trust. At least that had been her initial impression, but had she misjudged him? She remembered that funny look of relief he'd had when he talked about Gail's death the day they'd had coffee in Buttermere. He'd talked about his marriage feeling like a prison at times. She now wondered whether he'd tried to escape that prison and strayed from the marital home. Had John felt trapped in their marriage? Is that why he'd had an affair? Was it all her fault?

It had been a couple of weeks since she and Chris had gone for coffee and ended up sharing a bit of their lives, but since then, they hadn't spoken to each other apart from general chitter-chatter before and after swims. Anyway, Holly had always been with them. After the Yorkshire Dales weekend when she'd had a whole body reaction to Chris enjoying Karen's company, Stevie was beginning to wonder whether she had just imagined the connection in the cafe. She looked across at Chris again, but he seemed to be very emotionless and reserved, quite the opposite to how he'd been on the Yorkshire weekend. Was he finding this trip difficult because the company of others was being forced on him for hours, for days? For someone who had so obviously avoided the company of others after his wife's death, it was a big ask. Perhaps that's why he had offered to drive them. It was a brilliant way to stay focused, not have to interact too much, and to feel more in control.

If he was finding it difficult, so was she, but for other reasons. First, it was the culmination of a crazy idea she'd had several months ago as a way of building herself back up and proving to herself that she was still a strong, fairly competitive woman. Second, not only did it cement her friendship with Holly and Angela – which was important to her because, otherwise, her social outlet was desperately limited – but it also connected her to the bigger world, not just Cumbria. It would also be good to see Emma and the Oxford team again. A bit of friendly competition, perhaps?

The third, and final, reason was to do with jealousy. What was becoming an irritating road trip and difficult to deal with was largely down to an attractive, flirtatious woman half her age and how that woman, Karen, seemed to have everyone, including Holly, jumping to her attention.

But here they all were. Parked up in a lay-by en route to everything they'd been training for. *Time to stop all this internal fretting,* she told herself. *Just get on with it!*

Her firm chat with herself helped a little and as she pushed open the door and was about to climb down from the van, she stole a last glance across at Chris who was still in the driver's seat, but stretching his arms up above his head and yawning. He dropped them down and shook his head from side to side like a cartoon character, his jowls slapping from side to side. *Delightful,* she thought, but grinned to herself. It was good to see him messing around a bit. It seemed to be for her benefit, judging from how he then turned and grinned at her. It was all she needed to lift her spirits. In a moment of playfulness, she yanked at Holly's arm to wake her up.

'Hey, wakey-wakey! We're here.' She pulled again and waited until she got a response.

To further boost her team spirit and rally the troops, she marched down to the lakeshore with the things she needed for this quick dip and found a rock to perch on. The others joined her and one by one everyone stripped down to swimming costumes. She put on swim shoes to protect her feet from the rocky shore, but noted that she and Holly were the only ones who had thought of this.

Chris and the Yorkshire men stood at the edge of the loch flexing their muscles and posing for pre-championship photos. Stevie smiled and waved at them. She'd grabbed her phone and was about to take their photograph when she noticed Holly creeping up from one side while they were distracted. She waved at Stevie to not give her away, then suddenly ran and splashed into the water behind them. The perfect photobombing opportunity.

Stevie watched in stunned silence as Holly then took it one step further and continued to splash the men. Their shrieks rang out through the drizzle and it was game on. She could feel herself start to relax and put everything else aside until this was all over. Maybe this halfway coming together had been a good idea after all? Break the ice and start the weekend with plenty of childish humour and silliness.

Then there was a different sort of shriek, which at first everyone ignored because they were now swimming out into deeper water, each one dealing with the cold water in their own way: swearing, squealing, talking loudly, or just zoned out. Stevie was on the verge of tucking her phone into her furry boot to keep it safe while she swam when she heard someone in pain. She looked up, expecting to see one of the swimmers messing about again, but it was Karen sitting on a rock a bit away from where everyone else had walked in.

'Are you alright?' called Stevie and started to walk over to her. It was now drizzling more heavily and she wished she'd kept her swim cloak on.

'I've cut my foot on that glass,' moaned Karen, bending her head over her foot, which she had up on her other leg, trying to turn the foot over slightly so that she could inspect the wound. But there was just too much blood. Stevie could see that from where she was. This looked pretty serious, she thought as she got nearer and saw the broken bottle scattered over the ground. Some of it was pushed well into the ground, but other pieces were ready to do damage to anyone who trod on it in bare feet. Someone would need to clear that up to avoid a repeat accident. But first she needed to help Karen.

'*Hey!*' she called out to the others, most of whom were starting to swim back to shore anyway. 'Anyone got a first-aid kit? Karen's cut her foot!'

'I feel a bit faint,' the younger woman said. Stevie knelt down next to her and instinctively put her arm around her as she would've done with one of her daughters. She didn't want to actually touch the wound and knew that there was no point suggesting putting pressure on it to try to stop the bleeding. That would only drive the glass in further, causing more damage.

'Who's got a first-aid kit?' she called again. Chris was the first to walk out and came straight across to the women, looking concerned. Holly and another of the Yorkshire women arrived next, while one of the men ran as quickly as his bare feet would allow him and rooted around for his car key in his black dustbin bag. He managed to push his cold feet into Crocs before heading back up to the lay-by to find the first-aid kit in the boot of his car. Someone needed to go and fetch the kit from him to speed things up, so Stevie left Chris with Karen who was looking extremely pale, and made her way back up to the vehicles. By the time she'd taken the kit and run back down to the lakeshore, the others were all out and getting themselves dressed in a hurry. The childlike horseplay atmosphere had vanished, replaced with an air of fear and anxiety.

Chris was now kneeling and pouring water over the wound to wash the blood away. Stevie could see where the puncture wound was, but then the blood kept flowing, so it was impossible to pinpoint it exactly. She unzipped the green first-aid kit and searched amongst the little packages until she found some antiseptic wipes and a gauze bandage. Glass was so difficult to deal with. If she tried to push it out, she risked driving it in deeper. She'd once had to try to get some glass out of her own foot and, in the end, having got herself home in the car, hopped up the stairs to the bathroom and used tweezers and a magnifying glass to grab hold of the end and pull it out. She remembered the excruciating pain up until the point of extracting the glass and then just feeling rather faint from the shock.

She caught Chris looking up at her, urging her to hurry. Finally, she gently placed the wipe on the wound, but it immediately became blood soaked and useless. She pulled another wipe from the packet and this time she did press it down gently, bracing herself for the woman's squeal. But she was unable to stem the flow of blood and she felt a wave of panic. Karen appeared to be losing consciousness – or was she just leaning into Chris for support and comfort?

'Stevie, stop. I know we need to stop this blood flowing, but this just isn't working. She needs to be seen,' said Chris quietly. 'Let's just try and staunch it enough by applying some gentle pressure and wrapping it tightly. But, whatever, there's no way we can drive on to Loch Tay like this.'

'Hospital?' squeaked the woman, looking scared. Her face was pinched and a shade of blue, which made Stevie worry that she was also probably getting cold, even though she did now have her swim cloak around her.

'Yes, I think we should get you to the nearest one,' Chris replied. 'Just as a precaution,' he added, standing up and beckoning over to one of the Yorkshire men who had got dressed and was ready to help carry Karen in a cross-handed lift with Chris up to the lay-by. She leant against the other man while Chris opened the passenger door to his campervan. 'Right, slide her up onto the seat.' He wedged his swim towel under her foot and then wrapped it in one of his fleeces for comfort and to soak up more blood.

Stevie was puzzled. Chris was taking her to hospital? Why? Surely, it was up to one of the Yorkshire men to take her? A slightly sick feeling came into the pit of her stomach and she tried to ignore it. The ringing in her ears was getting louder as if her blood was whispering evil things to her. She hated herself for even questioning what was happening. It was almost as if she'd been triggered to react, more likely from old trauma rather than anything Chris was actually doing.

The truth was, in her mind, this was all going horribly wrong. She knew it had been a bad idea to stop off here. Holly came up to her and put her arm round Stevie's shoulder. 'You okay?'

'Yep, just not sure why it's Chris who's taking her,' she responded in a monotone voice, but it was the only way she could keep control of the horrible feeling of panic.

Although Stevie had told Holly about her ex, would she understand why Stevie was now reacting to this situation in such a strong way? Did everything always have to make sense? Could memories of being betrayed by her husband have somehow got tangled up with her growing feelings for Chris? Was the fear of being vulnerable stronger than the connection she had felt with Chris?

'Come on, let's go and get our bags and put them in the other vehicle.' Holly pulled at Stevie's arm to get her to move quickly. She knew what Stevie was probably thinking, but she also knew Chris needed to get off as soon as possible and it was sensible to transfer their bags, not just themselves, to the other car.

Chris reckoned the nearest hospital was Edinburgh, probably closer than driving on to Perth. One of the Yorkshire men had been googling hospitals and confirmed that he was right – it was closer by about twenty miles.

Stevie let herself be guided to the other car, trying to block out the sound of the campervan scrunching on the gravel in the lay-by as Chris turned it around and headed back the way they had come. Holly and the Yorkshire team shuffled stuff about and pulled down extra seats in the big silver seven-seater. Holly once again made no fuss about being prone to car sickness and climbed into the back, pulling a face at Stevie as she did so. As soon as they were settled, Stevie pressed the button to slide the window down a crack.

'Well, that was exciting,' said one of the Yorkshire women, turning round and raising her eyebrows at Stevie and Holly.

'It'll be fine,' said the burly driver, whose twinkly eyes

suggested that he was the type of man who only took things seriously when absolutely necessary.

Stevie used the sleeve of her fleece to wipe across the steamed-up window and concentrated on the drizzle-dull scenery that flashed past. What a disaster. It seemed that their brave team was now doomed to failure. To add to the misery, she didn't even know these people whose car she was now trapped in. She only knew Holly, whose skin was gradually turning green and sweaty.

'*Stop the car!*' Stevie shouted to the driver.

As soon as he had brought the car to a squealing halt in the first safe place he could find by the side of the twisty road, she flung open her door and held back Holly's long blonde hair while her friend leant as far as she could over her and spewed up half-digested hummus rolls into a puddle.

'Oh, Holly,' sighed Stevie as she helped her shaky friend out of the car and stood with her in the drizzle until the retching had stopped. Someone had found a child's potty under their seat, which made a perfect receptacle for anything else that came up during the next couple of hours as the silver car rolled slowly through the valleys and isolated outposts of the cloud-covered and rugged Southern Highlands.

'The snowy peak of Ben Lawers is over to our left somewhere,' said the man with now subdued twinkly eyes as he took every bend as carefully as he could for the benefit of his delicate passenger.

Chapter Forty-Seven

STEVIE

February: The Night Before

She felt like a teenager waiting for the phone to ring. Like Bridget Jones constantly checking to see if there was a message, but at least she hadn't left a thousand messages on Chris's answer machine. She told herself to push aside any personal feelings she had towards either Chris or the injured Karen. As team leader, she needed to know where her team was. She didn't want to even look at herself in the hotel room mirror for fear she'd see the old Stevie, the one who had been broken because her emotions had been trampled on: disregarded and disrespected.

The fact that she was even going down that self-pitying road scared her. Just because Chris was being a gentleman and taking care of a wounded woman. Part of her felt like crawling back under a stone, like the proverbial toad. *Shame on you, Stevie,* she told herself. *But I am afraid. I'm scared of being hurt again. I don't want to feel like that again.*

The pub in the village had become increasingly packed as

331

more and more swimmers arrived for the next day's event, some wearing their swim cloaks to keep out the cold night air. She and Holly had walked down to it from their B&B to get some food. Holly was fully recovered from earlier and declared she was starving.

'Come on, Stevie,' she'd said. 'Stop staring at your phone and let's go and eat!'

After their delicious meal, they hung around the table chatting, but Stevie suddenly had had enough. She needed to get some fresh air. As she was pushing past laughing and chatting strangers to get to the door, she felt her phone vibrate against her chest from the inside pocket of her down jacket. Anxious to see if it was Chris, she pushed a little more insistently and with a sigh of relief practically fell out of the door.

Standing to one side of the entrance to the pub, she reached inside her robe and extracted her phone from the pocket.

It was the news she had been dreading from Chris. Texting from the hospital he said the wound had been deep enough to require minor surgery and stitches, which meant that, after that had been done, he would need to drive the woman back to her home in Harrogate. The text had been matter-of-fact, but she could tell he had tried to make it less blunt by including a 'Sorry' and a 'sad face' emoji. 'Will keep you posted. Promise to be there on time,' he'd added as a PS.

The Stag Inn was located only a few hundred yards away from the loch side, so it only took her a couple of minutes to walk down onto the shingly beach. The night air felt refreshingly chilly after the combined heat of overexcited swimmers and stoked up log burners in the pub, but even so, she felt the need to zip up her swim cloak as she walked.

So, was this fragile ship, which she had built and manned with an able-bodied crew, actually going to manage to drop anchor and come into port? Time after time, Fate had tried to capsize the ship as it sailed unsteadily further and further north to this very long, dark, and currently rather unwelcoming loch in Scotland.

She picked up a small stone, turned it around in her hand, and then tossed it out into the loch, watching for its splash, white against the darkness. The lights of the event HQ were still twinkling from the jetties of the marina; the organisers hard at work doing last-minute adjustments and checks. The forecast was for strong winds during the night, so men were pegging down the guy ropes attached to the gazebos over the barbeque areas. Everything that could blow away was being weighted down or turned upside down. The hot tub was being filled, ready to be switched on first thing in the morning, the gang of cleaners were ensuring the changing facilities and huge 'hot box' – a temporary sauna – was spotless, even though they'd have to clean it all over again on Sunday morning.

It was exciting. This was what they had been planning and working so hard for. What a shame Fate had turned it on its head. Nothing could have been predicted or prevented it. So why did she feel so churned up inside? Chris had done what any decent person would have done in the same circumstances; she would have done the same if she had been driving her car up here. It certainly wasn't something he'd planned nor was it just a very cowardly way of getting out of swimming in the event. She felt guilty and uncharitable now. *What the hell was wrong with her?*

Standing on the beach made her feel cold, but also held the key to flipping the switch. Loch Tay was not a tidal sea loch, but even so, she caught a vague salty smell on the gusts of wind that ran down its twenty-three kilometres. Or perhaps it was the pub ventilators. She laughed to herself. Should she take an impromptu skinny dip now, here, on her own, with a belly full of Peroni and pizza?

Come on, she told herself. *He's promised he will be there on time.* She had tried to work out if it was actually feasible for him to drive down to Harrogate, probably try to grab a couple of hours' sleep, then turn round and drive the five hours or so back up north tonight. She counted on her fingers and shook her head. He'd have to set off at three in the morning to be sure of getting there in time – the relay races started at 9.30, so he'd have to allow time to park, get changed, do the briefing. And whose bed would he be sleeping in?

'Hello,' Holly's voice interrupted her downward spiralling thoughts. She felt an arm round her shoulders and leant against the other woman. They both shivered slightly in the cooling Scottish night air. 'You okay?'

'Yep, I'm fine, Holly. Just stressed. Seems everything that could have gone wrong has gone wrong.' She read out Chris's message in a monotone and tired voice.

'Oh. Oh bugger! Look, I know that's not what you wanted to hear, but we're here, it's a stunning place, we've got other people who will swim with us. No one's died.' Holly hesitated. 'Well, apart from Angela's mother-in-law!'

Both of them laughed wickedly and almost immediately felt guilty.

'You know what I mean,' said Holly. 'Chris will be here, you know. He promised you and I know he will do everything he can to keep that promise.' She looked at Stevie and added, 'Have you stopped to think how he might be feeling?'

'What do you mean?' asked Stevie.

Holly frowned. 'It's not that long since his wife died and since he was nursing her, you know.'

'And?' Stevie still didn't see the connection. But, slowly, the penny started to drop.

'Come on, Stevie, I know you're cross with him, but if you actually think about it, he's not done anything wrong!'

'No, I know!' Stevie snapped a bit too quickly. She was beginning to put two and two together. 'You mean... yes, I think I know what you mean now. He's had his fill of looking after people, caring, coping with trauma, medical emergencies…Oh, Holly!'

Stevie twisted under Holly's arm and turned to face her. 'I feel awful. I mean, I was a bitch!' She crumbled. 'How could I have even assumed there was anything other than caring and looking after?'

'Stevie, stop. Come on, I mean, I understand how you reacted – no, hang on.' Holly took Stevie by the shoulders and squared her up. 'Look at me.'

Stevie lifted her head and held Holly's eyes. She was shaking, not from the cold, but from a desperately unhappy emotion: panic.

'Stop blaming yourself. Stop feeling sorry for yourself especially, but also forgive yourself. How you reacted is in no way less important than how Chris reacted to the incident. You are both starting to let go of the past and the difficult emotions connected to how other people treated you. It is not surprising that everything feels so intense at the moment.'

Stevie hugged Holly and held on tight. Most friends she'd had in the past would have tried to console her with sweeping statements about 'men', or told her not to worry, everything would work out. With nothing helpful or concrete in between. But here was someone who was telling her bluntly that she had been in the wrong, not about needing to protect her own feelings, but how she had jumped to the wrong conclusions. The feeling of guilt that hung over her was palpable. She desperately wanted to wind the clock back. Thank goodness Chris wasn't here now to see what an emotional mess she was.

'You are allowed to be irrational and overreact, Stevie,' said Holly. 'We all are. Remember how accusatory and scared I was when I thought Simon was having an affair?' She waited. Nothing. Stevie didn't respond so Holly just held her and let her cry. It seemed the only way to show how much she cared for this woman who had brought them into her dream, guided them through weeks of cold water without a day missed or word of complaint. Stoical and warm-hearted, she was the perfect team leader, but she had absolutely no idea how to navigate her way through all the twists and turns of a full-on adult relationship. Nor had Chris. *God help them both.* Holly chuckled to herself. *But they'll have fun teaching each other.*

After a few minutes, she felt that the storm had passed. Now maybe was the better moment to bring her back into the now. 'Let's get down to basics, Stevie. You fancy him,' Holly stated, surprising Stevie with her frankness, but it was enough to break the hug. It reset the tone of the night to one of practical strategic planning, something both women were normally good at.

'You think so?' Stevie hadn't been prepared for this change of direction in their conversation.

'It's obvious. And he fancies you.' Holly shivered again and grabbed Stevie's hand. 'Come on, back inside, get another drink down you and stop fretting!'

Chapter Forty-Eight

The Day of the Championships

'Holly?' Stevie called from the bathroom, where she had been staring in dismay at the bags under her eyes. This mirror was surely faulty. She couldn't believe how saggy her whole face looked this morning. Was that the alcohol from last night? Or the level of stress that had peaked yesterday following the cut-foot incident?

'Yeh, what?' said a sleepy voice from the single bed near the window.

'Time to get up. We need to go and have breakfast or we'll be late.'

'Any word from Chris?'

A couple of minutes later, Holly appeared at the bathroom door yawning and stretching. She pushed Stevie to one side so that she too could examine her face. 'God! Wish we'd done the fancy dress thing. We could have come as zombies!'

'Hah! No, not heard a thing, have you?'

Holly shook her head and squeezed a blackhead out from the end of her nose.

'Ugh Holly!' complained Stevie, pulling a face. That was the trouble with sharing a room with someone: you got to see all their horrible habits. 'Right, I'm going down like this.'

She pulled on jogging bottoms and a hoodie over her pyjamas.

'Why not? Me, too,' agreed Holly.

The B&B was like a home away from home. The owners were a couple who both swam in the loch, so were in tune with the needs of outdoor swimmers, and offered relaxed, warm, and reasonably priced accommodation, complete with delicious home-cooked breakfasts to suit all, whatever the preferences or dietary requirements.

The dining room was busy, mostly with other swimmers. Excited conversations moved from table to table as everyone seemed to want to share information, experience, and recommendations for other places to swim in the area.

'Are you nervous?' asked Holly in between mouthfuls of delicious hash browns and beans.

Stevie, who had gone for the vegetarian sausage and hash browns, shook her head. She just felt strangely numb. What would be would be. Her reactions had already been stretched to the limit and she was feeling drained of emotion and energy.

Fortunately, there was endless coffee along with a huge temptation to sit and wallow in post breakfast slumber and conversation. Holly, on the other hand, was clearly twitchy and nervous. She kept looking at her watch. Stevie preferred not to look at the clock on the dining room wall too often; she had resigned herself to the possibility that Chris would not get there in time.

'I think I've forgotten how to swim. I'm that nervous!' joked Holly as they walked back up to their room.

'You'll be great,' said Stevie. 'You're a strong swimmer,

remember.' In the back of her mind, she knew there was something she had to mention about the race itself to Holly. Oh, yes, she remembered now. Holly's phone pinged and when she didn't say who it was from, Stevie assumed it was Simon wishing her luck. Time to ditch the pjs, get dressed for action, and check she had everything she needed with her for the race and immediately afterwards.

'I think when we get down to the venue, I'll go and grab a couple of those people who offered to be in our team. This not knowing is just too much!' Then Stevie frowned. It was only an hour and a half before the race briefing started. Chris wasn't just cutting it very fine, he was likely going to miss it. She glanced down at her phone and there was a notification. Chris had messaged her; how had she missed it? He confirmed that he'd reached Harrogate safely, had grabbed a couple of hours' sleep, then turned his car round and was heading back up. It looked as if he'd sent it at about three a.m., but for some reason it had only just arrived on Stevie's phone.

'There you are then! I told you he was coming,' said Holly when Stevie read the message out. Now, it was Stevie's turn to feel nervous. He was on his way, did she get two swimmers ready to race, or just one? And she felt another emotion too: gratitude that he was doing what he said he'd do and he was doing it for her.

As they left the B&B and walked down the road, they could hear loudspeakers making announcements, music interrupting the voices, and the general sound of a busy event starting to gather pace. The Yorkshire swimmers had already set off to stake their claim on the terraces so they could watch the other teams racing. They'd be easy enough to find in their matching teapot bobble hats all hand knitted by a clever member of the team.

Stevie left her rucksack with Holly who had squeezed in between the teapots. As she worked her way back through the groups of swim cloaks, she couldn't believe how many of them there were at the event. All those smiley, bobble-hatted adults in one place, all here for one reason: to freeze themselves in a cold Scottish loch in the middle of winter. Crazy? Probably.

She caught a not unpleasant whiff of barbeque smoke, mixed with a good dose of lighter fuel or petrol, as she reached the area behind the terrace. Here, there were several fire pits and one enormous hot tub, like a swimming pool, all prepped and ready for cold swimmers to warm themselves up in.

A vibration in her swim cloak pocket prompted her to unzip it and pull out her mobile. Hoping it would be Chris confirming he had arrived, she was disappointed to see a message from her Internet service provider, reminding her to claim her free gifts for February or she'd lose them. Who cared? She deleted the message with an irritated swipe left.

She spotted the man who had said he was up for swimming in a relay although he was also doing the 400-metre event a little later in the day. Awkward! It was so difficult to judge whether she needed him now, but when he walked over to her with his arms out to hug her in a swimmer's hug, it seemed easier to hug back and say, 'Yes, please! See you at the briefing.'

He nodded and went off to change.

Just as she was walking back towards the rows of swim cloaks, she heard a shout from behind her. It was a woman. Spinning round, she was shocked to see Angela running towards her.

'I'm here, I'm here!' called her excited friend. Behind her was a large-framed man carrying a huge bag. *That must be her husband, Ed,* thought Stevie in complete astonishment and confusion.

'But what are you doing here?' asked Stevie, squeezing Angela tightly in a hug.

'I've come to swim, of course,' Angela said with a smile.

'But—' Stevie's last words were inaudible because Holly's voice drowned them out.

'*Angela!* You made it! Ed, lovely to meet you.'

A bewildered Stevie was caught up in the round of hugs and handshakes. What the heck was going on?

'Come on, Angela, you need to get changed,' urged Holly. 'Oh, and we've got a slight problem. Did you get my message?'

'Yes, he's happy to.' Angela and Ed nodded in unison.

'What?' Stevie was completely confused now.

'No time, sorry. Come on, you two.' Holly virtually dragged the new arrivals off to the changing rooms, leaving Stevie standing on the grass with her mouth open.

Five minutes later, the three of them emerged. The only one not wearing a swim cloak, and probably the only person not wearing a swim cloak at the whole event, was Ed. Instead he had his old full-length wax cotton coat wrapped round his not insubstantial body. He was also barefoot and on his head was a black beanie that appeared to be smeared with mud. Stevie couldn't believe what she was seeing. Rural Cumbria comes to wild Loch Tay!

'Go on, Ed, show her!' squawked Angela and Holly in perfect harmony. As if that's all the validation he needed, this solid farmer, more used to wearing the same practical work clothes day in day out, yanked open his coat and flashed a pair of parrot bright Speedos at Stevie, as if to say, 'I'm ready and willing.'

'Oh. My. God.' Stevie covered her eyes and shook her head in disbelief. 'But what...? Why?' What the heck was Ed doing? It just didn't make any sense at all. There was no time and no escape from the fact that she now had more members of the team than she needed. The irony of it!

'Come on, Stevie. Briefing. We need to hurry!' Holly pulled at Stevie's hand to break her from a near catatonic state and all four made their way down through the swim cloaks to the small gazebo where there was a narrow bench, another couple of teams, and an official-looking young woman with a clipboard.

Angela gave Stevie a squeeze and a happy little grin, promising to tell her everything after their race.

'Just getting my own back.' Holly grinned wickedly. Stevie was completely helpless. Nothing made sense anymore. She gave up, did as she was told, and tried to focus on cold water and how she was going to pull her way through it as fast as she could. Next to her on the bench, Ed was drumming his hairy feet up and down on the decking, not from cold, but sheer terror. The poor man had probably never swum in cold water before. What on earth had possessed Angela and Holly – yes, Holly – she looked across at Holly who was sitting with a grin on her face next to Ed, muttering reassurances to him. What on earth had they been thinking to force this upon him?

Then the man she'd recruited at the last minute appeared, ready to take his place on the bench. Stevie apologised profusely and explained that she'd tried to find him and let him know that their team member had turned up after all and she was so sorry. He just shrugged his massive shoulders and wandered off into the sea of swim cloaks. Once he'd gone, she took a moment to take a few deep breaths.

Stop it, she told herself. *Just trust them. You can make a scene, pull out of the race, or just do as you're told. But just don't be a prat.* She forced herself to focus on what the lady with the clipboard was telling them. Then she heard her name being announced over the loudspeaker, along with the other three, except that Ed was now called Chris.

Next, they had to walk down to the top of the ramp where they were told to wait until the heat before theirs was finished and all the swimmers were out of the water. From somewhere over near the briefing gazebo, she heard her name being shouted.

'Stevie! Stevie!'

Who the hell was shouting at her? She ignored it because in a few moments, the signal would be given and they'd be walking down the ramp to the pontoons. Timing was crucial at this event to achieve a smooth transition for the swimmers and complete visibility of anyone in the water for the safety crew.

'*Stevie!*' More urgent this time.

It was Chris. He had arrived and he was running towards the briefing gazebo wearing just his down jacket and swim trunks. His feet were bare and he had his goggles on top of his head.

Stevie watched as he reached the official, said something to her, pointed at the ramp, waited for her to nod in agreement, then ran towards them with a worried look on his face. Although the music was still thumping in the background and people were cheering on the swimmers who were in the heat before them, Stevie felt as if everyone's eyes were on them, this motley team from Cumbria, which now numbered five swimmers. If she hadn't sent the substitute away, it would be six!

'I'm here,' Chris gasped when he reached them, a smile breaking out on his red face. Ed shook his hand and patted him on the back. The look of relief on his face was tangible. Stevie's mouth dropped open, but before she could say anything, the marshal instructed them to walk down towards the pontoons that floated on the dark surface of the loch.

The marina had been roped out into separate lanes, each about the same width as in a standard swimming pool. Red and white floats were attached to each rope and the ropes themselves were attached to the bottom rungs of a ladder on one end and the pontoon itself on the other.

Each team had to assemble just before the final pontoon in swimming order. Then the first swimmer walked across the slightly wobbly decking to the team's lane and stood next to the spotter.

'Take off your clothes,' was the first instruction and there was a wave of good-natured whistling and cheers from the onlookers. Everyone knew that this was the standard instruction given at all the international ice swimming events, usually spoken with a heavy Eastern European accent and more of an order than a request. It was guaranteed to make everyone laugh.

The Number One swimmer handed their swim cloak and footwear to their spotter and then climbed backwards down the wooden ladder and submerged with one shoulder under and made ready to swim on a count of three. A false start occurred if the first swimmer set off before the whistle, so everyone listened and concentrated. No one relished the thought of being in that water for any longer than necessary. It was only four degrees, colder than Crummock, and would be a real test for each of them.

Stevie was their number one swimmer and they all wished her luck as she marched onto the final pontoon to take up her position.

'Take off your clothes.'

She felt a shiver run across her body as she disrobed and stepped towards the ladder. Pausing briefly to look around her and enjoy the moment, she remembered wondering back in October if they'd ever get to this moment. This was it! Arctic Flappers Rule!

Calmly, she lowered herself into the water, deliberately flexing and unflexing her pelvic floor muscles as if to say to the world, 'Hah! Never underestimate what you can do. I've got this.'

The bite of the dark water on her legs, pelvis, waist, and chest immediately focused her attention on what was to come next. She had a few seconds to check her swim cap and pull down her goggles. She wriggled round, grabbed the ladder with her right hand, jammed her feet up against the bottom rung, and scrunched her body up into a pre-launch ball. Her left hand was reaching out in front of her, ready to whip back through the water when the whistle blew.

And go! No false start, just eight swimmers launching themselves into one of Scotland's most iconic lochs, challenging their cold-water swimming ability and nerves to the far jetty and back using heads-up breaststroke: the classic ice swimming stroke.

~

Holly was next to go and she started to lower herself down the ladder when Stevie was about six strokes away from completing her swim.

The water seemed inky black and she shuddered briefly, but no sooner was she in than Chris, Stevie, Angela, and their spotter shouted at her to go.

Driving through the cold water, she tried to control her breathing while pulling as hard as she could. This was nothing like the training swims. It was a high adrenalin race, which automatically compelled her to swim faster, but she didn't know whether she was doing well or not. At the turn, she glanced briefly over to her left and couldn't see a swimmer in the next lane so plunged her arms forwards and pulled back, kicking off from the boards she thought were attached to the pontoon. Nothing there! A moment of panic meant she swallowed a couple of mouthfuls of loch and coughed a couple of times. But she kept pulling herself through the water, trying to regain some of her momentum. She could hear people calling at her, urging her on. She knew Angela was next and as she got nearer the end, she saw she was already in the water, waiting for Holly to touch the board so she could go.

'Go Angela!' she yelled and then started to pull herself back up the ladder out of the water. The spotter held out her swim cloak and she pulled it over her arms and wrapped it round her. She saw that Chris was handing his down jacket to the spotter, so she wished him luck and watched him climb down the ladder. Angela had almost reached the end of her swim and Chris was ready to go as soon as she touched the pontoon.

Holly had to leave the pontoon and walk back towards the ramp because, for safety reasons, every competitor had to leave the pontoon after they'd swum and head towards the sauna or changing rooms. She looked up and saw Stevie, who was watching Chris like a hawk as he powered his way down the first twenty-five metres.

From halfway up the ramp, Holly turned and watched him swim back towards the ladder, heads down front crawl and killing it. Although breaststroke was the 'official' ice swimming stroke, they could do any stroke in the mixed relays and Chris had switched to front crawl to try to beat the other teams.

Holly whooped loudly, grinned, and clapped her hands, calling out his name. A bearded giant next to her clapped too and grinned at her with twinkly blue eyes. He had a Viking helmet dangling from one arm and it bashed into the rail that ran right across the front of the terrace. But Holly had gone off Vikings since the encounter with Tors. Besides, she had her own Egyptian back at home waiting to smother her with lubricant and have his wicked way with her. She giggled. Simon had offered to come up to the championships with them, which had seemed like a good idea at first, but after the Yorkshire Dales weekend and seeing how Stevie had reacted to Chris and Karen, she had a gut feeling that she might be needed as emotional support. She decided to treat the weekend away as an Arctic Flappers adventure rather than a couples getaway.

The race was over and they had done well, but they didn't win. But they'd done it. The Arctic Flappers had got to the winter swimming championships by the skin of their teeth.

Stevie saw Angela scanning the sea of faces as if she was looking for someone. Ed? Her fellow team members? Chris was putting on his down jacket and when he looked up into the spectators, she waved at him – he must've seen her because he smiled and waved back, picking up his pace as he trod back along the pontoons and up the ramp.

He appeared at her side, his face clearly jubilant, and the rush of endorphins lighting up his brown eyes. He gave her a huge hug and then the others pushed in around them for a group hug, even Ed. Time to get warmed up before the adrenalin buzz disappeared and any of them started to lose body temperature. And the hot tub looked steaming and the hot box intriguing.

'We did it!' said a jubilant Holly. 'Well done, everybody!'

It was a tight squeeze in the giant sauna because so many of the competitors wanted to be in it for at least a few minutes, with some of them staying longer while they chatted to other swimmers.

'Imagine if there was one of these down at Crummock,' Stevie said with a sigh, though she wouldn't really want one down there because it would change the place from somewhere relatively wild to something approaching civilisation.

'Who's for the hot tub?' asked Holly.

They all agreed it was a good idea.

The enormous swimming pool-like hot tub was quite empty, so they hung their cloaks over the back of a chair next to it and climbed in one at a time. Big Ed stepped in gingerly as if he'd never experienced anything like it, but soon relaxed in between Angela and Chris.

'So, Ed. Would you really have swum?' Stevie asked. Had he been practising? Since when? How had he managed to keep that from Angela all this time? She wondered whether Chris had known about it too. Probably. It seemed that she was the only one who had been kept in the dark.

'First I heard of it was just now,' Chris said. He must have read her mind. 'Do you think I would have risked getting points for speeding if I'd known this man was going to stand in – sorry, swim in – for me?'

'Hmm.' She still wasn't sure how all this had been organised, but at the end of the day, did it matter? She was sure all would be revealed on their first swim back in the lake.

She closed her eyes, put her head back against the rim of the hot tub, and sighed. Done. They'd done it.

More than 700 swimmers from all over the country and as far afield as Russia, Poland, Slovenia, Sweden, Norway, and even the USA had taken part in the championships that day – a mixed bunch of experienced ice swimmers, veteran wild swimmers and complete newbies – all drawn to a Scottish loch at the end of February to celebrate winter swimming. Now, as twilight crept out from the surrounding hills and forests, about 100 of them had stayed for the evening's celebrations: a ceilidh around the fire pits and hot tub, guaranteed to warm those parts of the body still cold from the black waters of Loch Tay.

Dress code was informal and gradually, as the evening drew on, most people shed the lifesaving post-swim layers until they appeared more like human beings rather than Michelin men. Faces glowed and smiles shone.

Holly gave first Stevie, then Chris, each a rather emotional hug and kind of pushed them together a bit with a silly grin on her face.

'Be nice to each other,' she murmured, her words just a touch slurred.

Stevie looked across at Chris to see how he reacted to Holly's slightly out of place comment. He just raised his eyebrows and gave Holly a big bear hug that almost lifted her off her feet.

'Thank you,' Stevie mouthed at Chris and laughed. He knew just how to handle Holly and wasn't afraid to defend his own and Stevie's privacy.

Stevie felt grateful to him for having brought a potentially embarrassing conversation swiftly to an end. She liked his assertiveness and sensed that he did too. She felt excited to spend more time with him. There was more to him than she'd realised, that was for sure.

The emotion sitting with her now was like a precious creature just taking its first breaths, waiting to be nurtured and grow stronger. Should she suggest meeting up for a swim once they were all home? All of them together, or just Chris and her? Would they just go for a swim? Or something more?

Stevie realised she was holding her breath as if in anticipation of their first intimate moment. She knew that's what she wanted now, with this man who had become such an important part of her journey. She looked at him and hoped her eyes wouldn't give away what her body was feeling, how much she wanted to press up against him and find out what he smelt like, skin on skin. Thankfully, he disappeared off towards the bar with Holly in tow – hopefully, to get her a soft drink.

She walked towards the group who were standing by the fire pits eating delicious barbeque food. Ed and Angela were there with their arms around each other, her head on his chest. Their closeness made Stevie's heart ache. Would she be doing this with Chris one day? Perhaps he wasn't a cuddly sort of person.

'Please be cuddly,' she whispered to the Love Gods.

The other questions started to fly into her head once more and she parked her fantasies about Chris. How had they all managed to keep their plotting and planning secret from her? How long had they been messaging each other to organise back-up plans? Surely none of them could have predicted that the Yorkshire swimmer would cut her foot. It seemed such a tangle of circumstance, coincidence, accidents, and what ifs, but ultimately, it came down to bravery.

As the stories and answers emerged over the evening round the fire pits, the hot box, and the hot tub, Stevie realised they'd all done it for her. This amazing group of friends had taken it upon themselves to ensure that she had her dream team for the winter swimming championships in spite of their own personal dramas and issues. What stunned her most was Ed's story of how Angela had found him up by the beck, having just had his secret dip in the cold water. How come he'd never let her know what he was doing? If he loved the water, why had he reacted to her going swimming with them? It just didn't make sense.

'Look at them, though.' Holly's voice interrupted her thoughts. 'Happy as teenagers in love. I reckon it was the old woman, don't you? Wanted to keep her son for herself. Jealousy is a dangerous trait in anyone.'

Was that a dig? Stevie looked at her friend, but just received a smile and slight raising of the eyebrows and a bottle of Pepsi.

She kept her response unemotional, but honest. 'Yes, it can jump into the smallest chink and spoil things, can't it? And we're all susceptible, I guess, however old or cynical.' A few mouthfuls of delicious burger later, she added, 'I think we're lucky, you know, Holly. We're all vulnerable to self-doubt and over-thinking stuff and quick to put up the barriers.'

Holly nodded but didn't say anything.

'But this swimming thing… we all feel its magic and we have all found it works for us. Look at Ed. A Cumbrian born and bred farmer, stoical as hell, gentle as can be, but even he believes in letting the water take away his worries and releasing his inner strength.'

'Inner child,' corrected Holly, pointing at Ed and Chris who were dancing together around the hot tub.

Stevie wiped tomato ketchup from the corners of her mouth and laughed with Holly at the two men, who seemed lost in their own world of mischief. Wistfully, she said, 'If only more people knew about it, maybe the world would be a happier place?'

'Nah,' said Holly, 'it's just not something that appeals to most people. I love swimming, but, to be honest, until I met you, I'd never have considered that I'd be loving something like this. I wish Simon was here.' She waved her arm around the HQ with the fairy lights twinkling on the dark waters of the loch and small groups of fleece- and jogging-bottomed men and women dancing, drinking, talking, and relaxing around them.

'He'd have loved to see all this and had a giggle about it with us. But I wanted to be here with you on my own so that I could focus on supporting you. Besides, he's making sure the pool is finished for when I get back – you must all come round. We'll have our very own Cumbria Winter Swimming Championships!'

Chapter Forty-Nine

CHRIS

The Day After

C rummock is a wild, remote lake which has many faces, and Chris had stared into most of them over the years. Sometimes, they were benign, often smiling, and sometimes roaring and fierce.

Today, Crummock's face was hard to read – she was in a teasing mood. The subtle lines of light rippling across her surface were gentle, but strong. No white horses, but a weird kind of undulation down at Rannerdale Knotts by the diver's car park. Maybe there were divers down there, he thought, as he paused briefly above the little bay. No trail of bubbles, so it was unlikely.

He pedalled on slowly, taking pleasure from the feel of his muscles working up the hills and relaxing down the curves of the snaking road. But his mind was far from relaxed. He was as twitchy as hell and couldn't stop thinking about Stevie and hoping she might just possibly be down at the lake too.

In his rucksack were two thin thermal layers and he was already wearing a thick Castelli windproof that would keep him warm after swimming. His feelings were all over the place. He was desperate to see Stevie, but wasn't sure what she was thinking or whether she even wanted to see him again. When he had dropped them off on Sunday after driving back from Loch Tay, he had asked her and Holly if they wanted to meet up for a swim the next day, but both of them said they were busy. So, he'd gone home to his empty house feeling disappointed and lonely.

He played over and over in his head what had happened during the last few days, trying to see if he could have done anything differently: from the first trip to the Dales and the way that Karen woman had latched onto him, the cut foot and him driving her all the way to Harrogate! It had been a rash decision, he knew that, but at the time, it had seemed the right thing to do. Thank God he'd got back in time, even though it had half killed him – madness, sheer madness, looking back on it now. Not only to risk everything they'd trained for together, but to upset the woman he'd fallen in love with.

There, he'd admitted it. He was crazy about her. Simple. But even though he'd kept his promise to be at the championships on time, maybe that's all that had mattered to her? Perhaps it was just wishful thinking that she might think of him in any other way than a rather unpredictable member of her team.

On the night they arrived back in Cumbria, he'd given up on sleep at about three in the morning, dragged himself out of bed, and made a mug of tea. But it was no good. His brain had gone into overdrive. He tried to distract himself by doing some chores. All he could think of was Stevie: her face, her voice, the way she looked at him, how she always fiddled with her hair, the way she walked and held herself. He felt compelled to tell her how he felt, but wasn't sure how.

He had time though. Everything he'd learnt about himself while training to swim at the championships was healing him from within. His grief had become a dull ache, lying where it needed to and allowing him to move on, but not forget. He was in touch with his emotions again and it felt good.

He wanted Stevie to trust again. Trust him. He wanted her to feel again. Feel what he was feeling. But he knew he'd upset her. If only he could turn back the clocks, start Friday all over again, put a magical rug over the broken glass by the loch, or suggest to the Yorkshire swimmers that they needed to take Karen to hospital. Why had he offered?

He felt empty as he cycled along past the lake, barely taking in his surroundings, locked in his own head, his thoughts spinning round and round like the wheels on his bike.

Nope, no one was here. His big, sad sigh matched the mood of the dank, grey morning. Thick clouds hung heavy over the mountains and the lake did not look inviting. This landscape could be brutal and unwelcoming. He sighed again and the tall, whispering conifers sighed back. He peered out to the island across cold, dark water hoping he'd see her. But, no. Nothing.

Should he go on to the cafe? Tom wouldn't be there though. His replacement was someone Chris knew, but it wasn't the same. He just didn't fancy it somehow. Go home? Go to the other end of the lake? *Aha*, he thought. *Lanthwaite Woods. Of course. Why hadn't he gone there first?* After taking a quick sip from his water bottle and jamming it back in the bottle cage, he clipped in, pushed off hard with the other foot, and began to power back along the narrow road as fast as he could.

Head down and really going for it – a quick glance at his Garmin told him that he was doing thirty miles an hour along the straight. *Whoop! Go on, you can do this.* He grinned.

As he approached the sharp bend at Rannerdale, he had to slam the anchors on. The tarmac here was badly eroded in places, with potholes waiting to swallow him up. And then he pushed down again on the pedals. Up and down the undulating road, praying nothing was coming the other way.

As he approached the old telephone kiosk at speed, he noticed a car parked in the lay-by. Someone was closing the boot. He called out her name. It was her. It was Stevie. And she was on her own.

She didn't seem to have heard him. He shouted louder and this time she looked up. As he skidded to a stop by her car, she finally seemed to recognise him and smiled. His heart was beating so hard he thought it was going to burst right out of his chest.

'Hi.' He smiled back at her. 'I've got my swim kit.' He wriggled his back and the rucksack bounced slightly. He grinned, feeling a nervous excitement rising up from his belly. He felt like a child wanting to know if he could join in the game.

'Oh, but I'm not swimming at the lake today,' she said. Disappointment replaced the spark of joy. 'But I am going up to a little river pool, if you fancy coming with me?'

He looked down at his bike. 'What about my bike?' He lifted it up by the handlebars and then let it bounce gently back down.

His heart flipped as Stevie tucked a strand of dark hair behind her ear.

She was thinking and then made a suggestion. 'Would it fit in the boot? I can put the back seat down if that helps.' Her blue eyes invited him to accept the offer.

'Let's try,' he said without hesitation. 'I can take the front wheel off,' he added, reaching down for the quick release.

'What about your cycling shoes, will they be okay?' Stevie pointed down at his feet. He slowly closed the boot to make sure he didn't bend any part of the bike. It was a tight squeeze, but it worked.

'Oh, yeh, hmm, I guess they'll be alright.' He twisted round and lifted his foot up to peer at the metal cleats on the bottom. 'Might be a bit slippery, but, hey. What's the worst that can happen?'

'You slip into the river!' Stevie laughed. Then she was off, across the narrow road and up a steep grassy bank on the other side. He had to run to catch up with her.

It took them about ten minutes to walk across to the valley between two mountains: two Ice Age truncated masses of rock. That was the easy part and conversation flowed, all random stuff. They jumped from tussock to tussock over the muddy section, praying the stiff clumps of grass would hold their weight – especially Chris, who was conscious of his impractical cycling shoes. He hadn't anticipated how sketchy the next part of the path would be. *In fact,* he thought, *is it even a path? Where is she taking me?* He glanced back at the wooden bridge they had walked straight past and asked where that went.

'Oh, it's the footpath up to the summit,' she responded, 'but we don't want to go that way.'

As his foot scooted across the wet surface of the rock above the tumbling water, he nearly lost his balance. He thought about taking off his cycling shoes and walking in socks or even bare feet.

'Not much further,' she said, holding out a hand to steady him as he slid on his backside down the rock and back onto what looked like a path again. It was just a sheep path, but at least it was easier walking. He watched Stevie's bum as she stepped from rock to rock. It looked so good he wanted to bite it. My God, did he really just think that? But he couldn't take his eyes off the way she moved and how beautiful she looked. The little rucksack on her back just exaggerated her athletic shape. He was so happy to have spotted her just in time. A few minutes later and he'd have missed her and probably not even noticed her car. Even if he had done, he would have had no idea where she'd gone and certainly would not have thought of walking up here.

And the fact that she'd seemed pleased to see him... Surely, that was a good sign? All these thoughts rushing around like little ants in his head while he moved and negotiated slippery rocks, boggy moss, and places where both he and Stevie had to take a small leap of faith across a gap between two large rocks.

Excited was an understatement of how he was feeling right now up here, in this new and stunning landscape, with the woman of his dreams.

'Where are you taking me?' he asked and when she laughed with him, he relaxed a little bit more. Whatever they did while they were up here would be amazing. He could feel it in his bones.

'Last tricky bit,' she said. He noted where she put her feet as she crouched down and moved across a dryish boulder. Then he tried to copy her. The rock sloped down at a crazy angle to the beck. There were a few wide cracks in the surface where water had collected and a few other places where moss grew, but otherwise it looked fairly straightforward.

She lowered herself off the boulder, turned round, and waited for him. It was harder than it looked, especially if you knew you were being watched. He tried not to overthink where he was putting his feet or what he could hold onto to steady himself. The metal cleats of his shoes and the marble-like surface of the boulder were a recipe for disaster. In a split second, even though he grabbed at the heather with both hands, his feet had gone from under him, and he was heading towards Stevie. She tried to step out of the way, but his body weight propelled him down too fast. In an attempt to avoid crashing straight into her, he grabbed her and pulled her down with him as he landed, thankfully straight onto the soft moss and heather-planted slope rather than into the rocks.

It worked. As he hit the ground, he felt the lump of his rucksack push uncomfortably into his back, but there was nothing he could do to move because Stevie was now lying on top of him. They both burst into laughter and for a brief moment he was acutely aware of her body, her warmth, her breath in his face – and then she moved away. But she was still close enough and his arm was still round her. She was lying on her side and looking down at him. A million thoughts flashed through his mind, all of them inappropriate.

He could feel his heart thumping wildly in his chest. He ignored the dampness of the moss under his bum and the rucksack digging into his back. Time stood still and then she kissed him.

The kiss was soft and her lips stayed still for a few seconds. Did he dare kiss her back? He pressed his lips onto hers, hoping – but she moved away.

Disappointment and uncertainty paralysed him. Her face was still close to his and he watched her beautiful eyes staring down at him. What was she thinking? He couldn't remember the last time he had felt this nervous. It was like being kissed for the first time and feeling that awkwardness that follows.

He swallowed and held his breath, waiting for her lead. Would she kiss him again, or was that it? The rucksack was getting uncomfortable now, but he daren't move and lose the moment.

Then, incredibly, she put her warm hands either side of his face and bent down to kiss him again. Every nerve in his body was on fire. This couldn't be happening. This gorgeous woman who was in his thoughts constantly was kissing him. Kissing him as if she really wanted him. Her lips and tongue were exploring his, and his body and mind were responding. He couldn't remember the last time a woman had aroused him so deeply and completely.

Her hand was moving across his chest, then over his left arm and shoulder. She pulled at the strap of the rucksack and together they released him from it so that she could unzip the neck of his windproof and run her hands across his skin. The kissing had grown more passionate, more intense, and left him wanting more. But did she? Where would this stop?

Then he felt her hand move from his chest down to his stomach and over his hip bone, down his thigh. The tension was excruciating and he found himself willing her hand to explore, keep exploring. He desperately wanted to touch her too, not just feel her shape through the layers of clothes. When he felt her hand move across the front of his cycling shorts, he gasped in shock, but then almost immediately began to panic that she might be disappointed with what she felt.

She was pushing her hips into him and rubbing her hand against him with more urgency, then, unbelievably, he felt her pull back the Lycra at his waist and move her hand down inside the front of his cycling shorts.

But then she stopped kissing him. Her hand slid out of his shorts and she moved away. No! Don't stop! Had he actually said that out loud? Or was he just silently begging her to come back to him?

Maybe she had been disappointed. Perhaps she'd come to her senses and decided they'd gone far enough? But she was now sitting up and unzipping her boots, then pulling down her jogging bottoms and knickers. He got rid of the rucksack, then waited. She glanced across at him and half smiled. It was a sexy smile and he reeled at the intensity of her eyes: raw sexual desire and a hint of playfulness. She was giving him the cues he needed. Those eyes, that smile, the way she was now moving back, releasing him from his cycling shorts and putting her naked leg over his hips and looking down into his face. She wanted him as much as he wanted her.

He ached for her, so much that when she rubbed him against her, teasing both of them, he gripped her thighs and closed his eyes, lost in the feel of her. Opening his eyes, he lifted his head slightly so that he was able to see down his body and groaned as she slowly slid down onto him.

That delicious feeling of being right inside her, feeling her heat all around him, and then looking up at her body and face as she moved herself, gently at first, and then, oh, God, he didn't want this to stop. This amazing woman wanted him and was making love to him. Here, outdoors, on a mattress of moss and heather, moving to the sound of a mountain beck.

He watched her face intently. Every time she closed her eyes, he felt her slow just slightly and then she looked down at him and smiled. Once or twice, she bent right over him and as her hair fell around his face, she kissed him deeply.

As she sat up she pulled his hands round to her bum. He pulled her closer, pushing in deeper. She moaned.

Then, he felt his heels slipping on the mossy bank and struggled to concentrate for a second or two as he kicked them in again. If he slipped, they could both slide down – and the moment would be lost.

Her breathing had changed; it was faster and he knew she was building up to her orgasm. He wanted to hang on, make sure she got there, but he felt so close. An old trick saved him: biting down on the nail of his little finger. The pain just took the edge off and stopped him losing control. He could feel her suddenly tense up around him. It was like a trigger and he felt a white hot pulse deep down in his groin – and then he was completely lost in the feeling, no longer aware of anything, not even Stevie, just an intense emptying and merging of bodies, emotions, souls, and needs.

Afterwards, she lay on him and together they felt him growing smaller and then leaving her body. Passion's gift was sticky, but they didn't care. Neither of them dared move; neither of them wanted to move. Everything was heightened and on fire. Chris felt in awe of her and just wanted this moment to last forever. They had made love, it had been magnificent, she had been the one who took control, who took what she wanted and needed – it had been more, so much more than he had dared to imagine. He listened to their breathing and the sound of the beck. Overhead, the sun had broken through and there was a tiny patch of blue sky. Colour was back in the world.

When he moved slightly, so did she. They carefully untwined their legs from each other and pulled themselves up to sit staring at each other. Two grinning people, immersed in each other. It was as if they were asking themselves: what just happened? Did we really?

Without a word, Stevie pulled herself to her feet, grabbed her rucksack, jogging bottoms and boots, shot him a cheeky grin, and then ran barefoot off up the winding track towards a little tree that hung over the beck. He laughed as she deliberately wiggled her bare bum at him as if to say, chase me, chase me. So he did, pulling up his cycling shorts with one hand and holding onto his rucksack with the other. He wanted to catch her. He hadn't had enough of her. He wanted more.

At the tree, they both stopped. Under a little waterfall was the most gorgeous river pool, the colour of a Bahamian sea with white froth and swirling bubbles.

Stevie was first in, giggling and squealing as the little rocks dug into her feet. Shoes off and pulling at his clothes, he couldn't get them off quick enough. He wanted to be in that water with her. She was watching him undress, waiting for him like a temptress. Those eyes, that smile. Oh, Jesus! That was cold! He screwed his eyes up tight. It felt as if his balls were being sucked up into his neck. Down he sunk, trying to breathe as the bubbling water enveloped his shoulders and pain ran up his neck and into his teeth. He didn't know how much he could stand of this – it hurt! Far more than in the lake.

Stevie was on the other side of the little pool watching him with that smile on her face. Damn her! How could she be so relaxed when he felt as if he was in a deep freeze? Then she tipped her head back into the waterfall and her long hair became darker, mermaid's locks around her shoulders and neck. He watched this amazing woman as she abandoned her human trappings and became a water creature; content and confident in her own being.

Already the lake had reached deep into his soul to heal his sadness and this place was bringing out joy. A few months ago, he'd not have dared to imagine being here with such a gorgeous woman who seemed to want him as much as he wanted her. This tiny, cold pool of pristine mountain water was even more magical than Crummock and he knew that Stevie felt the same.

He reached out through the bubbles and his cold fingers met the tips of her cold fingers, and in a whisper, he said, 'I want you.'

Chapter Fifty

STEVIE

The Day After

S tevie May stood in front of her full-length mirror and realised she liked what she saw. An attractive, middle-aged woman who had a few grey hairs; tall, yes, but she carried her height rather than tried to hide it. Below her broad shoulders, her body curved in and out gently, from her average-sized but rounded breasts through to her subtle waist and narrow hips.

Her blue eyes smiled through long lashes and her mouth curved up at the corners. She saw happiness, excitement, and passion in her reflection. Emotions she now trusted and felt deeply. This body was absolutely fit for purpose, she told herself. It could swim in cold water and it could make love with the man who had turned her world upside down. Chris.

She touched her breasts and trailed her fingers down her stomach. Chris. It had been a long, long time since she had felt that combination of lust and emotion so strongly. She sighed, remembering how nervous she had been while he had put his bike in her car, how she had not really known what to say to him as they had walked up to the beck.

He had been on her mind constantly. On Sunday night, she had tossed and turned until she had given up and gone to sit in her duck-egg blue study sipping hot, sweet tea. But even that calm oasis had not sorted her out. That was when she had decided to go to the Whisky Pool, thinking it was probably the only place she would find any peace. She just wanted to immerse herself in its cold bubbles and allow them to cleanse her of everything confusing or upsetting that had happened in Scotland.

When she'd seen Chris on his bike and heard him shouting her name, her heart had done a somersault. She had not expected to see him that day, or possibly ever again. Everything she had hoped she might get a chance to say to him went right out of her head. But then his eagerness to follow her, even though his shoes were totally inappropriate for the slippery rocks, had amused her. All the questions he had asked about where they were going had reminded her of her children. It was almost as if he was putting himself in her hands like a child, trusting her to know where they were going and how they were going to get there. His excitement at being with her had been almost tangible and she had had no idea how to respond.

But everything had changed for her when he had slipped.

He had put her safety before his own, tried to protect her from falling onto the rocks, and had taken the brunt of their weight when they landed. The penny dropped. He cared about her. She meant something to him. Whatever misunderstandings or overreactions had come between them, the fact was this man, who had braved Crummock's cold winter water, not just once, but several times a week for the last couple of months, had been doing it just for her. Not out of the kindness of his heart, or to brag about it to his mates, but for some deeper, more emotional reason. Love.

Chris had been falling in love with her.

On the mossy bank that first kiss had been impulsive. The second had been a risk. His eyes had told her it was a risk worth taking. His response had shown her that he wanted her as much as she wanted him. She remembered how the kissing had turned into full-on snogging like a pair of teenagers. How long had it been since she had lost herself in a kiss? She felt as if Stevie the woman, not the mother, or the jilted wife, had surged into existence again. She had given up believing that she would ever do this again.

All those nagging doubts about whether her body would actually remember what to do and how to respond had vanished. Any initial shyness had given way to raw sexual passion and need. Everything would be alright. And it had been.

Afterwards, lying on the damp moss with their legs still entwined and their arms holding each other close, it had been as if they were one body, one mind, and one heart. Then, as she had felt him slowly slip out of her, that feeling of completeness had opened up to one of utter joy and happiness.

Whisky Pool. *Come on, Chris,* she had thought, *let's go and wash ourselves in that cold-water Jacuzzi.* She had watched him walk into the water, had seen how he gritted his teeth and submerged himself. Tipping her head back into the shocking iciness of the waterfall exposed her to his gaze. She was the mermaid, the living, breathing water sprite, who had captured his soul.

Blinking back the water from her eyes and gasping for air, she had seen Chris moving slowly through the bubbling pool towards her. He had been submerged so low that only his eyes and nose were visible.

A mixture of love, delight, and anticipation raced through her entire body. I am sensuality and spirit. I am softness and strength. I am Stevie May.

Acknowledgments

My Great Aunt Millie told me over afternoon tea in a shabby hotel in Hove that one day I would be an author. I was about eleven years old and had just received A* Commended for my children's storybook *Quest for Two Girls* from the headmistress at Cambridgeshire High School for Girls. This illustrated adventure story was inspired by a traumatic experience while high on gas and air at Mr Wolfendale's dental practice while I was having several wisdom teeth removed. One day, it will be published and made into a film, I already have the prototype 'Toothface' doll, which I fashioned out of clay and fired as a present for my late mother. All enquiries to my wonderful agent, Broo Doherty, at DHH Literary Agency.

Back to reality, or at least, what has become my 'normal' life: being a published author, after a lifetime of wanting and believing that one day I would be one. To get here it has taken the last 30 years of remaining positive after many rejections of synopses and first few chapters, alongside working as a freelance copyeditor within the academic publishing world, looking after an astonishing array of books written by professors from around the globe. But, in spite of reading every single word, comma and full stop, I am none the wiser about: concrete, Kant, or how to curate cherubs in Canada. But, I have acquired good editing skills and solid self discipline, which have helped enormously when it comes to the steep learning curve on which I've been over the last couple of years since being lucky enough to be invited to the other side of the magic publishing table.

Thanks must go first to my immediate family: my late mum and dad, who were always quietly proud of my overactive imagination; my daughter, Emily, who has always protected me fiercely even when she was a little girl; my son, Robin, with whom I fell in love feet first when he was born on our sofa at home and who is so like me in many ways, and, finally, to our British Blue cat, Baloo, who we have known since the tip of his tiny tail was no higher than my laptop screen.

Next, I feel especially grateful to my cold water adventure family, including one whose strong hand is ready to steady me when the going gets tough, but also to all those beautiful men and women who light up my day with their insane, cold water induced grins and giggles and who are always up for a long-winded discussion about how, why, where and when.

I wrote the first draft of *The Winter of Our Lives* back in about 2018 as a love letter to how daily cold water immersion had helped me fall back in love with myself after some serious surgery, which made me feel pretty low and worthless. I was also scared of growing older and facing a lonely future, albeit surrounded by stunning nature. I remember staring out of my kitchen window at one of the tallest mountains in England, Skiddaw, feeling very disturbed by the notion that you cannot live off beauty alone, you need something more than views and weather patterns. That was when I came up with the idea of bringing a team of four people together to face the challenge of entering a winter swimming competition. At the time, I had no idea that it would become the hook on which I was to write a different love letter, *The Winter of Our Lives*, a story about characters who are navigating the path of ageing in a positive and mutually supportive way.

A small word of thanks must go to a fellow swimmer, Nida, who told me about the One More Chapter open submission window while we were getting dressed with blue lips and numb fingers on the shores of Bassenthwaite Lake after a particularly chilly January swim. I went home, Googled OMC, edited my love letter to cold water, outlined a plot and pressed SEND. It was over three months later that I received an email from Charlotte Ledger, publisher at OMC, saying she loved my submission and was I okay to bear with her for just a little longer while she gave it further consideration. I was more than okay as you can imagine and the next few weeks were torture, but in a good way! With both Broo and Charlotte on board with my writing and my vision as an author, the adventure began. Working with both of them has been such an eye opener and I have loved every piece of constructive criticism and feedback. We're all working towards the same place: where words and images live and breathe and characters evolve into three-dimensional beings.

Thank you everyone who has had my back throughout this journey and thank you for choosing to read this book. I really hope it makes you feel as if you've stepped into a different, but familiar world, where age is immaterial and love is every bit as wild as when you were a teenager!

ONE MORE CHAPTER

YOUR NUMBER ONE STOP

FOR PAGETURNING BOOKS

The author and One More Chapter would like to thank everyone
who contributed to the publication of this story...

Analytics
Emma Harvey
Maria Osa

Audio
Fionnuala Barrett
Ciara Briggs

Contracts
Georgina Hoffman
Florence Shepherd

Design
Lucy Bennett
Fiona Greenway
Holly Macdonald
Liane Payne
Dean Russell

Digital Sales
Laura Daley
Michael Davies
Georgina Ugen

Editorial
Laura Burge
Arsalan Isa
Charlotte Ledger
Laura McCallen
Jennie Rothwell
MFE Editorial Services
Kimberley Young

International Sales
Bethan Moore

Marketing & Publicity
Chloe Cummings
Emma Petfield

Operations
Melissa Okusanya
Hannah Stamp

Production
Emily Chan
Denis Manson
Francesca Tuzzeo

Rights
Lana Beckwith
Rachel McCarron
Agnes Rigou
Hany Sheikh
Mohamed
Zoe Shine
Aisling Smyth

**The HarperCollins
Distribution Team**

**The HarperCollins
Finance & Royalties
Team**

**The HarperCollins
Legal Team**

**The HarperCollins
Technology Team**

Trade Marketing
Ben Hurd

UK Sales
Yazmeen Akhtar
Laura Carpenter
Isabel Coburn
Jay Cochrane
Tom Dunstan
Gemma Rayner
Erin White
Harriet Williams
Leah Woods

**And every other
essential link in the
chain from delivery
drivers to booksellers
to librarians and
beyond!**

ONE MORE CHAPTER

One More Chapter is an
award-winning global
division of HarperCollins.

Sign up to our newsletter to get our
latest eBook deals and stay up to date
with our weekly Book Club!
<u>Subscribe here.</u>

Meet the team at
<u>www.onemorechapter.com</u>

Follow us!
 <u>@OneMoreChapter_</u>
 <u>@OneMoreChapter</u>
 <u>@onemorechapterhc</u>

Do you write unputdownable fiction?
We love to hear from new voices.
Find out how to submit your novel at
<u>www.onemorechapter.com/submissions</u>